TEMPTING SIN

"This is sinful, though, isn't it?" Ivy murmured. "Lying with each other like this."

Drake smiled into the darkness. "We'd have to do a lot more than this to make our nights together sinful."

Meaning to let his cheek rest against the silky hair at her temple, Drake bent his head toward her.

At the same moment, Ivy looked up, meaning to ask him a question. Though neither of them intended for it to happen, their lips touched in the darkness.

Suddenly Drake's blood was pounding hotly through his veins, and his kiss deepened. A melting sensation poured through Ivy, making her feel strangely lethargic. Though she knew she should push Drake away, somehow her body didn't want to listen.

Drake's fingers unfastened the front of her nightgown and she felt the cool night air as it swept over her . . .

FIERY ROMANCE

CALIFORNIA CARESS   (2771, $3.75)
by Rebecca Sinclair
Hope Bennett was determined to save her brother's life.
And if that meant paying notorious gunslinger Drake Fra-
zier to take his place in a fight, she'd barter her last gold
nugget. But Hope soon discovered she'd have to give the
handsome rattlesnake more than riches if she wanted his
help. His improper demands infuriated her; even as she
luxuriated in the tantalizing heat of his embrace, she
refused to yield to her desires.

ARIZONA CAPTIVE   (2718, $3.75)
by Laree Bryant
Logan Powers had always taken his role as a lady-killer
very seriously and no woman was going to change that.
Not even the breathtakingly beautiful Callie Nolan with
her luxuriant black hair and startling blue eyes. Logan
might have considered a lusty romp with her but it was apparent she was a lady, through and through. Hard as he
tried, Logan couldn't resist wanting to take her warm slender body in his arms and hold her close to his heart forever.

DECEPTION'S EMBRACE   (2720, $3.75)
by Jeanne Hansen
Terrified heiress Katrina Montgomery fled Memphis with
what little she could carry and headed west, hiding in a
freight car. By the time she reached Kansas City, she was
feeling almost safe . . . until the handsomest man she'd
ever seen entered the car and swept her into his embrace.
She didn't know who he was or why he refused to let her
go, but when she gazed into his eyes, she somehow knew
she could trust him with her life . . . and her heart.

*Available wherever paperbacks are sold, or order direct from the
Publisher. Send cover price plus 50¢ per copy for mailing and
handling to Zebra Books, Dept. 3380, 475 Park Avenue South,
New York, N.Y. 10016. Residents of New York, New Jersey and
Pennsylvania must include sales tax. DO NOT SEND CASH.*

Pirate's Angel

MARSHA BAUER

ZEBRA BOOKS
KENSINGTON PUBLISHING CORP.

In loving memory of Florence Bauer—
we'll never forget you;

For Robin Kaigh and Wendy McCurdy—
thanks for making this third book happen;

And as always to Ken, Brooke, and Brent—
you make me remember to stop to smell the flowers.

Also by Marsha Bauer:
   Sweet Conquest
   Treasured Embrace

ZEBRA BOOKS

are published by

Kensington Publishing Corp.
475 Park Avenue South
New York, NY 10016

First printing: April, 1991

Printed in the United States of America

Prologue

July 1791
Off the coast of England

Her hair was as bright as the sun—and as beautiful, long enough to tangle around her slender waist as she sat upon his bed.

"Sunny," the pirate captain murmured, calling the lovely captive by the name he had given her because of that glorious hair. "I can't resist you." He let his fingers run through the golden mane, so different from his own hair, as black as the wing of a raven.

Sunny sighed at his touch. This man was so different from any other she had ever known. As his fingers moved from her hair, stroking over the curve of her shoulder, all else was forgotten as he brought his lips to hers, arousing a passion she had never felt before.

"I can't resist you either, Keils Cauldron," she whispered. As he reached for the final piece of clothing she wore, slipping the sheer muslin shift off her, she made no protest, nor wanted to.

The light shining in through the leaded windows that spanned the rear wall of the cabin made an array of soft colors dance over the pale satin of her skin.

Cauldron touched his lips to where one splash of tints turned Sunny's bared breasts into a swirl of reds, blues, and yellows. As the ship rocked, making the colors flicker over her, he followed one glimmer of red over the lush fullness of her bosom, ending at a nipple that needed no prism of light to give it a rosy hue. He brought it into his mouth, savoring the feel of that tautening flesh.

As he heard Sunny's soft moan of pleasure, the ship shifted again, making the red tint he had trailed before move lower. His mouth followed it, caressing the smoothness of her stomach and then delving lower still, parting those silken thighs to reach the treasure hidden within.

"Keils . . ."

The word, though spoken with the low timbre of growing passion, showed Sunny's shock at where he was venturing. Not wanting to go too fast for this gently born lady, Cauldron followed the swirl of colors back up to her breasts, letting his lips linger over their softness.

He would have the days ahead to show Sunny that nothing was too shocking when it came to the passion that flared between a man and a woman. But until then, there were still so many things to teach her.

He laved his attention on those rosy crests, turning them slick with his caresses. As she arched against him, showing her increasing readiness, he let his fingers slowly trail down to the golden curls he had possessed before.

Gently he caressed her, his fingers moving with soft strokes across the weeping flesh. As she moaned again, lifting her hips, he let one finger slowly delve further.

The way her thighs tightened around his hand, riding his deep caress, showed him he needn't tarry any longer.

Untying the cord that fastened the lounging robe he wore, he shrugged it off, exposing a body whose musculature was honed by the rugged life he had led.

Sunny looked up at him, the sight taking her breath away. "Be with me, Keils," she murmured, holding out her arms to him.

"I will, Sunny," Cauldron said with longing, easing himself between her thighs. "I will." Knowing he was the first, he proceeded with care, mindful of the virgin territory he would soon be entering. Parting her with his fingers, he slowly shifted forward to claim her, feeling the slight barrier that marked her innocence give way to the hard, unyielding length of him. As she gasped softly, tensing beneath him, he stilled his loins and smoothed several long strands of golden hair away from her face.

"There will only be pleasure now," he promised.

Sunny's lips slowly curled into a smile. "There already is pleasure, Keils," she whispered, the heat she had been feeling before once again sweeping over her as she grew used to the feel of his strong body.

Cauldron gave a delighted chuckle as she began to move her hips to make his still ones respond.

"Ah, Sunny," he sighed, "you're everything I thought you would be. And much, much more." No longer needing to curb the impatience of his loins, he surged strongly into her, responding to her eager, enticing movements.

The words Sunny had been going to say were forgotten as the exquisite sensations of passion began to claim her. Holding her pirate lover tightly, she eagerly received the rocking, rendering motions of his body, gasping for breath as pleasure that was more intense than anything she thought possible began to pour over her.

"Keils, oh, Keils," she cried, wrapping her legs around him to better receive the sudden, explosive arcing of those taut loins. When his seed spewed forth, spilling hotly onto the entrance of her womb, producing one last shuddering response from herself, she knew nothing would ever make her forget this unforeseen, magical moment in time. . . .

Within her body, one small seed took root.

Chapter 1

Fall 1814
Chesapeake Bay

With quick, impatient strides, Drake Jordan walked past the line of captives gathered on the deck of the captured ship. He gazed with disinterest at their cold, huddled forms, hardly noticing the two women who were standing at the far edge of the men. As he strode closer, he was aware that both nervously tightened their arms around the child that each was holding.

His lips twisted wryly at the frightened gesture. Though the women didn't know it, they were safe enough from harm since the pirate crew of the *Black Cauldron* were under strict orders to keep their minds—and their bodies—only on the task at hand. With hostile frigates patrolling the surrounding waters, there was no time to spare if they wanted to finish up with the *WildSwan* and disappear safely into the coming dusk.

When he walked past the first woman, she stared openly at him, her plain features reflecting her fear as she cradled the heavily swaddled newborn baby in her arms. The second woman had her face averted, almost hidden in the dark curls of the young boy she was holding. She was shivering, but he didn't know if it was from fear or the brisk, chill wind since she had apparently only had time to slip a coat onto the boy before being forced up onto the deck.

Drake slowed his steps and then halted, intrigued by the little he could see of her. The child in this woman's arms was dark-complexioned, while she herself had skin that was the color of fine alabaster. The father of this boy had to be very swarthy, he decided, to have produced such a child by this fair-skinned creature.

Thoughtfully, he assessed the men in the group to find the husband. While the woman with the newborn baby was pressing nervously against the tall man at her side, no man seemed to be attached to the female who had caught his interest.

As he watched her nervously clutch the boy even tighter to herself, he noticed the slim fingers that were stroking the child's small head in an apprehensive movement. No wedding ring encircled the third finger of her left hand. So there was no husband, he mused.

His eyes swept downward, seeking to see more of the captive despite the boy who was blocking his view. The high-necked dress she wore was dark gray and made of wool. Though plain in design, its cut revealed the feminine contours beneath it were softly slender.

Drake's gaze returned to her face, moving in interest over the averted profile. It was as striking as the beautiful figurehead of a sea maid he had recently felt compelled to buy. The nose was small and straight and the bone structure as delicate as a porcelain doll. Beyond that, he

10

couldn't tell much more, for the gray bonnet completely concealed the color of her hair and the tightly closed eyes kept him from seeing their hue.

His sea maid had ebony hair and amethyst eyes, but this woman was probably a blue-eyed blonde, Drake guessed, assessing the pale satin of her skin. Curiosity suddenly made him want to see if his speculation was true.

Parting the open front of the leather greatcoat he was wearing, he tucked his pistol into the waistband of his breeches and stood there patiently, waiting for the woman to open her eyes and face him.

Ivy felt the pirate's eyes boring into her. When he didn't move on after a few seconds, her heart began to beat at an increasingly frantic pace. The captain of the *Wild Swan* had assured everyone that the trip from Georgetown to Norfolk would be perfectly safe since the ship would never leave the bay. The British blockade would not affect them, he had promised, and he had obviously thought they would be equally safe from marauding pirates, for though there had been recent attacks, they had only involved ships foolish enough to venture out into the Atlantic. It was now all too clear the captain's thinking had been wrong.

Afraid of the pirate's intentions, she nuzzled deeper behind the shield of the child's face, praying he would leave.

When Drake realized the captive wasn't going to look at him, he cleared his throat. She continued to ignore him.

"You can pretend I'm not here," he finally offered in a conversational tone, "but I'm not going to go away until you look at me."

11

Feeling almost faint at the order, Ivy reluctantly opened her eyes as she raised her face from behind the child she held.

Drake took a startled breath as he looked into eyes that were violet, not blue, and which were staring fearfully at him from a distractingly lovely face. No wonder she had tried to hide her features, he reflected as he took in her oval face, high cheekbones, and sensuously full lips. She was a beauty.

Ivy shuddered as she met the pirate's gaze, for there was no mistaking the interest that shone from the pale blue depths of his eyes. The brisk bay wind roughly tousled his hair, the color of burnished gold, drawing her attention to the contours of his face as the tawny strands whipped against his cheeks. It was an attractive face, a small part of her mind registered, with a strong chin and generous mouth, but there was something in his expression that bespoke a man who was used to giving orders and taking what he wanted.

Nervously she swallowed, apprehensive of the strength that was apparent from the way the pirate's leather greatcoat molded to the tall, powerful length of his body. When a sudden gust of wind parted the open front of his coat, revealing a white cambric shirt unfastened nearly to the waist, she caught a glimpse of wiry, golden chest hair and a shocking expanse of corded, male muscle.

Ivy shuddered again, the sight of such virility making her more and more worried about the man's open interest in her.

Now that Drake had seen the color of the captive's eyes, he couldn't resist finding out the color and texture of her hair. He reached out to remove the bonnet.

Frightened by the thought of him touching her, Ivy

quickly stepped back, involuntarily clutching the child in her arms. As the boy began to wail in protest, she crooned frantic words into his ear to quiet him.

"Mama!" the boy shrieked, sensing Ivy's fear.

"Hush," Ivy pleaded in a taut whisper, bouncing him slightly in an attempt to stop any more outcries. To her consternation, he broke into tears.

"Mama!" the boy cried again. Turning to the woman standing next to Ivy, he held out his little arms.

At the child's revealing action, a slow smile spread across Drake's face. "Give the boy back to his mother," he ordered. When the captive didn't comply, he gestured to the real mother of the child.

"Take your boy," he demanded. He waited while the mother hastily handed her newborn to her husband so she could gather her older child into her arms.

Now that the boy no longer concealed his view, Drake quickly revised his first impression. He had thought the captive was softly slender, which was true, but the way the bodice of her wool dress fit across the curves of her torso made the word voluptuous spring to his mind.

"What's your name?" he asked softly.

Ivy felt a frightened lump form in her throat. "Ivy," she finally managed to whisper when she was able to form the word. "Ivy Woodruff."

The mate standing guard suddenly shouldered his way through the other captives, his eyes gleaming with a heated interest as he gazed at Ivy.

"I didn't realize this one was such a ripe little piece," he exclaimed.

Drake frowned at the words. Now that the mate was aware of Ivy's abundant charms, he hated to leave her unattended while he finished up with the *Wild Swan*. He held out his hand to her.

"Come below with me, Ivy," he suggested. "You can keep me company until I leave."

They were the kind of words Ivy had dreaded to hear. Shaking her head, she backed rapidly into the gunwale, her hands behind her back to refuse him.

Drake's frown deepened at the sight. There had been a time in his life when he had enjoyed the heady power that came with his adventures on the high seas, but the sight of Ivy reacting to him in such fear gave him no pleasure.

He started to reach out to grasp Ivy's arm but stopped as she pressed even harder against the gunwale. She looked so pale and was breathing so erratically he was afraid she might faint if he laid a hand on her.

"If I promise not to touch you," he murmured, "will you come with me?"

Ivy gave her head a quick, negative shake.

Drake leaned closer so that his next words would reach only Ivy. "Would you rather I left you alone with him?" He gave a curt nod in the direction of the mate.

Ivy cast a nervous glance at the man in question. His face was disfigured with battle scars, and he was missing several fingers on his left hand. Worse than that was the unconcealed lust in his dark eyes as he looked at her.

"No." The word was barely audible.

"Then come along." Drake motioned for Ivy to accompany him, wanting her to come of her own accord.

With slow uncertain movements, Ivy straightened away from the gunwale, taking a hesitant step toward Drake.

"Captain Cauldron said no ruttin' on this haul," the mate reminded Drake, his voice hoarse with envy, "but since ya be on such good terms wid him, mayhaps he

14

won't care if ya make it quick."

"Captain Cauldron?" Ivy whispered, disbelief filling the words. Craning her head, she looked over to the pirate ship to see its Jolly Roger. The twelve-cannon schooner sat high in the water, its two-masted, square-rigged sails luffing in the wind to prevent any movement. At the top of the foremast, a black flag with the picture of a skeleton pulling riches from a large cauldron confirmed the identity of the pirate captain. At the sight, angry sparks suddenly replaced the fear that had filled her eyes.

She glared up at Drake. "History will *not* repeat itself!" she said savagely. "Not with me! *I* won't bear a pirate's child!"

The sudden transformation from fear to sheer, vibrating animosity fascinated Drake. "Did I ask you to?" he answered dryly, a touch of humor lacing his words. He grasped her wrist. "Now come with me."

Ivy was determined to avoid the fate she felt sure was waiting for her below. "I want to speak to Captain Cauldron!" she demanded.

"He's too busy."

As Drake's grip tightened, bringing her after him, Ivy dug her heels into the deck to remain where she was.

"Which of you worthless thieves is Captain Cauldron?" she cried loudly to the pirates milling around on deck, knowing the insulting nature of her question would guarantee an audience with the infamous pirate leader.

A hush fell over the crew as their eyes turned in the direction of an attractive, older man standing near the helm. Dressed in a black calfskin jerkin that emphasized his height and wide shoulders, he had a commanding presence that had nothing to do with the gold-trimmed pistol he carried at his side.

15

"What," Drake muttered into Ivy's ear, "are you trying to do?"

Ivy ignored the question, her eyes fastened intently on the pirate captain. "I see your crew recognizes you for what you are," she called out to him, her deep animosity toward the man evident in her voice. "I demand to speak to you."

Cauldron frowned as he looked up from the entry he had been making on the list of *Wild Swan* passengers, annoyed both at the woman and the mistake the distraction of her words had caused him to make.

Before deigning to answer her, he dipped his quill into a vial of ink one of his men was holding, meticulously scratched out the error, and then wrote the entry properly. When he finished, his eyes were wintry as he turned his full attention to the captive who had so scornfully called out to him.

He stared at her, the wind ruffling his thick black hair, tinged with silver at the temples. "I'm Keils Cauldron," he finally acknowledged, the clipped words carrying easily across the deck. He handed the quill and list to the pirate at his side. "Bring her over here, Drake."

Ivy didn't wait for the pressure of Drake's hand to bring her forward. Boldly, she closed the distance.

Cauldron scowled as Ivy came to a halt in front of him, staring up at him with undisguised hostility.

"You're lucky you're a woman, or you'd be feeling the back side of my hand right now," he informed her curtly. He braced his long legs apart as a ground swell rocked the ship beneath him. "Now what is it you have to say to me?"

Ivy raised her chin. "I have no intention of allowing this man"—she cast a quick glance at Drake—"to have

16

his way with me."

Considering Drake had temporarily given up command of his own ship to help him raid the *Wild Swan*, Cauldron knew Drake was too involved in their mission to be thinking about a quick tumble.

"I don't exactly see Drake with his breeches at half-mast," he observed with cold impatience.

"He was going to take me below!" Ivy insisted.

Having more important things to attend to, Cauldron was fast losing interest in the captive's melodrama. But as he considered the grimness of the days gone past, he could see how Drake might benefit from a brief dalliance. He only wished he could find a way to temporarily suspend his own pain, but he knew nothing short of revenge could ever do that for him.

"If you've a mind to be with her, Drake," he said, turning away, "just make it quick. We'll be leaving soon."

Icy fear coursed down Ivy's back at the carelessly spoken words. As her eyes flew to Drake, the steely fingers that were still clamped around her wrist suddenly seemed to burn into her flesh.

"Captain," she cried desperately to Cauldron's retreating back. "Would you let your own daughter be at the mercy of one of your men?"

Chapter 2

No sooner had Ivy uttered the words than she found herself hauled tight against Drake's broad chest.

"What the hell are you trying now?" he gritted. But the damage had already been done, he saw, as Cauldron spun around, his face bitter as he came back toward them.

"I don't have any children," Cauldron stated harshly, a small muscle working in his jaw as the face of his dead son Geoff came to his mind. "Not anymore."

Held as she was, Ivy could feel Drake's heart pound against her own. The shocking sensation was a potent reminder of what her fate would be if she couldn't enlist Cauldron's aid. She jerked away, facing the pirate captain.

"I wish to God it weren't true," she said urgently to him, her fears overweighing her anguish at having to admit to such a disgrace. "But I *am* your daughter. Look at my eyes—I got them from you!"

Cauldron stared into violet eyes that were indeed a mirror image of his own.

"It's an uncommon color," he agreed, his voice losing none of its brusqueness, "but that *hardly* makes us kin."

Ivy brought her hand up to her bonnet, yanking it from her head. Long raven locks spilled down, the rays of the low-lying sun highlighting its silky texture.

"My hair is your doing also!" she cried, shaking out the long, loose strands.

Cauldron's interest was caught as he looked at the thick mane of hair that was as black and shining as his own. Only the touches of silver that now graced his temples set the deep color apart from hers.

"And who might your mother be?" he asked with wary speculation.

"Marianna Edwards."

The name invoked no memories. "Don't know her," he said, his words again clipped. Once more, he turned away, dismissing the pointless and painful conversation.

Ivy stared after him, speechless with indignation that the man had taken her mother's innocence and didn't even remember her name.

"Let's go!" Drake said sharply, his hand settling on Ivy's shoulder. "And don't say another word to Keils," he warned her, seeing the direction of her gaze. "You're touching a painful memory for him." And for himself, he added silently, for Cauldron's son had been as much of a brother to him as if they had been born in the same family.

As Drake began to force her along with him, a small, vital piece of information leaped into Ivy's mind. She twisted one last time toward Cauldron.

"You called my mother Sunny," she cried out to him, "because of her blond hair."

Cauldron stopped abruptly at the words. He remembered the woman well. She had caught his fancy twenty some years ago on an English ship he had preyed upon in his early pirating days. After a couple of weeks of enjoying her lithe and lovely body, he had let her go.

Turning slowly, he walked back toward Ivy. "I remember her," he said, drawing out the words. "She was a pretty lady."

At that new development, Drake dropped his hand from Ivy's shoulder. He crossed his arms over his chest, his eyes not leaving her face as he waited to see the outcome of this unexpected revelation.

Though Ivy finally had Cauldron's complete attention, she was outraged at his casual acknowledgment of her mother. Without stopping to think of the consequences, she brought her hand up in a hard slap that connected sharply against the taut planes of Cauldron's cheek.

No sooner had Ivy completed the blow than she found both her wrists caught in a crushing grip from behind as Drake yanked her away from the pirate captain.

"Are you trying to get yourself killed?" he growled into her ear.

Ivy was suddenly aware that all the pirates' desultory talk as they went about their tasks had come to a halt as everyone waited to see what punishment Cauldron would inflict at receiving such unheard-of treatment.

Her hand still stinging from the blow, she had ample time to realize just how unwise her action had been, considering how much she needed Cauldron's aid. But despite the punishment her slap would undoubtedly bring, she couldn't regret hitting the man, for he deserved that—and more—for what he had done.

Frowning darkly, Cauldron raised his hand to his reddened cheek and rubbed at the area. Several long seconds

21

slipped by. Then a slow smile spread over his lips, the first since Geoff had died.

"You're certainly spirited enough to be mine," he told Ivy. "You can let go of her now, Drake. I think this little lady has already given me the best she's got."

While he spoke, his gaze moved in an assessing sweep over the raven-haired woman in front of him as he weighed the truth of her allegation. Sunny had had golden blond hair and sky-blue eyes, but he had to admit this woman had the same porcelain skin and delicate features that had made Sunny so breathtaking.

"So you claim to be my baseborn daughter," he mused.

"I'm *not* illegitimate," Ivy answered stiffly. And then, aware such a statement might endanger her claim, she quickly added, "My mother was betrothed before you captured her, and that man married her to give me his name."

"And what might that name be?"

"Woodruff." Ivy uttered the name with pride. "And I'm Ivy Woodruff." As she spoke, she was aware that Drake was shrugging out of his greatcoat. When he went to wrap the garment around her, she shook her head, not wanting any connection to him, but found it dropped about her shoulders anyway. The warmth permeating the inside was unsettling, a reminder that it had just left Drake's strong frame. It strengthened her resolve to come out of this unscathed.

"So when did this Woodruff fellow marry your mother?" Cauldron asked, speculation in his voice.

"Soon after she got back."

"Then what makes you so sure"—the question was asked very softly—"you're not his?"

22

"My mother died a year ago, not long after my . . . my father died." Though Ivy now knew Ian Woodruff wasn't her real father, she couldn't think of him in any other way, for his love had been as caring as any father's. "On her deathbed, she told me who my real father was. I don't think she meant to, but she was so delirious it slipped out."

The thought of Sunny's vibrant beauty being gone made Cauldron aware of the relentless march of time and the inevitable touch of death. As Geoff's face again rose unbidden to his thoughts, he forced his attention back to the woman standing in front of him.

"Sunny and I were only together for a very short time," he stated, unconvinced.

"You took her innocence!" Ivy flung the words at him fiercely. "And I was born nine months from when you took it!"

"Is that so?" A little more curiosity came to Cauldron's eyes. "I can look in my old log books to find out the date I took the ship your mother was on, but can you prove the day of your birth?"

The sudden interest in the question made Ivy's desperation ease slightly. "It's written in the family Bible."

"Do you have it with you?"

There was an intensity to the question that suddenly made Ivy afraid to give the answer. "No."

Cauldron brought his face down to Ivy's level, his expression now hard. "It's well known that my pirating has made me a wealthy man. Maybe once you heard about your mother's stay with me, you thought you could falsely claim me as your father so you could get your hands on some of that wealth."

Ivy stared at Cauldron uneasily, not liking the

23

unexpected direction the conversation had taken.

"If I had *wanted* to meet you, I would have sent—" She broke off as she realized a wanted pirate like Cauldron would have no address to which to post a letter.

"I can't exactly be reached in the regular ways, can I?" Cauldron finished for her. "In order for someone to meet me, they would have to do it just as you did."

"You're making it sound as though I was traveling on the *Wild Swan* because I knew you would raid it." Ivy gestured around at the captured ship. "I would have had no way of knowing that."

"I'm sure it's well known I recently raided other ships in this area," Cauldron shot back. "And the *Wild Swan*, being so heavily laden with cargo, would certainly make an enticing target for me. A smart woman might have gambled I would capture this particular ship."

His mocking words showed Ivy how increasingly perilous her position had suddenly become. She felt the blood drain from her cheeks.

Cauldron's lips twisted in a sardonic smile at Ivy's pallor. "My speculations ring true to me," he continued, "because you certainly wasted no time making sure you met me once I boarded this ship."

Ivy was beginning to feel like an animal cornered by a fierce hunting dog intent on its destruction. "I only called out to you because I was afraid of *him*," she told him sharply, her eyes flashing for a moment toward Drake. "I'm not interested in your money! I just want to be left alone until you leave this ship!"

Cauldron stared back at her, not answering. His face grew brooding. "If by some chance you *are* mine," he added meditatively, "I wouldn't want you to slip through my fingers."

24

"What do you mean?" Ivy's question came out as a strangled whisper.

"You're coming with me until I can look into your story."

Vehemently, Ivy shook her head. "I'm just the unfortunate result of a few careless nights with my mother!" she protested, her voice rising higher on each word. "I couldn't possibly be of any real importance to you!"

"You might be my *daughter*." Cauldron ground out the word. "You don't call that important?"

"Considering the life you've led, you probably have a score of children like me!"

Pain suddenly shone in Cauldron's eyes. "The only other child I had was a son, Geoff, but he's dead." Conscious his last words had ended in a tortured rasp, he placed a tighter rein on his emotions. "So if you're mine, you better believe I'm interested!"

Then his face tightened. "But if this is a clever lie you've spun to try to claim some inheritance from me, then you'll wish to God you hadn't thought of it!"

Ivy took a step back at the harshness of the threat, nearly bumping into Drake. Feeling threatened from each side, she stared mutely up at Cauldron, her eyes stricken.

Cauldron waved over one of his men. "Find Ivy's belongings from below and put them on my ship."

"No, please," Ivy cried, finding her tongue.

The mate paid no heed to Ivy's objection. "Where should I put 'em, Capt'n?" he asked. "There ain't no empty cabins on board."

"Any objection to using your cabin, Drake?" Cauldron asked.

Since Drake's stay on the *Black Cauldron* was only a temporary measure while he helped Cauldron find his son's killer, he didn't mind giving up his cabin.

"None," he answered easily. "I'll find a place among the men."

Cauldron shook his head, his eyes flitting over the rough members of his crew, none of whom could be trusted around a beautiful woman.

"That's not what I'm asking. Ivy's going to need more than a locked door while she's with us," he clarified. "She's going to need a man's protection, too, to keep her safe and to stop any escape attempts." He paused, his next words thoughtful as his gaze went to Ivy. "I want you to watch over her, Drake—day and night."

"You can't mean that," Ivy protested in horror. "I've . . . I've never—" She broke off, too mortified to complete the thought.

Ivy's stammered words and the heightened color that accompanied them made it plain to Drake just how innocent her past had been when it came to men. And as he glanced around at the pirates within hearing distance of that confession, he saw from their expressions they had all come to the same conclusion. Their faces now had the sharp, predatory look of wolves that would like nothing better than to pluck that innocence.

Ivy would certainly need a man to guard her in the days to come, Drake conceded, but to put the two of them together in a cabin that only had one small bed . . .

As Drake gazed into the eyes of the man who had always treated him like a son, he knew he would do whatever Cauldron asked. He nodded his assent.

Ivy looked from one man to the other, feeling panicked as Drake sealed her fate. "But—"

"This topic is closed!" Cauldron snapped, his eyes scouring the bay for frigates. "I want to finish here

26

before any ships spot us." He waved over one of the older pirates. "Take her to my ship, Tinny," he ordered, "while Drake and I finish up."

As the pirate clamped a calloused hand around her arm, Ivy had no choice but to follow him toward the plank that spanned the two ships. With a heart full of fear, she left the safety of the passenger ship to face a future that seemed fraught with danger.

"Do you think she could really be my daughter?" Cauldron said thoughtfully as he watched Ivy step onto the *Black Cauldron*.

"She certainly has your hair and eyes, Keils," Drake had to admit.

"That she does," Cauldron agreed. "But that still doesn't make her mine. This could all be a clever story."

"Maybe," Drake agreed. "But you should have seen the way she acted when she heard your name. Like that"—he snapped his fingers—"her fear changed to fury."

Cauldron just shrugged. "Maybe she's a good actress," he argued.

"And when I told her I was going to take her below to keep me company," Drake continued, "she said something about not letting history repeat itself because she wouldn't bear a pirate's child."

Cauldron absorbed that interesting piece of information. "Well, we'll see what proof turns up about her, but I'm suspicious," he admitted. "If there's one thing I've learned, when there's money involved, people will go to great lengths to get it."

He gave Drake's arm a friendly slap as he turned toward one of the hatchways leading below. "Now let's see if there's anyone else on this ship."

27

Chapter 3

With a feeling of despair, Ivy watched as the pirate crew returned to the *Black Cauldron* and removed the thick ropes and grappling hooks that had bound them to the *Wild Swan*. As the two vessels floated apart, ending all hope of freedom, her eyes went worriedly to Drake when he left the other men, heading in her direction. She chewed on her lower lip, trying to control her rising panic.

When he reached Ivy's side, Drake dismissed Tinny with a gesture, placing one foot on a crate of cannon shot as he regarded his new charge.

Ivy had wrapped her arms around herself, but considering the warmth of the coat he had given her, he was sure it was more of an involuntary response to fear than the coldness of the air around her.

He suddenly hoped for her sake she could prove her claim, because if she couldn't, he knew there would be hell to pay for falsely making Cauldron think he had another child.

"Whenever possible," he told her, "I'll keep you with

me. With this crew, I don't want to leave you by yourself any more than I have to. Even with a locked door . . ."

He glanced around at the pirates, now climbing the rigging to set the sails. Though involved in their busy task, all had their eyes trained on Ivy.

"Keils told the men he'd geld anyone who tries to touch you, but—"

"Does that include you?" Ivy hadn't meant to voice her concern, but the words sprang unbidden to her lips. Despite her sheltered upbringing, she had heard whispered accounts about men and the primitive urges that ruled their bodies and was afraid of what those urges would do to Drake. Not really wanting to hear his response to that blurted question, she looked awkwardly away.

"—but that might not stop a few men from trying," Drake finished. "This is a very rough crew."

Ivy gave a small, worried sigh. "I've noticed. This is exactly the kind of ship I always imagined Cauldron would command."

Drake was struck by the change in her. The bravado that had possessed her in the pirate captain's presence was now gone, fear once again shadowing her violet eyes.

"His name happens to be Keils," he reminded her.

Thinking of her pirate father by his first name was far too personal for Ivy. "He'll always be Cauldron to me," she said emphatically, hostility returning to her eyes as her thoughts dwelled upon the man. "And I'll *never* regard him as anything more even if he *does* ever believe I'm his daughter!"

The fiery spark was back, Drake noticed, fascinated by the quicksilver change. "Keils will want to talk to you later about that particular subject," he warned her.

"Until then, I'll show you to your cabin. A frigate's been spotted, so we'll be heading out the bay as soon as the men finish with the sails."

As he saw Ivy crane her head around to see if help was on the way, he added, "They're too far away to catch us, and even if they did, it wouldn't help you. They'd just shoot us out of the water."

With that dismal thought, Ivy accompanied Drake down the narrow, aft hatchway to the quarters below.

At his cabin, Drake leaned against the doorjamb while Ivy stepped inside. "One of the men will be rigging up a blanket to give you some privacy," he said, nodding toward one corner, spanned on the sides by a bolted-down washstand and a set of drawers.

Ivy gazed unhappily around her, knowing a partitioned corner wouldn't offer much privacy. The cabin was very small, with one little porthole letting in the rays of the rapidly setting sun.

There was no room for a hammock and the arrangement of the washstand and drawers made it impossible to place a pallet on the floor. There was only one place to sleep—and that was the bunk built into the opposite corner of the cabin.

Drake's bed. Her eyes moved worriedly over the narrow bunk that was edged along the outer side by a restraining board. Within its confines was a thin pallet that appeared to be filled with straw.

"I could sleep curled up on the floor," she suddenly suggested, desperation filling her words.

Drake rejected the idea. "There's nothing but ballast under here and it's cold as ice at this time of year. But even if it weren't cold and cramped," he added meaningfully, "you'd still be sharing my bed—no matter what

31

lodging we share in the days ahead. Because other than tying you up, keeping you by my side is the only way I'll be able to keep my eye on you."

"I'd rather be tied up," Ivy offered.

"Why doesn't that surprise me?" Drake murmured, the words dry. "Well, Keils doesn't want you tied up."

"He doesn't want me tied up, but doesn't care I'm in your bed?" There was considerable disbelief in Ivy's question.

"Apparently not—since you're sleeping with me."

The harsh reality of her situation made Ivy feel increasingly trapped. Suddenly she felt like crying.

Drake saw the mist forming in her eyes. "Someone will bring your trunk in soon," he said, purposely changing the subject to a less threatening topic. "You can unpack when it arrives," he added, indicating the drawers.

Ivy paid scant heed to Drake's suggestion. Since Cauldron would probably want to find out immediately if she was his daughter, she hoped she wouldn't be on board long enough to settle into this tiny cabin.

"We'll be eating soon in Keils's quarters," Drake continued, nodding toward a doorway at the stern of the ship. "I'll come back for you then."

As Drake left, locking the door behind him, Ivy sank down on the narrow bunk, positioning herself in the place where the restraining board dipped to allow easy access to the pallet.

Dear Lord, she thought, lowering her face into her hands. *What's going to happen to me?* For a long while, she sat there like that, lost in her frightened thoughts, then she rose, resolutely squaring her shoulders. She wouldn't wallow in self-pity, she chastised herself, not when she could go through Drake's belongings and find something that could help her escape.

Pulling Drake's greatcoat from her shoulders, she hung it on a peg set into the rough-hewn wall and then turned toward the drawers. Inside the top one were Drake's clothes. She riffled through the garments, but other than several spare shirts, there was nothing of use. The drawer beneath it was just as fruitless, containing a pair of leather breeches and an extra pair of boots. Pirates certainly led simple lives, she decided, if Drake's possessions were any indication. She reached for the bottom drawer.

Gleaming from a wooden box was a shaving razor. With an excited intake of air, Ivy reached for it, picking up the blade. Gingerly, she tested it against her finger. It was honed to a fine, fine edge.

Slipping the razor under the cuff of one of her tightly fitted sleeves, Ivy surveyed the result. Only the slightest bulge gave away its presence. Now all she had to do was . . .

What was she going to do? she thought, suddenly discouraged as she weighed her options.

Kill Cauldron? Even if she had the courage to do that, it would only spell her own death.

Hold Cauldron hostage until she could get away from the ship? Even if she could somehow manage to make him her prisoner, getting safely away with such a scheme on a pirate-filled ship would be next to impossible.

Perhaps the blade might not be of much help in escaping from the ship, she conceded, but at least it would be an effective weapon against Drake tonight if his primitive male urges made him go against Cauldron's orders.

Feeling a little calmed by the blade's presence, Ivy

33

wandered over to the small porthole and gazed out into the approaching dusk as she waited for Drake to return.

When the door finally opened, Ivy turned swiftly toward it, hoping nothing would give away the fact she was now armed. When she saw Drake's eyes travel over her in a slow, thoughtful fashion, she fought the urge to look down at her cuff to make sure the blade wasn't noticeable.

"You ready?" Drake asked at last.

"Yes."

"After you," Drake said with a sweep of his arm.

"So gallant—for a pirate," Ivy couldn't help but observe as she stepped past him into the narrow passageway.

"I just don't want to put my back toward you," Drake replied, giving her an easy grin. He patted the top of a trunk that was now sitting along the wall. "Someone will put this into my cabin while we eat," he said as they headed for Cauldron's door. When they reached it, he knocked once, then turned the knob, letting it swing open.

Cauldron, already sitting at a table with his meal in front of him, pointed toward an empty chair. "Have a seat." It was an order more than a request.

Ivy bristled at the command, her dislike of the man showing in her eyes. As she sat down, spreading a linen napkin over her lap, she glanced around the cabin. Being the captain's quarters, it was far more spacious than the small cabin she shared with Drake. And far more luxurious. All the furniture was teak, the floor was covered by a lushly thick Turkish carpet, and the walls were paneled with beautiful, polished mahogany. Along the rear wall, a row of leaded windows sparkled like prisms as the last rays of the sun shone through them. And from overhead, a lamp fashioned from fine crystal swung gently with the roll of the ship.

It was all pirate's bounty, she thought with displeasure, eying the expensive silver mug in front of her. Having no taste for the ale that filled it, she ignored it, picking instead at the salted beef and boiled potatoes that made up her meal.

Though she kept her gaze on the plate in front of her, she was very aware of the eyes of both men often moving in her direction. She didn't know which disturbed her the more—Cauldron's coldly assessing appraisal or Drake's blatantly interested one.

"What day were you born?" Cauldron abruptly asked between bites.

Ivy put down the hardtack she had been nibbling, knowing an interrogation was beginning. Before answering, she glanced at Drake. His eyes were still upon her, the interest in them making it frighteningly clear what her fate would be if she couldn't convince Cauldron she was his daughter. Unnerved, she looked back at the pirate captain.

"April 16, 1792."

Cauldron reached behind him, pulling an old-looking log book from a nearby shelf. "Can you read?" he asked, opening it to a certain page.

"Yes."

"Read this aloud," Cauldron ordered, jabbing his finger at an entry.

The page was filled with descriptions of taken ships, and from the way several words were scratched out with a carefully corrected word inked in beside it, Ivy surmised Cauldron hadn't had the benefit of any lengthy schooling. Considering that, she was surprised at how well he spoke, which, apart from Drake, was far different from the rough men he commanded.

As Cauldron tapped impatiently at the words he wanted her to read, she focused her attention on them. "It says 'Captured the *Guardian,* bound from Southampton to London.'" She looked up. "That was the ship my mother was on." She pointed to the date entered alongside the entry. "And I was born nine months from that time."

"If you were born when you say, that's so," Cauldron agreed, his voice noncommittal.

Ivy's nerves suddenly felt as taut as a bowstring. "The date written in my family Bible will prove—"

"Nothing," Cauldron finished, cutting her off. "Babies can come early," he reminded her, studying her through narrowed lids. "And dates can be changed," he added ominously. "You can be certain I'll examine it carefully."

In the brittle silence that followed, Ivy had the grim feeling that no matter what Cauldron saw in the Bible he wouldn't easily accept it. As she tensely sat there, she didn't need to look at Drake to know his eyes were still upon her.

"You were born in England?" Cauldron's next question put an abrupt end to the silence.

Ivy shook her head, trying to swallow the knot that kept forming in her throat. "To get away from the scandal of my mother being with you, they moved to Georgetown." Despite the circumstances, she couldn't prevent the note of bitterness that crept into her words.

36

"That's where I was born."

"Was there a midwife present?"

"Yes."

Cauldron's fingers drummed an absent-minded rhythm on the tabletop. "Providing she's not part of some scheme, she might be able to confirm the date."

Considering Cauldron's cold skepticism, Ivy didn't want to admit the next words. "She won't be able to tell you anything because she's dead."

"How convenient," Cauldron muttered. "Were you baptized?" He pursued the topic with relentless determination.

With a growing sense of despair, Ivy managed to nod. "Trinity Church." It came out a whisper.

"She's looking a little pale, wouldn't you say, Drake?" Cauldron observed.

Ivy was looking very pale, Drake decided. He had a strong urge to place his hand over Ivy's trembling ones but, of course, did nothing. Cauldron was purposely intimidating her, but he had to get to the truth.

"Why so glum, my dear?" Cauldron persisted. "Is there going to be something wrong with the church records? Perhaps a fire that just happened to destroy the information we need?"

"The records are still there." Ivy tried to keep her voice steady. "It's just that my mother had childbed fever after I was born so my parents delayed my baptism until she was well."

"Oh?" Cauldron smiled a grim smile. "How long a delay?"

"Over a fortnight." Ivy dragged out the answer, knowing her case was getting weaker and weaker in Cauldron's eyes.

"That's not going to be of much help in proving the date of your birth, is it?" Cauldron offered the comment with considerable cynicism in his voice.

"The church warden, who was a friend of my family, was at my christening," Ivy added in desperation. "Perhaps he'll remember I was a little older at the time. His name is Jonathan Moore and—" Her words faded into an uneasy silence as Cauldron gave her a look that said louder than words that the chance of a man who had witnessed countless baptisms being able to remember such a small detail after all those years was almost not worth discussing.

For all that Cauldron was skeptical over Ivy's responses, Drake wasn't. She was giving answers to the badgering questions that a conniving woman simply wouldn't give. A woman intent on deceit would have paid some midwife to support her story and would have said she had never been baptized rather than reveal the event didn't particularly support her allegation.

"I guess there's really not too much proof I fathered you, is there?" Cauldron observed after a pregnant pause.

"Mabel Starn," Ivy blurted, a fragment of hope coming to her shaken voice. "Perhaps she can prove what I say."

"Who's she?" Cauldron demanded.

"She's the woman who helped me care for my mother before she died. We took turns looking after her, so maybe she heard some of my mother's story." From the way Cauldron rolled his eyes heavenward at the word "maybe," Ivy knew he was far from convinced.

"She lives in Georgetown?" Cauldron finally asked. At Ivy's nod, he added, "I'll talk to her—and your friend

38

Jonathan Moore."

He speared another piece of salted beef. "When Sunny was dying, did she mention whether she had ever told this Woodruff fellow that you were my child?"

There was a subtle difference in his voice that told Ivy the interrogation was over, at least for now.

"She said that she had."

"And did he treat you well despite that?"

"I couldn't have asked for a nicer or more loving father." Ivy said the words with heartfelt sincerity as her many memories of him passed through her mind. "I was always so proud of him when I listened to his sermons."

Cauldron almost choked on the meat he was swallowing. "His sermons?" he finally got out. "He was a clergyman?"

"Yes," Ivy said with pride.

For a moment, Cauldron was silent, then he laughed out loud, appreciating the irony of a man of the cloth raising a child supposedly sired by a notorious pirate.

"I remember Sunny was betrothed," he said, the words coming between laughs, "but she never mentioned he was a preacher!"

For all that Cauldron was caught off guard by the revelation, Drake somehow wasn't surprised. There was a primness about Ivy that bespoke an orderly and very proper upbringing.

Ivy's ire began to flame as Cauldron continued to laugh. "I see nothing humorous in the fact that he was a man of God," she said stiffly.

Cauldron gave one last hearty chuckle. "Well, I'll say one thing for the man. He must have raised you well because you certainly are refined."

At the words, Ivy began to wonder if Cauldron had

other motives for holding her prisoner. "If part of your interest in me is because you hope there's money in either of my parents' families, then you'll be disappointed," she told him. "After they died, what little money there was went toward some debts, and since then I've had to work as a governess to support myself. The people whose baby I was holding on the *Wild Swan* were my employers. So there's *no* money in my background for you."

All laughter left Cauldron's face at the accusation. "You're the one who stands to gain," he reminded her bluntly. "And considering the plain dress you're wearing and the even plainer ones in your trunk, the thought of gaining any money from you frankly never crossed my mind."

The idea of Cauldron rummaging through her personal belongings made Ivy's temper flare even more. "You looked through my trunk?" she seethed. The fact that she had done the same thing to Drake's possessions, she pushed aside. Her search had been necessitated by the need to survive, not from any prurient interest.

"Keils and I both went through your trunk," Drake answered her, purposely deflecting Ivy's indignation onto himself. As Ivy turned stormy eyes in his direction, he added softly, "Just as I imagine you went through my things when I left you alone in my cabin."

Taught to always tell the truth, Ivy knew she would stumble over a denial. She just hoped nothing in her expression would give away the fact she had taken his razor.

"Drake wanted to make sure you didn't have a pistol tucked away in your trunk," Cauldron continued. "And I had to see if there was anything in it that could support your story." He reached into a pocket of his jerkin. "There was only this." He pulled out a small, intricately painted miniature, placing it on the table.

Ivy stared down at the two faces in the tiny painting. The woman was blonde and lovely, with delicately formed features. The man had dark brown hair, and while his face was not conventionally handsome, it contained a look of gentleness and refinement.

"How dare you take my parents' picture from my trunk!" She went to snatch it from the table, but Cauldron placed his hand over it, preventing her.

"It's a good likeness of Sunny," he murmured, picking up the miniature. His eyes were thoughtful as they moved over the finely painted faces. Sunny, though older here than when he knew her, was still just as beautiful.

"Except for the hair and eyes, you resemble your mother," he said gruffly. Then he glanced at the man in the picture, the man whom Sunny had married. Ivy had none of the clergyman's features, but since Ivy resembled her mother, it proved nothing.

He handed the picture to her. "You can have this back." As she clutched it in a protective gesture against her chest, he added, "Is that family Bible of yours in Georgetown too?"

Ivy nodded. "It's at my employers' house—Havenrest."

"I know of it." Owned by a wealthy dilettante who liked to mingle with the social and political elite of Washington, it was one of the most expensive mansions in the area. "Are they going to be in Norfolk for a spell?" Cauldron asked, thinking of the *Wild Swan*'s destination.

"Several months. They haven't been at ease since Washington was burned, so they decided to go away for a while." Wanting as brief of a captivity as possible, Ivy gave the answer truthfully, wanting Cauldron to know it would be safe to immediately begin his investigation.

"Havenrest is closed up," she continued, "but I have the keys in my trunk."

Cauldron took a long sip of his ale as he digested all that Ivy had told him. "Drake and I were planning to go to Georgetown anyway to handle some unfinished business," he finally said. "So it will be easy enough to look into your claim too. If all goes as planned, we'll be there by the end of the week."

"By the end of the week?" Ivy echoed, the brief captivity she had envisioned suddenly shadowed by the thought of spending a number of nights in Drake's care. "It shouldn't take that long to sail—"

"This is a pirate ship," Cauldron interrupted her, "so boldly sailing up the Potomac wouldn't be a very wise thing to do. We'll be going in by horseback, and after Drake and I finish up what we have to do, we'll look into your story."

After they finish up what they have to do? The length of her captivity, if she couldn't somehow escape, seemed to be growing in disconcerting leaps and bounds.

"But I . . . I thought you would want to look into my claim right away," she stammered.

Cauldron's mouth set into a grim line. "I have other things to deal with that are more important than you."

The nights that stretched ahead with Drake made Ivy's already frayed emotions suddenly explode. She threw her napkin onto the table, her anger with Cauldron again making her forget how foolish it was to openly show that emotion.

"Why are you doing this to me?" she flared. "Even if

you finally do convince yourself I'm your daughter, you must know I'll never accept you as my father! I hated you before I met you and now I hate you even more!"

Cauldron's face grew forbidding at the insult. Swallowing the last of his ale, he thumped the empty mug down onto the table.

"You better hope there's enough proof I fathered you," he said with a rough edge to his voice. "Because if there isn't . . ."

Ivy stood up, hostility apparent in her every movement. "I hate you for what you did to my mother," she said in a low, furious stream of words, "and I hate you for what you're doing to me now! But most of all, I hate that I have your blood running in my veins, because it's *tainted!*"

When she ended the sentence, Ivy ran toward the door and, throwing it open with a loud crash, raced through it.

Cauldron's lips twisted in a grimace as he heard Ivy flee into Drake's cabin and then slam that door shut behind her. Moodily, he stared at the empty doorway, his eyes brooding.

"I sure wish I knew if she was mine," he grumbled to Drake, "because until I find out, it looks as if I'm going to have to take a lot of back talk from that little lady."

Drake's lips curved slightly at Cauldron's baleful expression. "She must be yours, Keils. Who else would be foolish enough to talk like that to the captain of a pirate ship?"

Cauldron rejected that reasoning. "A conniving female might be scheming enough to think of that very thing," he argued. Then he sighed heavily. "I just wonder what else I'll have to put up with."

"You do seem to bring out her claws," Drake admitted.

Then he paused as he thought of the way Ivy acted when she was around him. "But I don't think her claws come out too often," he added. "She seems . . . gentle, demure."

"Are we talking about the same woman?" Cauldron muttered with considerable disbelief.

"She does have strong feelings when it comes to you," Drake conceded, "but she's also scared, Keils. Really scared. Can you imagine what this must be like to someone who was raised by a clergyman?"

Cauldron gave another long sigh as he thought about the other father in Ivy's life. "There's no doubt in my mind that Ivy is Sunny's daughter," he said after a moment. "But the question is, is she mine?"

Ivy leaned against the door, her breath coming in angry spurts. She glared around at the small cabin, her mood not improved by the fact there was no other place for her to go but here.

"I'm glad I told you what I think of you, Cauldron," she muttered to herself. But most of her satisfaction faded as she thought about how angry her rash words had made him. Warily, she backed away from the door, expecting it to burst open.

As the minutes went by and there was total silence from the passageway, some of the tautness left Ivy's shoulders. She glanced down at the miniature she had forgotten she held. The light from a lantern nailed to the wall softly illuminated the two people in the small painting.

"Oh, Mama, Papa," she whispered. "What am I going to do?" Depressed, she carefully set the delicate piece onto the area above the drawers and then regarded the changes that had taken place in the cabin.

As Drake had promised, someone had strung a blanket across the one corner. Though it would add a small measure of privacy, the cabin was so tiny that if Drake were in it while she dressed, he would practically be within touching distance. Trying not to think about that, Ivy turned to her trunk, which now sat at the foot of the bed. Though not large, it barely fit into the area between the door and the end of the bed.

Mindful of the path the door would take when it opened, Ivy knelt down at the side of the trunk, lifting its heavy lid to see what havoc the pirates had caused to its contents. Inside, everything was out of order, showing that each article had been carefully scrutinized. The garment on top was her white flannel nightgown and beneath that, some delicate cotton underthings. Her cheeks grew warm at the thought of Drake's handling her most intimate apparel. With that unsettling thought churning through her mind, she began to remove the contents of the trunk so she could neatly repack everything.

She was almost finished when she heard the knob turn. She tensed, not sure if it would be Cauldron or Drake, and not sure which man would be the worse to see.

Drake stepped inside.

Looming above her, his large frame seemed to fill the small cabin, reminding Ivy just how close she and Drake were going to be while they shared his quarters. Her fingers shook slightly as she folded the last garment. Was he already planning to turn in for the night?

Drake was silent as he watched Ivy place the dress she held into the trunk and smooth the folds of material. The way her fingers delayed needlessly over the task showed her uneasiness.

"For your sake," he finally said, "I hope you can prove you're Keils's daughter because he's not a man you want to cross."

Before answering, Ivy pulled two miniatures from a pouch fastened to the interior of the trunk. "Regardless of whether I can prove it, it's still true, unfortunately."

She came to her feet, placing the tiny paintings alongside the one of her parents. Their presence was somehow fortifying and Ivy clung to the feeling, needing whatever strength she could glean from them.

Drake had seen the other miniatures as he and Cauldron had carefully sifted through Ivy's belongings. One was of an attractive man wearing the white collar and black frock of a clergyman and the other was a religious scene, a profile of Moses holding up the Ten Commandments.

He had wondered about the identity of the man from the moment he had seen it. "Your brother?" he guessed, since the man was as blond as the woman in the neighboring miniature and obviously had the same religious calling as Ivy's clergyman father.

"My betrothed," Ivy corrected him, emphasizing the word in the hope that knowing about the man in her life would make Drake less interested in her. "My parents never had any other children."

Drake picked up the miniature to better study the man Ivy wanted to marry. Considering her proper upbringing, he could understand she would be drawn to a man of God, a man like Woodruff. But there was a current of sensuality about her that made it hard for him to picture her as a clergyman's wife.

"What's his name?" he asked, putting the piece back with the others.

Ivy was trying to keep her thoughts away from the approaching bedtime hour. "Allen Badgley. He took over the church after my father died."

She straightened the three portraits, her fingers lingering over the small task in an effort to delay the inevitable.

"Jonathan Moore, the man who was at my christening, painted all three of these pictures," she continued, searching for conversation to prolong the time. "I was supposed to deliver this one"—she lightly touched the religious scene—"to a friend of his in Norfolk."

She bit her lip as she turned away from the miniatures, wondering if she would ever deliver the piece now, considering the dilemma she was in. As she met Drake's eyes, the interest that still shone in their blue depths continued to unnerve her.

"It was Allen's sermons that first attracted me to him," she continued briskly, trying to hide her increasing anxiety behind talk. "He often uses Cauldron as an example of improper behavior."

Drake couldn't help but grin at the information. "He must like *long* sermons."

Ivy was hardly in the mood for such a flippant response. "Allen just feels people should lead honest, productive lives."

Drake's grin grew wider at the prim retort. "Keils is giving clergymen all over the world something to preach about," he said with a chuckle. "What could be more productive than that?"

Ivy gave Drake the disapproving look his words deserved. "I guess I shouldn't be surprised a man like you wouldn't understand the morals of a man like Allen."

Far from feeling chastised, Drake was enjoying the conversation. In comparison with many of the women he had known, Ivy's demure ways and wholesome attitudes were a welcome change. Still, he couldn't help but tease her.

"So what does this saint of yours think about Keils Cauldron being your father?" he asked, cocking one eyebrow at Allen's likeness.

Ivy's eyes dropped for a moment.

"Don't tell me you haven't revealed that interesting little fact to your saintly betrothed?" Drake said.

Ivy brought her eyes back to Drake's. "Since Allen just recently asked me to be his wife, I didn't have time to tell him about my"—she faltered—"my heritage."

"How long have you been seeing him?" Drake asked with a seemingly casual air.

"About a year," Ivy answered warily, having a feeling what question would come next.

Drake didn't disappoint her. "And the subject just never came up?"

"Until Allen proposed, it wasn't something that needed to be aired!" Ivy said stiffly, drawing herself up. "But I fully meant to tell him as soon as I returned from Norfolk."

A teasing light came to Drake's eyes. "Aren't you afraid you might become the subject of one of the saint's sermons when he finds out?"

The look Ivy gave Drake conveyed how impossible it was for a pirate to judge a clergyman. "Allen's hardly the type of man who would hold such a thing against me."

"Since Allen is such a good man, perhaps he *will*

forgive your unfortunate heritage," Drake continued to tease. Then he paused, his smile becoming more pronounced. "But what is he going to think about you and me sharing a bed?"

That was something Ivy didn't want to think about. Allen was a man who felt strongly about proper conduct and who felt that intimacy should only occur within the sacred bond that existed between a husband and a wife. All through their courtship, he had conducted himself with the utmost restraint, carefully keeping his kisses within the bounds of propriety.

"I guess you're not going to tell him about that either," Drake prompted when Ivy didn't respond.

"Of course, I'll tell him," Ivy said after a moment. "I'll sure . . . he'll understand."

Drake couldn't imagine that, but instead he said, "I'm glad he's going to be so understanding because it's time for us to go to bed."

Chapter 4

At the words, Ivy took an involuntary step backward, her face showing distress at the news.

"I'll give you a few minutes to yourself to get ready," Drake suggested.

"That won't be necessary," Ivy said, her voice strained. "I am ready."

Drake's eyes moved over the itchy-looking wool of her dress. "You planning to sleep in that?"

"Yes," she answered, gaining courage from the blade hidden in her sleeve. She was armed and Drake no longer was, the pistol and knife he had been wearing before now conspicuously absent. She guessed he had removed them to ensure she didn't grab for them during the night, but that ploy was to her advantage.

"Think again." Going to her trunk and flinging open its lid, Drake knelt down to rummage through its interior. When he found the white flannel nightgown, he stood up and held it out.

"Put this on."

The idea was too awful for Ivy to contemplate. "No."

Drake looked over the modest, high-necked garment, fastened down its voluminous front by a row of plain wooden buttons.

"This *has* to be less revealing than what you have on now," he pointed out.

Self-consciously, Ivy tugged at the fitted bodice of her dress. Drake's words were true, but it didn't alter the purpose of such a garment.

"It's a nightgown," she stressed.

"So?"

"Only a *husband* should see me in such a thing."

"Well, I guess I'm going to see you in it too."

Ivy raised her chin with determination. "No, you're not."

"Ivy," Drake said with all the patience he could muster, continuing to hold out the primly designed nightgown, "this *isn't* the type of garment that gives a man any ideas." He stepped toward her.

Ivy backed up to the wall, her fingers inching toward the razor in her cuff. "Cauldron said *no one* is to touch me," she reminded him sharply.

Drake stopped at the words. "Despite your feelings for Keils," he said dryly, "you're quick to name him when you think it will help you, aren't you? Well, don't count on him to come to your aid every time you feel threatened. His protection will only go so far."

He tossed the nightgown to her. "Now go behind that blanket and change," he ordered. When she didn't comply, he added ominously, "Either you do it or I'll do it for you. And if I have to take off your clothes, I can't say what else might happen. A man only has so much control."

Ivy stared at the virile male in front of her, believing

the threat. Even though she had a razor and Drake was unarmed, it seemed like such an insignificant weapon against a man like him.

"Well?" Drake demanded.

"I'll change," Ivy relented, deciding to save the blade for when she might really need it—to keep Drake at bay once they were together in that small bunk.

"Good." Turning away from her, Drake started to strip off his cambric shirt, his heavily muscled shoulders coming into view.

Disconcerted at that sight, Ivy hurried toward the blanketed corner so she wouldn't see him disrobe. When she was safely behind it, she reached for the buttons at the back of her dress and unfastened them, all the while listening to Drake as he moved around the tiny cabin.

What would he sleep in? she wondered tensely as she stepped out of her dress. Her father had always worn a nightshirt to bed. Surely that would be what Drake wore. Undoubtedly, one had been in his drawers.

As she heard him settle into the bunk, she pulled her flannel nightgown on over her shift and petticoat, unwilling to remove any more clothing than necessary. The garment in place, she carefully tucked the razor into one of its loose, long sleeves.

The wooden floor was cold beneath her bare feet, but she knew that wasn't what was making her teeth chatter as she prepared to join Drake in the tiny bunk. Taking a deep breath to fortify herself, she walked out from behind the partition.

Drake was sitting up in bed, leaning against the wall. The blanket was drawn to his waist, but above it, his torso was bare. Having expected him to be decently clad, Ivy stopped in shock.

53

He's naked under that blanket, she thought in panic, her gaze flying over the broad shoulders, muscled arms, and golden wedge of hair that tapered to a vee as it reached the ridges of a distinctly male abdomen.

From Ivy's expression, Drake had no trouble guessing her thoughts. He tossed the blanket aside so she could see he was wearing a brief swatch of cotton.

Ivy gasped as the blanket billowed around Drake, sure the sight of a nude male body would greet her eyes. She shut them tightly so she wouldn't view such a forbidden thing.

At Ivy's tightly closed eyes, Drake couldn't help but laugh. "I guess you've never seen a naked male before?" he teased, his eyes moving languidly over her frozen form. Dressed in white, with her long raven hair flowing around her shoulders, she could have been the model for his beautiful sea maid figurehead. But while that woman was carved of cold, unresponsive wood, this one was made of warm flesh and blood.

He hadn't expected the prim flannel nightgown to be at all alluring, not with its high neck and loose-fitting design. But somehow—draped on Ivy's voluptuous figure—it was. He wondered how he could sleep alongside her night after night without giving in to the desire to touch her.

Her eyes still closed, Ivy started to back toward her partitioned corner. "One of the children I cared for was a male," she reminded Drake, trying to keep the panic from her voice.

Drake grinned at her retreat. "That hardly counts, though, does it?" he drawled. "If you'll open your eyes," he added with some humor, "you'll see I'm not naked."

Afraid to believe him, Ivy slowly opened her eyes. One

glance at the brief cotton garment that molded all too closely to his distinctly masculine form made her squeeze them shut again. With a shocked gasp, she turned on her heel and disappeared once again behind the blanket.

"Is *that* what you're going to sleep in?" she stammered from the shelter of the blanket. The image of Drake's bronzed, hard body seemed etched into her brain.

"I usually wear nothing," came the laconic reply. "I'm wearing this much for you."

Ivy put her hands to her flaming cheeks. "I thought you would be wearing a nightshirt."

"I don't have a nightshirt."

"But it's too cold to just wear that."

"With the two of us under one blanket, Ivy, I'll be anything but cold."

Ivy didn't want to picture such a thing let alone try it. "I don't want to sleep with you."

"You'll probably like it once you get over your reluctance," Drake tried to cajole her.

Ivy couldn't imagine she could ever overcome her reluctance. "I don't want to find out."

"You have no choice," Drake reminded her. "Since Keils doesn't want you tied up, you'll be sleeping with me every night we're together so I can keep a watchful eye on you." To give her a sense of privacy, he reached up to turn down the wick in the lantern set onto the wall above him. Moonlight, streaming in through the small porthole, softly lighted the cabin.

His voice became coaxing. "Come on out, Ivy."

"I'll come later," Ivy hedged, the darkness not making it any easier. "You go ahead and sleep."

Drake put his hands behind his head and chuckled.

55

"This feels like a wedding night—except I won't have the pleasure of consummating the marriage once I get the *frightened* virgin to bed." He purposely made the word a challenge, hoping to lure her out.

Ivy stayed where she was.

"If you're really Keils Cauldron's daughter," Drake tried next, "you're going to have to show more backbone than this."

His taunting words galvanized Ivy into action, for her future depended on the pirates accepting her claim. Gathering her courage, she moved from behind the partition and stepped quickly across the cold floor. When she reached the bed, she lifted the blanket and determinedly climbed in. The straw in the pallet rustled beneath her as she positioned her back against the wall as Drake was doing.

"I'm *not* afraid," she told him, placing her hand near the cuff of her sleeve to keep her weapon ready.

Drake gave a derisive snort. "No? Then why are you clutching at that razor you've been carrying all evening?"

Ivy started, her heart thudding at the words. "You've known all along I had it—and didn't care?" Her fingers crept closer to the blade as she spoke.

Drake crossed his arms, purposely presenting a non-threatening posture so Ivy wouldn't feel compelled to draw her weapon.

"I think you're smart enough to know that killing me or Cauldron won't get you off this ship—not alive anyway," he amended. "And I thought you might be a *little* less scared if you had a weapon."

His light tone made it clear to Ivy that Drake didn't consider her any threat, even though she was armed.

"Then you'll let me keep it?" she asked with a guarded caution to her voice.

"As long as you let me use it tomorrow to shave," Drake replied dryly, "I don't care what you do with it. But it is very sharp, so sleeping with it isn't a good idea. Why don't you put it on the floor for now? That way it will still be within easy reach in case you feel threatened for some reason during the night."

Once again, his words were said lightly, making Ivy feel a little foolish about her plan to sleep with a razor-sharp weapon sliding around in her loose-fitting sleeve. Since Drake knew about the blade, its effectiveness as a weapon was now limited, but without it . . .

As she weighed what to do, her eyes went to the three miniatures, dimly illuminated by the moonlight. Their watchful, loving presence once again gave her the fortitude she needed.

"I'll put down the razor," she conceded. "But if you try anything, I *will* use it."

As gently raised as Ivy had obviously been, Drake couldn't imagine her doing such a thing, and he was willing to trust his instincts.

"I'll keep that warning in mind, Ivy." His words were drier still as he settled into the bed, lying on his back.

Keeping a watchful eye on him, Ivy pulled the blade from her sleeve and placed it on the floor. When Drake made no move toward her, she gingerly eased down beside him, holding onto the board that edged the length of the bed so the sag in the middle wouldn't bring her to him.

Drake smiled into the darkness at her futile attempt. "We're going to be touching, no matter what you do. This is a *very* small bed."

Ivy could hear the amusement in his voice. After a few more seconds of struggling to stay where she was, she gave up and released the side of the bunk. Drake's greater weight immediately brought her snugly up against his side.

Ivy felt the long length of his leg, the warmth of his hip, and the solid strength of his torso. Clasping her hands together, she said a quick prayer for being in bed with a man who was not her husband.

"I never had a woman pray while she was in bed with me," Drake said wryly, seeing Ivy's lips move slightly as she voiced her thoughts to God. "But then, I never had a woman get into bed with me carrying a razor, either."

Ivy unclasped her fingers. "I was asking the Lord for forgiveness for being here," she said primly.

The chastely spoken thought brought another smile to Drake's lips. "I'm sure He won't blame you since you have no choice." Purposely, he rolled over, placing his back toward her.

As Ivy lay there, keeping self-consciously still, she was acutely aware of the warmth that radiated from Drake's body and the way his large male frame so completely overshadowed her own feminine one.

She was so tense that, after only a few minutes, she was taken aback to hear Drake's breath even out into the unmistakable sound of sleep.

He's sleeping, she thought, a little resentful that he was at such ease, even knowing she had a razor, while she lay in a state of mortification.

Hoping to find a less intimate sleeping arrangement, she carefully shifted onto her side to face away from him. But the way Drake's buttocks now touched her own made her even more conscious she was sharing a bed with a virile male.

Daunted by the sensation, she started to shift again and then stopped, facing the reality that no matter which way she turned, she and Drake were going to be intimately touching, considering the narrow confines of the bed.

For a long, long while, she stared into the darkness, sleep totally eluding her. Finally exhaustion took its toll, and she gratefully sank into oblivion.

The feel of Drake's lips nuzzling at the nape of her neck jolted Ivy awake. Even as she registered the fact that he was now turned toward her, she realized from the even rhythm of his breathing that he was still sound asleep. Her first shocked inclination was to shove him away, but she quickly rejected that idea, afraid that if she woke him from an obviously amorous dream, he might want to continue where the dream left off.

She decided instead to ease herself away from his touch. But as she started to move, his arm slipped around her waist, stopping her, and his nuzzles grew bolder, becoming soft, moist kisses that caressed her neck in the most sensual way.

Suddenly Ivy's skin felt flushed and her heart was beating in a strangely erratic tempo. Shocked, she forgot her plan and gave Drake's shoulder a sharp push.

"Stop that!" she cried.

Groggily, Drake propped himself up on one elbow, brushing his hair from his eyes as he regarded Ivy in the shadowed darkness. She looked flustered and on the verge of flight.

"What did I do?" he asked, aware of the aroused state

59

from which he had awakened. As she mutely stared back at him with wide, shocked eyes, a score of sensual possibilities began flashing through his mind.

"You . . . you—" Ivy halted, not really wanting to discuss the way his lips had caressed her.

"What?" Drake demanded, his voice suddenly hoarse as the visions playing through his mind became increasingly erotic. "What did I do?"

"You kissed me," Ivy blurted. "On . . . on the back of my neck." One hand crept up to touch the still-tingling spot.

"I kissed you on the back of your *neck?*" Drake echoed the words in disbelief as one by one, his sensual fantasies crumbled. "That's all I did?" The question was half disappointment, half incredulity.

Ivy was still trembling from the encounter. "That was enough!"

Considering how strongly he was attracted to Ivy, Drake felt his instinctive, male reaction to her feminine presence had been a minor trespass compared to what his body actually ached to do. Since he certainly couldn't say that, he simply turned his back to her once again.

He settled back into the bed and gave a wry chuckle. "I guess I'm lucky you didn't go for your razor."

Ivy didn't answer as she warily lay back down. The encounter with Drake had ended so quickly she hadn't even thought about reaching for the razor. But she had an unsettling feeling that even if she had, Drake would have easily taken it from her if he had wanted to continue his amorous inclinations. That thought made sleep completely elude her.

As she tensely lay there, the constricting layers of clothing she was wearing under her nightgown began

60

adding to her discomfort.

When the stillness of Drake's body convinced her he was asleep, she eased into a new position, hoping to loosen the binding material. It didn't help, not with so many clothes swaddling her. Restlessly, she shifted again.

Suddenly, Drake spoke. "If you want these sleeping arrangements to stay brotherly," he warned her gruffly, "you better stop squirming around."

With that warning weighing heavily on her mind, Ivy kept very, very still. Not until long past Drake's even breathing convinced her he had indeed fallen asleep was she finally able to rest herself.

Chapter 5

The sound of a door closing woke Ivy the next morning. As she opened her eyes, blinking a little at the brightness of the early sun streaming in through the porthole, she realized Drake had left. Alone in the bunk, she stretched, trying to sort out the many confused feelings about sleeping with a man.

The worst of her fears had been unfounded, thank God, and she had emerged as untouched from the narrow bed as she had entered it. Well, not completely untouched, she amended, flushing as she thought of the sensation of Drake's lips brushing across the back of her neck.

Her pulse raced at the memory, making her feel oddly warm despite the chill that permeated the cabin. It was just nerves, she decided, pushing aside the disturbing reaction.

As she sat up in the bed, trying to find the strength to face a new day on the pirate ship, she saw the straight-edged razor was now on top of the washstand, lying carelessly between the pitcher and basin that were set into indented areas on its wooden surface.

Ivy sighed as she swung her legs over the side of the bunk. It was obvious Drake had taken the razor to shave and then had purposely left it behind, showing her once and for all how little he cared she had it. The action made her feel all the more vulnerable, for it proved more than words she was at the pirates' mercy.

Disheartened by the fact, she went to her trunk and, shifting her weight from one bare foot to the other to avoid the cold floor, pulled a dress from its interior. As she shook out the folds of the modestly fashioned beige dress she selected, she tested the door to the cabin. It was locked, but at least she knew Drake couldn't surprise her while she performed her morning ablutions. In a matter of minutes, she had the nightgown off and the wool dress in place. She was at the washstand, running a comb through the long length of her hair when there was a sharp rap on the door.

Ivy jumped at the sound.

"Are you up?" Drake called in to her.

Without thinking, Ivy started to reach for the blade, the need to have it close by still within her. Then her hand stopped in midair as she remembered the little good it would do her.

"Just a minute," she called out to Drake. Suddenly feeling awkward about facing him after sharing his bed and feeling his caresses, she felt her cheeks flush. She reached for the pitcher and poured a little water into the basin. Quickly, she splashed the cold liquid onto her face. Its bracing effect helped, she decided as she patted away the droplets with the small towel that had been looped through a metal ring on the side of the washstand.

"I'm ready," she said, turning toward the door.

Drake stepped inside. He was glad to see the razor was still on the washstand because it showed Ivy had accepted how little it would help her. As she faced him, with the trace of a blush touching her cheeks, she looked fresh and wholesomely appealing—an enticing contrast to the women who had shared his bed in the past.

Considering the circumstances, those were unwise comparisons, Drake reminded himself. "We'll be joining Keils for breakfast," he told her, bringing his thoughts back to the present.

Though Ivy felt uncomfortable about being alone with Drake, she preferred that to sharing another meal with Keils Cauldron.

"Do we have to join him?" she asked. "I really don't have anything else to tell him about my background."

"That may be, but Keils wants to get to know you better."

Ivy couldn't help but grimace at the idea. "I know him as well as I want to."

"He's not a fire-breathing dragon, Ivy."

Ivy tossed her head, sending her hair tumbling back over her shoulder. "That's easy for you to say."

A glimpse of a smile touched Drake's lips at the disapproval implied in the statement. "Why? Am I a fire-breathing dragon, too?"

"You're just like him, a pirate." Ivy's strong feelings about that particular subject flavored each word.

"There are worse things in life than being a pirate," Drake said easily.

The man obviously had no remorse for what he did, Ivy decided, censure shadowing her eyes. It made her wonder what influence Drake had on her pirate father.

"Are you the reason Cauldron is now attacking

American ships?" she asked abruptly. "It was bad enough before, knowing my real father was a pirate, but at least he never used to attack ships from his own country."

That had been Cauldron's only redeeming grace in her eyes. In the course of his piracy, he had never preyed upon his own country's ships. When he had taken her English mother, she had been aboard a British vessel, and later he had centered his attacks on foreign ships. And then, when the second war with Britain had started, he had preyed heavily on the English warships that were trying to blockade the coast. So even though he was a pirate, he had at least been patriotic in his own way. Now, there was nothing to exonerate his actions.

"It was a joint decision," Drake answered her, "and we had good reason to do it."

Undoubtedly the valuable cargo, Ivy thought, even more disapproval filling her eyes. The lavishness of Cauldron's quarters attested to the bounty he had garnered over the years.

As Ivy's eyes took on the angry gleam they always did when her thoughts dwelled at any length on the pirate captain, Drake knew the morning meal wasn't going to be any more pleasant than last night's repast.

"Before we join Keils," he said, "give me the keys to Havenrest. We'll need them to look at that family Bible of yours." As Ivy got them from the trunk and handed them over without a word, he could see by the combative tilt of her chin that his little dove was once again making that intriguing transformation into a warlike hawk as she prepared to meet Keils Cauldron.

Then he frowned when he ran that thought once again through his mind. *His* little dove? Where had that notion come from? She was anything but his, and from the look in her eyes, it was apparent she wasn't pleased to be in his company—or Cauldron's.

When they entered the captain's quarters and Ivy faced her adversary, Drake knew as he looked from one set of violet eyes to the other that it would be only a matter of time before the two clashed.

Ivy gave Cauldron an appraising glance as she sat in the same chair as before. A shadow of a beard on his jaw this morning gave him a fiercer, more predatory look. Not wanting to talk to him, she turned her attention to the bowl of oatmeal in front of her.

"My son Geoff went to boarding school in George- town," Cauldron began without preamble, carefully con- trolling his emotion as he brought up the memory. "It's surprising I never caught sight of your mother the times I foxed my way in to see him."

Ivy didn't expect the words, but as she recalled how familiar Cauldron had seemed with Georgetown the night before, she should have guessed there was a reason. The thought that she had had a half brother living in the same city as she did was unsettling, but even more unsettling was the fact that Cauldron had often been there as well.

She had never heard he had any connections to that area. From all accounts, he had been born and raised in South Carolina before turning to his infamous life on the seas. And once he had become entrenched in his pirating ways, he had never been known to return to his early haunts, let alone Georgetown. Certainly, if her parents had known, they never would have moved to America. She said a silent, brief prayer of thanks that her mother had been unaware of the pirate's clandestine visits to the city.

"My mother and you would hardly have traveled in the same circles," she told him.

At the words, Drake was sure the sparks would fly, for Cauldron was quite aware of his lack of proper schooling. Only by his own diligent efforts had he learned to read and write, and he had spent years teaching himself to speak in an educated manner. One of the reasons he had insisted Geoff go to boarding school was to ensure his son had the kind of education he had never had. So Drake was surprised that Cauldron, other than regarding Ivy with narrowed eyes, let the words pass unchallenged.

Cauldron's thoughts were centered too much on Geoff to take offense at Ivy's comment. "I'm sure Sunny and I lived in separate worlds," he agreed, "but it's still surprising I didn't catch a glimpse of her, considering how many times over the years I was in Georgetown to see Geoff."

Despite how Ivy felt about the pirate captain, the sorrow in his voice each time he spoke about his son touched a responsive chord within her. Having felt a deep loss for her parents when they died, she could empathize with his grief.

"Until I met you, I had never heard you had a son," she said, her voice losing much of its tightness.

Maybe Geoff could bring the two together, Drake mused, feeling a subtle easing in the tension. As he watched the tautness leave Cauldron's face and eyes, he hoped some good could come from his friend's senseless death.

Cauldron rose from his chair and went to a desk tucked in a corner of the cabin. Opening a drawer, he pulled out a brass frame and brought it back to the table. As he sat down, he handed it to Ivy.

"This is a picture of Geoff."

Though Ivy had never known her half brother had existed until yesterday, Geoff was suddenly no longer just a name. As she gazed upon the young man in the painting, she saw that his face was friendly and open, with laughter apparent in the easy set of the eyes and lips. The sight of him unexpectedly tugged on her emotions. Regardless of the circumstances, she and Geoff shared a bond of blood, and now he was dead. She felt a loss she hadn't expected.

She looked for similarities to herself, but Geoff, with his light brown hair, hazel eyes, and square face, bore no resemblance to herself—or to Cauldron.

"He resembled his mother," Cauldron said gruffly, guessing her thoughts. "You never heard of him because he went by his mother's maiden name when he was growing up so there would be no connection to me."

Ivy's gaze lingered on the portrait. "How old was he when he died?" she asked, her voice gentle as she assessed the youngish features. "Twenty?"

Cauldron shook his head. "He was about that when that picture was painted, but he was the same age as Drake. That's how they became friends. Being so close in age, they roomed together at boarding school."

It took Ivy a moment to realize the importance that lay behind those casually spoken words. *Geoff was the same age as Drake?* The knowledge shocked her to the core, for Drake had to be several years older than she was.

"Geoff was older than me?" she hissed at Cauldron, the sympathy suddenly gone from her voice. "You mean you were *married* when you were with my mother?" That appalling thought had never occurred to her. When she had heard about Geoff, she had assumed he was a product

69

of a marriage that had taken place after the pirate knew her mother.

As tension once again filled the room, Drake knew Geoff wasn't going to be a balm to soothe the trouble between Ivy and Cauldron. And as he watched Cauldron's lips twist at Ivy's accusation, he also knew the sparks were finally going to fly.

Cauldron leaned forward, his face set in harsh lines. With Ivy's sheltered upbringing, the thought that he had compounded his evil deed by being an adulterer was probably more than she could endure, but he wasn't in the mood to bear any more disapproval.

"My wife died giving birth to Geoff," he said with a gritty undertone, "so adultery is one sin I've missed."

All empathy gone, Ivy shot back, "I'm sure you haven't missed many!"

A muscle worked in Cauldron's cheek as he fought for control. "No," he said with a bite to his words, "I probably haven't." Pushing himself away from the table, he strode from the cabin, his dark mood apparent in the way his boots struck hard on the floor beneath him.

As Cauldron's footsteps faded, Drake folded his arms, regarding Ivy with a disapproving look. "For a brief moment," he told her, "I thought you and Keils might almost carry on a civil conversation."

"About Geoff?" Ivy asked wearily, sighing as she looked down at the picture she still held. "Though I didn't know him, he was my half brother, and it affects me to think of his death." For a moment, she was silent as she gazed at the picture, and then she asked softly, "How did it happen?"

"He was murdered." Drake's words were suddenly grim. "In Georgetown."

Ivy had half-expected to hear of an illness since both her mother and father had succumbed to contagious maladies. But the curtly spoken words reminded her that Geoff was the son of a notorious pirate and that such an end would hardly be unexpected in the kind of world in which he and Cauldron lived.

"I'm sorry Geoff is dead," she said with candor, putting down the picture, "but it doesn't change the way I feel about Cauldron."

"Keils is a good man, Ivy."

"He's a *pirate*."

"When Keils began that life, he didn't have much choice," Drake tried to explain. "Geoff was born too early, and for the first several years of his life, he couldn't keep down most of what he was fed. The only thing that helped was an expensive medicine, and Keils couldn't afford it, not as a sailor. So he turned to piracy to keep his son alive."

The explanation hardly appeased Ivy. "While that story has a very noble ring to it," she answered, "apparently Geoff outgrew his frailty. Yet Cauldron still continued his life at sea."

"By that time, he already had a price on his head."

Ivy met Drake's eyes in a long stare. "But he also liked what he was doing, didn't he?"

Drake paused and then said with honesty, "Yes."

Ivy continued to hold his gaze. "That's what I thought. And he still likes it," she added pointedly, "even now."

"It's not a liking for adventure that made us attack the *Wild Swan*." Drake's face grew somber as he thought about the circumstances that had made such a raid necessary. "We were trying to find out who murdered Geoff."

The news took Ivy by surprise. "His killer was on the

71

Wild Swan?"

"No, but we hoped another man who was part of the plot would be on board—a man with only one ear."

"There wasn't anyone on the ship like that," Ivy said with certainty, knowing she would have noticed a man maimed in such a way.

"As it turned out, there wasn't," Drake agreed, disappointment in his words. "We didn't find him on the other ships we thought he might be on, and the *Wild Swan* was our last chance. He was supposed to be carrying some information with him. Something that cost Geoff his life—stolen military secrets." His tone turned harsh. "Keils and I figured once we had that one-eared man, we'd get the name of the killer from him."

There was no doubt in Ivy's mind that torture would have been the method to loosen that tongue. As she thought about the situation, a sinking sensation suddenly settled in the pit of her stomach.

"Is discovering who killed Geoff the task Cauldron wants to do before he looks into my claim?"

"Yes."

"But that could take a long time!"

Drake gave a careless shrug. "It will take as long as it takes to find—and kill—the murderer and his friends."

Ivy felt a shiver pass through her that was caused as much from the deadliness of Drake's promise as the thought of spending night after night in his bed.

Ivy was looking decidedly uneasy again, Drake decided. "Finish your oatmeal," he suggested, "and then we'll go above. I think the fresh air will do us both some good."

*   *   *

The wind was brisk, but with her heavy wool cloak wrapped securely around her, Ivy was warm enough. Not wanting to talk to Cauldron again, she was glad to see he was busy at the other end of the ship. As she and Drake walked along the deck, she tried to ignore the blatantly interested stares of the men.

Though she didn't like to be grateful to Drake for anything, she had to admit his solid presence at her side made her feel safe among the rough crew. None of them, for all their interest, approached her or even tried to speak. She had a feeling if she were alone, it would have been far different.

"What are your plans now to catch Geoff's killer?" she asked, hoping he and Cauldron had something definite in mind to speed the process.

Drake reached into a pocket of his leather greatcoat, pulling out a small tin used for holding tobacco. He handed it to her.

"This was lying not far away from Geoff when I found him," he answered. "It was empty. Keils and I figure the killer probably threw it away."

Ivy examined the container. On its lid was painted a gold tobacco leaf. "How is this going to help you?" she asked, handing it back. "Can't tins like this be bought in any tobacco shop?"

Drake shook his head as he pocketed the clue. "It's a very expensive brand of tobacco and an expensive container so not all shops sell it—and not all men buy it. It will still be a difficult search so we'll bring some of the crew to help."

"You think the shops will be able to give you the names of the people who buy such a tin?" Skepticism crept into Ivy's voice as she tried to picture such a plan working. "Wouldn't it be easier to hunt for the one-eared man?" she ventured. "There couldn't be many of them around."

Considering the life Ivy had led, Drake didn't doubt that one-eared men would seem like a rarity to her. But in the rough waterfront sections of Georgetown, Washington, and nearby Alexandria, the loss of an ear was a fairly common penalty among the sailors who worked on the many ships and barges that traveled the area.

"How many one-eared men have you seen on this ship?" he gave as an answer.

Ivy had seen more than she wanted. "Three."

"It's not uncommon—not among a certain kind of man," he told her. "We'll look for one-eared men too, but the tin will probably lead us to the killer." He gave Ivy a quizzical glance. "You live in Georgetown. Are you familiar with any of the more expensive tobacco shops?"

Ivy wrinkled her nose at the thought. "I've never even been inside a tobacco shop," she confessed. "My father didn't use tobacco, and neither does Allen. Both felt the shops that sell it weren't the type of place I should enter."

If Ivy thought tobacco shops weren't proper, Drake couldn't help but wonder what her reaction would be to the place where he was taking her tonight. Considering her sheltered background, he had a feeling she wasn't going to be pleased.

"I don't suppose you've ever been in a tavern?" he hazarded.

"Of course not."

"By tonight," Drake warned her, "you will."

It could hardly be worse than being on a pirate ship, Ivy decided. And perhaps she could escape. "Where are we landing?" she asked, trying not to sound too interested.

"Cay's Cove."

The name was unfamiliar to Ivy. "Where's that? I've never heard of it."

Drake wasn't surprised, thinking of the kind of place it was. "It's south of Norfolk and it's not much of a town," he admitted, picturing the few dwellings that were sheltered in the secluded inlet. "Kind of rough," he added, trying to prepare her for it. "But we need a place to buy horses and supplies without worrying that someone will talk about our being there. If we want to catch Geoff's killer, we have to keep him from knowing we're coming after him. As soon as the *Black Cauldron* drops us off tonight, she'll head back toward the Chesapeake to make it look as though we're still at sail."

It was a clever plan, Ivy acknowledged. She just hoped she could find a way to escape and not be a part of it.

"One of the men wants to talk to me," Drake excused himself, looking past Ivy to where a pirate was motioning for him to come over. "Wait there, out of everyone's way," he told her, pointing toward the foremast, only yards from them. "I'll be back in a moment."

Ivy went to the mast and leaned against the smooth, rounded base. From above her, the sound of the wind ruffling through the sails was soothing to her troubled thoughts.

They grew even more troubled when two pirates, walking past carrying crates, leered openly in her direction, mouthing words she was glad she couldn't hear. It was enough to make her wish that Drake was still at her side, shielding her from the men's crudity.

As her eyes turned in Drake's direction, she was struck

by the contrast he made with the man he was talking to. Whereas the mate was short and stocky, Drake was tall and muscular. And where the mate had broken teeth and a shaved head, Drake had a flashing grin and thick, tawny hair.

He was handsome, she had to admit, and the fact she could think so, given her circumstances, did not sit well with her. Drake was a pirate and her captor—hardly the kind of man she should feel attracted to. She only had to think of her mother to remind herself of that.

The dissonant sound of metal bumping against wood brought Ivy out of her musings. It took her a moment to realize the noise was coming from above her. As she tipped her head back, looking up at the mast for the source of the clamor, she heard Drake yell out to her.

"Jump to the right, Ivy! Quickly!"

For a moment Ivy froze, held in place by the look of alarm on Drake's face as he ran toward her. But as she registered that the clanging sound above her was suddenly louder, she came to life, leaping to the side as he had instructed.

"God damn it!"

Drake's oath was loud in Ivy's ear as he caught her in a rough tackle that sent them both tumbling hard onto the pine planks of the deck. A scant second later, an even louder noise sounded as a heavy block and tackle attached to a loose line came crashing onto the deck beside them.

Jarred by the fierce jolting, Ivy lay still, her breath almost knocked from her body by Drake's weight landing on top of her.

For his part, Drake was suddenly aware of how soft Ivy was as she lay pinned beneath him. Despite the dangerous situation that had brought them together, his blood begin to thicken and pound at the sensation.

Ivy caught her breath and stared up into Drake's face. She felt the sudden heat that seemed to radiate from him despite the clothing separating them. And reflected within his blue eyes, she saw desire.

"Drake," she said uneasily, stumbling a little over his name as she said it for the first time.

The way Ivy's voice caught was Drake's undoing. Without thinking, he brought his lips to hers and kissed her as he had wanted to from the moment he had set eyes on her.

Chapter 6

At the touch of Drake's lips, a swirl of sensations bombarded Ivy's senses. The only other kisses she had ever received from a man had come from Allen, and his had been light, carefully restrained caresses that had ended almost before they had begun. Those chaste kisses were a far cry from the way Drake's mouth was moving over her own, his tongue skillfully urging her lips apart. And certainly Allen had never kissed her while pinning her shamelessly to the ground.

The brazenness of such an embrace shocked her. Even more disturbing, she found the feel of Drake's lips and body unexpectedly sensual as well, and she felt weak inside and strangely passive. Her fingers, which had been aimed at his broad shoulders in an effort to push him away, suddenly seemed unable to complete the motion. Lying quietly beneath him, she accepted without resistance the deepening, teasing advances of his tongue.

At the sound of feet running across the deck, Drake suddenly came to his senses, knowing that in an instant the area would be filled with men, curious to see the source of the loud crash.

He raised his head and looked down into Ivy's face. As her eyes slowly opened, the dazed bewilderment in them showed more clearly than words that she had never been kissed as he had just kissed her.

Drake swore to himself at his loss of control. Clamping a tight rein on the attraction he felt, he began to push himself away from her. A sharp slap on his face was his reward.

"You're not supposed to touch me!" Ivy hissed as she struggled to a sitting position, her embarrassment at the way she had yielded to his kiss adding to her indignation.

"Then don't end up sprawled under me!" Drake shot back. "You jumped left when I told you to jump right!"

Ivy glared at him. "I didn't have time to think straight!"

"Well, neither did I!" Drake came to his feet, bringing Ivy with him, and then waved away the men who were gathering around. "But at least what I did," he added in a low growl, "wouldn't get us both killed!"

Ivy was trembling, but she knew it was more from Drake's kiss than from the brush with danger. "When you yelled at me to jump," she said heatedly, "my mind went blank for a moment, but that didn't give you the right to—"

"Kiss you in a way you've never been kissed before," Drake cut in with just as much feeling. "Your response made *that* very clear!" As he looked down into Ivy's violet eyes, seeing the same fiery spirit that was usually reserved for Cauldron, he found he liked having that spirited emotion directed at him. It made him feel stimulated, full of yearning, and—frustrated, he reminded himself as Ivy abruptly turned toward the gunwale.

80

Seeing the stiffness of her back as she stared out at the ocean, he immediately regretted what he had said. He knew Ivy, with her proper upbringing, would be particularly sensitive about her response to the kiss they had shared. As he was about to join her, a hand on his shoulder made him turn around instead.

"What happened with the—" Cauldron's question came to a halt at the sight of the red imprint of fingers clearly marking Drake's cheek. He grinned broadly.

"Ivy's not quite as sweet natured as you thought, is she?" he remarked, enjoying seeing someone else tangle with the spirited captive.

Drake rubbed at the reddened area, giving Cauldron a rueful smile at the ribbing. "I guess I deserved it," he admitted.

Cauldron chuckled as he turned his attention toward the broken tackle. "With that little lady," he tossed over his shoulder, "I'm sure it's just the beginning."

Cauldron might be wary of Ivy's claim, Drake reflected, but her presence was certainly easing some of his grimness. He joined Ivy at the gunwale, and when she pointedly ignored him, he stared out at the ocean as she was doing.

"Neither of us was hurt," he said in a low voice, "so let's forget it happened."

Ivy didn't know if he was referring to the kiss or the loose tackle, but she was so appalled by her behavior, she didn't want to talk to him. She should have pushed him away, she chided herself, to clearly show she didn't want to receive his kiss. Instead, she had passively lain there, allowing him to do so.

Not answering, she continued to stare unseeingly out at the water.

Not particularly surprised by her response, Drake decided on a different tack to make Ivy acknowledge him.

"There's a possibility Keils may not be a pirate for much longer," he threw out as bait.

At the words, Ivy turned toward Drake, her chagrin at her behavior indeed forgotten. "What are you talking about?" she demanded.

"After Geoff died, I mentioned the spy ring to a friend of mine in politics. Some people in power came back with an interesting proposition." He paused, noting he had Ivy's full attention. "They thought since Keils had a personal interest in going after the spies, he would have a better chance of catching them than they would." For a moment his lips twisted in a humorless smile. "Revenge and piracy do make a deadly combination," he conceded.

As a captive taken from one of the ships they had raided, Ivy was quite aware of the power and freedom that pirates had to pursue their own course of action.

"So what does Cauldron get in return for that favor?" she asked with a bite, her emotions still brittle from before. "Enough money to retire?"

"You really do think the worst of him, don't you?" Drake gently chided. When Ivy gave him a look that wasn't the least repentant, he answered her with, "The government will give him a pardon."

Ivy's expression didn't soften. Even if Cauldron were pardoned—which was unlikely since he had so few clues to finding Geoff's killer—she knew it wouldn't change the way she felt about him. Nothing could pardon him in her view for what he had done to her mother.

"I'm sure it's important to the government to stop a spy plot," she said, "but Cauldron doesn't deserve to be pardoned, not for all he's done."

It wasn't the reaction Drake had hoped for. "Considering the number of British warships Keils has preyed upon," he reminded her, "he's been of great service to his country."

"He also preyed upon my mother and me." When Drake had no answer for that irrefutable fact, Ivy added, "What happens if Cauldron *doesn't* end the spy ring?"

The question, filled with unconcealed speculation, made Drake grin. "At least this answer should please you," he answered. "He'll be held accountable for the American ships he had to raid."

"He'll still be wanted for piracy, you mean," Ivy clarified. As Drake gave a shrug of assent, Ivy realized one part of the explanation didn't fit. "If Cauldron has an agreement with the government, why did we run from the frigate in the bay?"

"Only a few people in Washington know about the pact since Keils didn't want anything forewarning the killer and his friends." Drake's gaze swept the horizon. "So the *Black Cauldron* is fair game to anyone who wants to blast her out of the water."

It was hardly a comforting thought. "That's some deal," Ivy muttered.

"Keils would have attacked those American ships with or without the government's permission," Drake pointed out, "because the people who killed Geoff are going to pay for what they did—with their lives."

The deadly promise sent a chill down Ivy's spine that had nothing to do with the brisk air about her. When it came to revenge, the pirates were relentless; that was becoming more and more apparent. If Cauldron decided she was trying to deceive him, she would hate to see what happened if that harsh revenge was turned on her.

Pardoned or not, she knew it wouldn't change whatever plans the pirate captain had for her. He had already made that very clear. And if the government didn't care what methods Cauldron used to catch his prey, they probably wouldn't care about one hapless victim taken from one of their ships, particularly if they found out she was his daughter.

She glanced toward Cauldron, still with his men at the mast. "If Cauldron accepts I'm his daughter, what will he do with me?"

"If I were you," Drake answered, "I wouldn't worry about your fate if Keils accepts that you're his. I'd worry if he decides you're not—and that you deceived him."

Ivy turned back to the gunwale, staring once again at the sea. "What would be my fate then?" she whispered.

"I don't know, Ivy," Drake replied after a moment. "I honestly don't know."

That night, with the moon hidden behind a blanket of clouds, the *Black Cauldron* dropped anchor in the secluded inlet at Cay's Cove. The longboat was lowered and Ivy held tightly to the rope ladder as she made her way down to the boat.

When she reached the bottom, she stiffened as Drake placed his hands around her waist to help her into the narrow craft. Locked alone in the cabin most of the day while the pirates sailed toward the cove, she had seen very little of him since morning. The feel of his hands spanning her waist and the nearness of his face as he steadied her made her remember all too clearly the kiss she had been trying hard all day to forget.

"I may nibble," Drake murmured into her ear, feeling

her body tense beneath his touch, "but I won't bite."

If that was supposed to reassure her, Ivy decided, it didn't. Between his sleep-induced, languid kisses the night before and his deliberately sensual kiss this morning, his "nibbling" seemed instead to arouse her fears. She could only hope her link to Cauldron would keep him from "biting."

After Drake had stowed the canvas bag containing a few of their things under the plank seat at the stern of the craft, she situated herself over it to make sure the softly constructed piece of luggage wasn't inadvertently trampled by the other men filling the boat.

It was only large enough for their most basic necessities, but when she had asked Drake if she could include her miniatures, after only a moment's hesitation over the wisdom of transporting such fragile objects, he had agreed. She was sure he had relented for the same reason he had been willing to let her have the razor—to put her at ease—but that wasn't why she wanted the tiny portraits with her. Their presence seemed to give her an inner strength, and Ivy needed that to face the days ahead.

When Drake settled beside her, his arm carelessly resting on the edge of the longboat behind her, she self-consciously tried to shift away but was immediately jostled back as a vicious-looking pirate known as Drager crowded onto the seat on her other side.

She found herself crushed tightly against Drake's side with her shoulder pressed against the soft cambric of his shirt, his greatcoat being open. The clean, masculine scent emanating from him was in sharp contrast to the particularly loathsome odor of the man flanking her other side. But that clean, masculine scent also reminded

85

her of the taste of his lips and the feel of his body as he had pinned her beneath him. They were sensations she wanted to forget.

"Isn't Cauldron coming with us?"

Ivy asked the question more to divert her thoughts than out of caring what the pirate captain did. With the men busy with their preparations, she had been spared any more meetings with him, and that had been to her liking.

Drake held back his reply until the pirates shoved the longboat away from the ship and began to row toward a small cluster of buildings nestled in the isolated cove.

As the boat's oars settled into an even rhythm, he said, "Keils has already gone ashore to arrange for the horses and supplies we'll need. We'll meet him at the tavern we're going to."

Even with her cloak acting as a barrier between them, Ivy was pressed so closely against Drake's side she could feel the steady beat of his heart as he talked. She tried to ignore the intimate sensation but couldn't, conscious that Drake's eyes were boring into her.

"You look like the figurehead of a sea maid I recently bought," Drake told her, his words reflective.

"Sea maid?" Ivy asked the question distractedly, disconcerted by his steady stare.

"It's another name for a mermaid," Drake explained. "You remind me of her."

His words made Ivy look up at the prow of the *Black Cauldron*, now looming right above them. The female figurehead that graced it was bare to the waist, the naked breasts thrusting wantonly through long strands of dark hair.

Ivy was scandalized at the comparison. Is that how

86

Drake envisioned her, with her breasts naked? Only the fact that she had nowhere to go kept her in her seat.

Following her gaze, Drake threw back his head and laughed. "That's *not* what I'm comparing you to. That's not even a sea maid," he added. "She has legs. And in the daylight, you'd see her hair is red, not black. I'm talking about the figurehead on *my* ship, the *Sea Maid*."

"*Your* ship?" Ivy asked in surprise. "I thought you were part of Cauldron's crew."

"No, I just joined Keils to help him catch Geoff's killer. The *Sea Maid* isn't my pirating ship, though," Drake clarified. "She's a pretty sloop I use when I want to be free of that. You'll see her when we get to Georgetown. I left her there when I brought her in to meet Geoff before he died." Bringing his lips close to Ivy's ear, he murmured, "And the woman on *her* bow isn't bare."

The way he said the last words made Ivy feel as though he was picturing her like that anyway. She searched for a safer topic.

"How do you and Cauldron know about Cay's Cove?" she asked, nodding toward the lights of the little town they were fast approaching.

"Every pirate along this coast knows Cay's Cove."

A town that catered to thieves and ruffians, Ivy thought gloomily. Her life had certainly made a turn for the worse. When the longboat reached a rickety pier, she was further dismayed by a group of drunken men tossing dice in a dark corner. She saw other roughly clad men lurking in the shadows of a nearby ramshackle building, and it was with great reluctance that she followed Drake from the longboat.

"This is a frightening place," she murmured uneasily as they left the pier area behind, turning into a dark, forbidding alley. As their feet crunched over the shells that paved the narrow lane, she couldn't help making frequent glances over her shoulder.

"Couldn't we be attacked in here?" she asked worriedly.

Drake's teeth flashed white in the shadows. He gestured at the members of Cauldron's crew who were preceding them.

"The men who sail on the *Black Cauldron* are more dangerous than anyone who's already here," he said dryly. "It's everyone else who has to be afraid." His point was proved as several men standing at the end of the alley quickly moved aside to let them pass.

"If you have escape on your mind," Drake continued, his voice suddenly filled with warning, "don't try it. In this town, men have lust or murder on their minds, and that includes our own crew."

Just then Ivy heard a strangled scream come from the pier area behind them; she didn't need Drake to tell her she wouldn't survive on her own in a place like this. Escape was important, but staying alive was even more so.

"It would be suicidal," she agreed. But when she was in the right place, she added to herself, it would be different.

"Even when we're clear of this town," Drake added, guessing her thoughts, "don't think we'll let you escape. Keils and I won't risk *anything* ruining our plans to catch Geoff's killer. So even if you somehow managed to get away—and that won't be likely since I plan to watch you like a hawk—we'd track you down, to the ends of the earth if we had to. And that's doubly true since you claim to be Keils's daughter."

It was a discouraging thought, not that Ivy was dissuaded from contemplating her freedom anyway. But as another scream ripped through the night, it emphasized the fact that such plans would have to wait.

She stayed close to Drake's side as they approached a shabby tavern that had a steady stream of rough-looking patrons flowing in and out. The name, Dirk and Dagger, painted in faded letters on a sign hanging above the door, hardly began to describe the deadly weaponry that everyone—including one blonde woman lolling by the entrance—carried.

As the men of the *Black Cauldron* shouldered their way into the place, the blonde broke away from the conversation she was having to stop Drake from going inside.

"It's been a long time, Drake," she purred, "but you grow more and more handsome each time I see you."

Ivy eyed the blonde with shocked fascination, for she was the kind of woman she had only heard about. A fox cape was flipped negligently over her shoulders to reveal an off-the-shoulder red satin dress that barely covered her generous bosom. Kohl outlined her blue eyes, and rouge had been liberally applied to her lips and cheeks to enhance their color. With her carelessly tousled golden hair, she was undeniably provocative.

Drake gave the woman an easy grin. "It's been awhile, Lola."

"Too long," Lola pouted. She threw Ivy a quick, appraising look and, after taking in the plain cloak and the unadorned wool dress that peeked from beneath it, pointedly dismissed her. Slanting a coquettish glance at Drake through her darkened lashes, she laced her hand through his arm, pulling him a few paces away from the tavern entrance.

As Ivy watched Lola raise herself on her toes to whisper something into Drake's ear, the muted conversation that followed made her feel as though her presence was an intrusion on their intimacy. Strangely bothered by the feeling, she turned her back to them to shut out the whispered words. As two men stepped from the tavern, she moved to the side to let them pass.

"All alone, sweeting?" the more muscular of the two asked, his question a low invitation.

Ivy was aware of the men's eyes roving over her in an indecent, hungry gaze. She tensed under their perusal, conscious of a predatory aura that seemed to radiate from them.

She gave her head a quick, negative shake to make them move on. To her chagrin, they didn't.

"You look alone to me, darlin'."

Ivy shot a swift glance back at Drake but saw he was still engrossed in his tête-à-tête. Though he was only a few yards away, she knew he wouldn't have heard the muttered words that had been said to her. And as he laughed at something Lola was saying, Ivy had a feeling he wouldn't welcome an interruption—particularly not for something he would probably think was trivial. Still, his nearby presence made her feel not as threatened.

"What's your answer, violet-eyes?"

The words snapped Ivy's attention back to the men. "I'm with the *Black Cauldron*," she told them firmly, certain her connection to the dreaded pirate ship would make the two depart.

Neither man moved.

The predatory aura that surrounded the two suddenly seemed stronger, more dangerous to Ivy, and she sensed their interest in her had, for some inexplicable reason, just magnified.

"Let's go find a dark alley," the second man suddenly rasped with a lusty eagerness to his voice, "so you can show us some of the tricks you learned from *that* crew."

Ivy's first reaction to the crude suggestion was to flee to Drake's side. But as she remembered his comment about showing more backbone if she was really Keils Cauldron's daughter, she decided otherwise.

"I wouldn't go anywhere with the likes of you," she threw back at them. Sure that such an emphatic refusal would finally send them on their way, she grew alarmed when the men's expressions suddenly grew forbidding. As they came toward her, she began to back away.

"Are you trying to get yourself killed, Ivy?" Drake growled as he stepped to her side.

"You were the one who told me I should show more backbone," Ivy tried to defend herself.

Drake's eyes didn't leave the two men. "You've shown enough backbone since then," he gritted as he pushed her safely behind him. "And *this* isn't the time to show some mettle even if you hadn't. I'm outnumbered."

Chapter 7

Drake ducked as the more muscular assailant suddenly lunged toward him, swinging a hard blow. Before the man could regain his balance to throw another punch, Drake straightened, bringing his fist against the side of his opponent's face in a bone-crunching swing. Without a sound, the man sank unconscious to the ground.

Graceful as a lethal panther, Drake turned to face his next attacker. He met the man's leap toward him with a swift, hard kick that connected solidly. Clutching at his groin, the thug toppled over, immobilized by the waves of pain pouring through him.

Satisfied the men were no longer a threat, Drake turned to Ivy, his expression showing his displeasure at having to do battle.

"What on earth did you say to these men"—he motioned toward the downed assailants—"to make them decide to take you to an alley so you could show them your tricks?"

Ivy was still staring in shock at the two men lying on

the ground. The complete ease with which Drake had defeated them made her increasingly aware of just how dangerous a man he was. No wonder he hadn't cared that she had a razor last night. Taking it from her would have been but a moment's effort.

Reluctantly, she raised her eyes to meet his, knowing by the tone of his voice he was angry. The grimness of his expression made her step away warily, uncertain if he had Cauldron's permission to punish her if he saw fit.

"All I said was that I was with the *Black Cauldron*," she struggled to explain, not understanding herself what had made the two men suddenly so insistent. "With the ship's reputation, I thought they'd go away when they heard that."

Drake frowned at the answer. But as Ivy took another leery step away from him, he realized he was frightening her. Immediately his ire faded, for he knew from her explanation she hadn't purposely provoked the fight.

"What you said made them think you were a ship doxy," he told her. "And a talented one at that since only the best ever make it onto the *Black Cauldron*."

Drake's bluntly spoken words embarrassed Ivy, not only because of the frankness of the topic but also because she had given the two men such an erroneous impression.

"Oh."

"If you had wanted to send those men on their way," Drake continued, "you should have told them Keils Cauldron is your father."

Ivy's embarrassment disappeared at that bit of advice. "That's a fact," she said with feeling, "that I'd just as soon not have known."

94

"It's also a fact that could have saved us both some trouble."

"If you hadn't left me to talk to *her*"—Ivy glanced toward Lola, still standing in the street—"*we* wouldn't have had any trouble at all."

Drake couldn't refute that. When Lola had come over and whispered a sultry invitation in his ear, he had been sorely tempted to take her up on her offer so he could slake the desire that had been building since he had met Ivy. But as he gazed down at Ivy's lovely face, he suddenly knew another woman wouldn't ease the tension gathering within him.

"Let's go inside," he growled instead, not liking the whole ridiculous situation Cauldron had put him in.

The tavern was crowded and smoky, its sand floor littered with broken glass and stained in several places by the dark spill of blood. Torches made of twisted, lard-soaked rags cast wavery shadows of the men who were milling about as they drank their ale. Their conversation—loud, lewd, and boisterous—filled the air.

It was not a place Ivy wanted to be. Dismayed by such surroundings, she reluctantly followed Drake to a long table where Cauldron was sitting, surrounded by his men.

"Another round of ale," Cauldron called to one of the serving girls as he caught sight of Drake and Ivy.

Several men shifted over to make room for them on the bench, and Ivy found herself sandwiched between Drake and Cauldron. On the far side of the room, a violent fist-fight broke out between two men, wildly cheered by a score of drunken watchers. Ivy couldn't help but mutter to herself, "Oh, Allen, if only I were with you."

Cauldron caught the lowly spoken words. "Allen?"

"Allen Badgley, my betrothed," Ivy informed him. "He's a clergyman," she added stiffly, expecting Cauldron to laugh over the occupation as he had done before, but this time, the revelation brought nothing more than a shrug.

Considering Ivy's upbringing, Cauldron could have almost guessed her betrothed's calling in life. And as with her mother, the match suited her.

"Ale?" he asked, taking the new pitcher from the serving girl.

Ivy shook her head. "I don't care for ale."

"Considering you didn't touch it last night, I didn't think you did." Cauldron pushed a steaming cup of tea over to her that had been sitting in the middle of the table. "That's why I ordered you this as soon as I saw my crew come in through the door. The ale is for Drake." He poured Drake a mugful, pushing it toward him.

Ivy sipped at the hot liquid, surprised Cauldron had thought to get it for her. "Thank you," she finally said, feeling awkward at saying such words to a man she despised, but saying them anyway since etiquette demanded they be said.

"You're welcome." Cauldron's response was cautious, showing he had no trouble guessing Ivy's reasons for being polite.

All in all, Drake decided, it was an encouraging attempt at civility. But one look at their faces, both taut with tension, made him decide to steer the conversation elsewhere before it deteriorated. A public tavern was no place for these two to spar.

"Did you make all the arrangements, Keils?" he asked, speaking over Ivy's head.

As the two men talked, Ivy sipped at her tea and watched the other people in the tavern. In addition to the serving girls, a few other women were scattered around the room, their revealing clothes and bold actions identifying them as the prostitutes they were. She wasn't particularly surprised that Lola, sauntering into the tavern on the arm of a large man, seemed to be one of them.

Ivy was more than a little shocked at the casual way each woman disappeared up the stairs with a man, only to return a short while later to repeat the process with someone new. Even with her sheltered background, she knew why they sought a place to be alone.

As her gaze moved idly over the room, a swarthy man at one of the tables caught her eye and gave her a broad wink in an obvious invitation. Ivy quickly looked away but she was conscious of him standing up and moving in her direction.

"If no one here is needing your services, I have gold that's crying to be spent," the man offered.

At the words, Drake started to rise, a dangerous warning in his eyes, but Cauldron slammed down his mug before Drake could speak.

"That might be my daughter you're insulting, Jonesy," he snapped.

The man paled at the magnitude of the mistake he had just made. "My apologies, Cauldron," he said contritely, backing away. "I didn't know you had a daughter."

Cauldron gave Ivy a sideways, unreadable glance. "Until recently, neither did I."

Though Cauldron's words showed his wariness about believing the claim, Drake didn't miss the touch of pride in the pirate captain's voice at the thought that the raven-haired beauty at his side might be of his own blood. Once again, Drake found himself hoping Ivy could prove her claim, for he could see how badly Cauldron would be hurt if he began to accept Ivy only to find out there was no truth to it. And what would happen to Ivy, if Cauldron thought she had played him false, was something he didn't want to imagine.

Cauldron stood up. "It's late," he said to Drake, "and we'll be rising early. I arranged for some rooms upstairs. Mine is the one at the end of the hall and yours is the one to the right of it." He waved over one of the maidservants, passing by with a bucket of water. "See that we have clean linen in our rooms," he ordered.

As the girl scurried away to do Cauldron's bidding, Ivy said weakly, "We're going to stay *here?* I assumed we would be going to an inn."

"This is as much of an inn as this place has," Cauldron answered before turning to his men with some last instructions.

Drake headed toward a narrow flight of stairs, and Ivy followed him. She didn't know what bothered her more—another night with Drake or staying at a place like this.

At the top of the steps, she stopped in shock.

Standing in the hallway, his pants down around his knees, was a man entwined in a decidedly amorous embrace with one of the tavern girls. And she was just as indecent, her pendulous breasts fully bared and her skirts hiked to her waist, showing an expanse of naked thigh as she wrapped one shapely leg about her eager partner.

The man's taut buttocks began thrusting forward and the huge breasts began to heave wildly. Ivy suddenly realized with even greater shock that the couple was making love. The frantic arching of the naked loins gave her unwanted glimpses of glistening, taut male flesh burying itself into the yielding softness of the tavern girl's body.

As their loud, lustful groans filled the narrow hallway, Ivy turned to flee back down the stairs. Drake's hand on her arm stopped her and forced her instead to step around the grunting couple toward their room.

"Don't let it bother you," he said curtly. "If we wait for the hallway to clear, we'll be downstairs all night, especially since we're taking up one of the rooms." He thrust Ivy into their chamber, effectively separating her from the passion in the hall.

Ivy was so mortified by what she had seen and especially by having seen it in Drake's presence she couldn't look at him. As the grunts and moans from the hallway suddenly exploded into wild, wanton cries of delight, she kept her eyes steadfastly on the maidservant busily putting fresh linens on the bed. The girl seemed totally oblivious to the sounds of the mating, but Ivy could seem to hear nothing else.

When the noises peaked, ending with a sharp outcry from the woman and a deep, satisfied groan from the man, Ivy tried not to think about what they had been doing to reach that final state. Nor did she want to think about who had used the bed the maidservant was now changing or what had been done on its soft surface.

Instead, she channeled her thoughts onto the interior of the room. It was even more bare than Drake's cabin, containing only a bed and a battered washstand that had a dented metal basin on it. One small window was on the facing wall, but its shutters were drawn shut and tightly padlocked. Cauldron's orders, she guessed, the man taking no chances she would escape.

He needn't have worried, she thought unhappily as she heard the couple in the hall laughingly discuss intimate aspects of their passion. If she hadn't already decided that being on her own in this town was suicidal, she would have quickly reached the same decision by now.

When the maidservant finished her task and hurried out the door, Ivy felt very awkward at being left alone in the room with Drake. Her awkwardness increased at Lola's sudden appearance at the door.

Striking a sultry pose, Lola drawled to the man standing possessively beside her, "Honey, wait for me in there"—she pointed to the doorway right across from her—"and I'll be with you in a moment." Her current swain eagerly doing her bidding, she sauntered over to Drake. Ignoring Ivy, she suddenly pressed herself to him and gave him a swift, intense kiss.

"It would be good," she said in a sultry voice, moving her hips from side to side to brush provocatively over the firm feel of him. "Very, very good." As she felt Drake's body tauten more under her touch, his eyes darkening with desire, Lola's lips curved in satisfaction. Turning away, she threw a last, enticing smile over her shoulder as she went to join her gentleman friend.

Though Ivy was apprehensive about spending another night with Drake, the thought of spending one without him in a place like this suddenly worried her even more.

"Are . . . are you going to be joining her, Drake?"

From Ivy's reluctant question, Drake could tell it was difficult for her to ask. Before answering, he watched the door close on Lola and her eager lover. Though he had already accepted he would get no real relief from being

100

with another woman, he envied the satisfaction Lola's partner would feel. For himself, there would be no such pleasure. The only thing that loomed ahead of him was another night of frustration.

"I'm not going anywhere," he said, his voice tight. As he saw the relief that passed over Ivy's face, some of his frustration faded. Considering what she had seen in the hall, he was sure she would be even more skittish about sharing a room with him tonight than she had been last night. At the same time, it was obvious she didn't want to be alone in it either. Not in this town.

"I'm not going anywhere," he repeated, gentling his voice. He set the canvas bag containing their things onto the bed. "I'll give you a few minutes to get ready. Until then, I'll be right outside."

As he entered the hallway, closing the door behind him, the sounds of a wildly creaking bed began to come to him from Lola's room. Gritting his teeth at the images that noise provoked, he tried not to think of himself and Ivy in a similar passionate embrace. Already aroused by what he had witnessed at the top of the stairs, he totally failed.

Inside the room, Ivy prepared for another night with Drake, little butterflies forming in her stomach. Leaving on her petticoat as she had done the night before, she reached for her nightgown with the intention of sleeping that way again. But when she started to slip on the garment, the thought of such binding discomfort made her pause.

Sleep was difficult enough, she decided, without adding other difficulties. She would shed the petticoat but keep on her cotton shift. That way she could be comfortable and still not feel too bare.

By the time she had the nightgown in place, there seemed to be a whole colony of butterflies in her stomach. To help bolster her flagging courage, she pulled the miniatures from the canvas bag, carefully unwrapping them from the woolen scarf she had wound around them for protection.

Once again, their presence seemed to strengthen her. After placing them onto the washstand, she got into the bed and pulled the covers modestly up to her chin as she sat there. The sheets were cold, but from her one night with Drake, she knew how warm they would be once he joined her. And join her he would, for Drake had made it clear they would be sharing a bed, no matter what their lodgings, so he could keep an eye on her without tying her up.

Suddenly she felt like a new bride waiting for her husband, and the feeling unnerved her. Taking another bracing look at her miniatures, she called out to Drake.

"I'm ready." Her voice wavered as she said the words.

Drake entered the room. The sight of Ivy waiting in bed for him, looking alluring as she modestly held the covers to herself, was like a powerful aphrodisiac, intensifying the stirring in his loins.

He saw she had set out the miniatures just as she had the night before. If she hoped the sight of her betrothed would dampen his interest in her, her efforts were all for nothing, he decided, to judge by his body's reaction.

Knowing the effect such evidence of his desire would have on her, he quickly doused the lamp. With only the moonlight that filtered in through the slats of the closed shutters to guide him, he divested himself of the pistol and knife he was carrying, and laid them on the floor.

Considering the smallness of the room, the pistol was

close enough for Ivy to think of making a grab for it, but after looking at it with longing, she didn't try. Like the razor Drake had let her have, she knew a one-shot pistol wouldn't be enough to gain her freedom—not in this rough tavern, in this rough town. Drake knew it and so did she.

Still, she couldn't help remarking, "You're very confident I won't use your weapons against you, aren't you?"

"*I'm* not your enemy, Ivy."

Ivy wasn't so sure of that as she watched Drake tug off his boots in preparation for bed.

Chapter 8

Drake gave a small chuckle as he tossed his boots aside. "If I were Keils, though," he added, "I'd *never* put a weapon within your reach. The way you flare up around him, you'd shoot him for sure." He began unbuttoning his shirt. "I'm as much of a pawn in all this as you are." He gave another low chuckle. "Maybe we should *both* shoot Keils for putting us through this."

Ivy saw no humor in the situation. As Drake turned away from her, shedding his shirt, the faint moonlight played over the strong contours of his back, making each well-defined muscle stand out in bold relief.

This man was going to share a bed with her again, Ivy thought, swallowing hard. And tonight, thanks to the couple in the hall and Lola's brazen invitation, she was sure mating must be going through his mind.

Suddenly, the idea of grabbing for the pistol didn't seem like such a useless idea.

From the corner of his eye, Drake was watching Ivy to make sure she didn't. Considering how rough the tavern was, he wanted his weapons within easy reach. He hoped by putting them openly in front of her, emphasizing they would be as little use to her here as the razor had been on the ship, that her common sense would again govern her actions.

Just in case he was wrong, he watched her stealthily as he unfastened his breeches. Last night, he hadn't been particularly concerned about the razor because wrestling it from her would have been an easy enough task. But a pistol was a far more dangerous weapon, and Ivy was looking increasingly skittish as he stepped out of his pants.

Ivy's throat constricted at the way the shadows danced over Drake's physique. Tall, muscular, and well-proportioned, he had all the beauty of a Greek statue as he stood there clad only in a brief swatch of cotton that took only the smallest bit of imagination to picture as a fig leaf.

He was the kind of man who was undoubtedly used to success when it came to women, and as he turned to face her, she could only hope she wasn't going to be one of them. Even in the concealing darkness, it was evident that Drake was heavily aroused.

The sight made her heart pound with hard, erratic thuds. Again, Ivy glanced at the pistol, the temptation to grab for it overwhelming. While her emotions cried out for her to do it, her common sense held her back. As Drake had said, though he was her captor, it was Cauldron who was her foe. Shooting the one wouldn't free her of the other, not in this town.

The weapon would only be useful to keep Drake from joining her in the bed, and now that she had seen him fight, she was certain he wouldn't docilely go along with that. If it came to a skirmish, she didn't want to think what could happen after he had wrestled the gun from her. As he had told her last night, a man only had so much control, and from the look of him now, he was already at the brink.

From where he stood, Drake began to relax when he saw Ivy wasn't going to do anything foolish. The uneasiness in her eyes made him want to take her into his arms; the fullness in his loins told him how unwise that would be.

"You made the right decision," he told her as he came toward the bed. "You know those weapons can't help you here."

The sight of Drake coming purposefully toward her, looking so aggressively male and so ready to mate, was Ivy's undoing. She lunged for the pistol even as she knew it was a foolish thing to do.

Her fingers were just wrapping around its handle when Drake's bare foot came down, pinning her wrist and the pistol hard onto the floor.

"Let go of it, Ivy."

The command, though said in a low voice, was filled with a definite threat of what would happen if she didn't. Ivy looked up at Drake. From her crouched position on the floor, the sight of him was even more intimidating than before.

"I'm afraid to," she whispered.

Drake sighed at the words and then reached down and hauled Ivy to her feet, jerking the pistol from her as he did so.

Held tightly against the almost-naked length of Drake's body, Ivy felt the mating part of him press intimately against her loins and then felt it tauten and stir at the feel of her. She flinched at the sensation.

Drake abruptly released her. "Get back into bed," he ordered.

Ivy couldn't obey, not now. Instead, she began backing toward the door.

"If I have to chase you around this room and then wrestle you into that bed," Drake gritted, "I *know* I'm not going to be able to stop myself when I get you there, not the way I feel tonight."

The blatant state of his body convinced Ivy he was telling the truth. Although she dreaded doing so, she returned to the bed, reluctantly sliding once again under the covers.

Drake picked up the knife, adding it to the pistol he held. "I guess a pistol was a little too much temptation," he muttered. "Well, since I can't trust you around these, I'll have to put them where you can't get them, though I hate to have them out of my reach in a place like this." Pushing them deep under the mattress, he joined her in the bed, its frame groaning under his weight.

Ivy was afraid he was going to reach for her. As the minutes passed and he didn't, she realized he meant to keep his distance. Side by side, they lay next to each other, each very aware of the other's presence.

Drake tried to think of the quest he and Cauldron were on, but his awareness of the soft, tempting body lying so close to his own made it impossible to keep his mind from straying in that direction.

Ivy tried to think of Allen, but the image of the muscular, aroused body at her side wouldn't leave her. Tonight was even harder than last night, she decided. Then, everything had been so new, so frightening, her thoughts had dwelled as much on her captivity as on her captor. Tonight, after seeing Drake clad in so little and looking so blatantly male, she found she could think of nothing else.

The tension between them was almost tangible.

"Can you tell me more about Geoff?" she finally asked to break the strain.

Drake was glad to think of something besides Ivy and the desire he felt for her. "After we met at boarding school, Geoff was like a brother to me," he answered. "My parents were dead and Keils was off pirating, so we did everything together. And whenever school wasn't in session, we'd join Keils on the *Black Cauldron*."

"He made you both into pirates." Disapproval of the man's actions stole into Ivy's words.

Drake shifted in the bed, coming up on his elbow to face Ivy in the dim moonlight. "That was a decision both Geoff and I made."

The way he now loomed over her in the bed made Ivy feel small and vulnerable. Intimidated, she tugged the blankets higher.

The gesture didn't escape Drake. He settled once again onto his back, but the tension between them, which had momentarily lifted, was back.

Ivy tried to focus her thoughts back onto Geoff. Though she had only known of his existence for a short time, the idea of having lost a brother, even a half brother sired by a man she held in contempt, was sobering.

"How was Geoff murdered?" she finally asked.

That particular day was etched forever in Drake's mind. "I received a message from him that he and Keils would be coming in to Georgetown to see Keils's great-aunt, who was very ill. Martha was the one who took care of Geoff when he was a sick baby and Keils was at sea," he added to clarify the importance of the woman. "She was like a mother to him—and to me too, once Geoff and I became friends. Because I was close to her, Geoff and Keils wanted me to meet them at her cottage."

Ivy tried to envision Drake as a boy in need of mothering, but the man lying beside her now was so far removed from that innocent state she couldn't picture it. Geoff, though, was much easier to imagine. With his open, friendly face, she had no trouble thinking of him as a schoolboy. He had grown up so near to her and yet they had never known the other existed. It was a thought that saddened her.

"When I arrived," Drake continued, "I found Geoff lying face down in a pool of blood." He drew a long breath, the image as vivid now as it had been then. "He was still alive, but I could see it would only be a matter of minutes before he died."

It was a terrible image for Ivy to picture. "How awful," she murmured.

For a moment, Drake didn't speak, silently agreeing with her. With the kind of life he had led, death had been no stranger to him, but he hadn't realized just how devastating it could be until he had held Geoff's dying body in his arms.

"Before Geoff died," he said with painful remembrance, "he told me what had happened. Keils had been delayed, so he had gone on alone. When he reached the cottage, he heard two men talking from inside his aunt's shed. One seemed to be an American informant and the other a British spy, and they were discussing how the next information would reach its destination. The informant said he would send it with someone he trusted on a particular shipping line—a man with only one ear." Drake paused. "Geoff must have made a noise, because

110

the next moment he was shot. And he never had a chance to see who did it."

Drake relived the terrible memory in his mind. Until Geoff had been killed, the shed had always been the source of good memories. As boys, it was the place where they went to discuss the kinds of things young males needed to discuss in private. And when they were older, it was inside the shed's rough-hewn interior that he and Geoff had both lost their virginities on the same night to two lusty tavern girls. The shed had been a place of fun and excitement, but in an instant, it had become a place of death.

"To think Geoff died because he had the misfortune to overhear some plot," Ivy murmured sadly. "What terrible, terrible luck."

"Bad luck had nothing to do with it."

Ivy didn't expect the harsh statement. "What do you mean?"

"Right after Geoff was shot, he heard one of the men say, 'That's not Keils Cauldron. If he's anywhere around, he'll be on his guard after hearing that shot.' They left immediately."

"They were there to kill Cauldron?" Ivy asked in surprise. "Why?"

"We can only guess, but with the number of British ships Keils had captured, he was probably interfering with the stolen messages getting through to England. The spies must have somehow found out he had a relative in Georgetown and schemed to get at him through her."

Again Drake paused as his thoughts swept back to that grim day. "I found Martha's body inside her cottage. When Keils arrived and saw the deaths, he was torn apart. He loved Martha like a sister, and Geoff, he loved more than life itself."

For a minute, both Ivy and Drake were quiet, absorbed in solemn thoughts. Then Ivy said softly, "I really am sorry about Geoff. I wish I had known him."

"You would have liked him."

"Was he like Cauldron?" Ivy asked, hoping to hear a list of qualities that would set him apart from his infamous father.

"He was a lot like Cauldron."

Not the answer Ivy wanted, she had no polite reply.

When her silence told of her feelings, Drake added, "You'd like him too if you gave him a chance."

"I can never forgive him for what he did to my mother." Ivy's low words were adamant. Then as her eyes moved over Drake's large frame beside her, she added with a catch in her throat, "or for what he's doing to me now."

With that, she shifted to her side, facing away from him. But just because she couldn't see him didn't mean she wasn't still very much aware of his presence. His every movement, his every breath burned into her consciousness.

In her wildest dreams, she had never imagined she would be sharing a bed with a man who was not her husband. It went against everything she had ever been taught. But as a door slammed shut in the hallway, accompanied by loud, lewd laughter, she had to admit Drake's presence made her feel safe from the roughness of the world surrounding her.

With that thought soothing her and with the heat radiating from his body warming her, she finally fell asleep.

Drake didn't find the same escape. The muted sounds

112

of men and women laughing, flirting, and loving kept him awake, making him constantly think about the woman lying beside him. As a couple paused right outside the door, carrying on a conversation filled with husky laughs and suggestive murmurs, he felt Ivy stir beside him in her sleep.

She didn't wake, but as the conversation grew louder and the man's advances grew bolder, she turned toward him as though she were instinctively seeking protection from the roughness of the male voice. Coming into contact with his side, her body immediately stilled its restless movement as though comforted by his presence.

Drake suppressed a groan at the feel of the soft body now lightly pressed against his own. *You can't touch her,* he reminded himself as his skin began to grow warm where it touched hers. When sleep finally claimed him, it was the image of doing just that that was still playing through his mind.

The motion was pleasant and massaging, softly soothing Ivy even as it slowly aroused her from her sleep. For a moment, she lay with her eyes closed, enjoying the feel of the ship as it moved. Wrapped as she was in the warmth of the surrounding blankets, she felt as snug as a baby in a gently rocking cradle.

Suddenly she remembered she was no longer on the ship and that the bed didn't have a particularly warm set of covers. Her eyes flew open. It was Drake's sleeping body, turned now toward her own, that was warming her. And as for the soothing sensation . . .

Ivy gasped, shocked, as she realized Drake's hand was lightly caressing the curve of her hip in his sleep. But

113

even more shocking was the hard, male feel of him as he nestled closer yet.

"Don't do that!" she cried sharply, jerking away.

Drake came awake with a start. Aware of the taut state of his body, he groaned to himself at Ivy's distraught words.

"Was I kissing your neck again?" he hazarded, sitting up beside her.

"It was worse!" Ivy blurted. "Much, much worse!"

Had he— As sensuous images began forming in his mind, Drake clamped a firm damper on his imagination. As he had learned before, Ivy's thoughts on certain subjects were far different than his own.

"Maybe you just better tell me what I did," he suggested.

His actions were too embarrassing to put into words. Ivy shook her head.

"If I have to start guessing," Drake said dryly, "I think you're going to be shocked by the kinds of things *I* come up with."

A guessing game of embarrassing situations was more than Ivy wanted to contemplate. "You pulled me . . . against you," she finally managed.

There was a moment of silence as Drake sifted that vague comment through his mind and arrived at its proper meaning.

"Uh, sorry," he finally said. "It won't—" He broke off. "I can't say something like that won't happen again, Ivy, because it probably will," he said with complete honesty. "I know that's not what you want to hear, but we're sharing a bed and I'm attracted to you."

That was certainly not what Ivy wanted to hear. Uneasily, she shifted in the bed.

"But since I've never made love in my sleep," Drake stressed, "try not to get upset at anything else I do."

"That doesn't exactly put my mind at ease, Drake." Nor did the fact that Cauldron, sleeping in the next room, had to have heard her loud, shocked outcry but hadn't even bothered to shout through the wall to find out what had happened.

Drake reached out, cupping Ivy's face. "Do you think it's any easier for me?" he demanded. "Before, when there was a woman in my bed, I was bedding her."

The feel of Drake's hands on her face disturbed Ivy even more than the blunt honesty of his words. She tried to pull away, but his fingers tightened, stopping her.

"I want you, but I can't have you." Drake said the words with quiet emphasis. "So stop worrying that I will." Releasing her face, he lay back down. "Come on back to sleep."

There was something in the deep timbre of Drake's voice that made Ivy believe his promise. But as she lay once again beside him, long after his even breaths told her he was asleep, she could find no rest herself. She was staring restlessly into the dark when Drake rolled toward her, his arm slipping around her waist.

She didn't know what was more unsettling—the feel of Drake's warm, sleeping body pressing lightly against her own or the feel of his relaxed breath softly fanning her neck.

Immediately, she raised her hand to shake him awake but, after a moment, let it drop back to her side. Waking Drake and telling him about his transgressions was, at best, futile and, at worst, embarrassing. As he had made it clear, he couldn't help what he did in his sleep, and it appeared she was going to have to resign herself to that fact.

She would just move away, she decided. But as she tried to do so, the arm about her waist tightened possessively, stopping her. Uncertain what to do, Ivy lay there stiffly, hoping Drake would turn away on his own.

He was warm, she had to admit, the heat from his body a pleasant contrast to the coldness of the room. As his lips began to gently caress the side of her neck, strange little shivers began to course through her. Allen's kisses had never given her such a feeling, she acknowledged to herself, but then he had never kissed her on the neck or lain half naked with her in a bed either.

To her dismay, she began to find the caresses pleasurable. He's a pirate, she reminded herself sternly. A handsome one but still a pirate, not the kind of man a woman should ever want to touch her. Her mother's experience with Cauldron was certainly proof of that.

Still, when Drake's languid kisses stopped as he slipped deeper into sleep, she found herself inexplicably missing the touch of his lips.

His arm, however, still lightly encircled her waist, its touch possessive enough to keep her near him. Like his lips, it would probably slip away as Drake settled deeper into his dreams, she decided. Lulled by his warmth and feeling secure despite the rough world around her, she fell asleep waiting for that to happen.

A light rap on the door followed by Drake saying, "That's Cauldron, letting us know it's time to get up," brought Ivy awake.

To her chagrin, she was lying half on Drake's chest, with both his arms wrapped around her. Her cheek was

116

now resting on his shoulder, her arm was sprawled across the broad expanse of his torso, and her leg was intimately entwined between his. It was a far cry from the way Drake's arm had lightly held her before. All she could conclude was that he must have gathered her even closer to him as they slept.

Awkwardly, she pulled away, her cheeks flushed as she sat up. "You pulled me to you again last night," she tried to explain.

"I'm sure I did," Drake agreed easily. "And I'm sure you realized just how useless it would be to keep waking me up."

It had been nice, he reflected, waking to find Ivy cradled in his arms. He had lain there for some time like that, enjoying the soft feel of her body. And though he didn't doubt he had been the one to initiate the closeness, each time she had stirred, she had snuggled deeper into the circle of his arms. Awake, Ivy was coolly proper, but asleep, she was sweetly responsive, seeking his warmth and needing his security.

"Could you get out of bed now and turn your back?"

The primly spoken request reminded Drake that Ivy was now awake and the closeness between them gone. He was about to comply with her request when a sudden loud pounding on their door made him tense instead. His hand was snaking around the side of the mattress to get to his pistol when a voice came through the panel.

"Open up in there!" The command was punctuated by hiccups and a laugh as the caller continued to bang on the door.

Drake's hand returned to his side. "I know that voice," he quickly reassured Ivy, seeing the sudden fear in her eyes. "He's—" Just then the door crashed open.

Two men stepped into the room, broad grins appearing on their faces at the sight of Drake in bed with a raven-haired beauty.

"Didn't know you had a wench with you, Drake," drawled the taller of the two. There was no remorse in his voice as his eyes raked over the beautiful woman in his friend's bed.

Ivy stared at the men in dismay, appalled to be caught in such indecent circumstances. Without thought, she slid behind Drake's broad back, holding tightly to his shoulders as she used him to shield herself from the men's bold gazes.

The fingers that were digging into his flesh showed Drake how mortified Ivy was. He scowled at the intruders.

"Get out, Tobias," he ordered, "and take Jonas with you." The good-natured way he said it didn't disguise the fact that he meant what he said.

Tobias held up his hands in a gesture of complete understanding. "When I heard you were in town, Drake," he said, backing up in compliance, "I thought you might want to have a dram with Jonas and me for old time's sake, but I can see you're far, far too busy!"

The words made Drake aware of the softness of Ivy's breasts as they pressed into his bare back and the feel of her nipples jutting sensually into his flesh. Feeling aroused despite the ridiculous situation, he gave Tobias another scowl to take out some of his frustration on his old acquaintance.

With a bark of laughter at the mix of emotions crossing Drake's face, Tobias pushed Jonas toward the door.

As it closed behind them, Ivy realized she was holding onto Drake with what could only be described as an almost indecent embrace. Suddenly conscious her breasts were pressed against a totally bare torso, she abruptly released him.

"Old friends of yours?" she asked in a weak voice, warmth suffusing her cheeks.

Drake slid quickly from the bed, still feeling too much of his own particular warmth. "Yes."

As he reached for his clothes, even more warmth came to Ivy's cheeks as she took in Drake standing there with no concealing darkness to soften the impact. He was still as magnificent as a Greek statue, but the touches of sunlight that streamed in through the slats of the closed shutters emphasized he was a living, breathing man—and one with desire still stirring his blood. The masculine bulge that last night's darkness had mostly concealed was now fully revealed. Before, the sight had frightened her; now, it held an unexpected—and unwanted—fascination.

Disturbed to have such an interest, Ivy quickly averted her eyes and kept them averted until Drake pulled on his breeches. Just as he was ready to slip into his shirt, the doorknob began to turn, the sound rusty and loud.

"Tobias," Drake said sternly, facing the door as it began to open, "enough is enough!"

But instead of his old friends, the two men he had fought before stood in the doorway, their pistols drawn and their faces harsh with revenge.

Chapter 9

Automatically, Drake reached for the waistband of his breeches to draw his own pistol only to remember his weapons were under the mattress. He swore under his breath as the two men came in, kicking the door closed behind them.

At the sight of them, Ivy frantically clutched the blankets around her.

"Well, well, well," said the more muscular of the two, his eyes flickering between Drake, standing there in only his breeches, and Ivy, sitting in the bed. "Looks like your man just finished with you," he sneered. "Now it will be *our* turn, once we kill him for what he did."

Ivy shuddered at the words, her eyes flying to Drake to see what he would do. But unarmed against two men with pistols, there was little he could do, she realized with growing horror, not with his own weapons tucked beneath the mattress. Nor could she reach them.

If only she hadn't grabbed for Drake's pistol last night, forcing him to put it out of her reach, he would now be armed and this wouldn't be happening. But she had, and now it was going to cost Drake his life and her, her virtue.

"Let's let him watch, then we'll kill him," suggested the other man, advancing toward Ivy with a lustful gleam in his eyes. "I'll be the first."

"Drake!" Ivy cried out as the blankets were torn from her hands, but she knew he was as helpless as she was to stop what was going to happen.

The man who had grabbed away the blankets gazed down at Ivy in surprise, his eyes puzzled as they moved over her prim nightgown.

"Flannel?" he wondered aloud, having expected silk, satin, or velvet from a woman skillful enough to tumble the crew of the *Black Cauldron*. But as he took in the voluptuousness of Ivy's body, apparent even in the plain nightdress she was wearing, he forgot the thought.

"Unbutton that nightgown, pretty thing," he ordered, "so I can see what you've got under there."

Mutely, Ivy shook her head at the order.

"Do as he says, Ivy."

Drake's command made Ivy look at him in shocked disbelief. In many ways, he had frightened her since she had met him, but he had at least always made her feel safe from other men.

"Drake—" Her word of protest came out as a whisper.

"If you want to live, Ivy, obey them." Drake's voice brooked no further delay.

If you want to live ... With shaking fingers, Ivy started unfastening the buttons of her nightgown.

Expecting the sight of bare skin, the man watching Ivy frowned when he saw a layer of cotton as prim as the flannel nightgown over it.

"Whatever that is," he snapped impatiently, "unfasten it too!"

Ivy's hands shook even more as she unfastened the cotton shift, finally revealing the full swell of her breasts.

"Looks like she's going to be quite an eyeful!"

As the man guarding Drake glanced over at Ivy at the excited words, wanting to see for himself, Drake saw the chance he had been waiting for. He launched himself into the air and crashed hard into his captor. As they both hit the floor, the pistol went skittering across its wooden surface, coming to a halt beneath the bed.

At the commotion, the second man swung around, Ivy forgotten. At the sight of his friend frantically wrestling on the floor, he leveled his pistol at Drake, trying to get a clean aim amidst the tumbling bodies.

For a moment, Ivy was immobilized by the sudden change of events. But as Drake rolled on top, his fists thundering into his opponent's face, the sound of a pistol being cocked galvanized her into action. Flinging herself off the bed, she grabbed the metal basin from the nearby washstand and swung it hard against the back of the man's head. With a groan that was half surprise, half agony, he sank to the floor.

As Drake rose from the body he had rendered unconscious, Ivy stared down at the one she had dealt with. Blood was streaming profusely from the man's scalp. Despite the circumstances, the sight shook her badly.

"I killed him, didn't I?" she asked, horror at the deed creeping into her voice.

Drake reached down and lifted the man's head by the hair to look into his face. "You just knocked him out, Ivy," he reassured her. He released the hair, letting the thug's head fall back to the floor. "And he certainly deserved what he got."

Ivy's legs suddenly felt weak in reaction to everything

that had occurred. She sank onto the edge of the bed, more shaken than she had realized.

"Take a few deep breaths," Drake suggested, sitting down beside her. "It'll help."

Drake's voice sounded calm, as though being attacked was a common occurrence. Which it probably was, Ivy realized, considering the life he led. For her, it was far different. Following his advice, she took one deep breath after another until she began to feel better.

That feeling suddenly changed as she looked down at herself, catching sight of her forgotten, still-open night-gown. Unfastened past her breasts, it gaped immodestly, almost showing her nipples. She grabbed the material together, glaring at Drake as she did so.

Take a few deep breaths, he had said. And all the while, he had been sitting there beside her, getting quite an eyeful! Then she glared even more as she thought back over the terrifying events.

"You told me to open my nightgown so I would distract those men," she accused him.

"You made a nice distraction," Drake admitted, not contrite at all. As Ivy looked even more affronted, he added, "I don't know why you're upset. It's not as though they got to see very much before I jumped the one."

"Even *then* you were watching me," Ivy fumed, "when our lives were in danger."

"We weren't in any real danger by that time," Drake corrected her. "As soon as they said they wouldn't shoot me until they were done with you, I knew we'd be free. There was no way they could keep an eye on me if they were ogling at you."

"Ogling at me!" Ivy sputtered. "You . . . you—"

"My only real worry," Drake added, suddenly grinning, "was if you had on any *other* layers of clothing beneath that nightgown. Any more, and they probably would have shot me rather than wait."

"I wish they had shot you!"

Ivy's pallor was gone, Drake noted with satisfaction, replaced by the fiery spirit he enjoyed. "I was lucky my plan worked," he teased, wanting to see more of that spirit. "That one man was so stunned at the sight of you wearing flannel, I was a little worried he might not go for the bait."

"Go for the *bait?*"

"I probably should have waited until you took everything off," Drake admitted. "With a distraction like that, I could have just walked over and plucked the pistol from the man's hand instead of fighting him. But I decided to be chivalrous."

"Chivalrous!" Ivy flung the word at him in disbelief. "You used me!"

"I had to, considering I didn't have my pistol or knife handy—thanks to you, I could add. But I did get us out of danger."

"I wouldn't be in any danger at all," Ivy reminded him fiercely, "if you hadn't walked over to me on the *Wild Swan* in the first place! And as for getting us out of danger, *I* did as much as you!"

"You certainly had a chance to show more of that Keils Cauldron backbone—and a couple of other things too," Drake added chuckling.

A couple of . . . Ivy clutched her nightgown even more firmly over her breasts. The seething retort she was about to fling at him was interrupted by a loud groan from the floor.

Ivy jumped to her feet, warily regarding the stirring men.

"I guess you're not going to want to change out of that nightgown with these two lying here, are you?" Drake asked, the humor still in his voice as he collected his weapons as well as his victims' pistols. "I'll bring them out into the hall with me." It took him only a moment to drag the men from the room.

As he gathered up the rest of his clothes, taking them with him into the hall, Ivy was still frowning in his direction as the door closed behind him.

When Ivy stepped from the room, two of Cauldron's crew were dragging the thugs toward the stairs while Drake stood casually talking to his friend Tobias. As Tobias gave her a slow, appreciative stare that went from her head to her toes, Ivy included him in the glare she still had for Drake.

"It looks like she's as much of a wildcat out of bed as she is in one," Tobias observed, giving Drake a wink.

As Ivy's eyes began glittering even more, Drake growled, "That's enough, Tobias."

"Not going to share this one, Drake?" Tobias teased. "You weren't quite so possessive about that little red-haired wench who—"

"Leave, Tobias," Drake interrupted, grasping the man's shoulders and turning him toward one of the rooms opposite them.

"Can't say I blame you," Tobias said, grinning back over his shoulder as he took the none-too-subtle hint. "She's a beauty. I wouldn't let her stray from my bed either if I were you."

As Tobias opened the door, Ivy caught a glimpse of one of the tavern girls waiting for him before he shut it behind him. Her indignation grew as she considered Tobias's words.

"Did you tell him that you and I—"

"No."

"Then why was he talking like that?"

"He caught us in bed together, Ivy," Drake reminded her, "so he just assumed we were lovers. That's all."

That assumption didn't sit well with Ivy. As Drake headed toward the steps, she stared moodily at his back as she followed him, not liking the idea of people thinking they were intimate. On the ship at least, all the men knew the truth, but here, in everyone's eyes she was a—

She grimaced as terms like lightskirt, loose woman, and soiled dove sifted unhappily through her mind.

"Next time," she said to Drake in a fierce whisper, coming alongside him, "tell people the truth about us!"

Drake gave her a sideways glance. "Do you think the truth is any better?"

"The truth is always better, Drake."

At the bottom of the steps, they almost collided with Tobias's friend Jonas, coming up with a large mug of ale in his hand.

"I'm surprised you pried yourself out of bed, Drake," Jonas drawled, his eyes settling on Ivy in frank approval. "Not when you're with someone like her."

Ivy gave Drake a nudge with her elbow.

Complying with her wishes, Drake said, "It's not what it looks like, Jonas. This woman might be Keils Cauldron's daughter."

"And you're sleeping with her?" Jonas asked the question with considerable awe. "I know you're like a son to the man, but Cauldron strikes me as the type who would kill—"

"Ivy and I don't have that kind of relationship," Drake continued. "I'm just bunking with her to keep her safe until Keils finds out about her."

Jonas was fascinated by the story. "She's quite a temptation. It must be hard to sleep next to her and not—"

"I manage," Drake interrupted.

"And if she's not Cauldron's daughter?" Jonas pressed, his imagination obviously whetted by the situation. "What happens then?"

Ivy was beginning to regret she had insisted that Drake explain, for Jonas's prurient interest was worse than Tobias's simple assumptions.

"We'll face that when the time comes," Drake answered, sidestepping the issue.

The gleam that came to Jonas's eyes showed Ivy he was picturing something that was far more erotic than the straightforward images Tobias had conjured. As she stared at the floor, wishing the conversation would end, she acknowledged that Drake was right. Telling the truth was worse than saying nothing.

"I'd sure like to be in your boots if Cauldron finds out she isn't his," Jonas said to Drake, his voice filled with envy. Giving Ivy a last raking look, he added philosophically, "But since I'm not, I think I'll just hurry on up to the little brunette who's waiting for me."

As Jonas climbed the steps two at a time, obviously intent on slaking his just-aroused desire with one of the tavern girls, Drake asked, "Was that any better?"

"No," Ivy admitted, "that was worse." Not feeling like talking, she followed him silently into the main part of the tavern and sat down while he ordered breakfast.

They were just finishing when Lola came down the stairs and walked over to Drake with a provocative swing of her hips.

"I missed you last night," she purred.

"It couldn't be helped, Lola," Drake reminded her, gathering his things as he came to his feet.

The sight of Lola clinging shamelessly to Drake's arm as she accompanied them to the entrance of the tavern bothered Ivy though she wasn't sure why it should. Drake's amorous interests were, after all, certainly none of her concern.

When they stepped outside the tavern, her mood grew inexplicably worse as she watched Lola reach up, tenderly pushing a lock of Drake's hair away from his forehead as she bid him farewell.

"Maybe next time you come," Lola murmured, the cold morning air making misty wisps of her words, "you won't be saddled with playing nursemaid to Cauldron's by-blow."

Saddled with playing nursemaid to Cauldron's by-blow? Was that how Drake had described the situation to Lola? As the blonde whispered a last few, and probably impassioned, words of farewell, Ivy, feeling more than irritable, looked away.

Her gaze met that of a lanky man standing in the shell-paved street. Staring boldly back at her, he pulled a piece of silver from his pocket and held it out in a gesture that made it obvious it would be payment for services rendered.

If Drake felt he had to play nursemaid to this particular by-blow, Ivy decided, then he could darn well earn his keep.

"All the silver in the world wouldn't make me be with

129

the likes of you," she said in a loud, clear voice. From behind her, she heard Drake order Lola inside. Then he was beside her.

Ivy ignored the admonishing glance he gave her for uttering such fight-provoking words. As the lanky man approached, his face ominously angry, she waved her hand airily in his direction.

"Handle this for me, won't you, Drake?" she said lightly, knowing he would have to protect her. With his superb fighting skills, she knew it wouldn't take him long to defeat this one skinny man, but at least he would have to exert himself a little in his role as watchdog.

"What the hell are you trying to do, Ivy?" Drake muttered. As the man confronting him drew the knife strapped to his side, he unsheathed his own wicked-looking blade.

"Move back, Ivy," he ordered.

Ivy had only pictured a quick, bare-fisted fight such as she had seen before, with Drake easily winning the bout. But even as a part of her told her she shouldn't care about Drake's fate, she knew she didn't want to see him hurt in a fight she had purposely and needlessly provoked.

"Move on, mate," Drake warned the man, his voice deadly.

"Why should I?" came the swift, careless reply.

Ivy looked on worriedly as the two men began to circle each other with wary steps, each one waiting for the other to make his move. When the thin man suddenly lunged forward, there was a loud clash of metal hitting metal as Drake parried the thrust with his own blade.

Again the men circled, Drake deflecting each fierce thrust of the knife with the same effortless fighting skills

130

he had shown before. When his opponent lunged again, his blade swinging in a savage arc, Drake placed a hard kick to the man's booted foot, toppling him onto the street.

Before the man could move, Drake placed the tip of his knife to the man's throat. "I have no argument with you," he said flatly, "but that won't stop me from killing you if you want to continue this needless fight. What's your answer?"

The man gulped in fear, his face ashen. "Just let me go," he croaked. When Drake released the pressure on his neck, he scrambled to his feet, practically running by the time he disappeared into an alley.

Ivy had thought Drake invincible before and now, having seen his skill with a knife, he seemed even more so. She knew even before he turned to face her that he was far angrier about this fight than about the one she had unintentionally provoked.

Abruptly, Drake sheathed his blade. "Were you hoping to get me killed, Ivy?" he asked, anger in each word. "This time, you started that fight on purpose!"

His words made Ivy remember why she had started the fight in the first place. "Since you consider yourself a 'nursemaid to Cauldron's by-blow,' I thought I'd let you play the part."

"Those were Lola's words, not mine. And she heard them from one of the other men, not me!" Drake caught Ivy's shoulders, his fingers tightening around them to emphasize his next words. "Don't *ever* force me into a fight again!"

Only yesterday, hearing a pirate speak to her in such a fierce manner would have frightened Ivy. But she knew Drake better now and glared up at him, defiantly meeting

131

his eyes.

"I'm not afraid of you!" she said, suddenly meaning each word. "Not anymore!"

As Drake gazed into Ivy's stormy eyes, he sensed the spirit that was so fiery when she was angry would be just as fiery when she was writhing in passion. His ire suddenly faded at the thought and he released her, letting her step back.

"Good," he murmured, his voice suddenly throaty instead of threatening. "I don't want you to be afraid of me."

The words should have been reassuring, but the raspy sound of want in them made them otherwise. Ivy knew she didn't need to fear Drake's interest for now, but what would happen if Cauldron rejected her was something else entirely.

Chapter 10

The sound of hoofbeats clattering on the shell-paved street was a welcome distraction to Ivy. It was Cauldron and his men coming around a corner, leading two horses, one with a sidesaddle. She could see the stubble on the pirate captain's face was more pronounced, showing he had once again not shaved. It altered his appearance considerably.

Cauldron nodded as he came nearer. "Morning."

Drake was sure that Ivy, schooled strongly in social etiquette, would feel compelled to give Cauldron a polite, though begrudging, nod in return. Her curt response didn't disappoint him.

Cauldron tossed the reins of a roan stallion to Drake and then held out the reins of a large black gelding to Ivy.

"This one is for you," he told her.

Reluctantly, Ivy took the reins. "I'm not much of a rider," she admitted, looking askance at the height and breath of the animal.

"Didn't Woodruff have horses?" Cauldron demanded, foreseeing an unwanted delay to his plans.

Immediately Ivy felt defensive, certain there was a slur in the words. "We had a horse," she replied, "but we usually rode in a small rig, so I haven't had much practice."

"You'll keep up," Cauldron said impatiently.

There was a threat to the statement that rankled Ivy. "Or what?" she challenged. "I get left behind?"

Cauldron gave her a sharp glance. "Or you'll ride pillion with Drake."

"Now why didn't I guess that answer?" Ivy replied in a mocking lilt, her hostile feelings toward the man again surfacing. "Considering I'm already sleeping in Drake's bed, don't you think that threat pales a little in comparison? After all," she added, warming to the subject, "Drake and I are already practically joined at the hip, aren't we? I'm just surprised you don't want us to eat out of the same plate."

Drake stifled the smile that Ivy's words brought to his lips, for he could see Cauldron didn't find the same amusement. Unaccustomed to anyone talking back to him and used to dealing harshly with anyone who did, the pirate captain was obviously nonplussed by how to react to Ivy.

"Maybe I'll make you ride with me." Cauldron glowered as he said the words.

Though Ivy knew it was unwise to anger the man further, somehow she couldn't seem to help herself. "Now that *is* a fate worse than death," she said archly. "I guess I *better* keep up so I can avoid *that*."

Anyone else would have been dead by now, Drake reflected as he watched Cauldron's jaw tighten. He was sure Ivy didn't realize how lenient Cauldron was being with her. For entirely different reasons, he mused, Ivy was giving both himself and Cauldron frustrations that neither could alleviate.

"Let's get going," he suggested, hoping to keep more sparks from flying. His ploy worked, for at his words, Ivy's attention returned to the gelding.

As Drake held the horse still, Ivy cautiously eased herself up onto its back. They set out at a walk, but she was sure the slow pace was due to the unsteady footing caused by the crushed shells than to any allowance for her inexperience in a saddle. Regardless, she was grateful for the chance to adjust to the feel of the gelding beneath her. It wasn't a long reprieve, however, for as soon as they left the town behind, reaching solid ground, Cauldron nudged his horse into a gallop.

Ivy's gelding, following the action of the other mounts, leaped forward with them. It took all her concentration to maintain her seat in the saddle, but maintain it she did, for she had no intention of riding pillion with anyone.

By the time they stopped for a break, Ivy's entire body felt sore from the unaccustomed activity. Her mental state wasn't much better. She had been watched very carefully as they rode, giving her no chance to even consider breaking away from the men.

Without enthusiasm, she ate the simple meal of cold sausage and bread that Cauldron handed to her and drank water from the pouch Drake pulled from his stallion's saddle. When she finished, she wasn't surprised that the few moments of privacy Drake allowed her was done in such a way that made wandering off impossible. She was sure when they reached a populated, safe area, the watchfulness would even be worse.

As they set off again, she couldn't help but bristle as Cauldron brought his mount alongside hers, sandwiching her securely between himself and Drake.

"Aren't I being watched enough without adding this?" she asked him.

"There's some swampy ground up ahead," Cauldron answered her, nodding toward the terrain in front of them. "I thought I'd make sure you didn't ride into it."

For a moment, Ivy's heart softened, hearing that her well-being was at the source of Cauldron's watchful action. Then she immediately rejected the feeling.

"You didn't care enough about me last night to even see why I cried out." The words were out of her lips before she thought about what she was saying. When both Cauldron and Drake pulled their attention away from the swampy ground and focused it intently on her, she wished she hadn't blurted the thought.

"Why did you cry out?" Cauldron finally asked.

It was hardly something Ivy wanted to discuss, but as Cauldron looked pointedly at her, obviously expecting a reply, she finally said in embarrassment, "Drake did something that was . . . unspeakable."

"Unspeakable?" Cauldron repeated after a long, pregnant moment.

"Before your imagination runs wild, Keils," Drake said dryly, "keep in mind Ivy and I don't have the same ideas when it comes to 'unspeakable.'"

Considering Ivy's upbringing, Cauldron didn't doubt the truth of that statement for a moment. Since he had complete trust in Drake, he was sure the infraction, whatever it was, wasn't worth discussing any further.

"I'm sure the two of you don't have the same ideas

about anything," he said, turning his attention back to the dangerous ground.

Though Ivy was glad to have that particular topic dropped, Cauldron's reaction showed he wouldn't question anything that occurred between herself and Drake. In many ways, it was a sobering thought.

By nightfall, Ivy was more than ready to stop. Cold, hungry, and aching from the ride, she wanted nothing more than to get out of the saddle, even if it meant staying at another rough tavern. There was no town in sight, however the countryside populated by only a few isolated farmhouses. Wearily, she kept pace with the men.

As he rode alongside her, Drake was surprised Ivy had held up as well as she had since she wasn't used to being on horseback. She had learned quickly, he had to admit, handling her mount with a determination he was sure was born of a desire to remain on her own steed. With the brisk wind whipping her long hair around her shoulders, she made a striking sight as she galloped along on the back of the black gelding.

"It looks as if we'll be stopping just ahead," he called to her as Cauldron veered in the direction of a two-story farmhouse off in the distance.

"At a farmhouse?" Disappointment surged through Ivy at the news. A peaceful village might have offered a means to escape, even with watchful eyes on her. A solitary farmhouse offered considerably less hope.

They came to a halt outside the structure, and Drake stopped Ivy from dismounting with a wave of his hand.

"We'll wait here until Keils persuades the owner to let

137

us stay," he said.

At the news, Ivy's eyes filled with contempt. "What is Cauldron going to do to 'persuade' the owner?" she asked. "Threaten him? Maim him? Torture him?"

"Something even more persuasive." Drake's words were dry.

"He's going to *kill* him?" Ivy said in horror. As little as she thought of her pirate father, somehow she hadn't expected him to sink that low—not just to secure a place to sleep for the night.

"Actually, Ivy"—Drake's voice was drier yet—"he's going to offer him gold."

Ivy had the grace to feel a little foolish for letting her imagination run so free. "Oh."

"You really should stop thinking the worst about Keils," Drake added. "He might be a pirate, but he's not a bad man."

"Somehow, I don't think you and I have the same idea about what makes a bad man." Ivy watched Cauldron walk toward the front door. "What happens if the owner decides gold isn't enough payment to allow pirates to stay for the night?"

"They won't know we're pirates. Keils won't give his real name and the beard he's been growing will disguise who he is, not that most people would recognize him anyway. His face isn't nearly as well known as his reputation."

They watched in silence as Cauldron knocked on the door and then talked to the man and woman who answered it. After a few minutes, gold exchanged hands and the couple was motioning for him to enter.

"See?" Drake said, dismounting. "Everyone is happy. We have a place to stay and the farmer and his wife have enough gold to make it worth their while."

Ivy slipped tiredly to the ground and leaned against the gelding's flanks as her aching legs regained their strength. This was not the kind of place she had hoped for, but perhaps the farmer and his wife would somehow be able to help her. Some of her tiredness disappearing at the thought, she straightened away from her mount, suddenly eager to meet the occupants.

"Not so fast," Drake said, blocking her path. "If you tell those people Keils's real name, or anything else for that matter," he warned her, "he'll be forced to deal with them in a different way. And that's doubly true if you try to use them to escape."

Ivy's hopes crumbled, knowing she wouldn't be able to live with herself if she caused injury or death to innocent people.

"And you keep trying to tell me Cauldron's not a bad man?" she said bitterly.

"He does whatever he has to. Just keep that in mind." As they reached the doorway, the farmer's wife gave a nod of welcome.

"You must be Mr. Avery's ward," she greeted Ivy. "He said you were tired and wanted to go right to a room." Her eyes dropped for a second to Ivy's fingers, curled around the gloves she had just removed. "I hope you don't mind sharing a bed with one of my daughters, miss," she added. "Even with Mr. Avery's men staying in the barn, we only have so much space."

"She stays with me, ma'am."

A wave of embarrassment swept over Ivy at Drake's bold statement. It had been bad enough before having the low elements at the tavern assume she was Drake's paramour, but the idea of this respectable matron coming to the same conclusion was far more humiliating. And come to it, the matron would, for it was obvious she had already noticed the lack of a wedding ring.

That thought was confirmed as she watched the woman's eyes drop once again to her ringless finger, a disapproving line coming to her narrow lips.

"You're not wearing a wedding band," she observed, her voice tight with censure.

Ivy suddenly couldn't bear this woman thinking the worst. "I never wear any jewelry while I'm traveling," she blurted. It wasn't really a lie, she added in a quick aside to God, for she had left the few meager pieces she owned back at Havenrest.

To her relief, Drake said nothing to refute the statement, though she could sense his amusement over what she was implying. The matron, however, looked far from convinced.

"Funny that Mr. Avery didn't mention it when he was requesting rooms for the night," she said suspiciously. "But then, when someone chooses to stay at a private home instead of an inn and is willing to pay a large amount of gold to do it, there are usually reasons—none of them good." She placed her thin hands on her hips, regarding Ivy and Drake with piercing eyes.

"Are the two of you married?" she suddenly demanded. "Because if you're not, no amount of gold is going to persuade me to let you stay beneath my roof. This is a God-fearing household."

Ivy wasn't prepared for the point-blank, blunt question. Unable to answer it truthfully, she found herself faltering over a suitable response.

"Uh, well—"

As the matron's lips thinned still more, Drake stepped

quickly into the telling void. "What else would we be, traveling with her guardian?" His tone made it evident there would be no further discussion. "Now if you could show us to a room," he prompted.

"Very well." Said with a huff, it showed the woman still had considerable doubts on the subject. "If you will follow me." She turned toward a stairwell.

"Married?" Drake murmured as he and Ivy trailed behind the farmer's wife up the steep steps.

"Well, I couldn't very well have her think we weren't!" Ivy hissed back.

At a room halfway down the corridor, the matron ushered them into an austere bedroom dominated by a stern four-poster bed.

"I'll be serving a simple meal of cold ham downstairs in just a few minutes." Her voice was still disapproving as she lit a large candle.

"Could you serve it up here?" Drake asked, not wanting Ivy to mingle any more than necessary. "My wife"—he threw Ivy a quick glance at the word—"is very tired from the trip."

Considering the amount of gold Cauldron had probably paid, Ivy wasn't surprised when the woman gave a curt nod as she turned away.

While they waited for the meal to arrive, Ivy sank wearily onto a straight-backed bench situated at the base of the bed, her exhaustion catching up to her.

"Tired?" Drake asked.

"Yes."

"I am too. We'll turn in as soon as we have eaten."

Maybe she was tired enough to sleep easily and soundly, Ivy thought. When the farmer's wife returned with a light meal of sliced ham and warm biscuits, they

141

ate in silence.

When they finished, Drake turned his back on Ivy as he began to unfasten his shirt.

Ivy eyed him in consternation. "Aren't you going to go into the hall while I get ready?"

"Don't you think the lady of the house would wonder at that?" Drake answered. "A husband doesn't usually leave the room when his wife is getting ready for bed."

Given the woman's obvious doubts, it would probably be enough to confirm them, Ivy acknowledged. Still, the idea of undressing with no barrier to separate them was unsettling.

Keeping her eyes on Drake to make sure he didn't turn around before she finished, Ivy quickly slipped out of her dress. As she laid it aside, Drake's bare back came into view. Thick with muscle at the shoulders, it tapered sharply to a tautly trim waist. The sight made her decide to once again leave on her cotton shift, for though she no longer feared his interest—at least not for now, she amended—she knew she would feel too bare lying alongside him wearing only a nightgown.

She was buttoning her flannel garment securely up to her neck as Drake, after pulling off his boots, went to remove his breeches.

As he lowered them, Ivy realized she was now staring at that strong body more in interest than in ensuring Drake would not turn around before she was ready. Bothered by that knowledge, she turned away and busied herself with setting out her miniatures.

"Are you ready, Ivy?" Drake's back was still to her as he asked the question.

Ivy blew out the candle. "Yes."

In the moonlight, their bodies were shadowy and indis-

142

tinct, making it easier for each of them to face the other.

"Do you always sleep with those three miniatures beside you?" Drake asked, seeing the pieces on the night table as he placed his pistol and knife beneath the mattress.

Only since she had started sharing a bed with him, Ivy thought to herself. Not wanting to admit that, she said instead, "The ones of my parents and Allen, I always keep with me. The other one isn't mine," she reminded him. "It belongs to a man named Simon Whittaker—if I ever make it to Christ Church in Norfolk to deliver it," she ended weakly as Drake climbed into the bed, holding up the blankets so she could join him.

As they lay there, Ivy decided it wasn't getting any easier to share a bed with Drake. Trying not to think about the man beside her, she concentrated instead on her tired body in the hope that her exhaustion would make sleep come quickly. When she felt the first small tendrils slowly begin to claim her, she murmured a small prayer of thanks.

Chapter 11

The feel of Drake's arm sliding around her waist, drawing her close, brought Ivy back awake.

It appeared each night was going to be the same, she thought with a sigh as his lips began to move in a soft caress over the curve of her shoulder. But she was learning the sleep-laden caresses only lasted a few seconds before Drake slipped deeper into his dreams. All she had to do was wait. Still, the seconds seemed endless as his warm lips played havoc with her senses.

Allen had certainly never kissed her shoulder, or the back of her neck, she mentally added with a shiver as Drake's lips nuzzled there in the most intimate, stirring way.

A man's urge to mate must be so instinctive and so powerful that it controlled him even when he was asleep, she decided. As soon as that unbidden thought formed in her mind, she felt her skin flush hotly, for she had never really dwelled on what happened between a man and woman when they shared a bed and was taken aback to find herself thinking about it now.

It was hard not to. Lying alongside a nearly naked man, especially one as attractive as Drake, was proving to be a very distracting experience. Though she didn't like to admit it, the caresses that had once frightened her were beginning to feel increasingly pleasurable.

As Drake's body stilled, his lips sliding away from her neck, the combination of emptiness and yearning that remained left Ivy feeling totally awake and very restless. Easing herself from under his arm, she left the bed and made her way to the window nearest her. As she stood quietly in the moonlight, gazing out at the grounds beneath her, her thoughts were churning through her mind.

Would her life ever be the same after this? she had to wonder. Even if she were finally set free, would the experience of being with Drake ever leave her? She wouldn't have thought it possible when all this began, but she was growing used to being with him, even used to sleeping in the same bed.

On that disquieting thought, she glanced over to where Drake was lying. He would be warm, she knew, suddenly aware of the chilliness of the air around her. Though she wasn't ready to come back to bed, she knew that when she did, the heat from his body would quickly warm her. A part of her, she acknowledged with reluctance, was already looking forward to that.

She turned back to the window, lost again in her thoughts. Would Allen ever understand the situation when she confessed the details of her captivity to him? She thought—hoped—he would, for he was a very caring and understanding man. She tried to visualize his gentle face, but more and more, unless she was gazing at his likeness in the miniature, she found it increasingly difficult to do. With a troubled sigh, she continued to gaze out into the moonlight.

From the bed, Drake covertly watched her. He had awakened as soon as she had freed herself from his embrace. His first thought had been that she was trying to escape, but he had put that notion aside when she went to the window.

She looked beautiful standing there, with the moonlight streaming over her, making her long black hair a striking contrast to the whiteness of the flannel nightgown she wore. Its flowing lines, lit by the moonlight softly accentuated the feminine curves of her body. The familiar yearning that had become a part of his life since he had met her returned.

Was she thinking about him? he had to wonder. Certainly, he spent a great deal of time thinking about her. Cloaked beneath that demure decorum, he knew there was a wealth of passion just waiting to be unleashed. The kiss he had stolen had shown him that. The fire now banked within her could easily be flamed.

But not until things with Cauldron were settled, he reminded himself sharply. He watched as Ivy wrapped her arms around herself, trying to ward off the coldness of the room. When she turned away from the window, quietly making her way back to the bed, he closed his eyes so she wouldn't know he had been watching her.

He felt her slip under the covers, shivering as she settled on the mattress. Though she was cold, he knew she would never come near him for warmth.

He reached over, drawing her toward him.

Thinking Drake was simply reaching for her in his sleep, Ivy made no protest. She lay still, enjoying the heat from his body as it warmed the chill from hers. It wasn't until she noticed his body lacked the languidness of sleep that she realized this time was different.

"You're *awake*," she gasped, trying to roll away.

Drake tightened his arm, stopping her. "I'm going to reach for you as soon as I do fall asleep," he reminded her, "so I might as well start now so I can warm you."

Though there was logic—and certainly truth—in Drake's words, it was one thing to end up in his arms while he slept and another thing entirely to consciously begin that way. But when Ivy tried to sit up, she found herself cradled instead into the crook of Drake's arm.

"I'm not going to let you go," he murmured, "because it makes no sense for us to pretend we won't end up like this when we both know we will. You might as well relax."

Ivy couldn't. She was too aware of the way Drake's heart was pounding beneath her ear.

"Ivy is a pretty name," Drake remarked, trying to distract her. "But I'm surprised your parents didn't call you something biblical."

Considering the circumstances, it took Ivy a moment to collect her thoughts to answer him. "My mother wanted to name me something that would remind her of her home in England," she finally managed.

As Drake continued to ask questions about her life, Ivy slowly began to relax. Lying in his arms as they quietly talked in the dark was, in fact, very pleasant, she finally decided. And they were only talking, she mentally added—nothing more.

"Are you warm now?" Drake questioned, quietly breaking into the cordial silence they had eventually lapsed into. Ivy's body was soft and pliant now as she lay in his arms, all tenseness gone.

Ivy nodded sleepily against his chest. "Very warm." She was asleep almost as soon as she murmured the words.

Drake brushed a light kiss onto her forehead and then smiled as she gave a small sigh of contentment, nestling closer. Though he yearned for far more than the feel of Ivy in his arms, he was content for now to simply hold her so. Cradling her to him, he was almost asleep when the sound of the door opening made him tense warily. He was about to reach for his pistol when he made out who the intruder was.

"What is it, Keils?" he whispered as Cauldron silently came to the side of the bed.

At the words, Ivy stirred a little in Drake's arms, her head shifting slightly on his chest. In an absent gesture, Drake lightly stroked her hair, quieting her.

"I'm going to slip out for a little while to a tavern not far from here to ask some questions," Cauldron whispered in return. "I wanted that tin to show people."

"It's in my coat pocket."

The whispered conversation made Ivy stir again, her hand moving across Drake's chest to hold him close.

As Cauldron got the tin, his eyes moved over Drake and Ivy, lying so intimately entwined in the moonlight. Given the circumstances, he had pictured them lying stiffly apart, not sleeping like lovers.

"Have the two of you—"

"No."

Cauldron nodded, satisfied at the abrupt answer. "Good." The closeness he was seeing, however, somehow pleased him. If it turned out Ivy was his daughter, he knew nothing would make him happier than seeing her marry Drake, producing a passel of grandchildren for him to bounce on his knee. It wouldn't replace the grief he felt over Geoff—nothing would—but it would help it fade. With that interesting idea buoying his spirits, he slipped out the door.

As the room quieted, so did Ivy. Letting his cheek rest against the top of her head, Drake let his dreams join hers.

When Ivy woke, still nestled in Drake's arms, she didn't open her eyes at first, drowsily enjoying the contentment that still lingered at being held so. But as she became aware that her hand was wrapped in a loving way around his neck and that her upper thigh was boldly resting upon a very masculine bulge as her leg held him close, the contentment quickly faded.

Last night, as they had lain peacefully together in the dark, it had seemed innocent, making it eventually feel right. This morning, entwined as they were in the bright light of day, they seemed like lovers.

Daunted by the sensation, Ivy tried to carefully untangle her limbs from Drake's before he woke.

"Morning, Ivy."

Caught in the midst of trying to slide her thigh free from the masculine warmth of him, Ivy was sure her cheeks were as red as they felt. Then they got redder as she realized her hand was still wrapped lovingly around Drake's neck.

Quickly pulling away from him, she was relieved when Drake, after a quick look at her face, simply rose from the bed, facing away as he dressed.

Ivy quickly followed suit, each movement making the muscles in her body ache, a reminder of the unaccustomed ride of yesterday. Feeling awkward that she and Drake had awakened more like lovers than as a pirate and his captive, she didn't look his way even after they were both dressed.

Drake knew why Ivy was avoiding him. Her self-consciousness over the intimate way she had been embracing him made that quite clear. When he finished shaving, he was determined to make her acknowledge his presence.

"You have pretty hair," he said, watching her run a comb through the long strands as she stood before a small mirror hanging on the wall.

Ivy paused, then kept on combing. "Thank you," she finally said, not turning around.

Drake raked his fingers through his own burnished hair to tame it. Considering Ivy's good manners, he had known the compliment would force her to speak. Still, she didn't face him.

"It's very silky looking," he persisted. "Like that of a sleek black cat."

Common courtesy finally made Ivy turn to talk to him instead of keeping her back rudely in his direction.

"Allen"—she reached for his likeness as she spoke so she wouldn't have to look into Drake's eyes—"once told me the same thing. He said my hair reminded him of the coat of a stray black kitten he found as a child." As she stared down at that kindly face, it made her remember the many qualities that made Allen such a special person, so different from the pirate with whom she now shared a bed.

"Allen still has a soft spot in his heart for homeless creatures," she added, her voice suddenly tender. "The rectory and his office at the church are full of the strays

151

he's taken in."

"Are you one of them, Ivy?"

The question, filled with sudden speculation, made Ivy finally look at Drake. "I'm hardly a stray kitten, Drake."

"Aren't you? Your mother and father are dead and you don't have a place of your own."

"If you knew Allen," Ivy said with feeling, "you would know just how wrong you are."

"Believe me, I'm looking forward to meeting this saint of yours when Keils and I look at the register," Drake assured her. "And I'm sure he'll be just as interested in meeting me."

The confrontation between her betrothed and her increasingly intimate bunkmate was not one Ivy was eager to witness. As she repacked Allen's miniature, she just hoped he would understand.

"Did you and your husband have a nice sleep?"

It was the greeting she and Drake received from the farmer's wife as they came down the steps. Since Cauldron was standing nearby, sipping from a cup of coffee, Ivy was sure the question had been worded that way so the woman could gauge his reaction to the words. When Cauldron choked on the mouthful of hot liquid he was sipping, Ivy knew she had to speak fast.

"The room was very comfortable, thank you." While truthful, it gave the impression she wanted. While Cauldron cleared his throat, meeting her eyes, she willed him to say nothing. To her relief, he didn't.

As the matron disappeared in defeat into an adjoining room, Cauldron, after a shake of his head to Drake to indicate his nocturnal quest had proved fruitless, turned curious eyes on Ivy.

"Husband?" he asked dryly, a little intrigued considering the closeness he had witnessed last night.

Since Cauldron was the person responsible for placing her into a situation where she had to resort to such a deception, Ivy wasn't in the mood to be needled on the topic.

"I won't have respectable people thinking I'm some kind of lightskirt."

The way Ivy said the words made it plain she was determined to preserve her dignity. Cauldron chuckled at the ploy.

"If you want Drake to play your husband, I won't gainsay you."

"That's very considerate of you."

It was clearly not a compliment, despite the polite words. Rather than being affronted, Cauldron suddenly found himself smiling as he turned away. Ivy was proving to be as resourceful as she was spirited and beautiful. A man could certainly do worse than to have someone like her turn out to be his daughter. Then he caught himself, not wanting to think too much along that path until he knew if she really was his. Still, he couldn't help but be increasingly intrigued by her.

As they left the farmhouse, heading toward the barn where the men waited, he found his eyes often going in Ivy's direction.

"You really do take after your mother," he said with thoughtful reminiscence. "Both in the way you look and the way you speak."

Ivy couldn't think of Cauldron being with her mother without becoming hostile about it. "Thanks to your lust," she reminded him pointedly, ignoring the warning glance Drake gave her, "I also resemble you."

As Cauldron came to a sudden standstill, his eyes narrowing in Ivy's direction, Drake decided the time had come to leave the two alone together.

"I'll wait for you by the barn," he suggested, moving discreetly away.

"What your mother and I shared wasn't lust," Cauldron said in a quiet voice when they were alone.

"It certainly wasn't love." Ivy flung the words at him.

"It was its own kind of relationship," Cauldron agreed, choosing his words carefully. "But that doesn't mean it wasn't special."

"Special!" Ivy mocked the word. "You didn't even remember her name!"

"I only called her Sunny," Cauldron defended himself.

Ivy wasn't mollified. "You forced her to be with you."

"Did *she* say that?"

For a moment Ivy was silent. "No," she finally had to admit. "But why else would she give in to you?"

Cauldron tried to phrase the answer discreetly. "We were drawn to each other. And maybe if things had been different . . ." He paused, his thoughts going back to the short period of time when he had taken Sunny captive and she had briefly shared his life.

She had told him she was betrothed and that the courtship had been mostly conducted through letters since the two had lived a distance apart. Despite her betrothal, Sunny had been attracted to him—perhaps because it had been too long since she had seen her intended or perhaps because a pirate captain was a man unlike any other she had ever known.

He had been attracted to her as well, he acknowledged.

154

He had been charmed by her spirit, her intelligence, and her breathtaking beauty. The ships he had planned to capture in the weeks to come had been forgotten as the spark between them had ignited into a fiery flame. Their coming together had been as inevitable as the surge of the tides beneath them.

In his heart, he had sensed that Sunny's love for her betrothed, while temporarily suspended, hadn't ended. And he, needing to provide Geoff with the expensive medicines he required, had not been in a position to give up his pirating. Nor had he wanted to, for he loved his life at sea.

He was a pirate and Sunny was a lady. Though passion had brought them together, their differences soon set them apart.

Their parting, like their coming together, had been as inevitable as the waxing and waning of the moon above them.

How could he explain the passion he and Sunny had shared to Ivy, who was too unawakened about love to understand the desire that could flame between a man and a woman.

"It was special in its own way," he tried to explain. "For the short time your mother and I were together, we both forgot the reality of the world around us. There was only us and the attraction we felt for each other. And then we both accepted that it couldn't be. She had a man she had already given her heart to and I had my life at sea."

As Ivy thought back to the night her mother had inadvertently spoken of Cauldron as she had lain on her deathbed, she had to acknowledge that there had been no animosity in her mother's voice. Her words, though often mumbled and rambling as she sank nearer and nearer to death, had been gently spoken and there had been a soft shine of remembrance in her eyes as the story had spilled without thought from her lips.

For the first time, Ivy really looked at Cauldron, seeing him as a man and not as a pirate. He was tall and well proportioned, his raven hair and violet eyes emphasizing the rugged handsomeness of his features, evident even with the beard. Combined with his air of command and easy grace, he would be appealing to women. As she pictured how such a man must have appeared to her young mother, she had to face the thought that rather than being forced, her mother might have been attracted to the pirate captain, unwise as that had been.

"Perhaps she was drawn to you," she conceded, "but even if she was, you shouldn't have taken advantage of her youth and innocence."

Cauldron sighed, knowing he couldn't begin to explain the passionate feelings he and Sunny had shared. "There are some things, Ivy," he said quietly, "that are just too powerful to resist."

At the words, Ivy couldn't help but glance toward the barn, where Drake was standing by his roan stallion. Though she didn't like to admit to it, she was attracted to him—and if she were honest with herself, that attraction was growing. Is that how her mother had felt with Cauldron? Tempted against all good reason to be with a man so unlike the one she was betrothed to? It put the relationship into a whole new light.

Chapter 12

The pace proved to be just as fast on the second day of their journey as it had been on the first. By midafternoon, Ivy was again exhausted, her already aching muscles protesting more and more as the hours unfolded.

The thought ahead to the long, cold hours still awaiting her in the saddle added to her discomfort. Her only solace was the fleeting image of lying in Drake's arms at their destination.

As soon as the image entered her mind, Ivy chastised herself for having it. That was a dangerous way to feel, she reminded herself. Lying in Drake's arms had been pleasurable, she couldn't deny that. She had enjoyed the warmth, the security, the contentment, and the companionship. But the feeling that she and Drake were lovers that had accompanied those other sensations told her they were very unwise things to enjoy.

Casting aside that wayward thought, she concentrated instead on keeping up with the men. She knew her weariness must be apparent when Cauldron, after throwing several glances over his shoulder at her, indicated to

Drake to bring his stallion up alongside his so they could talk privately.

She wondered which of them she would be riding with, unsure whom she would prefer under the circumstances. When Cauldron and the others suddenly urged their mounts ahead, leaving her and Drake behind, it caught her by surprise.

"We'll catch up with Keils later," Drake explained, reining in his stallion to let Ivy reach his side. "There's a certain farmhouse he's already targeted to stay at tonight, so we'll get there at our own pace."

"I could use a rest," Ivy admitted, ready to dismount so she could stretch her aching limbs.

"There's a little more to it than that," Drake said, his words keeping her in the saddle. "Keils wants me to deliver a message to someone in a little town west of here."

Ivy perked up. "A town?" she asked, trying not to look too excited.

"I don't plan to let you get away," Drake cautioned her, "if that's why you're suddenly not looking as tired as you did before."

Not good at lying, Ivy didn't try to deny it.

"And I'm warning you not to try to talk to anyone," Drake continued, "because I don't think you'd like what I'd do to anyone you spoke to."

Suddenly Ivy felt tired again. "How far is this place?"

"Not far." Drake urged his stallion forward. "When we get there, you'll have a chance to relax a bit."

Though it was a small town, it looked prosperous, Ivy noted as they rode down the single road that went through the center of the place. When they approached a tavern, even though it was respectable looking, she expected it to be their destination since it was the kind of establishment where Cauldron would do business. To her surprise, they rode by it, stopping instead at a dress shop.

"*This* is where we're delivering a message?" she asked.

"Yes." The bell attached to the door pealed as they entered.

"May I help you?" The words were spoken automatically as a woman stepped from a back room, making her way through several beautifully attired mannequins. At the sight of Drake, her face broke into a delighted smile.

"Drake," she said in pleased welcome, "it's always a pleasure to see you!"

"You're looking beautiful as always, Elizabeth," Drake replied.

As Ivy watched them hug, she couldn't help but wonder if this was another of Drake's inamoratas. Though Elizabeth was considerably older than he, she was quite striking, with glossy silver-tinged auburn hair and a willowy, youthful figure. The thought of having to watch another woman brazenly flirt with Drake was oddly depressing.

"Is Keils in town, too?" Elizabeth murmured, her hand coming up to smooth a wayward strand of hair.

Drake shook his head. "His face is too well known in this town for him to stop by on this trip."

So the woman was her father's lady friend and not Drake's, Ivy mused. For reasons she didn't want to dwell on, the news made her feel relieved. Then that thought was forgotten as she appraised the woman in front of her.

She would have expected a pirate like Cauldron to cavort with the kind of women who worked at the Dirk and Dagger. But Elizabeth was nothing like those women. In fact, Ivy had to admit, she looked downright respectable, wearing a tailored cream dress that complemented her silvered hair and blue eyes.

Elizabeth's gaze flickered with interest toward Ivy. "Who is your friend, Drake?" she asked, her eyes alight with speculation.

Drake held up his hand in a halting gesture. "Before you start imagining all kinds of things, Elizabeth, I better tell you this woman might be Keils's daughter."

"His daughter?" echoed Elizabeth in surprise.

Ivy straightened defensively. "Not by choice," she said with feeling.

Elizabeth raised her brows at that emphatic statement, and Drake quickly explained the situation. When he finished, Elizabeth looked at Ivy with thoughtful eyes.

"If it's true," she murmured, "it will be good for Keils. It will help take his mind off Geoff."

Ivy didn't want to be a condolence for Cauldron's grief. As she prepared to say so, Elizabeth took her hand.

"I'm Elizabeth Lacey," she said, her fingers clasping Ivy's in a quick, welcoming gesture. "I'm pleased to meet you."

Even though the woman was involved with Cauldron, her open friendliness made Ivy's defensiveness fade.

"I'm pleased to meet you too," she answered, suddenly meaning it. "You have a lovely shop."

"I'm glad you like what you see, Ivy," Drake interjected, "because Keils wants you to pick out some dresses before we leave."

It was news Ivy didn't want to hear. "I don't want anything from Cauldron," she said decisively.

"He just wants you to have some fancier clothes than

160

the kind you owned as a governess."

As Ivy looked down at the serviceable dress she was wearing, partially revealed through the open front of her cloak, she didn't like the idea of a pirate like Cauldron having the audacity to pass judgment on her clothing.

"What I'm wearing may not be fancy," she pointed out with some heat, "but at least I earned it by hard work and not by stealing from others!"

Drake sighed at Ivy's usual tirade. "We're only talking about a dress or two," he told her.

Ivy crossed her arms, her stance adamant. "There's nothing wrong with what I'm wearing."

Drake's eyes moved over Ivy in an appreciative sweep. "You look fine in anything," he admitted, his gaze lingering over her. "But a color like that"—he nodded toward a lavender wool dress displayed on one of the nearby mannequins—"would look nice with those violet eyes of yours."

Feeling self-conscious under that frankly approving gaze, Ivy turned her attention to the dress. It was indeed pretty, and though it wasn't elaborate, befitting a garment worn during the day, it was very stylish.

"And that one"—Drake nodded toward an equally fashionable dress created in amethyst-colored cashmere—"would look nice with your coloring too."

It was even prettier than the first dress, Ivy acknowledged. And both dresses were the kinds of garments she had never owned. Even before she had become a governess, as the daughter of a clergyman, all her clothes had been plainly fashioned.

Though she hated to admit it, a small part of her was enticed by the pretty frocks. After a lifetime of gray, beige, and other somber, serviceable clothes, the thought

161

of wearing such becoming dresses was a true temptation. Still, considering the source of the offer, she knew this wasn't the time to give in to such fancies.

"I won't accept any gifts from Cauldron," she said firmly.

"Then consider the dresses a gift from me," Drake tried.

That was even more unacceptable in Ivy's viewpoint. "No."

"Whether it's from Keils or me, you're going to have new dresses before you leave this shop." Drake's tone made it clear he was not going to take no for an answer.

Whether she wanted the dresses or not, Ivy realized she was going to get them. That didn't make her like the idea of either man purchasing them.

If Cauldron bought them, he would think he could buy her affections if he finally accepted her as his daughter or, even worse, think that because she took the gift she was interested in gleaning whatever she could from him.

And if Drake bought them, he might feel she owed him something for the gesture, and it was already too clear what that payment would be if he were released from the chastity that bound him now.

Neither choice was in her favor.

A way out of the dilemma came to her. "I'll take the dresses," she conceded, "but only if *I* buy them. I won't be beholden to Cauldron or you." She turned toward Elizabeth.

"I don't have any money with me," she told her, "but when I'm finally free of the predicament I'm in, I'll send what I owe to this shop." As she spoke, she reached for the tags on the dresses to see their price. The amounts

162

made her take a sharp breath, for they were far more than she had anticipated.

"I'll only be able to send a little at a time," she amended in a weak voice, forced to qualify her promise, "but I will pay the whole amount."

On a governess's meager wages, it would take Ivy a long time, Drake knew, but he had to admire her integrity. There wasn't a doubt in his mind that even though she had made the offer under duress, she would make the payments until the debt was paid in full.

Elizabeth looked truly regretful as she shook her head at the offer. "I'm sorry, Ivy, but I can't accept an arrangement like that. I run this shop by myself and many of my expenses can't wait."

Drake saw Ivy's face grow wary as she obviously expected him to insist he or Cauldron buy the dresses, and he decided to try another tack. He had seen the way her eyes had lingered on the pretty frocks, and had guessed she had probably never worn dresses that weren't utilitarian. He was determined that she have them.

"I have an idea," he told her. "I'll pay Elizabeth for the dresses and you can pay *me* back." He didn't add he had no intention of ever allowing her to do so. "That way, you won't be beholden to anyone."

"I guess I don't have much choice but to agree," Ivy said in resignation. "But where would I send the money? I can't post something to the high seas."

Considering he was a pirate and her captor, Drake knew most people would never follow through with any payments. But just as he sensed Ivy would honor the agreement with Elizabeth, he knew she would honor it with him.

"Send it to Elizabeth, here at this shop," he answered, giving Elizabeth enough gold to pay for the clothes. "She'll see it gets to me."

Elizabeth stripped the two dresses from the mannequins, draping them over her arm. "Let's try these on," she suggested, drawing Ivy into a small, curtained dressing area. "This color will look nice on you," she observed as she held the lavender dress up to Ivy, "and I don't think it will take much more than a nip and a tuck to make it fit."

With Elizabeth's help, Ivy's serviceable dress was quickly removed and the lovely lavender one smoothed into place. Elizabeth made little tucks at the sides of the bodice, pinning the small alterations in place as she turned Ivy toward the cheval mirror tilted toward them.

Ivy gazed at her reflection, admiring the beautiful pale color and the simple but fashionable cut. With its graceful, scooped neckline and slightly flared skirt, it exceeded anything she had ever owned.

"I never had a dress as pretty as this," she confessed.

"It looks beautiful on you. I'm glad you're taking it. And the other one, too," Elizabeth added. "Keils will be pleased."

"I took the dresses because I had no choice," Ivy reminded her. "I couldn't care less if Cauldron is pleased."

"Since I'm often with Keils, I'm a little more interested in the state of his moods," Elizabeth said softly. "If he's displeased, I'll be the one who will feel it."

"Are you saying Cauldron would have taken out his displeasure on you if I hadn't taken the dresses?" Disdain suddenly filled Ivy's voice.

"Ivy's picturing you being beaten, Elizabeth." Drake's

words came through the curtain. "She always thinks the worst of Keils."

Elizabeth laughed at the idea. "Keils would *never* hurt me," she told Ivy. "But with all the pain he's been feeling lately"—suddenly her voice was somber—"I don't want anything else troubling him."

"Well, he should be a happy man tonight since he got his way about the dresses," Ivy conceded. And she was going to be in debt for a long time, she added silently, providing she ever got free of the trouble she was in to pay it. But as she regarded herself in the mirror, she couldn't really regret the dresses themselves, for they fulfilled a longing she hadn't even realized she had.

"Keils is really a very nice man if you give him a chance."

Elizabeth's words made Ivy pull her gaze away from the mirror. "His friends all seem to think so," was the only thing she would agree to.

When she put on the amethyst garment, it fit beautifully, needing no alterations. As Elizabeth drew the curtain aside, Ivy stepped out into the shop, feeling a little self-conscious about facing Drake in her new finery.

Drake drank in the sight of her. The high neckline emphasized the graceful length of her neck, the fitted bodice accentuated the feminine curves of her body, and the soft look of cashmere added just the right touch of elegance.

She was a beauty in anything, he acknowledged, but garbed in that deep amethyst color, she was breathtaking. That was a compliment he knew Ivy would hardly appreciate.

"You look very nice," he said instead. He was sure even those simple words would discomfort her. With her

165

lifetime of good manners, he also knew he would still receive a polite response.

A low, reluctant "thank you" accompanied by a becoming flush showed Drake how well he knew Ivy by now. Suppressing a smile, he handed her another dress he had selected.

Ivy looked down at a beautiful gown made of pale orchid silk. "Two dresses is quite enough, Drake," she said firmly, trying to give it back.

Drake didn't take it. From the conversation he had heard through the curtain, he knew he had been right about Ivy never owning a beautiful dress. When he had heard the delight that had come to her voice as she had admired the frocks, he had been determined to see her in something even prettier.

"One more dress. I insist."

The price was enough to make Ivy cringe. "This silk gown is too fancy for everyday wear," she argued, not wanting to be deeper in debt than she already was. "I could hardly wear it to ride in."

"If Keils accepts you're his daughter, you can wear it to the celebration I know he'll have."

From the tone of his voice, Ivy knew he was giving her no choice but to comply. "What do I wear it to if he doesn't accept me?" she asked with asperity, "My funeral?"

Not bothering to answer that comment, Drake gave Elizabeth enough gold to pay for the beautiful creation.

Elizabeth added the garment to the lavender dress hanging over her arm. "I don't think this one will need much in the way of alterations," she said, "but if it does, I'll use this other one as a guide. It shouldn't take long," she promised, heading toward her back room.

"Elizabeth surprised me," Ivy had to admit when they were alone.

"Why?"

"She seems so respectable. I guess I never would have thought a man like Cauldron would be involved with someone like her." Then she paused as she pictured her own gentle, cultured mother. "But then, he was attracted to my mother, wasn't he?" she added, her voice suddenly edged with the feelings that thought provided. "But being his captive, she was thrown into the relationship. Elizabeth seems to have entered it of her own accord."

"He's—"

"Not a bad man," Ivy finished for him, knowing by now what Drake was going to say.

Drake grinned at the quick response. "He really isn't."

"I wonder why I don't agree with that," Ivy retorted. "Could it be because he interfered with my mother's life and now he's interfering with mine? Even if I'm ever free of all this, my reputation will suffer as much as hers did from being held by pirates."

Restlessly, she moved to the window, gazing out into the street. As her eyes settled on the small goldsmith's shop up the street from them, a thoughtful expression crossed her face.

"Could you buy me a wedding ring, Drake?" she suddenly asked, swinging around to face him.

Chapter 13

The change of topic caught Drake completely by surprise. "You want *what?*"

"I want a wedding ring," Ivy said firmly. "If I have to share a room with you, I want people to think I'm married."

"We can just tell them we're married," Drake reminded her.

"You heard that woman last night. Because I didn't have a wedding ring, she didn't believe us." As Drake looked at her as though she had gone mad, she hurried to say, "I just want a simple band. And I'll pay you back, of course, just as I'll do with the dresses."

"Of course," Drake agreed, giving her an assessing stare. "Will a ring make you feel less embarrassed about being with me?" he asked after a moment.

"Yes." The word was spoken with a heartfelt sincerity.

"Then I'll buy one for you." For the first time since he had met her, Drake saw a smile light up Ivy's face, her features, always beautiful, taking on an even greater radiance. He found he enjoyed being the source of that pleasure.

"And Ivy," he added softly, "you don't have to pay me back. Not for the dresses and not for the ring."

The smile that had touched Ivy's lips faded. She had heard enough about men to know that when they bought women expensive gifts, they often expected certain favors in return. She had no intention of ever finding herself in that situation with Drake.

"I won't be beholden to you," she reminded him.

Since the words were spoken with a conviction that would have made her preacher father proud, Drake knew when to retreat.

"Have it your way," he conceded.

"I'll write you a promissory note for the dresses while we're waiting for Elizabeth to finish with them," Ivy decided, reaching for a quill and paper lying on the nearby counter. "As soon as I know the cost of the ring, I'll add it to this."

Not long after Ivy finished the note, Elizabeth emerged from the back room, carrying a carefully wrapped package.

"Here are the dresses," she said, handing the package to Drake.

Drake leaned down to give Elizabeth a kiss on her cheek. "Thanks for everything," he said warmly.

"My pleasure, Drake," Elizabeth responded with a smile. She turned to Ivy. "Regardless of how things turn out with Keils, I wish you the best."

Meeting her father's lady friend had made Ivy see him in still another, and more flattering, perspective. "I'm glad I met you too, Elizabeth. I'll include a note for you," she promised, "when I send the money I owe Drake."

Considering the way Elizabeth had seen Drake look at Ivy, she guessed it would be money he would never accept. A wise woman, however, she said nothing as she smiled her good-bye.

"Let's buy you that ring," Drake said as they left the shop behind. Passing the tavern, already bustling with activity, they moved on to the goldsmith's shop.

As they entered, the man behind the counter looked up from the bracelet he was polishing. "May I help you?" he asked.

"I want to buy a gold band for the lady," Drake told him.

The man beamed. "Getting married?"

Drake glanced at Ivy. "It appears so," he said with some humor.

The goldsmith placed a set of small iron circlets onto the counter. "Once I see what size fits her, I can have whatever kind of ring you want made in just a few days."

"We don't have a few days," Drake explained. "So we'd like to look at whatever you already have."

The goldsmith produced a small tray of rings from beneath the counter. "Take a look through these."

Most of the bands were set with gemstones. Ignoring those, Ivy selected the simplest one on the tray: a slim gold band. As she slipped it on her finger, she couldn't help thinking that she had expected to be shopping for rings with Allen.

Instead, here she was with a pirate, a man she hardly knew even though she was sleeping in the same bed with him. That was a difficult fact to ignore, she reminded herself as she brought her thoughts back to the reason she was now selecting a ring.

The golden circlet was too small. Ivy replaced it on the

tray and then tried on the only other unadorned gold band. It was smaller than the first ring.

Ivy could ill afford a simple gold band, let alone one with jewels. "Do you have any other rings?" she asked the goldsmith. "These other bands are too expensive."

"You certainly found yourself a frugal woman," the goldsmith complimented Drake. "Most ladies want to look at the most expensive rings in the store."

"That's one of the reasons why I'm marrying her," Drake agreed, even more humor coming to his voice.

Drake was enjoying the situation, Ivy realized, but the cost was a serious consideration to her. "Sir, about the rings," she prompted.

"I only have what's on the tray," came the answer.

A ring with gems would put her into the kind of debt Ivy didn't want to think about. "Are there any other shops that sell rings?"

"I have the only one in town," the goldsmith answered, his smile smug.

The thought of paying for such a costly piece of jewelry made Ivy wonder if she should forget about buying a wedding band. But as she pictured everyone assuming she was one of Drake's light-o'-loves in the days ahead, she decided the debt was a necessary expense.

Her next problem was whether Drake had enough money on him to pay for a jeweled ring. Since he had just purchased three expensive dresses, she didn't know.

"Are these too expensive for you?" she asked him hesitantly, indicating the glittering bands.

"A woman who worries about her man's finances is a rare catch indeed," wheedled the goldsmith, wanting Drake to be receptive toward the fancier bands. "I suggest you get a ring on this lady's finger as soon as you can." He pushed the tray closer to Drake.

"I intend to," Drake agreed, his eyes crinkling at the corners. In answer to Ivy's question, he reached over to the tray, plucking one of the jeweled bands from it. "This would go nicely with your eyes," he said to her.

The band contained an amethyst encircled by diamonds. It was the prettiest ring on the tray and by far the most expensive. The goldsmith beamed his approval as he anticipated a lucrative sale.

"That's *really* too dear," Ivy said firmly.

The goldsmith tried to keep his smile from slipping. "Where *did* you find this woman?" he praised Drake, valiantly trying to salvage the transaction. "She deserves the finest of rings just for being so thoughtful of your means."

Drake needed no encouragement from the goldsmith, for he wanted Ivy to have the ring. As with the pretty dresses she had never had, he was sure she had never owned a pretty piece of jewelry.

"Try it on," he urged, holding it out to her.

"I want something simpler," Ivy insisted, refusing to take it. She heard the goldsmith's disappointed sigh as she selected the simplest jeweled ring from the tray. It was too big. Ivy sighed also as she was forced to reach for a more expensive band.

As Drake watched Ivy try on rings, he felt as though he really were a bridegroom, helping his intended select a wedding band. To his surprise, the feeling was a pleasant one. After Ivy had tried on the small group of bands and had rejected each one because of the size, he reached for her hand.

"Looks as if you have no choice but to try this one on," he said softly. Before she could protest, he slipped the

173

diamond and amethyst ring onto her finger. It fit as though it had been designed for her.

Their hands still clasped, Ivy looked down at the wedding band that glittered there. The moment suddenly felt real, as though she and Drake were truly a betrothed couple, soon to be entering into the sacred bond of matrimony.

Drake felt the same shared intimacy. He leaned forward, wanting to seal that bond with a kiss.

But as his lips hovered over hers, only a moment away from touching, the illusion suddenly ended for Ivy. She and Drake were anything but a betrothed couple, she reminded herself, placing her free hand to his chest to stop him.

"I guess," Drake said lightly, aware of the goldsmith's raised eyebrows at Ivy's unloverlike reaction, "you're going to make me wait until *after* the wedding for this kind of sport."

The goldsmith laughed as he watched Ivy self-consciously pull her hand away from Drake's. "I can see why you're in such a hurry to place a ring on this one's finger," he observed to Drake, his smile broad as he again anticipated a big sale. "Will this diamond and amethyst band be the one?"

Though Ivy blanched as the price was named, she inclined her head. While Drake paid the goldsmith, she reached for a nearby quill, giving the glittering band a despairing glance as she added its exorbitant cost to her promissory note. When she finished, she handed the paper to Drake, her eyes already returning to the expensive piece of jewelry now adorning her hand.

Drake had to smile as he read the note that carefully detailed each amount Ivy owed him. When he saw the

174

price she had entered for the ring, he started to give the paper back to her, for she had inadvertently reversed the first two numbers, making the amount much higher than what she actually owed. Then he shrugged aside the thought and simply placed the note into his pocket. Since he had no intention of collecting any money from Ivy, what she had entered made no difference.

He could see, though, how she had made the mistake. Even now, her mind was obviously distracted by the glittering ring, her eyes containing both concern and admiration as she looked at it.

She was going to be in debt her whole life, Ivy thought with despair as she gazed at the gemstones flashing brilliantly on her finger.

It *was* beautiful, she acknowledged, the kind of band women dreamed of wearing. It was far different than the simple gold circle Allen would have placed on her finger.

Allen. As his face came into her mind, Ivy wondered what he would think about all this. She would deal with that when the time came, she finally decided. Right now, she had more immediate things to worry about, namely, this evening's sleeping arrangements.

As she and Drake left the shop and started back down the street, she said, "Tonight I'll go by the name Mrs.—" She broke off. "What *is* your last name, Drake?"

"Jordan."

"Jordan," Ivy repeated, getting a feel for the name. "From now on, I'll go by Mrs. Jordan. Mrs. Drake Jordan," she amended.

It had a real sound to it, Drake decided, making him feel as though his bachelor days were truly at an end. To his surprise, the feeling was just as pleasant as when he had helped Ivy select the ring.

175

As Ivy ran Drake's name once again through her mind, she wondered that he had told it to her. Other than Keils Cauldron, who was already too well known to keep his identity a secret, she had noticed that no one else on the ship ever went by a last name. She was sure the idea of an arrest warrant gave them just cause.

"You don't care that I know your last name?" she asked him curiously.

Drake gave his shoulders a careless shrug. "A lot of people know my last name." He glanced up at the low-lying sun, gauging the hour. "We still have a lot of ground to cover. So if you're ready, *Mrs. Jordan*"—he teasingly emphasized the name Ivy was now assuming—"we should be going."

"Mrs. Jordan?" exclaimed a voice from the tavern they were now passing. "Drake, you sea dog, when did you place a ring on a woman's finger?"

Drake turned toward the voice, breaking into a grin as he recognized an acquaintance from his past. "Actually it was just a few minutes ago, Jamie," he answered, slanting Ivy an amused look. His grin grew wider as he watched Ivy self-consciously twist the jeweled band, obviously not prepared for the reality of being taken for his wife.

"Then let's see a kiss for your pretty bride!" Jamie called, raising the mug of ale he was holding up into the air in a toast.

As Drake cocked an inquiring brow at her, Ivy gave him a quelling glance to show him he had better not try.

"A kiss for your bride!" Jamie called out again as the couple in front of him didn't comply. At the loud words, several other people poked their heads out the door of the tavern, all apparently feeling mellow enough to want to join in a celebration of any kind.

176

"A kiss! A kiss!" The words were suddenly a steady chant as the men got into the spirit of the occasion.

"If we don't go along with it," Drake murmured, "pretty soon we'll have every person in the tavern out here urging us on." Letting his package slip to the cobblestones, he reached for her.

"Drake, no—" Ivy's protest was silenced as Drake captured her lips.

The kiss on the ship had been unashamedly passionate, bending her to his will. This one was gentle, but in many ways, Ivy found it far, far more sensuous. The objection she had been going to voice was forgotten as his lips parted hers, his tongue delving within, exciting her in ways she had never imagined.

When Drake finally raised his head, Ivy felt languid, conscious it was only his strong arms, wrapped tightly around her, that supported her weak body. She took a shaky breath, trying to collect her bemused thoughts.

"It looks like you'll have no trouble siring a brood of children with *this* one, Drake," Jamie called out with a laugh. "She's certainly willing enough." Raising his mug in a last toast, he disappeared inside the tavern.

The words snapped Ivy from her dazed state. She hurriedly stepped away from Drake's arms, vividly conscious the other onlookers were grinning widely in her direction. Aware also that she had given them cause to grin, she glared up at Drake and channeled her embarrassment toward him.

"You took advantage of that situation to kiss me!" she accused him in a fierce whisper.

"It *was* only a kiss, Ivy."

Maybe to Drake, it was only a kiss, but to Ivy it was more serious and she still felt weak inside from it. To

177

make matters worse, she had made a spectacle of herself in front of the men watching.

"I'm so mad at what you did I could just"—Ivy searched for a word to express her agitated feelings—"just *scream!*" she ended between her teeth.

Expecting something a little more violent, considering Ivy's pause to find the right word, Drake laughed.

"Now *there's* a threat that has my knees knocking," he said with mock horror, his eyes alight with merriment. As Ivy continued to glare at him, obviously wanting to berate him more but also obviously unable to come up with anything really vile because of her genteel upbringing, he added with a chuckle, "And considering the lady you are, Ivy, we both know you're not even going to do *that.*"

The fact that he was right made Ivy angrier.

"How about *me* kissing the bride?"

The slightly slurred words, uttered by one of the men standing at the tavern door, gave Ivy the opportunity to vent her ire—and make Drake pay for the embarrassment she felt over his stolen kiss. She turned to face the man.

"I'd rather kiss—"

"Don't do it, Ivy," she heard Drake mutter.

"—a snake," she ended emphatically, ignoring the warning in Drake's words.

Though she had provoked the conflict, Ivy's stomach clenched as he drew nearer. He was a huge, powerfully built man, with a jagged scar slicing down one cheek and several days' growth of beard surrounding teeth that were uneven and yellowed. The idea of such a mouth possibly covering her own made her feel sick and increasingly frightened, for he didn't look like the kind of man who would easily be stopped.

He forced up Ivy's chin, ready to claim his prize.

"*No one* kisses her but me," Drake said, the words a definite threat.

Any other time, such a possessive statement would have annoyed Ivy, but now she felt only relief.

"I aim to kiss her," answered the man, confident enough of his own prowess to not be intimidated. In a movement meant to put both Drake and Ivy in their place, he pulled Ivy full against himself, deciding to have his way with her right in full view of her man.

His lips never made it to her mouth. Drake swung him away from Ivy, his fist clenching at his side. "It's easy to pick on someone half your size, isn't it?" he asked, his voice dangerous. "*Now try me!*" His tightly balled fist shot out in a hard right to the man's prominent jaw.

In the other fights Ivy had seen Drake in, such a blow had easily felled his opponent. This time, while the man staggered back, shaking his head to clear it, he remained on his feet. And the look in his eyes made it plain he now had murder on his mind.

Although Drake was a big man, this man was even bigger, Ivy realized with dismay. She had thought Drake was unbeatable, but with this dangerous opponent, she suddenly wasn't so sure. Afraid of what she had started, she watched worriedly as the two men prepared to battle.

When the hulk of a man suddenly launched himself at Drake, his big fists flying, she cried out. They came together in a flurry of blows that soon ended up with both men rolling on the ground.

Ivy couldn't tell which man was winning. Only when Drake pinned his opponent to the cobblestones, his fists connecting with the force of a mule's kick to the underside of the man's jaw, quickly rendering him unconscious, did she realize he was the victor.

Confident his foe would stay down, Drake craned his head toward where Ivy had been standing, fully expecting her to have run off during the fighting. In this town, tame compared to Cay's Cove, he knew escape would have been possible.

To his surprise, she was still there. The sight made his anger at having to fight completely disappear.

"You would have to pick the biggest thug in this town," he said with irony between hard breaths as he rose to his feet.

Expecting anger, which certainly would have been justified, Ivy felt even worse about what she had done.

"I am sorry, Drake," she said contritely. "I won't do that again."

Knowing Ivy as he did, Drake believed her promise. "Good." He gave her a curious glance. "Why didn't you run away?" he asked. "In a town like this, I thought you would."

It hadn't even occurred to Ivy to run off, not when she had put Drake's life in danger. But that was a thought she didn't want to acknowledge, let alone share.

"Everything just happened too fast," she said instead.

The calculating look Drake gave her in return made her wonder if he believed her.

Chapter 14

The sun had been down for several hours when they reached the farmhouse where they were to meet Cauldron. As they knocked on the door, Ivy removed her gloves so her new ring would not be hidden. Its presence on her finger made her feel considerably better about facing the occupants.

The door opened to two robust people, obviously husband and wife.

"I'm Drake Jordan," Drake introduced himself. "I believe you're expecting me."

"Yes, yes, we are," the farmer answered. "Mr. Avery said there were two people with him. I'm Donald Weaver and this is my wife, Sarah."

Ivy held out her hand to the wife, making sure her new ring caught the light from the lamp the farmer was holding.

"Pleased to meet you," she said. "I'm . . . I'm—"

Raised to always tell the truth, Ivy suddenly found herself floundering at having to say the bald-faced lie she had fabricated.

"She's Mrs. Jordan," Drake finally answered for her, filling the awkward gap. He could almost sense Ivy's relief at his intervention.

"Mr. Avery mentioned you were a married couple," Sarah said warmly, reaching forward to take Ivy's hand.

Ivy was surprised at the words, hardly expecting Cauldron to be so considerate. But seeing Sarah's eyes go to her ring, she was still glad she had it to confirm the story.

Cauldron suddenly appeared at the couple's side. "I'm sure glad to see the two of you," he said with feeling. "It was getting so late I thought something might have happened."

Despite herself, Ivy was touched, for the worry in his eyes seemed to encompass her as well as Drake.

"We were delayed," she said, her eyes going involuntarily to the ring on her finger.

Cauldron's brows rose at the sight. "A wedding band?" he murmured as Drake and Ivy brushed by him to come inside.

Drake could hear the humor in the pirate captain's voice. "It's a long story," he said under his breath.

"I can imagine," Cauldron said, the words wry. Still, he had to admire Ivy for the way she continued to turn an awkward situation into one she could live with. Then that thought gave him pause, for it also showed Ivy could have been clever enough to have manipulated that first meeting with him. More and more, though, he found he didn't want to believe that of her.

Sarah waved them all into her kitchen, the room nicely warmed by the fire burning in the huge fireplace. While Cauldron and Drake lingered by the door, speaking in low tones with each other, Ivy removed her cloak, then

182

moved closer to the fire, needing its warmth after the long, cold ride in the dark.

"Are you hungry?" Sarah asked. "I have stew and biscuits I could heat up."

Ivy shook her head. "We stopped at an inn shortly before we got here." She was sure Drake had suggested that arrangement to keep her contact with the people at the commandeered houses at a minimum. That thought was confirmed as she watched Drake throw frequent, watchful glances in her direction as he kept one ear cocked on her conversation to make sure she said nothing she shouldn't.

"At least let me get you something to drink," Sarah suggested. "What would you like? Tea or coffee?"

Ivy rubbed her chilled fingers in front of the hot flames. "Tea, with one lump of sugar."

"And your husband? What would he like?"

A wife would be expected to know such a thing, Ivy acknowledged to herself, but she had no idea what Drake liked.

"He'll have what I'm having," she hazarded. While Sarah bustled over the stove preparing the tea, Ivy eyed Cauldron warily as he joined her in front of the fireplace.

She didn't speak and neither did he. Instead, they both stared into the flames.

"Your new dress is nice."

The words were spoken with a slight hesitation, showing Cauldron was on unsure ground when it came to complimenting a woman who might be his daughter.

He was having as much difficulty with this relationship as she was, Ivy realized in surprise. That knowledge made her turn from the flames to face him.

"Thank you," she answered, her voice less guarded

than usual. "Elizabeth has lovely fashions." Then remembering Cauldron was the one responsible for her excessive debts, she added more formally, "Drake probably told you I'm going to pay for the dresses myself."

"I heard." The news had, in fact, pleased Cauldron, for it showed a woman of integrity. Or a calculating one, a small part of his brain tried to warn him. Again, he found he didn't want to listen to that warning voice. "Regardless, I'm glad you took them."

Ivy was affected by the effort Cauldron was making to be nice. "I'm glad I took them too," she confessed. "They're very pretty."

For a moment, silence stretched between them, but for the first time, it was a pleasant one, not strained.

"Well, good night," Cauldron finally said. "I'll see you in the morning."

"Good night."

This time, Drake reflected from where he stood at the kitchen door, they had actually carried on a civil conversation. It had been brief, but not one spark had flown. As he nodded his own good-night to Cauldron, he decided they were making real progress.

"This should warm you," Sarah said, turning from the stove to hand her newest guests each a cup filled with steaming liquid.

Drake took a sip and then tried not to grimace at the sweet taste. "I never had a liking for sugar," he apologized. "Or tea, for that matter. I'd like coffee if you have it. Black."

Sarah cocked her head in amusement as she looked over at Ivy. "The two of you been married long?" she asked.

"We . . . we—" Once again, Ivy found her self stammering as she tried to lie.

Drake came to her rescue. "As a matter of fact," he said easily, "I just put a ring on her finger today."

Ivy looked at him in relief, glad of an answer that, while truthful, fostered the impression she wanted.

At the news, Sarah broke into a broad smile. "So *that* was what delayed you," she murmured. Her smile suddenly got broader. "And that means tonight is your wedding night!"

At the words, Ivy started, almost spilling her tea. "Uh, well . . ." Again she stumbled, at a loss and not wanting to talk about something as intimate as a wedding night even if she could.

"I guess you could say that," Drake answered when he saw Ivy was again hard pressed to give an answer.

"Let me get your room ready—and add some special touches," Sarah added, obviously wanting to make their first night together special. She reached for two huge metal buckets banked by the fire, hefting their weight with ease.

"No, really, it's not—" Ivy broke off for Sarah was already out the door. Pretending she was married wasn't working out as she had imagined, she thought in dismay.

"I wonder what Sarah is going to do to that room?" Drake's question was filled with speculation.

"Remember, Drake," Ivy reminded him, "that *none* of this is real."

Drake had to grin at the primly spoken warning. "I'm surprised Sarah thought it was real," he countered. "You've got to be the worst liar I've ever seen." He gave a low chuckle. "Make that the worst would-be liar I've ever seen. You don't even get past the first word. We're going to have to work on your ability to spin a yarn if we're to pretend we're a married couple."

"I was raised to tell the truth," Ivy said defensively.

Drake chuckled. "Then I guess *I'll* be the one who does all the talking."

When Sarah returned and then showed them to their room, Ivy was more than pleased by the accommodations, by far the nicest she had seen since her capture. The bedroom was small but cozy, its walls painted a soft country blue. A large mahogany bedstead, whose intricately carved headboard was positioned between two windows, filled most of the space. It was covered with a beautifully stitched counterpane, its colors matching those of a braided rug that spanned most of the polished wooden floor. In a stone fireplace, a blazing fire nicely warmed the air.

Ivy loved the room. She had mixed feelings, however, at the special touches Sarah had provided. For the metal tub in the corner, filled with steaming, lilac-scented water, she had great interest, provided Drake would step discreetly into the hall while she used it. For the lovely white satin nightgown draped enticingly over the bed, she had no interest, knowing she would never wear such an alluring garment in Drake's presence.

Sarah saw Ivy's eyes on the nightgown. "I didn't know if you had anything special to wear for tonight, so I wanted to give you this." She said the words shyly as she lightly touched the beautiful fabric. "It was given to me for my wedding night, but I couldn't wear it. The aunt who sent it hadn't seen me since I was a child and didn't realize I had turned out so big. And with no children, I don't have any family to give it to." Her eyes were hopeful as she regarded Ivy. "So if you don't have anything special . . ."

"All she has is flannel," Drake volunteered. He knew Ivy well enough by now to be certain she would turn down such an item, but he couldn't help but tease her a little. Her answer was just what he expected.

"That's very generous of you, Sarah, but I really can't accept such a fine gift."

"A wedding night only comes once in a woman's life," Sarah urged, her voice wistful.

Ivy was touched at the woman's generosity for a total stranger. Not having the heart to refuse her, she decided to accept the gift and then simply not wear it.

"Well, thank you," she said. "It's very nice of you." She could sense Drake's curiosity at her surprising capitulation.

"I'm not going to wear it," she murmured for his ears alone as Sarah bent over to plump up the pillows.

"Good," Drake murmured back. "Satin on a woman is one of my weaknesses."

The statement evoked thoughts that Ivy knew she shouldn't have. Moving her thoughts to safer ground, she murmured, "About the bath, Drake . . ."

Sarah started toward the door, interrupting the request Ivy was going to make. "I've bothered the two of you enough," she said discreetly. "I'm sure you'll be wanting your privacy."

"I'll go out with you," Drake said, his gaze holding Ivy's. "I'm sure my new bride will want some time to herself to get ready." The appreciative look Ivy gave him in return made the simple gesture well worth it.

As the door closed behind him, Ivy knew from her

other nights with Drake that he wouldn't come in until she told him he could. In his own way, she reflected as she began stripping off her clothes, Drake Jordan was a gentleman. He wasn't at all what she would have expected of a pirate. For all that he was a fierce fighter, he could be considerate too.

Minutes later, she was immersed in the warm water. It felt marvelous on her skin, soothing the muscles that were still sore from being in the saddle all day. For a short while, she simply sat there, enjoying the comforting sensations, but then aware that Drake was standing uncomfortably in the hall, she reached for the scented soap by the tub. Lathering up her hair and body, she scrubbed them clean, letting herself sink totally under the water to rinse herself off.

When she was done, she stepped from the tub and reached for the thick towel Sarah had thoughtfully left behind, using it to dry herself.

With the fire still blazing, the room was quite warm. She decided to forgo the cotton shift she had felt compelled to wear before and slipped on the flannel nightgown. Kneeling by the fire, she used its heat to dry her hair as she combed it. When it flowed in smooth, clean ripples down her back, she hurried to do her other nighttime ablutions, mindful of Drake waiting patiently for her to finish.

"I'm ready," she called as she climbed into the bed. When Drake came in, she turned away to give him the same privacy he had allowed her. She heard him quickly divesting himself of his clothes. Though she should have expected it, the slight splash as he stepped into the tub caught her by surprise.

He's going to take a bath right here in the room with me.

That was her first thought followed quickly by: *He's naked.* Disconcerted, she tried not to picture what he was doing, but as small splashes continued to come from the tub, she couldn't help but think about it. The long, muscular lines of his body kept coming to her mind, disturbing her with images she knew she shouldn't be envisioning.

As Drake stepped from the tub, he looked over at Ivy, lying there on the bed. Everything about her intrigued him—her modesty, her honesty, her forthright nature, and her beauty. She was a woman unlike any other he had ever known and he was finding it increasingly difficult to keep his behavior chaste when he was around her. Even the bath water, cold now from sitting so long, hadn't dispelled the longing he felt.

Drying himself off, he felt the familiar tightening in his loins intensify as he thought about joining her in their supposed marriage bed. Trying not to think about the pleasure he would have if he could actually consummate that "marriage," he stepped into his brief undergarment and then put out the lamp.

When Drake joined her in the bed, lifting the covers that lay in the valley between their two bodies, Ivy knew he was going to reach for her, bringing her right into his arms as he had done the night before.

They were going to be together like this by morning anyway, she tried to remind herself as he pulled her close. And he would only be holding her, nothing more. Despite the fact that he must be as aware as she was that this was their pretend wedding night, until Cauldron made a decision about her, she was sure Drake would keep things chaste between them. Even so, she couldn't help tensing anyway at the intimate embrace.

"This makes us seem like lovers," she protested, glad Drake couldn't see her face clearly.

"That's what embarrassed you this morning, wasn't it?" Drake asked. "Well, we're not lovers. We're two people sharing a bed and that means we're also going to share the closeness that comes with it. They're nice feelings," he pointed out, "and considering the bounds of this particular relationship, they're nothing to feel self-conscious about."

They were nice feelings, Ivy acknowledged as she lay in his arms. It was just the way it made them seem like lovers that was making her feel uncomfortable. As Drake had said, they weren't lovers—nor would they be, she vowed. She would never let that happen, even if Drake were released from the bounds that held him now.

Able to enjoy the warmth and security of being with Drake without worry of any consequences, Ivy relaxed, sleep coming easily.

A cock's crow from outside awakened Ivy to a still dark sky. "Is it time to get up?" she asked in sleepy confusion, raising her face from Drake's chest as she looked toward the darkness of the window.

"Not quite yet," Drake answered. "That cock is just impatient for morning to come."

Ivy let her face settle once again onto his chest, her eyes closing. "This is a nice feeling to sleep like this," she confessed, her tone drowsily content.

Drake smiled into the darkness at the innocent pleasure in her voice. "I like it too," he admitted. Despite the frustration, despite the restraint he had to exercise, he enjoyed having Ivy in his arms. He laced his fingers companionably through hers.

"When I first saw you on the *Wild Swan*," he said with soft reminiscence, "you looked so frightened. Half of me wanted to put my arms around you in comfort, and the other half wanted to carry you off to my bed."

Just a few days ago, Ivy mused, such words would have panicked her. Now, as she lay in the shelter of Drake's arms, knowing no further intimacy could occur, she only felt contentment.

"You got both," she said shyly.

"*This* isn't quite the way I pictured it." Drake gave a wry chuckle. "Here we are talking in bed like an old married couple when what I really want to do is make love to you like the newly married couple we're pretending to be."

That would have panicked her too, Ivy mused, but since she knew Drake couldn't act upon it, she wasn't alarmed by the words. Or surprised. Drake had certainly made his feelings clear when it came to her. Knowing she was safe to simply enjoy the closeness, she nestled her head into a more comfortable position.

"This is sinful, though, isn't it?" she murmured. "Lying with each other like this."

Again Drake smiled into the darkness. "We'd have to do a lot more than this to make our nights together sinful." Intending to rest his cheek against the silky hair at her temple as he had done the night before, Drake bent his head toward her.

At the same moment, Ivy looked up, meaning to ask him a question. Though neither of them meant it to happen, their lips touched in the darkness.

Chapter 15

Suddenly, Drake's blood was pounding hotly through his veins. He instinctively rolled between Ivy's thighs, parting them with his own as his needs clambered for release. His kiss deepened, his tongue doing to her what his hot loins ached to achieve.

A melting sensation poured through Ivy at the feel of him on top of her so, making her feel strangely lethargic. Though she knew she should push Drake away, somehow her body didn't want to listen.

She felt Drake's fingers unfastening the front of her nightgown and felt the cool night air as it swept over her bared breasts. But all other thoughts were gone as his hands cupped her flesh, his fingers stroking over her nipples. Suddenly taut, they seemed to ache for his touch.

"You feel so beautiful, Ivy."

Drake's words were a groan as he caressed those turgid crests. He felt Ivy's breasts, already so lushly full, swell even more, overflowing his palms. The excited moans that erupted from her throat made his own desire sharply spiral.

Bringing his lips to one swollen peak, he laved it with his tongue. As Ivy arched against him in response, his hips begin to move. With only the nightwear they were each wearing keeping them apart, the feel of the most intimate parts of their bodies pressing together wildly excited them both.

As Drake brushed again and again over the part of her that was shockingly eager for his touch, Ivy found herself writhing beneath him. Even as she raised her hips to better receive that arousing, burning caress, her legs parted further, instinctively preparing for the mating her body knew would soon follow.

Drake felt the flannel dampen as Ivy's readiness grew. Inflamed by the sensation, he grasped the hem of her nightgown, tugging it up around her waist. As her heated flesh pressed against him, separated now only by the thin swatch of cotton he wore, his hips surged heavily against her even as he impatiently pushed his brief undergarment aside.

Eager, bared flesh met eager, bared flesh—the one hard and ready, the other soft and wanting.

The feel of Drake probing at the throbbing, tender flesh that was already inflamed to the point of explosion was more than Ivy could bear. With a wild, abandoned cry, she clasped her legs around Drake's hips, her body trembling as spasms of pure pleasure began pouring over her.

Drake, on the verge of burying himself within her, was brought harshly back to reality, back to the innocence he was about to claim. As he tried to pull away, wanting to keep that final union from happening, the slim legs that were tangled around his waist prevented him from doing so.

As raging desire coursed through him, making him want nothing more than to thrust himself into the warm sheath that was so ready for the taking, his seed spilled onto her, but not, to his immense relief, into her.

Drake's breath came in harsh, laboring gasps as he collapsed onto the softness of Ivy's body.

As she lay pinned beneath him, her body now free of the tremors that had claimed it, Ivy's mind slowly began to refocus. She felt the proof of Drake's passion at the still-throbbing apex of her thighs, felt the hardness of him still pressing intimately against her—and felt shame for what she had allowed. Though her virginity was intact, she knew it was only because Drake had stopped himself from taking it. She was her mother's daughter, beginning to repeat the same mistakes, and the thought appalled her.

"Let me up." Ivy's words were full of torment as she pushed at Drake's chest to get him off her. As he obliged, rolling to the side, she jerked to a sitting position, grateful for the darkness of the room while she yanked her nightgown down past her hips.

"I shouldn't have let you do that!" she cried, her hands shaking as she fiercely pulled the gaping flannel bodice back over her breasts.

Drake repositioned his own nightwear. "I was part of the passion too," he reminded her, his voice still ragged. "It wasn't just you."

Ivy put her hands to her cheeks, felt the warmth that passion had infused in them. "It can't happen again!"

Drake took a long, uneven breath. "No," he agreed, "it can't. Not yet."

"Not ever!" Tonight had been a mistake, but she

would not make the mistake twice, Ivy vowed. She would keep a tight, tight control on the attraction she felt for Drake. And as for him . . .

For now, his desire was slaked, she reminded herself unhappily, feeling his seed, warm and sticky, at the juncture of her thighs.

Abruptly leaving the bed, she made her way to the tub, thankful for the darkness that shielded her from Drake's eyes as she dipped the end of the towel into its cold water so she could wash away the remnants of his passion. Her body, still throbbing where her trembling fingers touched the area, increased her turmoil.

She had allowed a man whom she scarcely knew to do things that were only proper for a married man and woman. And worse, she had allowed it even though she was already betrothed to a caring, wonderful man.

"You all right, Ivy?" Drake's concerned words came to her in the darkness.

"I don't want to talk about it."

Drake could hear the anguish in her voice. Leaving the bed, he reached for his clothes, swiftly pulling them on.

"It's almost dawn," he said, seeing the faint lightening of the evening sky. "When you're ready, join me in the hall."

As Ivy dressed, she chastised herself again and again over the near-tragic mistake. She would *not* end up like her mother. It was a vow she repeated over and over as she combed the tangles from her passion-tumbled hair.

Her feelings grew worse as she went to make the bed. The linens were unmarked, showing her virginity was still intact. But not by much, Ivy reminded herself grimly as she straightened the rumpled sheets. When Sarah saw the unblemished linens, she would probably assume she and Drake had already been lovers. It was, unfortunately, not far from the truth.

Picking up the satin nightgown Sarah had given her and folding it so she could pack it in the canvas bag, she knew it was going to be doubly awkward facing the woman this morning. To Sarah, last night had been a wedding night. That alone would have made facing her embarrassing. Add to that the fact that she and Drake had come within a hair's breadth of consummating that pretend marriage, looking into Sarah's beaming eyes now would be as difficult as looking into Drake's knowing ones.

As Ivy placed the nightgown into the bag, she realized she hadn't set out the miniatures as she had always done before. Maybe if she had, she thought unhappily, picking up the portrait of Allen, she wouldn't have forgotten her commitment to him.

Allen was her intended, but Drake was her temptation. In the nights ahead, she would make sure all the tiny portraits kept their watchful eyes upon her to ensure she didn't forget that fact.

When she finally joined Drake in the hall, she couldn't meet his eyes. Nor could she meet Sarah's when they went downstairs.

"I'm sure you'll be wanting a big breakfast this morning," Sarah said with a beaming smile. "The others are eating in the dining room, but I have a private table set for two in the kitchen. I remember what those first special days of being married were like, when you just want to be alone together."

"I hate living a lie," Ivy breathed under her breath as they followed Sarah into the kitchen.

Drake didn't doubt the lowly spoken words. Every-

197

thing about Ivy was truthful, making him think she couldn't be lying about Keils Cauldron being her father. That was a question to which they would soon have an answer. But whether she was or wasn't, he meant to have her. The only difference was whether he would first need the pirate captain's blessing.

Though the breakfast was expertly prepared, Ivy couldn't enjoy it, not with everything that had happened. Still not wanting to look at Drake, she steadfastly kept her eyes on her plate.

By the end of the meal, Drake knew he was going to have to take the first step toward ending the awkward silence that stretched between them.

"Ivy, look at me."

Reluctantly, Ivy raised her eyes, knowing she would have to face Drake sooner or later.

"We came close to making love this morning—which we shouldn't have done, considering the circumstances," Drake conceded, "but it was a natural enough thing to happen between us."

The words made Ivy remember all too well the throbbing, intense pleasure she had experienced as she had lain beneath him.

"Just because mating is a natural instinct," she finally answered with difficulty, "it doesn't make it right."

"Between us, it will be right when the time comes."

"The time will *never* be right between us," Ivy corrected him. "Not with all that stands between us."

Though Drake didn't refute the statement, there was something about the thoughtful way he regarded her that made Ivy feel he was willing to bide his time on that particular subject. In many ways, it was a discomforting sensation.

Relieved to finally say good-bye to a still-beaming Sarah, Ivy had another awkward moment when she met Cauldron out by the barn. As Drake went to saddle their horses, leaving her alone with her father, she found she couldn't face him either, even though he couldn't possibly know what had happened.

"That dress looks as pretty on you as the other one," Cauldron told her, catching glimpses of the lavender frock as the brisk wind blew open the edges of Ivy's cloak.

In view of all that had been going on, Ivy had paid scant attention to the lavender dress when she donned it. Now, the kind words, coming as they did after that turmoil, made tears of regret well in her eyes.

"What's wrong, Ivy?" Cauldron asked gently, coming closer. "Did you and Drake have a fight?"

Ivy wiped away the tears with the back of her hand. "No, we didn't fight. I'm just . . . I'm just discouraged." Suddenly, her tears overflowed, glistening as they trickled down her cheeks. Without thought, she pressed her face against Cauldron's shoulder, needing the comfort that only a father could give.

"There, there." Cauldron said awkwardly as he patted Ivy's back. "Don't cry, Ivy. I know everything has been rough on you."

In that moment, Ivy felt close to her father in a way she had not felt before, but she could tell his feelings remained carefully guarded even as he tried to comfort her. Though she knew he was her father, he didn't know if she was his daughter, and his doubt was a barrier.

She stepped back, once again wiping away the tears as she stared at her father with thoughtful eyes. Now that she had had her first real brush with passion, she could better understand how her mother had ended up in his arms.

"Do you ever regret that things didn't turn out differently with my mother?" she asked, her question softly poignant.

For a moment, Cauldron was quiet. "It never would have worked between us," he finally answered. "We were too different, from two different worlds. And we each had commitments we couldn't forget."

Those were words Ivy understood all too well.

In many ways, Ivy found the ride that day worse than the others. While her body no longer ached from being on horseback, being near Drake proved to be a strain. Though he made no further reference to their passion and neither did she, they were both highly aware that it had happened.

Feeling uncomfortable around him, she spent most of the time talking to Cauldron. The tension that had marred their early conversations was now gone, allowing them to finally relax around each other.

"Do you ever regret the life you've led?" she found herself asking.

"Until recently, no," Cauldron admitted. "I liked my life at sea and being able to live as I wanted. But things are different now. I can see the age of piracy is coming to an end." He paused. "Did Drake tell you about the pardon?"

"Yes."

"It will come at a good time."

"I hope you get it," Ivy said with sincerity.

"It's just a matter of finding Geoff's killer when we reach Georgetown," Cauldron reassured her. "And I'd do that with or without the promise of a pardon."

"When will we get to the city?"

"Tomorrow morning."

The thought that her destiny would soon be resolved made Ivy aware of how different everything was since she had first been taken captive. Then, she had felt nothing but hate for Cauldron. Now, all that was changing.

She no longer viewed him as simply a notorious pirate. He was a man, too, who felt grief for the loss of his son and hope for the addition of a daughter. The idea of getting to know him better appealed more and more to her as her resistance to his being her father faded.

She was uncertain whether she could prove her relationship to him. That was still a source of concern about her future, for if the pirate captain decided she had tried to deceive him, he could be ruthless.

Since she had been honest with him, Ivy had to believe that Cauldron would accept her as his child and not reject her as a scheming adventuress. When that happened, she knew they would have the time to get to know each other.

And there brewed a very serious complication: Drake.

She was betrothed to Allen, yet was attracted to Drake. In many ways it was wrong. Not just because she was already promised to another, though that was an important commitment, but also because Drake was a pirate, the kind of man a sensible woman avoided.

The attraction she felt could only cause trouble, just as her mother's attraction to Cauldron had only caused trouble. If she stayed with the pirates for any length of time, she would have to be sure that her mother's fate didn't happen to her.

When they pulled to a halt that evening at an isolated tavern, Ivy assumed it would be their destination for the night. Cauldron's words ended that thought.

"We'll just stop long enough to ask a few questions and eat," he told her as they dismounted. "The place we'll be staying at later hasn't been lived in for years so there will be no food."

Ivy pictured a deserted house and then pictured sleeping on a cold, hard floor. The thought was unappealing, but she knew such accommodations would be less conducive to intimacy, and for that she was glad.

When they entered the smoky, noisy tavern, she saw it was of the same ilk as the Dirk and Dagger. Though she still felt awkward around Drake, she acknowledged his presence at her side made her feel safe despite the roughness of their surroundings.

As they made their way to a long trestle table, no one seemed to be aware that the notorious Keils Cauldron was in their midst, his beard now effectively disguising his features.

The food they ordered was surprisingly good. Ivy, sitting safely tucked between Drake and Cauldron, savored each bite of the meat pie she had been served whereas Cauldron didn't linger over his and finished quickly. Impatient to question a few people, he went over to a neighboring table.

A few minutes later, there was a loud crash.

Startled, Ivy looked up from her meal and saw Cauldron fiercely holding another man against a toppled table. The other occupants of the tavern scarcely bothered to look up.

"What's going on?" she worriedly whispered to Drake.

"The man didn't want to give Keils some information he hinted he had," he answered. "But he is now."

Keils Cauldron wasn't someone to cross, Ivy reflected as she watched the frightened victim babble what the pirate captain wanted to know. It must not have been what Cauldron sought because he looked over to Drake a moment later, shaking his head as he released his quaking prey.

"Let's go," Cauldron said as he returned to the trestle table.

As Ivy rose from her bench, one of the men sitting at the table next to her regarded Cauldron with a baleful stare.

"I sure wouldn't want to tangle with that mean son of a bitch," she heard him mutter.

The rude expression made Ivy fix her gaze on him. "That happens to be my father you're insulting," she curtly informed the man.

At the words, Drake and Cauldron exchanged glances, neither expecting to hear Ivy say such words. Drake could see from the way Cauldron smiled as he moved toward the door that he was pleased Ivy had championed him in such a way.

Having said her piece, Ivy turned away from the man. She could see the question in Drake's eyes at the reprimand she had just delivered.

"I couldn't let someone insult my own father," she told him, "even if he *is* a pirate."

Drake laughed when he heard her reasoning. "That

wasn't an insult, Ivy. It was a compliment. That's why Keils didn't deal with that man himself."

"Using words like that couldn't *possibly* be flattering," Ivy argued as she headed for the door.

As he followed her, Drake had to grin at that primly spoken response, Ivy's refreshing sense of propriety appealing to him more and more.

Their destination for the night was nothing like what Ivy had imagined, having expected some simple, dilapidated farmhouse. She was unprepared for the beautiful plantation house that loomed in front of them in the moonlight.

Made of brick with huge galleries gracing both the upper and lower floors, it was an imposing, elegant structure. The large casement windows were boarded shut, showing no one lived there, but it didn't distract from the inherent beauty or grace of the mansion.

It seemed a crime to break into such a place, but that must be what Cauldron planned since there was no one to buy off with gold.

"I know we need a place to stay," she protested, "but it just isn't right to break into a house like this."

"Ivy," Drake said dryly, "you're going to have to stop thinking the worst about Keils and me just because we're pirates. We're not going to break in." He reached into his pocket, pulling out a key. "I'm just going to open the door."

"You have a key?" Ivy asked in confusion.

"I own the place."

It was a revelation Ivy didn't expect to hear. "Pirate's bounty?" she had to ask.

Drake swung out of the saddle. "Inheritance."

"Oh." Chastised, Ivy said nothing more as she followed him to the door.

Drake unlocked the double door of ornately carved oak panels, letting them swing open. "I inherited this house when my parents died," he explained. "It's been locked up ever since, though I often have someone come in to clean it."

Inside, all the furniture was covered with sheets, but as Drake lit an elegant brass lamp, Ivy could see the place had been carefully maintained. She was astounded by the wealth so evident around them. Overhead, crystal chandeliers sparkled from underneath the cloths that had been draped over them. Beneath her feet, the finest of marble, wood, and carpets graced the floors. And on the walls, patterned silk complemented the fine oak that abundantly trimmed the house. A graceful curving staircase led to the floor above.

"If you inherited this," she finally asked when she and Drake were alone in the elaborate master bedroom suite, "why did you become a pirate?"

Before answering, Drake set down the lamp he had been carrying and pulled off the sheet that covered a finely crafted brass bed, encased in gray silk bed curtains.

"I met Geoff and Keils," he said simply, "and the adventure in their lives appealed to me more than running a plantation."

It was about what Ivy had expected. "What a waste," she murmured.

Drake didn't know if Ivy was referring to the plantation lying idle all these years or to the fact that a life of piracy had kept him from leading what she would consider a productive life. Knowing her, it was probably both, he decided.

He didn't regret the path he had chosen. He had experienced enough adventures to last a lifetime. And since he, like Cauldron, had attacked only foreign ships of war, he felt no guilt from that quarter.

After waiting in the hall to let Ivy get ready, he decided when he returned that she looked more skittish now about sharing a bed than she had their first night together.

Sighing at the sight, he climbed into the large bed and held up the covers so she could join him.

Ivy remained where she was.

"Staying away from this bed will gain you nothing but a cold, uncomfortable night," Drake told her. "There won't be any more passion between us, so come and sleep." Turning down the wick to place the room into darkness, he moved to the far side of the bed, facing in the opposite direction. "Last night caught me off my guard, but it won't happen again."

Ivy knew she and Drake had different motives for not wanting passion to flame between them again, but she also knew they agreed that it shouldn't happen. Still, she was reluctant to join him, considering his nature.

"You'll reach for me in your sleep," she reminded him.

"This is a big mattress, and we're both determined to stay apart," he answered her. "So come to bed."

His words were firm, reminding Ivy that Drake was still her captor and that she didn't have a choice when it came to sleeping arrangements.

Reluctantly, she got into the bed, keeping herself carefully on her side of it. Sleep, however, did not come easily as the memories of the night before spun again and again through her guilt-laden mind.

"Time to wake up, you two. The boarded-up windows make it seem like night, but the sun is up and I'm anxious to get to Georgetown."

Cauldron's words, accompanied by a rap on the door, jarred Ivy awake. It took her groggy mind a moment to ralize that it was Drake's arms, wrapped around her, that made her feel warm and secure.

The deep, yearning sensation that immediately followed told Ivy this was the last place she should be. Quickly, she pulled away.

Just as quickly, Drake released her, feeling too much yearning of his own. "I guess I must have reached for you during the night," he apologized.

"I guess you did." Inwardly Ivy was chastising herself as much as Drake. Obviously, she had accepted his embrace, letting him pull her to him.

When Drake left the bed, lighting the brass lamp so he could see to gather his things in the boarded-up room, the sight of that barely clad body no longer held any embarrassment or fear for Ivy. But in many ways, the unwanted yearnings that were replacing those emotions were just as alarming. She could only hope that when she was reunited with Allen, those foolish feelings would fade.

That afternoon, they were finally across the river from Georgetown. After they had brought their horses onto a local ferry to carry them across, Ivy watched the bustling activity of the tobacco port as they approached. Barges and small sloops, heavily laden with goods, filled the water, and people, hordes of them, filled the wharves.

Allen was so near now, and yet still so far, she thought with a bit of despair, knowing she couldn't see her betrothed until Cauldron finished the quest that overshadowed his interest in her.

Cauldron motioned to his group to gather close as the ferry neared the wharf. "I want you to find out who distributes this kind of tobacco," he told his men, holding up the tin, "and get lists of the shops they deal with. We'll meet at sunset at that tavern there"—he jabbed his thumb in the direction of a small, weather-beaten structure situated at the end of the line of piers— "to turn in what everyone got."

When the ferry docked, they split up into small groups to cover the area faster. Ivy was glad when Cauldron joined Drake and herself, for it kept her from being alone with the one while allowing her to become acquainted with the other. As they went from one distributor to another, showing the tin and getting the names and addresses of the shops that would carry such an item, she found herself liking more and more the pirate father she had once so despised.

By the time the sun was dipping below the horizon and they were heading toward the tavern to meet with the others, they had a sizable number of tobacco shops on their list.

They ate a quick meal while Cauldron collected the lists his other men had gathered. To cover the Georgetown, Washington, and Alexandria areas, he knew it would be a lengthy search, even with his men helping.

"The shops will be closed now," he told his men, "so we'll have to wait until tomorrow to pay them a visit. Until then, I want everyone, except for Tinny and

Drager, to go from tavern to tavern looking for one-eared men."

As Ivy watched Cauldron walk with his crew to the door, giving them more detailed instructions, she had a feeling she, too, would visit many rough taverns before the night was over. Though she was certainly growing used to such places, it still wasn't an appealing thought.

"How many taverns will we be going to this evening?" she asked when Cauldron came back to the table where she and Drake were sitting.

"None." Cauldron reached down, cupping his hand around Ivy's elbow to bring her to her feet. "We're going to Trinity Church to see those baptism records of yours."

The unexpected news made Ivy's heart start to hammer.

Chapter 16

With Ivy securely positioned between them, Drake and Cauldron entered the cool, shadowed vestibule of the church. When they saw no one was about, Drake quietly pushed open the massive oak door leading to the main chapel. Inside, candles lit up the area, illuminating the beautiful stained glass windows that graced each side. It was empty save for one person.

Ivy's heart leaped at the sight of Allen standing at the pulpit, practicing the sermon he would give at the next Sunday's service. His face, attractive and refined, was raised in the air, his pale hair making him stand out against the muted shadows. His deep voice, melodious and stirring, rang through the air.

The words came to a startled halt when Allen noticed the three people who had entered the chapel.

"Ivy!" he cried, dropping his notes. Rushing down from the pulpit, he met her in the aisle and excitedly threw his arms around her.

"You're free!" he exclaimed, pulling her close. "God has answered my prayers that you would somehow escape from those pirates!" His voice rose emotionally on the last word.

As Ivy sank against Allen's comforting solidness, she realized from his words that he assumed the men at her side were her saviors, not her captors. When she started to explain, Allen stopped her words by discreetly pulling her apart from the others.

"Are you . . . are you all right, Ivy?" he asked in a worried whisper, his concern apparent as he phrased the delicate question.

Many things—her night of passion with Drake among them—made answering that question difficult. She knew this was not the time or place to recount her transgressions. At least she still had her innocence, and she knew that was at the heart of Allen's concern.

"I'm unhurt," she finally murmured, striving for an answer that she could honestly say.

"Thank God!" Allen closed his eyes as he silently said a quick prayer of thanks. Then he turned to Drake and Cauldron, his eyes shining with happiness.

"I don't know how you gentlemen did it, but I can't thank you enough for rescuing Ivy!"

Drake and Cauldron exchanged a quick glance at the words, and then Drake said, "You might not be thanking us, Reverend, when you know who we are and why we're here."

"I'm afraid I don't understand," Allen said in confusion.

"I'm Keils Cauldron," Cauldron informed him.

Allen stiffened at the announcement. "Keils Cauldron?" he repeated warily, comparing the man's bearded appearance to the clean-shaven arrest posters he had seen of the notorious pirate. "But your ship has been spotted off the coast."

"Sometimes," Drake told him dryly, "things aren't what they seem."

At the words, Allen turned his attention to Drake. His face tightened as he realized the description he had heard of the pirate who had approached Ivy on the *Wild Swan* matched the man in front of him.

"What do you men want?" he demanded, his voice sharp.

"We're not here to hurt anyone," Drake assured him. "We just want some information."

"What kind of information?"

Cauldron spoke up. "We want to look at an old church register to see what date Ivy was baptized."

Allen gazed at him blankly, not expecting such an odd request. "Why would you want to see something like that?"

"To find out if Ivy is my daughter."

"Your daughter?" Allen echoed in surprise. "Why on earth would you think such a thing?"

Cauldron glanced in Ivy's direction. "Because that's what *she's* claiming."

Allen discounted the absurd idea. "It was probably just the first thing that came into her mind to stop *him*"—he frowned at Drake—"from touching her."

"That could be," Cauldron agreed, "but considering I was with her mother nine months before Ivy was born, there's a chance the claim is true."

The news took Allen by surprise. He had heard none of this from Ivy herself. And the only information about Ivy's capture had been that a pirate from the *Black Cauldron* had approached Ivy and that she had demanded to speak to the notorious Captain Cauldron. Beyond that,

213

no one had known anything ...cause once she had been granted an audience with the pirate captain, she had been out of the other captives' hearing. His eyes, full of questions, went to Ivy.

"Is there any truth to all this?" he asked.

Ivy met his eyes in a gaze that pleaded with him to understand. "I meant to tell you about it before we were married."

Allen took a long breath as he came to terms with the revelation. The woman he loved and wanted to marry was sired by one of the most infamous pirates to ever originate from the American shores. A man whose morals were beyond contempt.

Ivy could sense his troubled feelings. "If you can't accept my heritage, Allen, I understand. I really do."

As she started to turn away, Allen grasped her shoulders, making her face him. "It's difficult news to bear," he confessed, his voice soft, "but the fault of your parentage isn't yours. You're an innocent pawn, Ivy, and my love for you hasn't changed."

There was no doubt about it, Drake had to admit, the man was likable. And handsome, too, with a tall frame that had more strength to it than he had pictured. As he watched the tender way Allen reacted to Ivy, he knew the clergyman would make a caring, hard-working husband who would cherish Ivy and give her the kind of stable home and gentle marriage very much like the one her mother and father had shared. It would be a life Ivy had been raised to have.

Suited though Allen was for Ivy, as Drake watched him hug her again, Drake also had to admit he didn't like seeing Ivy in another man's arms. He had started to think of her as his, and he wasn't a man to share a woman.

"The register book," he prodded Allen, interrupting the embrace.

Allen dropped his arms from around Ivy. "If you'll step this way," he said stiffly.

Leading them from the chapel, he brought them to his office. As he opened the door, two cats, one black and one a tabby, which had been sleeping in the flickering glow of a painted porcelain lamp, jumped up to greet him. Winding around his legs for attention, they meowed softly.

Ignoring them, Allen went to the floor-to-ceiling bookshelves that lined one wall and ran his fingers over the leather bindings to look for the register he wanted. When he found it, he placed it on his desk and flipped through the pages.

While he waited for Allen to find the entry, Drake noticed a miniature on the corner of the desk. It was a portrait of Ivy, obviously done by the same man who had created the three miniatures she carried. The likeness captured all her beauty and, surprisingly, her personality too. Though the pose was demure, there was a hint of sensuality about it, a sensuality that the right man would one day unleash. Now that he had met Allen, Drake had to wonder which one of them it would be.

He picked up the black cat, stroking its silky fur. "This must be one of the strays Allen collected," he murmured to Ivy. "Her coat is as black as your hair."

Ivy didn't miss the insinuation. "I'm *not* a stray," she murmured back, moving to stand by Allen's side.

"Here's the entry," Allen said, pointing to several lines scrawled on the yellowed page. "It was written by Ian Woodruff himself," he said, indicating the initials following the words.

Cauldron read the neatly penned entry. The date, as

Ivy had told him, was a couple of weeks after the date she claimed to have been born since her mother's health had delayed the baptism. He had hoped the entry might contain some reference to her being a slightly older infant, but there was nothing.

"This doesn't really prove anything," he said after a moment.

"Then just let her go," Allen pleaded.

In response, Cauldron shook his head. "We still need to talk to someone who was at her baptism."

"Who?" Allen asked.

Drake tapped the miniature of Ivy. "The man who painted this."

"Jonathan Moore?" Allen glanced out the window to a cottage that bordered the church grounds. Though the darkness put the structure in shadows, the soft light of candles from within showed the church warden was at home. Hoping that cooperating with the pirates would help ensure Ivy's safety, he nodded in the cottage's direction. "He lives right there."

A few minutes later, they were knocking at the door. It swung open, revealing a wiry, older man with gray generously sprinkled throughout his brown hair.

The greeting Jonathan Moore was about to give Allen died on his lips as he saw Ivy.

"Ivy!" he exclaimed in delight. "You're free from Keils Cauldron!"

Cauldron moved from the shadows where he had been standing. "She's not exactly free," he corrected Jonathan, "since I'm Keils Cauldron."

Confronted by a notoriously dangerous pirate, Jonathan reacted without thought, lunging for a sharp letter opener on a small shelf just inside the door. Even as his

216

fingers wrapped around its handle, Drake was beside him, capturing his wrist in a crushing grip.

"If you want to live," Drake warned him, "you'll drop that. We're not here to hurt anyone. We just want some information about Ivy."

"Information about Ivy?" Jonathan gasped in confusion. When Drake nodded, he slowly loosened his grip on the letter opener, allowing it to drop to the floor.

"We just want to hear a little about Ivy's christening," Cauldron clarified.

"Her christening? Why—"

"Let's sit down somewhere so we can talk about it," Cauldron said, cutting him off. When they reached the tiny parlor, he motioned to Jonathan to sit in a high-backed chair.

As the others settled themselves on the couch opposite the church warden, Drake, going to a nearby desk, picked up a miniature that was lying on it to make room for himself to sit. Though the tiny piece was only partially completed, Drake could tell the finished art would be as beautifully created as the others he had seen. A portrait of Jesus wearing a crown of thorns, it was almost a silhouette, with only the barest touches of light across the cheek, ear, and eye giving soft definition to the face.

Aware that Jonathan was eying him worriedly, probably afraid that a pirate would destroy the delicate art just for the pleasure of wreaking havoc on a thing of beauty, he set the piece safely on the desk beside him.

"Your miniatures are well crafted," he told Jonathan, partly to give praise where praise was due and partly to relax the man so he would readily give them the answers they needed. "I particularly like the one of Ivy at the

217

church. It captured her beautifully."

To Ivy, the words sounded almost like a caress, and she could only hope it didn't sound the same to Allen. When he placed his hand on her arm, giving a reassuring squeeze, she knew he had heard the admiration in Drake's voice but was confident enough of the commitment they shared not to be concerned about it. That small gesture, showing his trust and his own deep caring, reminded Ivy of why she had become betrothed to him in the first place—and why she shouldn't do anything more to forsake it. She gave Allen a tremulous smile in return.

As Drake watched the interaction, it was obvious Ivy and Allen had a close relationship that was forged by the common values they shared. He found he didn't like it. Not one bit.

"About that baptism," he prompted Jonathan.

Jonathan didn't want to anger the pirates by being uncooperative. "What do you want to know?"

Cauldron fixed the church warden with an intense gaze. "Whatever you remember about that day."

Jonathan tried to think back. "It was a long time ago," he said. He paused, trying to recreate the events in his mind. "Ivy was wearing a satin christening gown that had been passed down in her father's family."

Would a man give a child that wasn't his own an heirloom christening gown? Cauldron wondered. He didn't think he would.

"She was a tiny thing, almost lost in that fancy gown she was wearing," Jonathan continued.

She should have been a big baby, not tiny, if her baptism had been delayed, Cauldron mused. Unless—and the thought had serious ramifications—Ivy had been tiny because she had been Woodruff's baby, not his.

218

"How small was she?" he demanded.

Jonathan looked nonplussed at the question. "All newly born babies are tiny," he said. "Especially little girls."

"Newly born?" Cauldron muttered the word under his breath, the term not agreeing with the slightly older child Ivy had said she had been at her baptism.

As he cast a quick glance at her, Ivy knew he was wondering if she had been lying about the date of her birth. His next question confirmed that.

"What day was Ivy born?" Cauldron demanded, suddenly addressing the question to Allen.

"April 16, 1792."

As Jonathan also nodded his agreement, Cauldron was mollified—at least until he saw the family Bible to see the date entered there. Willing to concede that Jonathan might feel a baby that was a couple weeks old was still a newborn, he then asked, "How old was Ivy when she was christened?"

Ivy found herself holding her breath as Jonathan hesitated over the question that would help verify her claim.

"I imagine the baptism occurred just after she was born," Jonathan hedged, trying to remember the specifics of that day so long ago. "That's when most babies are baptized."

It was obvious the man didn't remember. "We're not asking about most babies," Cauldron reminded him. "I'm only interested in Ivy. Was she a few days old? A week old? Several weeks old?"

Jonathan held up his hands in a gesture of defeat. "I just don't remember," he had to admit. "It's been too long and I've been at so many christenings."

Cauldron turned his gaze to Ivy, his eyes brooding.

"So far, there hasn't been any evidence to show I'm your father."

"You thought you might be her *father?*" Jonathan blurted the words in surprise.

"You'll have time enough to hear all about it," Cauldron said as he rose from his seat, "because you and the reverend are staying with me until I'm done in this city."

One impatient gesture of his hand stopped the protests he could see forming on the church warden's lips. Reaching toward a neatly stacked pile of parchment on the desk, he picked up a sheet along with the quill that lay beside it. Dipping the point into an inkwell, he handed both items to Allen.

"Write that you and Jonathan have rushed to the bedside of an ill parishioner and will return as soon as you can," he instructed. "I don't want anyone raising a hue and cry over the two of you." He expected the clergyman to balk at the command, but instead Allen began to quickly pen the words.

"I'll be glad to stay by Ivy's side," he murmured, his voice filled with caring.

After a quick glance to ensure it contained only what he had requested, Cauldron motioned everyone toward the door.

While they dropped the note off at the church and then made their way to the narrow alley where Tinny and Drager were waiting with the horses, Drake kept Ivy by his side. Though he murmured to her that it was to keep her from saying anything she shouldn't about their plans, he knew his action was based just as much on the fact that he didn't like seeing her with Allen.

"You two men can double up on Ivy's horse," he said,

indicating the black gelding. "She'll be riding with me." Even in the darkness, he could see the look Allen gave him was disapproving. Ignoring it, he swung into his saddle and held out his hand to Ivy.

Ivy had no choice but to place her fingers in his. As Drake pulled her in front of him, placing her sideways in the saddle so that she leaned against his chest, she knew the position had to look as intimate and possessive as it felt. Aware that Allen's eyes were upon them, she hoped he would stay forgiving when she confessed the full details of her relationship with Drake.

Cauldron brought his stallion alongside Drake's. "Let's go."

"To Havenrest?" Drake asked, speculation in his voice.

"Havenrest," Cauldron affirmed. "I want to see that Bible."

Located on the outskirts of the city, the stately red-brick Georgian mansion with its long, private drive and extensive grounds was beautiful. And it would also be a perfect place to keep the new captives, Drake reflected as he looked over the place. Not only was it isolated, but its locked, solid shutters, meant to keep the place safe while the owners were away, made it a perfect jail.

Using the house keys Ivy had given him, he unlocked the front door. Inside, Tinny and Drager groped in the dark for candelabra, lighting them when they found them.

As the darkness lifted, Cauldron shed his coat, throwing it carelessly over the banister leading upstairs.

"Find a room somewhere to put these two," he ordered

his men, gesturing toward the captives. As Drake tossed Tinny one of the skeleton keys from the ring of keys he had, Cauldron returned his attention to Ivy.

"Now," he said with anticipation, "where is that Bible of yours?"

"Upstairs . . . in my bedroom." The way she had trouble getting the words out showed Ivy just how important the moment had become to her.

Cauldron picked up one of the candelabra. "Drake, Ivy," he said to them. "Let's go take a look."

Ivy's room, situated on the third floor, was much as Drake would have pictured it. While feminine, it had no extra frills to brighten its whitewashed interior, just a prim, narrow bed covered with a russet quilt, a straight-backed rocking chair, and a smattering of other necessary bedroom furniture. It was probably not much different than the bedroom she had had while living with her parents and probably similar to what she would have in the future if she married Allen.

Drake knew Ivy well enough to know she could be happy with such an unfrivolous room, but it was not the kind of setting he would pick for her. As with the pretty dresses she had never owned, he pictured her surrounded with beautiful things.

Cauldron used a candle from the candelabrum to light a small table lamp. As the room brightened enough for the important task at hand, he said quietly, "Show me the Bible."

Ivy went to the bureau, opening its top drawer. Trying to ignore the sudden trembling of her hands, she pulled out the family Bible. On the inside cover was a list of births, deaths, and marriages that recorded her ancestors' lives. She pointed to the entry Cauldron wanted to see: the date she was born.

Cauldron took the Bible from her, holding it close to the lamp as he read the words. As Ivy had told him, the date was April 16, 1792, which was nine months from the time he had taken her mother's virginity. It was written in the same neat handwriting as the church entry, showing Ian Woodruff had entered it. It helped verify that this was the original family Bible and not some newly created copy, meant to deceive.

Looking higher on the list, he looked for another important date: Sunny's wedding to Woodruff. It was almost immediately following the short stay Sunny had had with him. Given the normal leeway of a baby's time in the womb, he knew Ivy could easily be the clergyman's. That thought was supported by the fact that Ivy was so tiny at her baptism.

"Nothing proves you're mine," he told her, feeling letdown.

Though Ivy had half-expected Cauldron to say as much, given the inconclusive evidence, it hurt her to hear the doubt in his voice. It was an emotion she had never thought to feel when she had first met him.

"Maybe the Bible and baptism don't prove anything," Drake pointed out, seeing Ivy's expression fall, "but they don't disprove anything either."

Cauldron shook his head. "That's not enough. Not for me."

As he closed the Bible, his eyes settled on a painting hanging on the wall opposite him. It appeared to be a family portrait, for in it was a young, coltish Ivy—about ten he guessed—along with her mother and clergyman father. What really caught his attention was the older woman posing with them, her hand looped lovingly around Woodruff's arm. Though there were streaks of silver in her hair, the strands that were untouched by time were jet black, making her light-colored eyes stand out.

Laying the Bible on the bureau, he picked up the lamp and took several long strides to reach the picture.

"Who," he asked, jabbing his finger at the raven-haired lady, "is *that?*"

The accusation in Cauldron's voice turned Ivy's dejection into sudden uneasiness. If he thought she had purposely set out to deceive him, she knew that despite the tenuous bond that had been forming between them, she would feel his wrath.

"She's my grandmother," she admitted.

Cauldron gave her a sharp glance. "*Woodruff's* mother?"

Ivy felt increasing concern. "Yes."

More and more it seemed doubtful to Cauldron that Ivy was his—not with Woodruff's mother having a mane of black hair. And as for the woman's eyes . . .

He held the lamp closer to the picture. "What color are her eyes?" he demanded. "I can see they're light, but I can't tell their shade from this small portrait."

This, at least, Ivy was able to answer without putting knots in her stomach. "Blue," she said, the word emphatic. "Definitely blue."

Providing Ivy's answer was true, blue still covered a range of shades, Cauldron mused, from those that held touches of green to those that held touches of violet.

"Is she alive so I can see those eyes for myself?" he demanded.

"No."

With the grandmother in the grave, he would never

224

see the exact color of her eyes. Cauldron was getting the grim feeling that if he had, they would have been tinged with violet.

The picture was highly damaging to Ivy's claim. So damaging, Cauldron couldn't imagine a scheming woman not getting rid of it. There was always the possibility Ivy had never expected to be taken off the *Wild Swan* and had thought she would be able to hide the picture before he sought her out to see the family Bible. It was a possibility he didn't want to acknowledge, but he also couldn't ignore it, for Ivy hadn't been the one to point out the portrait, he had.

As he looked at her with brooding eyes, Ivy shifted uneasily. "There's still the woman who helped me take care of my mother," she reminded him.

"Mabel Starn." Cauldron's muttered response showed he wasn't putting much faith in the woman knowing about Ivy's parentage or that he would even be able to believe her if she did. "Let's go downstairs," he said abruptly to Drake. "We have some serious thinking to do."

It sounded ominous to Ivy. Very ominous. She hoped they meant to discuss the search for Geoff's killer, but deep down she had a grim feeling it was going to be her future that would be decided—a very bleak future if Keils Cauldron decided she tried to deceive him to become his heir.

"May I see Allen?" she asked, feeling a need to talk to her betrothed on both a spiritual, comforting level as well as a very personal one.

Cauldron stopped at the door, looking back over his shoulder. "Not tonight. I'll let you speak with him tomorrow."

Seeing Allen tomorrow wouldn't provide any comfort for the worries she had tonight, Ivy thought somberly as the door snapped shut.

The rest of the evening passed slowly for her. Tinny, at Drake's request, brought up a metal tub and two large buckets of hot water so she could bathe. As he put them into a corner of the room, Ivy tried to find out how Allen and Jonathan fared, but other than telling her where the captives were housed, the tight-lipped pirate had nothing to say before he left.

Discouraged, Ivy turned to the water, hoping its warmth would soothe her. Instead, the feel of the heated liquid on her body made her think of Drake and the forbidden pleasure he had given her.

She should be thinking only of Allen, she chided herself, hurrying to finish. He was, after all, right in this house. But as she sat in the rocking chair, toweling her hair dry as she planned how to explain her brush with intimacy to Allen, it was Drake's face that kept intruding into her thoughts.

With all that was on her mind, Ivy wasn't surprised that sleep eluded her when she finally got to bed. As she lay there, restlessly tossing, she had to acknowledge that some of her sleeplessness was because she had grown used to sharing a bed with Drake. She was used to the warmth of his body, used to the strength of his arms as he held her, and used to the steadying beat of his heart as her cheek rested upon the broad expanse of his chest.

It was a very unwise thing to have grown used to, she reminded herself. As she continued to toss and turn, she found herself wondering how much longer it would be before Drake came to bed. That thought, as disturbing as it was, made her toss even more. When sleep finally claimed her, it was a fitful one.

On the floor beneath her, Ivy's restlessness was apparent, for the ceiling had first conveyed the sounds of her unceasing motion in the rocking chair and then the creak of the bed as she continually stirred.

"She has a lot on her mind," Drake commented.

"I'm sure she does," Cauldron answered, "but I think it's not having you with her that's making her so restless. She is used to having you at her side."

"Does that bother you?" Drake asked frankly.

"If it were anyone but you, yes." Cauldron paused and then added, "You like her, don't you?"

"Yes."

The brief word said it all. As the ceiling again creaked, protesting Ivy's restive movements, Cauldron waved his hand toward the door.

"We've pretty much settled everything, so you might as well join her." As Drake rose from the leather chair he had been sitting on, Cauldron added meaningfully, "After tomorrow, Drake, we'll know what Ivy's fate will be."

Drake quietly entered Ivy's room. In the darkness, he could hear the covers rustle as she stirred yet again. It took him only a moment to undress and then get into the narrow bed.

227

In her sleep, Ivy turned toward him. His prim little miss might want to deny it, he mused, but she wanted their closeness as much as he did. As she settled into his arms, he felt her fitful body relax, curving against him as she finally drifted into a deeper sleep. Within moments, he joined her.

Chapter 17

"Ivy," Allen called, opening her door even as he knocked, "Keils Cauldron told me I could speak to you this morning." He stepped into the room, holding aloft the lamp he needed to light his way in the darkly shuttered house.

He came to a sudden shocked halt as the lamplight penetrated the darkness, bathing the small bed and its two sleeping occupants in its soft glow. The covers, tangled around Ivy's and Drake's waists, revealed the swell of Ivy's breasts beneath her nightdress and all of Drake's naked, muscular torso. There was no doubt in Allen's mind that the rest of the pirate would be equally bare. All color washed from his face as the startled couple struggled to a sitting position.

"Allen," Ivy gasped in shocked dismay, "What . . . what are you doing in here?"

They were hardly the words Allen expected. On seeing Ivy and Drake together, his immediate reaction had been that the pirate had forced himself on her. But if that had been the case, Ivy would have greeted him tearfully, asking for his help, not why he had entered her room.

With stiff control, he said, "Ivy, I think the question should be: What is *he* doing in here?"

As Drake sat in the bed beside her, his hair tousled and his muscular, golden-furred torso bare, Ivy knew how incriminating the situaton looked. Panicked, she tried to remember how she had planned to explain the situation to her betrothed. Never in her imagined confession had she pictured being caught in bed with Drake as she explained.

"You led me to believe nothing like this was going on," Allen continued in an emotional gush, his voice suddenly anguished. "And I believed you."

"This isn't what it looks like, Allen!" Ivy cried, finally finding her tongue.

Allen set the lamp down on the bureau as his eyes traveled over Drake's imposing, naked chest. "No?"

"No! Drake and I just share a bed!"

The covers, still tangled around her waist, did nothing to conceal the agitated heaving of her chest, emphasizing the fullness of her breasts.

Drake reached over and placed the blankets in Ivy's agitated hands. As she flushed and then belatedly clutched at the material to cover herself decently, he was well aware how possessive his gesture must look, indicating that only he had the right to see Ivy in such a state. But that was the way Drake felt and Allen might as well realize it.

Spots of bright color began to form on Allen's pale cheeks. "I can see you share a bed, Ivy."

Ivy desperately tried to gather her thoughts into a more coherent pattern. "That's not what I meant! When I was taken aboard Cauldron's ship, he asked Drake to stay with me to keep me from escaping and to keep the other men away. That's the only reason he's with me now!"

She might want to deny it, Drake mused, but there was much more to their relationship than that. And though Allen was obviously shocked to find them together like this, Drake wasn't sorry it had happened. Once the clergyman bowed out of his betrothal with Ivy, it would be easier for Drake to win her. And bow out, Allen certainly would, because no man—clergyman or not—was going to be understanding about finding his betrothed in this particular situation.

"But we haven't . . . we haven't . . ." Ivy stumbled to a halt, unable to say that nothing had occurred when so much had.

As Ivy floundered, Drake provided the answer for her.

"What Ivy is trying to say, Reverend"—he leaned back against the bed's simple headboard, his hands behind his head as he spoke—"is that her virtue is intact."

To Allen, the statement was at odds with Drake's casual stance, which was that of a man at ease with all the intimacies of sharing a bed with Ivy. Combined with Ivy's stammered, unconvincing attempt at denial, he found he couldn't believe either of them.

"I accepted that Keils Cauldron was your father, Ivy," he said between jerky, labored breaths, "but this . . . this is just too much!" Taking another anguished breath, he fled through the door.

As his footsteps faded, Ivy put her face in her hands. "That couldn't have gone worse," she groaned.

"I don't think he understood about us quite as well as you hoped," Drake agreed.

It was such an understatement that Ivy raised her face from her hands, temporarily distracted from her dismay.

"I would say our betrothal is off."

Drake thought so too but gave a noncommittal shrug. At the sound of footsteps, he looked toward the door, expecting another bout with Allen now that the clergyman had had a few moments to compose himself. Instead, Jonathan Moore came through the door.

"Allen just came running—" His words stopped at the sight of Ivy and Drake in bed together. "I see now why he was so upset," he added stiffly, his eyes suddenly disapproving. "How could you betray Allen's love like this, Ivy? And with a *pirate?*"

"I . . . I—"

Jonathan cut her off. "Fornication is a sin, Ivy, and *this* is the worst possible kind. I'm very disappointed in you." Having said his piece, he turned to go.

A knife suddenly buried itself in the door jamb, only inches from his face.

"There's been no sin here," Drake corrected the man. "And the fact you saw Ivy and me in bed together better be a fact that doesn't ever get repeated."

Jonathan, giving one curt, frightened nod, bolted through the door.

"What a self-righteous prig," Drake muttered.

Ivy's eyes were still on the handle of the knife, quivering even now from the force with which it had been thrown. It had missed Jonathan by only the narrowest margin. Though she hadn't liked hearing the church warden's words any more than Drake had, they were near enough to the truth that she couldn't really protest that they had been said.

"Drake," she said weakly, "You almost killed someone

232

who's a friend of my family."

"If he had been anyone else, I would have added that I'd cut out his tongue if he talked." As Ivy groaned at that admission, Drake added, "I'm sure Allen will never say anything to anyone about this, but Jonathan doesn't have the same reasons to stay quiet. I didn't want him to set tongues wagging once he's free."

"Jonathan might be self-righteous," Ivy protested, "but he would never bandy my name about."

"Let's just say I wanted to be sure of that," Drake said, leaving the bed. "You have much more faith in your fellow man than I do."

With the downstairs lit by numerous candelabra, Ivy thought it had the look of a festive occasion as she and Drake came down the steps. That feeling was emphasized by the many men milling about, an indication that, sometime during the night, Cauldron's entire entourage had come to the mansion to reconvene.

The sight of Cauldron standing guard over Allen and Jonathan at the entrance to the dining room was a harsh reminder that this gathering was hardly a party.

As she faced Allen again, Ivy didn't know what to say.

Allen finally broke the silence that stretched awkwardly between them. "May I speak privately to Ivy for a moment?" His words to Cauldron, though polite, were strained.

"You can talk to her," Cauldron conceded, "but Drake will have to stay with you." He waved the others into the dining room, where Tinny had managed to create a breakfast from the provisions he had found in the pantry. "But don't be long."

With Drake listening in, it was hardly the circumstances Allen would have chosen to speak to Ivy, but certain things had to be said anyway. He drew her as far away as he could.

"You don't have to tell me the betrothal is off, Allen. I . . . I gathered as much before," Ivy said.

Allen caught at her hands. "That's not what I want to say, Ivy." He looked intently into her eyes. "Seeing you and Drake together this morning tore me apart," he confessed. "But once I calmed down and had a chance to clearly think about it, I believe you about Drake and that nothing happened between you."

It was the last thing Ivy had expected to hear. "You do?"

"You don't lie, Ivy. You never have. If you say you and Drake aren't lovers, then no matter what other circumstances exist, I believe you." His hands tightened around hers. "You've been placed into a very difficult situation. Now that I understand just how difficult it's been, I can understand the kind of relationship you've been forced into with Drake—and forgive it."

There was tenderness in the gentle smile he gave her. "I don't want to break off our betrothal because of what you've had to endure at the hands of the pirates. I care too much for you."

Ivy was overwhelmed by Allen's decision. "You're such a good person, Allen," she murmured, "to be so understanding."

It was certainly not the conversation Drake had expected to hear. He had thought Allen would bow out of his betrothal, not strengthen it by being so understanding. As the clergyman raised Ivy's hands, giving them a loving kiss, he knew the man was a formidable rival. His

234

steady love, similar background, and respectable profession were a strong lure to Ivy.

"What's this, Ivy?" Allen suddenly asked, staring at the diamond and amethyst ring she was wearing.

Drake hoped the man would show a side that wasn't quite so forgiving when Ivy, in her usual honest way, felt compelled to admit, "It's a wedding ring."

"*You're married to Drake?*" Allen's voice was as shocked as his face.

"No, no, Allen, I'm not," Ivy quickly tried to assure him. "I asked Drake to buy it because I wanted people to think we were married. I was embarrassed to have—"

Allen put his fingers to her lips, stopping her words. "I understand," he murmured. "Oh, Ivy, you've gone through so much."

There was no doubt about it, Drake decided. Allen—so forgiving, so stable, so kind—was going to be a very hard man to beat. To win Ivy's love, he would have to forge a bond with her that was so strong it would make her forget the ties linking her so closely with her betrothed. And the only kind of bond that could do that was the kind best forged in bed. Right now, he couldn't do that, but once things were settled. . . .

It was a thought he found often running through his mind during the simple breakfast Tinny had provided. Though Ivy was at his side and Allen was at the other end of the table, separated by several men, he was aware of the many caring glances the clergyman turned her way and the glances Ivy returned. It made him more and more certain of what he needed to do.

"Tinny and Drager," Cauldron said, pushing aside his empty plate, "the two of you will stay here with the preacher and his friend, so take them back to their rooms.

The rest of us have some things to discuss."

As Allen was escorted past Ivy, he held out his hand for a quick clasp with hers. "God be with you, Ivy," he breathed, barely getting out the words as Drager pulled him away.

"And you too, Allen," Ivy called softly.

Drake was glad to see the brief, put poignant, good-bye end. As Cauldron walked around the table handing each man a list of the tobacco shops to visit, he absently took his group of addresses, his thoughts as much on Ivy as on the quest.

"You all know what questions to ask," Cauldron told everyone, keeping one list for himself. "We'll meet tonight at Drake's *Sea Maid*, which is moored at the Tobacco Wharf. For the next few days, it'll be a more central place for us to work from than here. Be thorough," he added, "because I want some leads about Geoff's killer by tonight. Are there any questions? No? Then get started."

As his crew headed for the door, he placed a hand on Ivy's arm to detain her. "Before Drake and I part ways today," he told her, "we're going to pay a visit to Mabel Starn."

Ivy knew it was her last chance to prove her heritage and that it would be the catalyst—good or bad—that would determine her fate. Her nerves were taut as they made the ride.

When they reached the small white cottage, Cauldron's knock on the door produced no response, though the smoke coming from the chimney showed someone was probably home.

"You'll have to knock louder," Ivy said. "Her hearing—"

"Isn't too good," Cauldron guessed, finishing the sentence for her. "Considering everything else, why doesn't that fact surprise me?" He knocked again, harder.

After a number of seconds, the door slowly opened, revealing a frail, white-haired woman using a cane to help her walk.

"Why, Ivy," Mabel Starn exclaimed, her voice loud in the manner of someone who was hard of hearing. "What a pleasant surprise! You've come to visit and brought some friends, too. How nice! Come in, come in."

It was obvious the woman had heard nothing of Ivy's capture. They followed her inside.

"Do sit down," Mabel urged.

Ivy perched on the edge of a wing chair opposite the one Mabel eased herself into. As the woman gave her a questioning look, obviously waiting for an introduction to the two men who were now sitting on her horsehair couch, Ivy cast a look at Cauldron, uncertain how to proceed.

He gave his head a slight negative shake, indicating he would lead the conversation. "We're not exactly here for a social call," he told Mabel.

Mabel leaned forward, cupping one ear. "Could you repeat that?" she asked. "I didn't quite hear what you said."

"This is *not* a social call," Cauldron repeated, speaking much louder. "I'm Thomas Avery," he lied. "Mr. Jordan and I"—he nodded at Drake—"are solicitors who are supposed to settle a legal matter regarding some property that Miss Woodruff was to inherit after her mother's death."

Mabel looked confused at the request. "How can I help?"

"We just want you to answer a few questions about Miss Woodruff's mother right before she died. I believe you were with her at that time?"

"Yes, yes, I was," Mabel agreed. "Ivy and I took turns in the sickroom."

"I understand she was able to speak right up to the end?"

Mabel nodded. "She seemed restless, agitated. She spoke a lot, poor lamb, in a delirious sort of way."

"You could make it out, though?" Cauldron persisted.

"It was all kind of mumbled," Mabel said with an apology in her voice. "And I don't hear as well as I used to. But every now and then I'd catch a phrase or two."

It didn't sound encouraging, but Cauldron hoped the few phrases she caught were pertinent to his investigation.

"Did she speak about her younger days, before she married Ian Woodruff?"

"I don't recall hearing anything like that."

Cauldron knew he had to be more specific if he was going to uncover the information he needed. "Did you hear anything about Ivy's birth?" he tried. "I want to hear anything you might have heard, even if it's something you think was just gibberish."

Mabel's forehead wrinkled in thought. "Ivy's name was mentioned a great deal, but if there was anything about her birth, I couldn't make it out."

That information pretty much ended the interview in

Cauldron's mind, but wanting to leave no stone unturned, he finally asked, "Did she mention Keils Cauldron, the pirate?"

"Keils Cauldron?" Mabel asked in surprise. "Why would she mention him?"

Ivy knew the words sealed her fate, whatever Cauldron decided that would be. The breath she was trying to take was suddenly difficult, as though someone were squeezing her in a vise.

Cauldron stood up, knowing there was nothing else to ask. "Thank you for your time," he said to Mabel.

Mabel pushed herself up from her chair, surprised the questions were over. "Was I of any help?" she asked uncertainly.

Cauldron glanced over at Ivy, his expression unreadable. "More than you realize."

In some ways, it was for the best, Drake decided as they left the cottage, for if Mabel Starn had confirmed Ivy's claim, Cauldron would have had to then consider the possibility that Ivy had paid the woman to say so. Now at least, any doubts about Ivy being an adventuress could be put to rest.

It was now up to Cauldron to weigh all the evidence about Ivy, meager as it was, and make a decision. Drake could tell from the pirate captain's face it wasn't going to be an easy task. And he could tell from Ivy's face she was worried about the outcome.

Cauldron was also aware of Ivy's worry. As they reached the horses, he said quietly, "There's no proof you're my daughter, Ivy, but there's no proof you intended to play me false either."

The latter was a tremendous relief to Ivy, for she knew Cauldron would have been heartless if he felt she had tried to trick him. The former, however, was still of deep concern for her, for she had come to care for her pirate father.

"There's no definite proof about my heritage," she conceded, "but what do you believe?" Anxiously, she waited for his verdict.

"On that, I have some serious thinking to do." Cauldron swung onto his horse, looking down at her. "By tonight, when we meet at the *Sea Maid*, I'll have an answer for you."

But late that night, Cauldron still hadn't reached a decision. He paced back and forth in the small cabin he was using on the *Sea Maid*, taking a long sip of ale from the flagon resting on the washstand each time he reached it. And he had been reaching it often, he mused, considering the size of the cabin. On this ship, Drake was the captain, and the larger quarters belonged to him. Cauldron didn't mind the small size. It just made his pacing bring him more often to the ale and he had need of its bracing powers.

As he continued to stalk restlessly, he ran all the evidence about Ivy through his mind for the hundredth time. But no matter how he viewed it, it always came down to one fact: There simply wasn't enough to prove she was his.

The most conclusive evidence was the date of her birth in the Bible—nine months from the time he had taken her mother's virginity—but she could easily have been Woodruff's child, simply arriving a bit early. Ivy's small size at the baptism, the use of an heirloom christening gown, and the grandmother's black hair and light eyes helped support that thought. Jonathan Moore's vague memories and Mabel Starn's scanty testimonial had shown nothing.

He took another long sip of ale. Ivy had based her claim on her mother's dying words. He believed she had heard them, for Ivy had shown herself to be an honest, forthright person, but it appeared what she had heard was nothing more than the delirious ramblings of a dying woman.

He paced around again, coming back to take another long swill. With Geoff dead, he had wanted to believe Ivy was his child. It would have filled a void, giving him something to live for. But it appeared his hopes had been nothing more than a grieving father's desperate need to stave off unhappiness by claiming another child. He had wanted Ivy to be his, wanted it badly, but wanting didn't make it true.

Depressed, he paced some more, returning again and again to the ale. Though everything now pointed to the fact that Ivy wasn't his, he had come to care for her. He had begun to think of her as his daughter and even to picture a future together. It was a double loss to see it all crumble.

A knock at his door made him swing around. "Who is it?"

"Drake."

Cauldron quickly gulped the last of the ale, needing its numbing qualities to say what had to be said. Thankfully, his brain was rapidly reaching the state he wanted.

"Come in." Only the smallest slur showed the amount of alcohol he had consumed.

As they entered, Ivy was afraid. All day, her mind had been on nothing but the confrontation to come.

She had accompanied Drake from tobacco shop to tobacco shop almost in a trance. Though she knew they hadn't uncovered anything to help them find Geoff's killer, she couldn't have described where they had gone, what they had eaten, what they had talked about. And when the shops had closed and they had then visited taverns to search for the one-eared man, it had been more of the same. The hours had passed in a blur until, late in the night, Drake had told her it was time to head for his ship.

Even then, she had been only marginally aware of the *Sea Maid*, paying scant heed to the sloop's graceful design, its polished brass fixtures, and the whiteness of its furled sails, pale against the dark sky.

Only the figurehead gracing the prow had managed to penetrate her preoccupied thoughts. As Drake had told her, it was a sea maid—and the resemblance to her had been striking. They both had the same black hair, the same features, the same curves to their bodies. It had been uncanny, a mirror image of herself, but as they had passed the pirate posted at the gangplank and he had called that Cauldron was already on board and was waiting for them, her thoughts had immediately returned to the decision that awaited her.

As they had stopped momentarily at a luxuriously decorated cabin—the captain's quarters—to drop off their belongings, Ivy had given it as little attention as she had given the ship. Moonlight had streamed in through a row of brass-banded windows, softly revealing the polished oak of its furniture and the luxurious patterned rug on the floor. But its beauty had been forgotten when Drake had then guided her to the small cabin down the passageway from his.

As Drake now opened Cauldron's door, letting her precede him, Ivy felt shaky as she stepped inside.

"We didn't uncover any leads today," Drake said, knowing Cauldron would want to know that information before dealing with Ivy. The tired look on his friend's face showed how difficult making a decision had been.

"I didn't either," Cauldron answered. "Maybe one of the other men will bring back something. If not, there's always tomorrow." His voice was weary, affected both by the son he hadn't yet been able to avenge and the daughter he had lost. As he felt the numbing effect of the alcohol continue to claim him, making his world blessedly hazy, he sat down on the edge of his small bunk.

Though Cauldron hadn't yet said anything to her, the bleak look in his face as his eyes met hers told Ivy everything.

"I wanted to believe you, Ivy." A fine mist filled Cauldron's eyes. "But I just can't. It seems your claim was just the ramblings of a dying woman."

Ivy knew the words were coming, but somehow it didn't lessen their impact. The rejection hurt, more than she had thought possible. She found herself blinking back her tears. From behind her, she felt Drake place a comforting hand on her shoulder.

"What . . . what happens now?" The lump in Ivy's throat made the words difficult.

Numbnes continued to wash over Cauldron and he welcomed it against the pain he knew was in both their hearts.

"You'll have to stay with us until we catch Geoff's killer. I can't risk anyone finding out I'm in this city."

Already knowing how important secrecy was to Cauldron, it wasn't what Ivy was asking. "And when that's over?'' she whispered. ''What then?''

''That's up to Drake.'' Cauldron leaned back, letting his head rest wearily against the wall, the ale trying to completely claim him now that he had said what had to be said. ''You're his now,'' he murmured, his eyes closing as he let the alcohol have its way, ''not mine.''

Ivy could stand no more, the rejection crushing her. With tears spilling onto her cheeks, she fled from the cabin, stumbling blindly into Drake's cabin. Throwing herself onto the bed, she buried her head in her arms, letting the tears fall.

Drake entered the cabin, closing the door behind him. Though the cabin was in darkness, the moonlight pouring in through the windows illuminated Ivy as she lay crying on the bed. Sitting down beside her, he rubbed her back in a soothing gesture.

''Don't cry,'' he said softly.

Ivy sat up, turning to face him. ''It hurt,'' she said with a sob.

''I know it hurt. And it hurt Keils, too.''

''Did it?'' Ivy questioned through her tears. ''He turned me away . . . giving me to you.''

Drake reached over, smoothing away the glistening droplets. ''Are you still afraid of me, Ivy?''

His hand felt warm and loving as it touched her cheek, giving Ivy the comfort and security her wounded heart needed.

''No.'' The word came out as the barest breath.

Drake slipped his hand around the back of Ivy's neck to draw her closer. ''Then let me love you,'' he murmured, bringing his lips gently to hers.

Chapter 18

For a moment, Ivy held back a little, her conscience whispering that this shouldn't be. But as the pain of Cauldron's rejection cut into her heart, she gave herself up to Drake's kiss, wanting to forget everything but the feel of his lips and the heat of his touch.

The darkness of the cabin was soothing, making it easy for Ivy to accept her bareness as Drake undressed her. When she was naked, shivering slightly in the coolness of the evening air, he swept aside the covers, laying her onto sheets that were made of the softest lamb's wool. In a moment, he was naked beside her, pulling the covers up around them to form a cocoon that was as warm as it was comforting.

"I've wanted to love you since the moment we met," Drake murmured, brushing the softest of kisses over Ivy's lips.

Spoken with tenderness, they were words that soothed Ivy's hurting emotions.

"Then love me," she whispered. "And make me think of nothing but you."

Drake quickly began to fulfill her wish as his lips moved to the sweet curve of Ivy's ear and his hand moved slowly over the soft, smooth curves of her body. Her nipples responded immediately to his touch, swelling into tight, throbbing crests. As a small moan slipped from Ivy's throat, showing her pleasure, his hand moved lower, sliding between her thighs.

With gentle strokes, he caressed her, preparing her body to receive his own. She quickened beneath his touch, her body swiftly readying itself. As she arched against his fingers, he deepened his caress, taking full possession of her.

Caught up in the heat of desire, Ivy's body reacted one way to that intimate touch while her mind reacted in another. Her hips rolled and pitched, wildly riding the deepness of that caress; her mind flinched at the very personal invasion, making second thoughts begin to form.

"Drake." The groaned name was half euphoria, half protest as Ivy's mind battled with her body, her reason fighting with her desire.

Drake wanted Ivy to only feel euphoria, to have pleasure that was so intense, so fulfilling it would drive all thoughts of ever returning to Allen from her mind. The clergyman was the kind of man she had been raised to cleave to—and his compassionate, forgiving nature was a powerful lure—but Drake was determined to bond her to himself instead.

He moved between her thighs, easing her onto her back as his heavy arousal began pressing into her tender flesh.

Pleasure began to mix with pressure. Even though Ivy

was still caught up in passion, she instinctively pushed against Drake to make that pressure stop.

Just as instinctively, Drake surged harder, consumed with the need to fully make Ivy his own. The delicate membrane that separated her from him suddenly gave way, letting him sheath himself deep within her. The bond he wanted finally forged, he began to move.

With each steady thrust, the aching fullness receded, allowing the tremors that were still coursing through Ivy to intensify. Lifting her hips, she urged him deeper and deeper, seeking to reach that final, glorious release.

Ivy's body showed Drake what pleased her most. Each deep surge of his loins brought a gasp of pleasure; each rise of his hips brought a low moan of protest. Complying with what she wanted, he took her deeply, increasingly aroused by the way she eagerly accepted and then returned each penetrating thrust. As she finally shuddered in his arms, her hips arching to wildly mesh with his own, he surged heavily into her one last time, groaning in satisfaction as his seed exploded deep within her, completing the bond that his loving had begun. He held her close, his last spasms matching the ones that were still coursing through her.

"You belong to me, Ivy," he breathed, his words coming in gasps. "Only me."

Sated to the point of oblivion, the tender words were the last thing Ivy remembered as she drifted into sleep.

The knock at their door the next morning barely roused Ivy, so deeply was she asleep. Even when Drake rolled from the bed, tugging on his breeches so he could step out into the passageway to answer the knock, she didn't open her eyes, her body and mind still feeling lethargic.

"About last night, Drake . . ."

The muted sound of Cauldron's voice coming through the door jerked Ivy painfully awake. She sat up straight in the bed, straining to hear what came next.

"You gave up your claim to Ivy last night, Keils," she heard Drake respond. "It's a claim I've . . . staked for myself."

Drake's meaning was painfully, embarrassingly clear. Her nakedness suddenly shaming her, Ivy clutched at the tangled sheet, bringing it up to cover her. The motion revealed the glaring proof of her lost innocence. As she stared down at that dark, irrevocable stain, so stark against the whiteness of the bedding, she was appalled at what she had allowed in a moment of weakness.

Last night, Drake's lovemaking had seemed a balm to the hurt she felt over Cauldron's rejection. In the harsh reality of morning, giving in to the attraction she felt for Drake had gained her nothing but a fleeting moment of peace—and an everlasting loss of innocence.

She had forgotten the caring man she was betrothed to, betraying him by letting a pirate take her to bed—a union not only unsanctioned by God but also unpardonable for its breach of commitment.

"That's as it should be, Drake," she heard Cauldron finally answer, the long delay showing it had taken him a moment to fully absorb such a bold statement. "But once we're done in Georgetown, that kind of dalliance must end."

"I agree, Keils."

As Cauldron changed the subject, telling Drake the

other men had already left to visit more tobacco shops and that he would be leaving soon himself, Ivy stopped listening, too distraught to care about their quest.

Like her mother, she had given in to a foolish attraction. And like her mother, it was plain from the men's words she was just a passing fancy—a woman to be taken and enjoyed, and then forgotten. It made what she had done even worse.

Ivy knew she couldn't remain with Drake in the days to come, for despite her regret and despite her shame, he still held a strong attraction for her. He would reach for her each night, and knowing the pleasure he could give her, she was afraid she would foolishly forget both her morals and her commitment in the midst of the exquisite passion he would arouse in her. She refused to end up like her mother, loved for few passionate weeks and then released with a baby growing inside her.

She had to get away before that same fate happened to her, but how? The pirate posted at the gangplank made escape from the ship impossible and, on land, Drake always watched her carefully. That had remained true even when they had been at their friendliest, and now that he had taken the innocence he had seemed so determined to claim, she sensed he would guard her even more carefully.

Cauldron was leaving for Georgetown soon, she suddenly mused. Maybe, just maybe, if everything went as she wanted, she could go too. . . .

As Drake came back into the cabin, the sight of Ivy sitting in his bed, looking sweetly flushed and decidedly tousled, made his loins begin to stir. But he knew other commitments had to come first.

"We must get dressed," he said with considerable

regret. "We're supposed to meet Keils later today, and we have a slew of shops to visit before then."

The words didn't match Ivy's plan. To achieve her escape, Drake had to go back to sleep and that meant he had to get back into his bed. Once he was there, considering the little sleep he had gotten the night before, she hoped he would doze long enough for her purpose.

Instead of complying with his request, she said softly, "Can't we sleep just a little longer, Drake?"

"We have a long day ahead of us," Drake reminded her, holding out his hand to her. "So come on out of bed."

The firmness of his tone showed Ivy that Drake wouldn't easily be deterred from his plans. But sleep he must if she was to get away.

Instead of taking his hand, she forced her fingers to relax their grip on the sheet. It dropped to her thighs, allowing Drake to see her bared body. As she saw his eyes move slowly, interestedly over her, she hoped he couldn't tell how hard it had been for her to reveal herself so brazenly in the bright morning light.

Their lovemaking having occurred in darkness, it was the first time Drake had seen Ivy nude. He drank in the beauty of her. Her breasts, full and firm and pale, were accentuated by nipples that were tautly tipped and dusky. Her waist was narrow, emphasizing the womanly flare of the rounded hips below. And at the juncture of her smooth thighs was a small triangle of curls that was as richly raven as the long strands of hair that was now tangled around her shoulders.

It was a sight that stirred him more.

"Must . . . must we leave now?" Ivy asked the question with difficulty, feeling vulnerable as she used her nakedness to lure Drake back to bed.

Drake couldn't resist the temptation. "I guess a few more minutes won't hurt." Eagerly, he stripped off his breeches.

Ivy had never before seen Drake totally bared either. He was golden-haired all over, his burgeoning arousal adding to the picture of strength he exuded.

Her body suddenly yearned to feel him possess her.

The unwanted sensation showed Ivy just how necessary it was to get away before an extended time with Drake put his child inside her. That such a fate might already have happened, she had to put from her mind. Just because her mother had conceived from her initial union with Cauldron didn't mean she would.

As Drake joined her in the bed, his greater weight brought her smaller frame toward him. In the light of day, the meeting of their bodies seemed much more intimate than by night.

"You look just like my sea maid," Drake murmured as they lay side by side. "Same black hair"—he brushed several silky strands behind Ivy's shoulder—"and same beautiful breasts." He cupped the heavy warmth.

Ivy took a sharp intake of air at the sensation. "Your sea maid is clothed," she reminded him, flushing as he stared so closely at what he was now intimately caressing.

"Not in my mind, she's not." Lowering his mouth to one dark crest, he kissed its tip. "But she's just wood, and you're all warmth and softness, meant to be touched." He kissed the other dusky tip and then smiled as the crimson touching Ivy's cheeks traveled all the way down to the swell of her bosom.

"Am I embarrassing you?" he asked.

Ivy looked down to where Drake was nuzzling at her breast and then glanced further, first to the place where the raven and blond of their bodies almost met, and then to the jutting evidence of Drake's desire.

"This *was* a little easier in the dark," she had to admit. And it had also been much easier when she had been mindlessly swept away by passion at the time.

Drake sensed Ivy's hesitation, but attributed it to her basic modesty. "I like looking at you," he told her, raising his face to look into her eyes. "And touching you." Sliding his hands behind her back, he pulled her closer, bringing her prominent, dusky nipples into contact with his small, golden ones.

It was the only way in which she overshadowed him, and Ivy felt her pulse begin to race as the tips lightly touched. Then it raced more as Drake caught her hand, bringing it between their bodies to place it on himself.

"Feel my need for you," he breathed.

Beneath her fingers, Ivy felt his heat, his strength, and his desire. Despite the intimacy they had shared, caressing him so seemed somehow brazen, that feeling intensifying as she felt him tauten still more under her touch.

She pulled her hand away.

Drake gave a soft, throaty chuckle at the modest gesture. "My sweet, sweet Ivy," he murmured. "In the days to come, you'll find there's nothing a man and woman can't share."

If everything went as planned, there would be no days to come, Ivy silently corrected him. But right now, she had a man intent upon passion, a passion he meant to slake with her. She trembled as he cupped his hands around her hips, bringing her tightly against the masculine fullness of his loins.

"It will be better this time," he promised in a husky whisper, "now that we've been together once before."

Last night, there had been only a little talk sprinkled among the passion. The many intimate words Drake was saying to her now made what they were doing seem so much more real to Ivy. Just how real it would soon be became apparent as Drake drew one of her legs over his thigh to open her up to him.

"I'm going to love you now," he breathed, his hand kneading the round, twin curves of her hips as he spoke. For a moment his fingers lingered there and then they crept lower, caressing that most intimate part of her from behind.

Small ripples of wanting began to sweep over Ivy. Perhaps it was better this way, she mused, that he could excite her so. If this was to be so satisfying that Drake would doze afterward, it would be best if her passion were real, not feigned.

She felt his fingers part her, felt him shift his hips to bring that swollen part of him to her.

Ivy felt his gaze on her face. "You're watching me," she protested, the words ending in a gasp as he began to slowly claim her.

"In a moment," Drake promised in a rasp, "you won't care."

By the time he brought himself fully within her, Ivy found she didn't. Her own eyes fluttered shut.

Drake's hips began to move. "I want to give you enough memories to fill the hours until we can be together like this tonight."

It wouldn't be tonight—or ever. Even in the midst of passion Ivy knew that still had to be. But she also knew she might never again feel this kind of ecstasy.

"Give me memories," she urged Drake in a whisper. "Memories to take with me." As he responded, his hips moving in the long, deep strokes he seemed to know excited her most, she received the memories she wanted—the excitement, the passion, the loving, and the sharing. Their bond had been an unwise one, of that she had no doubt, but she would always remember the beautiful pleasure she and Drake had shared.

Freely, she gave herself to him, knowing this would be the last time. And just as freely she felt him respond, loving her with an intensity she knew she would never forget.

"Drake, Drake, *Drake!*" His name upon her mind, it burst repeatedly from her lips without thought. As she held him tight, her body shuddering, she felt his body violently shudder as he found his own pulsing release.

When Drake finally rolled away from her, breathing heavily as he stretched out at her side, Ivy lay very quietly, her eyes shut, tacitly encouraging him to do the same. When his breathing slowly went from ragged gasps to the long, even, breaths of sleep, she knew their vigorous loving and their previous night of passion had taken its toll. Feeling the same sated desire to sleep, she held on to her strong determination to get away to keep from succumbing to the same temptation.

Carefully, she eased herself from the bed, quietly picking up her cotton shift from where Drake had carelessly tossed it the night before. If he woke, she knew he would just think she was getting ready to go into town, but she hoped he would stay asleep long enough for her to leave the ship. Moving toward the door, she listened intently for the sound of Cauldron leaving his cabin but heard nothing.

About to step into her shift, she saw the traces of blood that still stained her thighs. Her heart pounded in slow, painful thuds at the sight of her lost innocence. She went to the washbasin, quietly poured a little water into it, and, with trembling hands, washed away the evidence of the passion she and Drake had shared. When she was done, she blinked back her tears as she again reached for her shift and swiftly put it on.

Don't wake, she prayed as she donned her amethyst dress and then ran her fingers through her passion-tumbled hair. Keeping an ear cocked for Cauldron, she went to the canvas bag that contained her scant belongings.

She couldn't take the bag with her, not without making the pirate standing on guard wonder why she had it, so she rummaged through it to get to the only things that were really important to her—the miniatures.

She picked them up, looking at the tiny pictures. Once again, they hadn't been out, and once again passion had flowered. But this time, nothing had stopped the passion from reaching its natural end.

Her mother had made the same mistake with Cauldron, but she had had Ian Woodruff to turn to once she had come to her senses. And that gentle clergyman had loved her mother enough to forgive the fact that she had lain with another man.

Ivy had no delusions about her own situation to comfort her. Allen loved her, of that she had no doubt. But while he had forgiven her before, she knew that once she told him her relationship with Drake had turned intimate, the betrothal would be over. Allen was a man of strong principles, and he wouldn't forgive her foolishly casting those principles aside.

With no reticule or pockets in which to put the minia-tures, Ivy strung their tiny golden hoops, meant for hanging on a wall, through the narrow, braided cord that fastened the neck of her cloak. Small enough to look like little decorative brooches, she didn't think the pirate on guard would pay them any heed even if he noticed them.

That done, she reached for the keys to Havenrest, lying at the bottom of the bag. She hadn't thought far enough ahead to know where she would go or what she would do, but she knew she couldn't leave Allen and Jonathan in the pirates' hands. Not now. Once the pirates learned of her escape and realized she might betray their presence in the city, they would be furious. Allen and Jonathan would bear the brunt of that anger if they were still held captive—and that she couldn't allow.

Not that she would ever betray the pirates, she acknowledged as she tightly held the keys to keep them from jingling. Geoff had been her half brother and she wanted to see his murderer caught. And Cauldron was her father. Despite his rejection, she wouldn't do any-thing to hurt him. As for Drake . . .

He had been her lover—as unwise as that had been—and she knew she would do nothing to endanger him.

But she couldn't risk Allen's and Jonathan's welfare either. She would try to free them, and if she succeeded, she would convince them to flee with her from the city until Cauldron caught his killers. She was certain Allen and Jonathan would comply, for doing anything else would be suicidal.

Ivy cast a look toward Drake, still sleeping soundly. Providing she could get off this ship, she hoped she would have enough time to free her friends before he woke. And that she would be able to free them, she added worriedly. Though she had the keys and could enter the house through the servants' entrance in the back, much depended on whether the two pirates standing guard would be positioned right outside their prisoners' doors. If they weren't, she thought she had a fair chance to free her friends. If they were . . .

Ivy didn't want to think about what would happen if the pirates on guard caught her—or how Cauldron would punish her for endangering his quest.

Trying to make as little noise as possible, Ivy searched through Drake's carelessly tossed pile of clothes for his pistol. It wasn't there, nor was his knife. As she realized he must have left them with Cauldron, she heard the sound of a door opening and then footsteps going toward the hatchway.

A furtive peek showed her it was Cauldron. Giving him just enough time to ascend the steps, she quietly opened the door. When she slipped out into the passageway, she couldn't help one last look toward the bed.

Lying on his back, one arm back over his head, Drake made a handsome figure, even in sleep. As Ivy thought of the passion they had shared, a swirl of emotions washed over her. Guilt, shame, and regret were at the center, but on the perimeter, there was also desire, even now.

Gazing at Drake and knowing she would never see him again, she acknowledged that a part of her wanted to slip back into that bed to be loved by him again. What a foolish, foolish thought, she chastised herself. With her mother's folly to guide her, she should certainly know better. But as she started to shut the door, she wasn't prepared for the achingly bereft feeling that washed over her.

"Good-bye, Drake," she whispered. "What we did was wrong, but a part of me will never forget you."

Chapter 19

Fighting back her tears, Ivy closed the door quietly behind her and headed toward the steps. At their top, concealed by the hatchway, she composed herself as she peeked to see where Cauldron was. When she saw he was walking toward the gangplank, she waited until he was near it and then stepped boldly into the open, right into the sight of the nearby guard.

Banking that Cauldron hadn't yet told his men that he had denounced her, she pretended to address the words she spoke to someone at the bottom of the steps.

"Cauldron is still here, Drake," she called, knowing the many noises from the nearby wharf would keep Cauldron from hearing the one-sided conversation. "So I'll just join him."

She turned brightly to the guard, mentally preparing to lie without stammering since her escape was too important to be jeopardized by her morals.

"I've changed my mind about going into Georgetown with Captain Cauldron," she said briskly, fastening her cloak around her neck as she did so. "When he asked me to go with him this morning instead of being with Drake, I first said no, but I've decided I should get to know my father better." She hoped the friendlier relationship she had been having with Cauldron would make her words convincing.

"I'll hail him," said the mate.

"Don't bother," Ivy told him, heading toward the pirate captain. "I'll be at his side before he even gets off the gangplank."

The pirate must have agreed with her, for though he followed her to the wooden ramp, he didn't call to his captain. Ivy knew she would indeed be right at Cauldron's heels before he stepped onto the wharf. All she could hope was that the sounds of the bustling wharf and the throbbing (she prayed!) state of Cauldron's hungover head would disguise that fact.

Feeling the guard's eyes on her, she moved quickly but quietly down the gangplank. Luck was with her, for when she reached the bottom and was literally a step behind her father, he hadn't realized she was there. She hoped that from the guard's perspective her close proximity to Cauldron would make it appear she was now safely in his hands. A quick glance back up at the mate showed her that so far he must have been satisfied, for he raised no outcry.

As she kept pace with Cauldron, Ivy positioned herself slightly off to his side to make it look to the guard as if she was walking with his captain, not behind him.

The wharf, teeming with activity and people, continued to mask any sound she made. And Cauldron, apparently deep in his own thoughts, never once looked over his shoulder.

Ivy hoped her luck would hold until she and Cauldron

moved out of sight of the guard. When Cauldron stepped off the wharf, turning onto the crowded street she knew led to the livery stable, she said a quick prayer of thanks at leaving the guard behind. Then she said another on seeing a small alley that gave her a place to conceal herself while Cauldron kept on walking.

Flattening herself against the brick wall at the alley's entrance, she tried to calm the accelerated pounding of her heart. She had made it this far, now she only had to wait for Cauldron to get his stallion and leave before getting her own mount. Since Havenrest was on the outskirts of town, a horse was the only way she could get there before Drake woke and came searching for her. With her friends imprisoned at the mansion, she knew it would be the first place he would look.

Cautiously, she peered around the corner of the alley, catching sight of Cauldron as he turned into the livery. A few minutes later, he emerged on his stallion, riding in the direction opposite her.

As soon as he was out of sight, Ivy hurried toward the stable. After taking a wary look into its interior to make sure no pirates were lingering there, she stepped inside. The same livery boy who had taken her horse from her late last night was busy cleaning a stall.

"That black gelding of yours is all ready to go," he said, looking up from his task. "Mr. Avery said you and your husband would be comin' shortly."

The boy's words made Ivy aware that she still wore the ring Drake had bought her. She should have left it behind, but her thoughts had been so occupied with her escape she had forgotten she wore it.

"My . . . husband"—it was still a thought Ivy faltered over—"has been delayed so I'll be riding by myself." To her relief, the boy simply dropped what he was doing to get her mount.

Moments later, Ivy was on her way to Havenrest, thankful she had learned to ride well enough to go at a full gallop.

When she reached the mansion's long drive, she guided her gelding into a dense patch of evergreens, leaving it there so she could covertly make her way to the back of the house.

Staying as much as she could in the concealment of the many decorative hedges that graced the grounds, she cautiously approached the servants' entrance and unlocked the door. All was quiet within.

She made her way up the narrow servants' staircase. As she peeked into the hallway, illuminated by several wall lamps, there wasn't a guard in sight. Tiptoeing to the room Tinny had told her Allen was in, she used her keys to open the door.

At the sight of her, Allen jumped up from the chair he had been sitting in. "Iv—"

Ivy put her finger to her lips to silence his outburst. "I'm here to free you and Jonathan," she whispered. "Let's go get him."

Instead of complying, Allen caught at Ivy's arm, pulling her inside the room and out of sight of anyone that might happen into the hallway. He shut the door behind her.

"Jonathan's not in his room right now," he told her. "One of the guards took him out to let him stretch his legs, but he should be back in a few minutes."

The news made Ivy look anxiously at the door, expecting it to open. "Are you next?" she asked worriedly.

"They already took me." Allen caught her hand in a caring gesture. "How did you get away?"

The movement made the ring Ivy was wearing press into her skin, reminding her of Drake and what she had done to be free of him.

"I was able to . . . slip away from the ship this morning." She knew the words sounded as awkward as she felt.

"I thought they watched you too closely for that."

"Today was . . . different." Ivy said the words haltingly, knowing the time for confession had come. "Cauldron decided I'm not his daughter because none of the evidence gave enough proof."

"That's good," Allen said, and then seeing Ivy's expression sadden, added, "Isn't it?"

"He's the only family I have," Ivy said, biting down on her lip, "and I had come to care for him."

That one sentence revealed a wealth of emotion. Sensing the sorrow and rejection she was feeling, Allen said softly, "Ivy, I'm sorry you were hurt. But the man *is* a pirate," he reminded her. "After we're married, you'll have me as your family."

Ivy's emotions, already low, plummeted lower. "That can't be now, Allen," she said with an ache in her heart. "When Cauldron renounced me, everything changed." Seeing the question in his eyes, she added in a shamed whisper, "Drake and I . . . we became . . . lovers."

Allen flinched at the words, closing his eyes for a minute as he absorbed the blow. But as he thought about Ivy's emotions, undoubtedly shattered over this latest development, he knew he had to put aside his own feelings to give her the comfort she needed. When he opened his eyes, they were filled with the compassion he felt. He brought her hand to his cheek.

"Once Cauldron disowned you, there was nothing to keep Drake away from you," he reminded her gently, only the tremor in his voice showing his own shattered feelings. "But that shame is his, not yours, for forcing you to be with him."

Allen's certainty that she had been a helpless pawn made Ivy's shame even worse. "There was no force," she confessed unhappily. "I was hurting and Drake was there, free from any commitment to Cauldron. It . . . brought us together. I shouldn't have let it happen, but I . . . I did. I know now it was a mistake, but that doesn't change that we were together."

Again Allen closed his eyes, struggling to accept the news that, in his heart, he had feared might happen if Ivy remained in the handsome pirate's care.

As Ivy saw the pain her confession had given him, she started to pull her fingers away from his grasp.

"I know things can never be the same between us now, Allen," she said softly, a sorrowful acceptance in her voice. To her surprise, Allen tightened his hand, preventing her from pulling away. His eyes, when he opened them, were filled with an understanding and forgiveness she hadn't expected.

"Ivy, what you've been through has been enough to make anyone stray from the path God intended," Allen murmured. "I won't deny I wish nothing had happened between you and Drake, but I care for you too much to lose you over circumstances beyond your control. The way the two of you were thrown together, I doubt either one of you could have prevented it. We'll put it behind us," he added firmly, "and start afresh."

Unknown to Ivy and Allen, Drake was right outside the door, listening to the whole conversation and not liking what he was hearing. Back at the cabin, he had stirred at the sound of Ivy closing the door and had immediately guessed that shame was making her run away. As he dressed to go after her, he had known he should have suspected something because the bold way she had lured him back to bed hadn't conformed to her modest nature.

If she was running away, he knew it would be to Allen, for as with her mother before her, such a caring man would be hard to resist. A quick check of the canvas bag for the keys to Havenrest had shown they were missing and had confirmed his guess. He had reached the gunwale just as Ivy had disappeared in the direction of the livery stable.

On the verge of stopping Ivy, he had suddenly decided to let her flee to Allen. After she had confessed her sin—and Drake knew she would feel compelled to do just that—surely the clergyman would break the betrothal. Even for someone as understanding as Allen, there had to be limits. And once that bond was broken, he would woo Ivy back to himself.

So he had let her get her gelding and, after giving her a moment's start, had carefully trailed her on his own steed, making sure she didn't see him.

But the conversation he had hoped to hear between Ivy and her betrothed hadn't occurred. Not only had the clergyman once again shown himself to be compassionate and understanding, he had even found it in his heart to be as forgiving of Ivy's lover as he had been of her.

There was no doubt about it, Allen was a forgiving man. Too forgiving, Drake added to himself as he heard

Allen continue to murmur compassionately to Ivy. He himself would have wanted to kill the man who had deliberately bedded his woman rather than to empathize with the circumstances that had made it happen. In many ways, Allen's love seemed too yielding, too passive, hardly the kind of fiery passion Ivy had shown she needed.

Regardless, the clergyman would tempt Ivy to put aside what had happened so he could make her his bride. But that mustn't be. She was his now, and Drake didn't intend to let her go.

With that, he opened the door.

At the sight of Drake standing there, Ivy's heart began to pound with hard, tense thuds. Then it pounded even harder as he held out his hand.

"Let me have the keys, Ivy," Drake said with soft emphasis. "And then you're coming with me."

"Let her be," Allen pleaded. "If there's a conscience within you, don't keep her with you."

"Believe me, Reverend, I have no choice." And it wasn't just the thought of Geoff that made Drake say the words. "The keys," he repeated to Ivy.

Ivy placed them in his hand and then quivered as he closed his fingers around hers, trapping her hand. With no choice but to comply, she followed him from the room. Instead of turning toward the servants' stairway to leave, he led her toward the main stairwell.

As Drake started climbing the steps, Ivy asked uneasily, "Why are we going up here?"

"We're going to your room."

"Why?"

"To talk."

"About what?"

"Us." Drake said nothing more until they were in Ivy's small room, a lamp lit against the shuttered darkness and the door closed to ensure the privacy of their conversation.

"Do you really feel that what happened between us was a mistake?" he demanded, shrugging out of his heavy greatcoat as he asked the question.

Ivy found she couldn't face him. Turning toward the wall, she stared instead at her family portrait. "What we did was unsanctioned, both by God and by society," she said unhappily. "And all the while, I was betrothed to another man, a wonderful, caring man. I . . . I acted just like my mother," she ended in despair, "forgetting my vows because I found myself attracted to a pirate. It was wrong!"

They were all the reasons Drake had imagined. He came up behind Ivy, standing close.

"It doesn't have to be unsanctioned," he said, his voice suddenly soft. "I could make that wedding ring you're wearing real."

At the words, Ivy stiffened in disbelief. "This morning, I heard you agree with Cauldron that our 'dalliance' would end as soon as you finished up in Georgetown. You meant to use me, then let me go!"

"I meant I would *marry* you."

Ivy swung around in surprise. She had never imagined Drake wanting to marry, not a man used to an untethered life at sea. As she realized Drake had never intended to abandon her, some of her shame faded. Not that there wasn't plenty left, she added despairingly. She had committed more than one sin when she had lain with Drake.

Her emotional side couldn't help but respond by picturing the two of them sharing a life together. But as soon as she ran those images through her mind, her sensible side rejected the notion when she considered Drake's livelihood.

"But you're a pirate!" she blurted before thinking how tactless the words were.

It wasn't the answer Drake wanted to hear, but it wasn't unexpected either in light of Ivy's upbringing.

"If Keils gets a pardon," he told her quietly, "so do I."

"Do you?"

"We're both involved in ending that spy ring." Drake paused meaningfully. "So my pirating days will soon be at an end."

At that, Ivy's rational feelings once again clamped down on her emotions. "They may not be"—she felt compelled to say—"considering how few clues you and Cauldron have to catch those spies."

"If there's one thing I can promise you, it's that we'll catch Geoff's killer."

"Even if you *do* get that pardon," she conceded, "it wouldn't change what you've been."

"No, it wouldn't. But *I* could change, Ivy. I could open my plantation, make a life for the two of us."

Although Ivy found his words tempting, she thought of the very different worlds she and Drake lived in. It would be difficult to make such a marriage succeed. She had come from a strict, proper upbringing. He had come from a notorious, wild life at sea. The union of a clergyman's daughter and a pirate was too much at odds.

"We're very different, Drake," she pointed out.

"That will be half the fun," he replied, lightly touching her cheek, "overcoming our differences."

The words made sensuous images begin to spin through

Ivy's mind, but images weren't reality, she reminded herself. The very pleasurable passion she and Drake had shared was luring her to consider his proposal, but there were other things that needed serious thought. Abruptly her mind went back to Allen.

"You forget I'm already betrothed," she said, her fingers coming up to the miniatures, dangling on the cord that fastened her cloak. She lightly touched the one containing Allen's likeness.

"A betrothal can be broken."

Ivy gazed down at the tiny portrait. "Not when it's to a man I care for, a man whose life is so suited to mine. And despite what I've done, Allen still cares for me."

"You come from similar backgrounds," Drake conceded, "and I grant you care for each other, but that's all it is, caring. There's not enough emotion between you to make it anything else. The two of you seem more like a brother and sister than mates."

Capturing her hand, he pulled it away from the miniature and brought it to his heart so she could feel its pulsing beat. She started slightly, her eyes showing her own heart had involuntarily answered with a matching rhythm, though she pretended otherwise.

"With us, it's different," he said.

"With us, it's passion," Ivy corrected him, quickly drawing her hand away. She placed it on her stomach. "I just pray there won't be a child as a result."

"I would welcome siring a child with you."

It gave Ivy a funny feeling deep inside to hear such words. "I've followed enough in my mother's footsteps without adding *that*," she said firmly, pushing aside the unwanted feelings he was arousing in her. "That's one of the reasons why I ran away this morning, so such a thing wouldn't happen. But there is one way I *do* intend to follow in my mother's footsteps."

This time, her fingers went to the miniature of her beautiful mother. "She realized the passion she shared was a mistake—and so do I."

Drake didn't want anyone else to influence Ivy. Pulling the cloak from her shoulders, he forced her to release the tiny pictures as he tossed the garment over the nearby rocking chair.

"Only *you* can decide your fate." He caught her shoulders. "Not Allen, and not your mother! Don't let what happened with her sway you now."

But Ivy couldn't discount that past. In the beginning, her mother must have felt her relationship with Cauldron was right or she wouldn't have been lured into the affair. It had to have been later that she realized she still loved her betrothed and that a permanent union with a pirate just couldn't be.

Both she and her mother had been tempted—and succumbed—to a pirate's passion, despite the fact they were already betrothed. But it was gentle, forgiving men like Ian Woodruff and Allen Badgley who made lifetime mates, not notorious men like Keils Cauldron and Drake Jordan.

The fact that she still desired Drake's touch was only to be expected, she decided, aware of the feelings stirring within her just from the feel of his hands on her shoulders. Temptation, even when it was unwise, was not easily dismissed or ignored.

But it was Allen—steady, caring Allen who still loved her even though she had strayed—with whom she should plan a future, not Drake. That the transition back to reality was difficult and filled with mixed emotions was the price she had to pay for her transgressions.

Ivy's eyes were solemn as she regarded Drake. "The miniatures make me remember things that are easy to forget when I'm with you. But I *am* making my own decision. And my mind tells me you and I can't be."

"What does your heart say?"

Ivy hesitated and then said with honesty, "My heart tells me I'm attracted to you. I guess I have been from the start. But I think it would be as unwise for me to make a life with you as it would have been for my mother to make a life with Cauldron."

"You're not your mother," Drake said with soft intensity. "And I'm not Keils. What might not have been right for them, is right for us. What we feel isn't just an attraction. It's more. Much more." He raised her chin, looking intently into her eyes.

"Marry me, Ivy. Let me show you how good it could be."

Bending his head, he let his lips lightly touch hers. He could sense both her attraction and her resistance. As she started to pull away, her resistance obviously taking precedence, he knew he had to bond her to him while she was still in his control, or else she would cleave to Allen as soon as she was free.

Drake refused to let Ivy slip out of his life, not when he had one bond that, by her own admission, drew her to him. Passion would be his web, and he would use it unmercifully to bind her to him until he could change her mind.

Chapter 20

Lacing his fingers through Ivy's hair to keep her from ending the kiss, Drake subtly deepened it, pressing his thigh with gentle intimacy between hers as he did so.

That part of Ivy that had been so newly initiated into the pleasures of love responded immediately to the touch. As she remembered the ecstasy they had so recently shared, desire once again began spreading through her veins.

It was a pleasure she wanted, even as she tried to disavow it.

"Drake." The word, gasped softly against his lips, was a breathless blur of the pleasure she felt and the resistance she clung to.

"I mean to make you my bride, Ivy," Drake murmured, recapturing her lips in a caress that was as insistent as it was gentle.

Drake's bride. The thought continued to be strangely appealing. As Drake kissed her, sweetly bending her will, her reasons for objecting to such a union didn't seem quite so clear.

Feeling Ivy's body grow softly yielding in his arms and not wanting her to have time to mull over the barriers between them, Drake pressed his advantage. His fingers moved to her breast, lightly touching its fullness through the fine cashmere of her dress. The nipple he found was taut, showing Ivy's blood was already beginning to surge heatedly through her body.

He heard Ivy's small moan of pleasure as he touched her so, and determined to see the obstacles between them crumble still more, he began unfastening her bodice, pulling aside the wool and then the cotton to find the soft fullness within. He cupped the warm flesh, his fingers stroking over the bared peaks as he set out to arouse her.

The coolness of the air on her naked breasts was a sharp contrast to the heat Ivy felt growing within her. Even as Drake touched her more intimately, flaming her senses so that her objections slipped further into the recesses of her mind, she was aware he was easing her toward the bed.

If he got her there, pressing her down with the hard length of his body, she knew every protest would be forgotten in the heat of the moment. With the small amount of common sense remaining in her, she pulled away, moving her head from side to side as she backed against the wall. Shakily, she began to draw her bodice together.

"You and I can't be," she reminded him between unsteady gasps for air.

Drake advanced toward her, placing his hands on the wall on either side of her. "We can be, Ivy." He pressed his lips to the hollow of her neck, kissing where her pulse was wildly luffing. "And we will be."

Ivy felt weak all over. Drake was making it very clear

he was determined to make her his bride, and as his lips moved slowly and sensuously over her throat, her reasons for resisting the proposal continued to fade.

As Drake caught her wrists, gently pulling them away from her bodice, Ivy, her objections fragmented by desire, let him. Her breasts, once again bared and now heaving with excitement, thrust boldly toward him.

Her yearning for the feel of his mouth on them shocked her with its force. Pleasure, intense and wonderful, jolted through her as Drake accommodated her, his tongue slowly circling one throbbing crest.

Weakly, Ivy leaned against the wall, her eyes closing as Drake began to suckle. She wasn't aware he had released her hands until she found her fingers stroking through the burnished locks of his hair, tacitly urging him to continue. She felt him ease up her skirt, felt him push down her undergarment—and hungered for the feel of his fingers touching that part of her that was pulsing as wildly as her heart.

The caress came, scaringly potent and achingly wonderful, but Ivy jerked within Drake's embrace as she realized it was his lips, not his fingers, that were claiming her so.

"Drake," she gasped, truly shocked. "That couldn't be proper!"

Drake gave a throaty laugh, not stopping his caress. "Some things, Ivy," he breathed against her, "aren't meant to be proper. They're simply meant to be enjoyed."

Slowly and deliberately he found his mark again, letting Ivy's undergarment slide down to the floor as he gave her pleasure he knew she would be unable to resist.

Ivy quivered at what was happening. It was shocking. It was indecent. It was . . . unbearably exciting. A fragment of her mind tried to conjure Allen's image to test the rightness of the passion that was rapidly leading to its inevitable end. But the only coherent thought that filled her passion-filled mind was that she couldn't picture Allen ever pleasing her so.

Again she found her fingers lacing through Drake's hair, their stroking movement indicating her unspoken compliance.

It was a compliance Drake sensed would end if Ivy had even a moment to clearly remember all her reasons for resisting him. As he felt her passion flower, felt her straining for release, he came to his feet, more than ready to sweep her into bed. He knew the kind of bond he needed to form would only come from the intimate entwining of their two bodies, not from Ivy finding satisfaction at how he was pleasuring her now.

But as he stood beside her, his hands still bunching her dress about her waist as he held her close, he saw from the slight focusing of her eyes that the delay of getting them both undressed and into bed would give her too much time to reconsider. Having brought her this far, he didn't intend to lose the battle now, for he had a feeling Ivy's resistance would quickly strengthen, making a second try much more difficult.

Lifting Ivy in his arms, he let her back rest for a scant moment against the wall as he swiftly unfastened his breeches, freeing flesh that was as unmistakably aroused as hers.

He was ready; she was ready, though he could see from the increased focusing of Ivy's eyes that that would

276

change in a second. Scooping her rounded buttocks into his hands, he brought her legs around him.

"Drake." The word held a hint of Ivy's returning sanity.

"I mean to make you mine, Ivy," Drake breathed, one sure thrust bringing him fully inside her. "Only mine."

The instant glazing of her eyes showed him there would be no more objections. Victory was apparent in his movements as he began to claim her, pinning her against the wall with the deeply arousing strokes she seemed to like so well.

Behind Ivy, the surface was cool and smooth, a sharp contrast to the heat and sensuous friction that Drake's fierce loving was causing. With her arms wrapped around his neck and her legs wrapped around his thighs, she was a ready vessel for his passionate possession.

Their panting breaths and the slight thuds as Drake pressed her again and again to the wall filled the room around them. The sounds heightened Ivy's passion, bringing her to the pinnacle of excitement.

"I won't let you go, Ivy," Drake groaned as he rapidly approached his own shaking pinnacle. "Not ever."

In the aroused state Ivy was in, the words somehow seemed right to her. The pace suddenly quickened, making the sounds of their passion more pronounced, more ragged, and pushed her over the edge. Sobbing out the pleasure she felt, she tightened her legs fiercely around Drake as he began pumping out a release that was undeniably as intense as her own.

When their bodies finally stilled, their ragged breathing sounded loudly in the quiet around them. Her back pressed to the wall, her legs wrapped around Drake's thighs, Ivy became aware they were both still fully clothed, only minor adjustments made to allow for their passionate joining.

She realized she had been taken like a dockside strumpet against the wall: her breasts bared, her skirts hiked up about her waist, and Drake's breeches hastily unfastened.

Though she could hardly deny she had enjoyed it, it still brought home all the differences between her life and Drake's. This was the kind of mating she had seen in the hallway at the Dirk and Dagger. It reminded her that Drake was a pirate, a man who had led both a hedonistic life and a ruthless one. As she thought of the men he had vowed to kill, it also reminded her that despite Drake's proposal, she was still his captive, as were Jonathan and Allen.

Allen. Gentle, caring Allen. Certainly he would never want to kill anyone, hold anyone captive, or ever be so wickedly experienced that he would know a woman could be pleasured so against a wall. He was a clergyman, a man who lived according to principles whereas Drake was a pirate and broke every one of them.

In so many ways, Allen was so right for her, yet she had once again pushed aside his memory as she had gotten caught up in the foolish fancy of imagining a life with Drake.

Drake wasn't right for her, she knew it in her mind if not her heart, and yet here she was again, lying spent in his arms. His unexpected proposal had temporarily clouded her judgment, making her give in to what she now realized had been a very deliberate seduction. It would not happen again.

"Put me down, Drake."

The words, spoken with a distinct chill, made Drake open his eyes. Violet ones, glittering with the emotions Ivy was feeling, met his own. He let her slide to the floor.

"There was nothing wrong with what we did, Ivy," Drake said with conviction as he fastened his breeches.

"There was everything wrong with what we did." As Ivy spoke, she fiercely shook her skirt down over her and then jerked at her bodice to close it. "You took advantage of the way I told you I feel, and what's worse, I let you!" Her resolve strengthened. "My future is with Allen, and I'm not going to let some foolish attraction for a pirate make me stray from that!"

"It is not a 'foolish attraction,'" Drake gritted. "What we feel is much more than that, but you won't give us a chance because you're convinced Allen is better suited to you."

"He *is* better suited to me!"

Since they could dance around this issue all day and still be at an impasse, Drake decided to drop the topic for now and picked up his greatcoat.

"I'll be out in the hall. As soon as you're ready, come out. We still have a number of shops to visit before meeting Keils."

As the door closed after him, Ivy stonily began to straighten her appearance.

Even with the fast pace Drake set, they were late for their rendezvous with Cauldron at the appointed tavern. As they made their way through the throng of people to where the pirate captain was sitting, Ivy felt awkward

279

about facing her father. That he knew things had changed between herself and Drake was evident in his eyes.

"You're late," Cauldron said gruffly. "Everyone else has already come and gone."

He probably thought she and Drake had dallied in bed all morning, Ivy thought in agitation. And they had, though hardly in a loverlike way.

"Ivy ran off." Drake knew Cauldron would hear of it as soon as he returned to the ship. "But she didn't talk to anyone about us," he quickly added as Cauldron's expression sharpened in concern.

"That could have ruined everything."

"It could have," Drake agreed, "but it didn't."

A tavern girl tapped Drake on the shoulder to ask what he wanted to order, and Cauldron turned questioning eyes on Ivy for an explanation.

Ivy was more than ready to give Cauldron an answer.

"I had good reason to run off this morning," she said pointedly. She knew full well Cauldron would know why she had done so, and that his own decision to renounce her had contributed to it. It gave her a small measure of satisfaction that he had the grace to look ill at ease by her reference to the passion she and Drake had shared.

For a moment, Cauldron was silent, and then he said uncomfortably, "I thought the two of you were drawn to each other."

That was undeniably true, but there were other considerations to bear. "You and my mother were drawn to each other," Ivy reminded him, "but sometimes that's not enough."

When Drake rejoined the conversation, Ivy fell silent and remained that way during the simple meal while the two men discussed the leads that several of the crew had turned up.

"I'm surprised no one came up with anything likely about a one-eared man," Cauldron said, "but at least the tobacco shops turned up some names of men who use that expensive tin." As he consolidated the leads, jotting them down in the order he wanted to investigate, he found his eyes straying toward Ivy, looking so solemn and staying so quiet. If only things had turned out differently . . .

Aware that his drifting thoughts had caused him to make a mistake on his list, he forced his thoughts back to the task at hand. When he finished, he pointed to the name at the top.

"We'll try this man first," he told Drake, "and then go through the others."

Five addresses later, the sun was just beginning to go down. Ivy gazed without expectation at the large brick house that was next on the list. So far, none of the men they had visited seemed to be the one they sought and she didn't have any reason to feel this man would be any different.

As Drake dismounted, leading his horse over to the door, she and Cauldron, as they had done each time before, rode their mounts around to the side of the dwelling. Since the killer would surely be familiar with Cauldron's face and might recognize him even with a beard, he didn't want to risk being seen. Only Drake talked to the men on the list, saying things that would trigger a certain response.

Each time she and Cauldron had been alone, there had been an awkwardness between them. Ivy was sure it was caused as much by his disowning her as it was by his knowledge of her resulting passion with Drake.

Now, when they were safely out of sight from the house, Cauldron said with difficulty, "I'm sorry things didn't work out between us, Ivy. I really did want you to be my daughter."

It was the first time he had broached the topic. Ivy felt a tight lump form in her throat. "I'm sorry too, Fa—"

She had never called him anything but Cauldron, but now, for some reason, she had almost called him Father. It was a word she knew no longer had any validity in his eyes. The lump in her throat got bigger and then subsided slightly as a new thought occurred to her.

"Maybe," she said, a bit of hope coming to her voice, "the papers at my father's church would show something about my heritage."

"Haven't you already looked through Ian Woodruff's papers?"

The quiet way Cauldron asked the question showed Ivy he thought she was clutching at straws.

"Not the papers at Trinity Church," she explained. "The papers he might have left behind at his church in England."

Cauldron sighed. "That was over twenty years ago, Ivy."

"I know. But they might be archived somewhere."

"*If* they exist," Cauldron answered. "And that isn't likely since it's not the kind of information a man would carelessly leave behind."

"Still—"

"The next time I'm in England, I'll look."

The words were said kindly, but it was apparent to Ivy that Cauldron was only placating her.

Neither knew what else to say, and the sound of Drake knocking on the front door was a welcome reprieve from a painful subject.

When the door opened, Drake faced a medium-built man with sandy brown hair. Unarmed and almost mousy in appearance, he didn't look the part of a spy.

"Yes?" the man asked politely.

"Are you Samuel Hockett?" Drake asked, not really expecting much result from this man. At the man's nod, he added, "Then I'd like a word with you."

"About what?"

Drake lowered his voice. "Certain information you might be interested in buying." As he spoke, he watched the man's face carefully for any indication the words meant something to him. There was no flicker in the hazel eyes staring at him.

"I'm afraid I don't know what you're talking about," Samuel said, starting to close the door.

Not yet ready to give up, Drake placed his hand against the panel to stop him. "The one-eared man proves that statement is false."

At the words, Samuel's eyes widened slightly. "How do you know about him?" he demanded warily.

Since his statement had finally elicited a response, Drake knew he had the right person, as unlikely as that person seemed.

"We'll discuss that inside," he countered.

After a moment's hesitation, Samuel opened the door wider. "Come in."

The minute the door closed behind them, Drake had his razor-sharp blade at Samuel's neck. "If you want to stay alive," Drake said harshly, clamping his other arm tightly around the man to stop his struggles, "you better answer my questions."

Lines of fear formed in Samuel's face as Drake's blade scored lightly into his flesh, emphasizing the words. A trickle of blood began to flow down his neck, and he stilled.

"What questions?" he gasped.

"I want to know about the plot to kill Keils Cauldron's son." Drake felt Samuel's body jerk in his arms.

"I don't know what you're talking about." The words came out in a gush.

"Don't you?" Drake pressed the blade a little harder to Samuel's throat, causing more blood to flow. "The tin we found by Geoff Cauldron's body says differently."

The feel of his own warm blood running down the hollows of his neck made Samuel panic. "If Cauldron paid you to do this, I'll pay you more," he pleaded. "Much, much more!"

Instead of easing the pressure of the blade, Drake increased it. "No deal," he gritted. "You're going to die for your part in that killing."

Samuel felt the new gush of blood trickling down. "I wasn't the one who killed him!" he babbled with fear, his body shaking violently.

Drake didn't know whether Samuel was telling the truth or just trying to save his own skin, but Drake's first goal was to find out the name of the other spy as well as that of the one-eared man. When he had all three, he would learn who had done the actual killing. All would die, but the murderer's death would be far, far the worst.

"Then who killed him?" The softness of Drake's question didn't disguise its intensity.

Samuel swayed dizzily as the blood continued to flow down his neck. He took a ragged breath. "It's . . . it's—" He slumped in Drake's tight grip, his eyes fluttering upward in a near faint.

Drake swore at the delay. "Don't pass out!" he ordered, lessening the pressure of the blade. No sooner had he done so than Samuel jerked strongly in his arms, ripping away from the deadly hold.

Drake smiled as Samuel backed away, but it was a deadly smile. "I thought you might be pretending," he said, brandishing his blade. "Let's see what happens *this* time when I cut you."

As Samuel took in Drake's height and weight and the dangerous glitter in his eyes, he knew he could never defeat the man, not unarmed. In a desperate bid for freedom, he suddenly launched himself at the nearby window, throwing his arms over his face for protection while he crashed through the panes.

At the sound of glass splintering and the sight of a man's body tumbling onto the ground not ten feet from where Ivy was waiting, she cried out in shock.

Cauldron, quickly grasping the situation, dismounted in a leap and ran toward Samuel to capture him before he could get to his feet and escape.

Cauldron's steps slowed when Samuel lay still, face down, blood profusely flowing from beneath him. While Drake climbed through the broken window to join him,

Cauldron knelt down and turned the man over. A large shard of glass was embedded deeply into Samuel's chest. Though he was breathing, it was apparent he would soon be dead.

"Oh, my God!" Ivy cried, rushing over to kneel beside the bloody body. "We have to get him to a doctor!" Even as she said the words, she realized with growing horror that the man would never live that long.

Drake knelt down also, grasping Samuel by the lapels of his frock coat. "The names," he ordered, giving the man a hard shake to revive him. "We want the names of the other spies."

"He's dying, Drake!" Ivy protested in horror, reaching over to touch Samuel's white cheek with shaking fingers. "Surely—"

Drake shook Samuel again. "I need answers, Ivy."

Samuel's eyes slowly fluttered open. Unfocused with approaching death, they sharpened slightly as he gazed at the three people hovering around him. His hand reached out in a jerky movement to touch one of the miniatures attached to the cord on Ivy's cloak.

It was the one of Moses that he grasped, and Ivy was glad the miniature's religious scene might provide the man with a final bit of peace.

Drake was more interested in answers than in the man's religious comfort. "The names," he grated. "We want the names."

Samuel's mouth worked to produce a word, but all that came out was a gurgle. Despite the fact that he was one of the men the pirates had sought, Ivy's heart went out for his suffering.

"God is with you," she tried to soothe him as Samuel

continued to try to speak.

"*You*," he finally croaked, his glazed eyes holding Ivy's. "Thought . . . one-eared man . . . safe with you." As he spoke, his eyes turned glassy with death. His hand, still grasping the miniature, fell toward the ground, ripping the tiny portrait away from the cord.

Chapter 21

Ivy stared at the dead man in horror, appalled by the implications of his final words. As both Drake and Cauldron turned to face her, their eyes suddenly full of suspicion, she stammered, "I don't know this man. I swear to God I don't!"

Without speaking, Cauldron reached over to pry the miniature from the dead man's hand. The portrait of Moses, done in profile, had only one ear showing.

"*This* is the one-eared man we've been seeking?" His words were laced with the pain of betrayal. "The miniature *you* carried?"

"I don't know anything about it!" Ivy cried out in alarm. "I really don't!"

Cauldron shot a quelling glance in her direction as he began to pry the back off the tiny picture. "No wonder there were no leads about a one-eared man," he said darkly as he found a carefully folded piece of paper inside. "He didn't exist except for here."

He scanned the sheet. "It's military secrets," he added grimly, handing it to Drake to read. "And *you*"—this he said harshly to Ivy—"were part of it!"

"No, I wasn't," Ivy beseeched him. "I was just supposed to deliver the miniature for Jonathan—" She broke off as she realized the terrible ramifications of the statement.

"For your friend Jonathan Moore," Drake finished for her, his voice as grim as Cauldron's. "To be delivered to a man in Norfolk." He paused as he thought back to what she had told him. "A Simon Whittaker," he added as the memories came back to him, "at Christ Church."

The pain and suspicion in his eyes rivaled Cauldron's, filling Ivy with anguish at the accusation even as it filled her with fear.

"I can't believe Jonathan would have anything to do with this, but even if he did, *I* didn't know anything about it! As God is my witness, please believe me!"

"I'm not so sure anymore," Cauldron said in a cold, assessing tone, "if God is a good witness for you."

Ivy turned in desperation to Drake. "Drake," she pleaded, placing her hand on his arm. "*You* must believe me!"

"I want to believe you're as honest as I always thought you were," Drake said with tight control. "But right now, Ivy"—he pulled his arm away from her as he stood—"I don't know what to think."

"I'm afraid I do," Cauldron said grimly as he rose to his feet, bringing Ivy with him. "It looks like you were in this with Jonathan Moore and his friend." He nudged Samuel's dead body with his toe. "Because according to Geoff's last words, the stolen information was to be sent with someone the spies trusted. That was *you*."

"I didn't know I carried it!"

"I was suspicious about you when we first met," Cauldron continued, "when I thought you had schemed to meet me to get an inheritance. Now I see I wasn't suspicious enough! Was it your idea to set that trap for me, the one that ended up killing my son? That would pay me back for capturing your mother, wouldn't it? As well as stop my attacks on British ships."

Ivy was shaking her head in a wordless denial, but he ignored it.

"And when that plan failed," he persisted with vehemence, "did you then think of an even better scheme? To claim you were my daughter? You probably thought that once I was childless, I'd leap at the chance to call you my own!"

He gave a bitter laugh. "And once you were my heir, how long would it have been before the authorities would have just 'happened' to find out where I was? You would have seen me arrested and then hanged—and ended up a very wealthy young woman!"

The barrage of accusations was so intense, Ivy hardly knew where to begin denying them. "I never plotted against you!" she tried, her desperation apparent.

"When we met, you made it *very* clear how you felt about me," Cauldron refuted her.

"I didn't like you then," Ivy had to admit. "I don't deny that, but I wouldn't have done anything to hurt you! And I would never have betrayed my country."

"Both your father and mother were English," Cauldron reminded her harshly, stabbing a finger at the miniature of her parents that was still dangling on her cloak. "And the only reason they came to America was because of *me!*"

Ivy tried to fight her spiraling fear so she could think straight. She pointed to the miniature Cauldron still held, the one containing the one-eared man.

"If I had been part of the spy ring, I would have wanted

that picture to reach its destination, not end up with you!"

"You probably just didn't think I would take you off the *Wild Swan*." Cauldron's eyes suddenly narrowed. "All this explains why you ran off right after hearing I wouldn't accept you as my daughter. And ran off with this miniature, too!"

"It's not true!" Again Ivy turned to Drake, her eyes pleading with him to believe her. "I swear it's not true!"

Drake tried to put his feelings for Ivy from his mind so he could objectively weigh the situation. Considering how he felt about her, it was a difficult task.

"She *could* be an innocent pawn in all this, Keils," he said after a moment. "Maybe only Jonathan Moore was involved."

"Maybe Jonathan Moore is the innocent pawn," Cauldron countered, "and Ivy was the one involved. But it looks to me as if they're *both* involved."

Drake looked into Ivy's eyes, so distraught in her pale face. "I hope that's not true," he said, his words heavy.

Cauldron knew the difficulty Drake was having because he felt it himself. "I know you've come to care for Ivy. Christ, we've both come to care for her," he admitted, pain coming into his voice, "but we can't let those feelings cloud our judgment."

Drake raked his hand in agitation through his hair. "No," he agreed, pulling his gaze resolutely away from Ivy, "we can't."

"We'll soon find the truth." Cauldron's words were a grim promise. "Because we're going to pay Jonathan Moore a little visit. Right now!"

* * *

"I want to see Jonathan Moore!" Cauldron growled to the pirate on guard when he reached Havenrest.

"He's right in there, Capt'n," Drager answered, pointing in the direction of the front drawing room. "Along with the preacher. Tinny was lettin' them stretch their legs a . . ." His voice faded as Cauldron stalked past him, followed closely by Drake and Ivy. Worried over the grimness of their expressions, he trailed after them as they entered the grandeur of the very formal room.

Allen and Jonathan were sitting on blue velvet chairs in front of a white marble fireplace, with Tinny standing guard over them. All three stiffened in wary readiness as Cauldron and his entourage burst in on them.

"I want to speak to you," Cauldron snapped, coming to a stop in front of Jonathan.

As Jonathan hastily came to his feet, Allen took in Ivy's tense, frightened face. "What's going on?" he questioned, coming to her side. The sharp glance Drake gave him made it clear no questions were to be asked.

Cauldron held the miniature toward Jonathan. "What do you know about this?" he demanded.

Jonathan glanced down at the piece. "It's one of my miniatures."

"Damn right it is," Cauldron gritted. "And hidden in the back of it was an interesting piece of paper."

Jonathan looked at him blankly. "There was?"

The man had only the look of innocence so far, but Drake wanted to see if it was a facade. He stepped closer.

"We just came from a little visit to Samuel Hockett," he informed Jonathan. "Who's now a very dead Samuel Hockett," he amended, watching Jonathan's expression carefully. There wasn't even the tiniest show of emotion. "It probably seemed like a good plan at the time to use the

293

miniature to smuggle secrets from the country, but unfortunately for you, Keils Cauldron's son was killed along the way."

The words got an exclamation of horror from Allen, but Drake silenced him with a gesture, his eyes remaining steadily on Jonathan.

"Tell us about it," he demanded.

Jonathan raised his hands in a gesture of confusion. "I don't know who or what you're talking about. I just make the miniatures. What happens to them after that is out of my control."

"You saying you're innocent?" Drake asked.

"Yes."

Drake drew his wicked-looking blade. "Samuel Hockett denied it too," he said with calm deliberation, "until I used this on him." He touched the razor-sharp tip to Jonathan's neck, making a tiny trickle of blood appear.

As Jonathan grew noticeably pale, he added, "And believe me, what I did to Samuel wasn't pretty." He paused to give his next words emphasis. "But he did talk." And then, because Jonathan would have no way of knowing Samuel had died without naming names, he blatantly lied as he said the next sentence, wanting to see Jonathan's reaction.

"And he named *you*, Jonathan."

Beads of sweat began to form on Jonathan's brow.

"Are you ready to confess now," Drake added, hostility sharpening his voice, "or do I need to show you *exactly* what I did to Samuel before he died?" To help persuade the man, he pressed the blade a little harder against his neck.

Jonathan swallowed with difficulty, a trickle of sweat slipping down the side of his face to join the trickle of blood. He could see from Drake's expression that denial would bring torture, and he knew torture would unveil a confession he didn't want to give.

"The killing was an accident," he blurted instead, hoping to lie his way out of danger. "A terrible, terrible accident! Samuel's pistol went off by mistake!"

Ivy had hoped that Jonathan's sudden nervousness was caused by the blade at his throat. With his words revealing he was indeed part of the plot that had killed Geoff, she felt her body grow cold as she thought of the implications to herself.

Though Drake had an admission of guilt, it didn't give him the answers he wanted. Samuel Hockett had denied being Geoff's killer and now Jonathan was doing the same thing. One of them had killed his friend and he was determined to find out who.

"Samuel's pistol?" he questioned with a deadly threat to his words. "Or yours?" He started to lightly slice the blade over Jonathan's throat, creating a thin, oozing line of blood as the knife moved. He heard Ivy cry out in horror over what he was doing, but he ignored it, adding fiercely to Jonathan, "I guess there's only one way to find out."

Jonathan saw his own terrible torture reflected in Drake's cold eyes and knew he would be forced to confess the deed he had done. Fear made his cunning mind swiftly change to a different tack to try to save himself.

"My pistol," he admitted in a gasp, the knife at his throat making it difficult to speak. "But it *was* an accident. I swear it was. I'll give you gold to help make up for it. A great deal of gold—all I've received!"

At the words, Cauldron pushed aside Drake's blade as he grabbed Jonathan by his shirt. "Gold won't replace my son," he said in a savage hiss. "And if his death was an accident, it was only because you wanted to kill *me!*" Finally having Geoff's killer in his hands, he let his fury burst loose. With all his might, he smashed his fist squarely into Jonathan's face.

As Cauldron's fists kept swinging, turning Jonathan's face bloody, Drake watched with eyes full of revenge, ignoring Ivy's frantic pleas to him to stop the terrible onslaught. It was only when Jonathan started to crumble that he finally stepped in and made Cauldron stop.

"Revenge is sweet, Keils," he admitted, "but we need to get more information from Jonathan before he dies."

Cauldron shook himself from the all-consuming rage that had possessed him. "You're right," he said, using one hand to keep Jonathan from collapsing. "Ivy," he snapped, "come over here."

"You can't believe Ivy had anything to do with all this!" Allen said in alarm, stepping in front of her in an involuntary effort to protect her.

As the pirates' attention was momentarily diverted from him, Jonathan, dazed and hurting though he was, saw his chance to escape. Forcing his battered body to obey his groggy mind, he curled his fingers around the gleaming brass poker beside the fireplace. The next moment, he was swinging it in a vicious, powerful arc right at Cauldron's head.

Catching the movement from the corner of his eye, Drake swiftly tackled Cauldron to the floor out of danger's way. With a loud swoosh, the deadly instrument swept by, barely missing its target.

Jonathan raised the poker to deliver another killing blow. As it began to descend, the loud explosion of a pistol shot rang through the air.

Jonathan, his hands still gripping the deadly poker, was suddenly swaying on his feet, a large red stain rapidly covering his chest. Drager, his smoking pistol in one hand, was now advancing with his stiletto in the other, ready to do whatever was necessary to protect his captain.

But nothing more was needed. With a strangled moan, Jonathan collapsed to the floor, his blood spilling onto the white marble hearth. His eyes, open and staring, showed he was already dead.

Ivy stared down at the body in horror, shocked into silence by the second violent death she had seen within such a short time. And this man, despite whatever he had been involved in, had been a family friend, someone she had known all her life. When Allen knelt down to close Jonathan's eyes and say a prayer, she tried to use the murmured words as a refuge for her own badly shattered emotions. Violent tremors began to rack her body.

"God dammit!" Cauldron swore, glaring at the lifeless body as he and Drake came to their feet. "Now we'll never get information about Ivy from him!"

With Jonathan dead, Ivy knew the truth about her innocence had died with him, making her afraid Cauldron would now think she knowingly was the courier and therefore guilty. And guilt, she knew, meant death, as it had been for both Jonathan and Samuel Hockett. Though they had died from attempting to escape, she knew death would have been their destiny anyway as soon as the pirates had gotten the information they wanted.

"Is it my turn to die now?" she whispered. "Even though I had no part in any of this other than unknowingly carrying the miniature?"

"Jonathan gave *you* the miniature to carry?" Allen's voice showed his dismay. "He involved you like *that?*"

"Stay out of this, Reverend," Cauldron said impatiently. "It doesn't concern you." His face was harsh with suspicion he didn't want to feel as he stared into Ivy's white face.

"As for you," he told her, "I won't make a decision until I talk to the man in Norfolk you were supposed to deliver the miniature to."

"You can't possibly think Ivy was—"

"Tinny!" Cauldron snapped as he cut off Allen's adamant words. "Take the reverend over to the sofa," he ordered, "and then do something with this body."

"But—" Allen's protest was silenced as Tinny forced him in the direction of a couch on the other side of the room.

Drake motioned toward Jonathan's dead body. "Maybe we can still learn something from him, Keils," he said. "When we first paid Jonathan a visit, he was working on a miniature whose portrait only had one ear. He left it on his desk."

"That's right!" Cauldron said eagerly as he waved Drager over. "I have something I want you to get for me," he told the pirate as he walked with him toward the door.

Left alone with Ivy, Drake looked appraisingly at her. She was very pale, her body trembling hard, but he didn't know if it was from fear for herself or from having witnessed two such brutal deaths. She was staring once again at Jonathan's body, her eyes having the glazed look of someone who had endured too much.

The part of him that had come to love her wanted to gather her into his arms, tell her everything would somehow turn out all right. The part of him that had to face her possible guilt warned him to keep his distance because if she was involved, she would have to be punished.

His emotions in conflict, he compromised the best he could by drawing Ivy away from the dead body, bringing her toward the couch so she could sit down and try to compose herself. As she passively accompanied him in a state of shock, he ticked off the evidence against her in his mind.

She had been a courier for the miniature, which had been created by her friend Jonathan. And Jonathan had killed Geoff Cauldron. That in itself was damning, but when he added the fact that Jonathan's real goal had been to kill Keils Cauldron, it became even worse. Because of her mother, Ivy had reason to want to see Cauldron dead. And because of her British parents, who had left their country because of the pirate captain, she had English loyalties that might have tempted her to join a ring of spies to exact her revenge. It all fitted, especially since Samuel Hockett, with his dying breath, had seemed to recognize Ivy as he pulled the miniature from her cloak.

There was so much evidence against her, and so little for her. Jonathan, at least, hadn't incriminated her, but since he had died before telling the whole story, that didn't mean he wouldn't have. Ivy really only had her basic honesty on her side, and even that now had to be suspect.

But she had always seemed so principled, so trustworthy. . . .

At an impasse, as he was sure Cauldron was, he knew he would have to wait until they reached Norfolk and talked to that last spy. Only then could they pass final judgment.

As Ivy sank numbly beside Allen on the sofa, she shuddered as she watched Tinny wipe away the bloody evidence that a man had been killed there. She felt Allen give her shoulder a gentle, reassuring squeeze.

"It will be all right, Ivy," he murmured.

Ivy heard the words as though from a distance. She wished she could believe everything would turn out all right, but she saw Drake give her a long, assessing stare as he pulled up a chair at a nearby secretary, and she was far from sure.

When Drager returned with the new miniature, if it mentioned she had been a courier for the first one, that would be highly damaging. And when they reached Norfolk, what would happen if Simon Whittaker recognized her? Jonathan had always been very meticulous in everything, so it was very likely he had written to Simon, giving her name and perhaps even a description. If Simon greeted her as though he knew her, Ivy didn't want to think about what Cauldron's reaction would be.

Her worried feelings increased when Cauldron, returning from walking Drager to the door, flung himself into a chair opposite her and gave her an intense, questioning stare that equaled Drake's. The tremors already gripping her seemed to intensify, making her feel icy cold all over.

"I can't believe Jonathan killed someone," Allen said in disbelief. "I just can't believe it. And to involve you! I wish I had known. Maybe I could have done something to stop it." He put his hand over Ivy's trembling one. "I'm so sorry it happened, Ivy."

Ivy suddenly felt like crying. "I . . . I am too," she said with a catch in her throat. She was aware that Drake, writing something now at the secretary, had paused to hear her answer. Any desire she might have had to say more faded. When Tinny hoisted Jonathan's body over his shoulder, another shudder racked her as she pictured her own body being disposed of in the same uncaring way.

Drake placed a seal on the paper he had been writing. "Wait, Tinny," he called to the pirate. "I have a note I want you to deliver after you finish with that body." He glanced at Cauldron. "There are people in Washington who will want to know we've dealt with two of the spies and will soon have a third."

"You were working with the government on this?" The words showed Allen's stunned disapproval. "They are willing to involve *pirates?*"

The clergyman was obviously so incensed by the idea that, despite the grimness of the situation, Drake's expression lightened slightly as he imagined the indignant sermon Allen would deliver.

"We'll even get a pardon for it, Reverend." Walking toward Tinny, he handed the pirate the note. "When you're done with the body and this message," he told him, "go to the ship and tell the men to prepare to sail." As Tinny left the room, Drake came over to the sofa, stopping in front of Ivy.

"Let's go to your room," he said quietly. "I have a few questions to ask you in private."

Passively, Ivy came to her feet, her eyes still glazed with shock.

"I'll stay with her," Allen said, starting to rise.

"Only Ivy." Drake's words brooked no discussion on the subject. "Call me when Drager gets back," he said to Cauldron, tossing him the house keys so he could lock up the clergyman. Picking up a candelabrum, he escorted

Ivy to her room.

Once there, he closed the door and set the candelabrum down. Its soft light played over the planes of his face that was taut with the turmoil he felt.

"Talk to me about it, Ivy," he asked her.

Feeling disoriented and shaky, Ivy closed her eyes and rested her face in her cold palms. "I knew nothing."

With all the evidence against her, Drake couldn't accept that simple answer. He raised her chin to make her look into his eyes. Hers, dilated with shock and fear, looked like deep pools of amethyst in the paleness of her face.

"Tell me something I can live with, Ivy. Did you join Jonathan and Samuel because you were so angry at Keils over your mother that you wanted revenge? Was that it?"

Mutely, Ivy shook her head in denial.

"You were hostile toward Keils when we first took you," Drake pursued with quiet determination. "But then you seemed to genuinely come to care for him. Could it be that after you got to know him, you regretted being part of that scheme? If that's so, maybe Keils and I could understand that—maybe even forgive it—if we thought your feelings had changed."

He wanted a confession, a confession that might possibly save her life, but Ivy couldn't admit to something she had no part in.

"I had . . . nothing . . . to do with it," she said with difficulty, the fine control she had been trying to hold over her shattered emotions beginning to crumble. Tears began to spill down over her pale cheeks. "Please believe me, Drake."

There was just too much evidence to the contrary, but

as Ivy stood before him looking so vulnerable and so fragile, Drake found himself pulling her into his arms, holding her close as he gave her the security and comforting he knew she so desperately needed.

For a long time Drake held her so, cradling her head against his chest as she cried. Ivy felt his lips lightly graze her temple in soothing, calming caresses and felt his hands gently massage her back, easing away the tenseness. Lost in the maelstrom of her tears and despair, she wasn't conscious when the caresses turned from ones of comfort to ones of passion or even who had instigated them.

All she knew, as Drake's lips met her own, was that she needed the strength and comfort of his body, needed the oblivion his passion would bring. His lips possessed hers with an urgency that showed he was just as afraid of the future as she was, and she knew he sought the same encompassing void.

It was her only thought as she found herself naked on the bed, Drake's bare body lying on top of hers.

The hands that had somehow never stopped stroking her as the clothes had dropped away were calming yet sensual, making Ivy focus only on the feel of Drake's touch instead of the death and disaster of before. The fearful tremors that had racked her body began to subside, to be replaced by the stirring tremors of desire.

"Think only of me, Ivy, nothing else."

At Drake's whispered words, Ivy felt her nipples harden against his palms and felt her skin, which only moments before had been icy cold, become heatedly warm.

She felt blessedly disconnected from reality, her mind entering a place where pleasure ruled and violence and danger were forgotten. There was only Drake, and the feel of his naked, male flesh now pressing into her.

She urgently received him, wanting to share his strength and glean a part of it for herself. As he came fully within her, the interlocking of their flesh immediately made her feel a little stronger, both in body and soul.

But she needed far, far more to overcome the depth of her despair. Looping her arms around Drake's neck, she lifted her breasts, pressing their swollen tips against his chest in a request she was unable to verbalize. When he responded, his thrusts deep and steady and wonderfully powerful, she welcomed each driving arc, reveling in the vital, life-confirming sensations that surged back and forth between them.

When she lay gasping and straining beneath him, her body rapidly reaching the final oblivion she wanted so badly, Drake's movements suddenly slowed.

Ivy opened her eyes in confusion, not understanding the delay that would prevent them both from reaching the goal they sought.

"I'll understand, Ivy," Drake breathed roughly, his words coming in ragged spurts. "Just tell me the truth."

The searching question, so unexpected and so unwanted in the midst of passion, gave Ivy a flash of anguish even as Drake's now-languid movements made her desire slowly continue to build. Her mind, bombarded by the bewildering swirl of pleasure, torment, and shock, struggled to find an answer.

"I have told you the truth," she finally cried. "I have!"

In answer, Drake's loins began rising and falling in tantalizing movements that would bring Ivy right to the brink of release and yet not quite send her into it.

"All I want, Ivy," he coaxed between labored breaths, "is something I can live with."

The words seemed to come from afar, cajoling and enticing her to spill her deepest thoughts while her mind was distracted by the confusing combination of passion and trauma. Even in the bewildered state she was in, Ivy knew she had nothing to confess.

"I wasn't part of it," she sobbed. The deepness of Drake's penetration brought her back to the quivering verge of release. By the slowness of his movements, she knew he didn't intend her to reach that release, not when he wanted answers.

But when his hips slowly shifted forward once again, claiming her as deeply as a man could claim a woman, Ivy finally reached the state she had so desperately been seeking. Heaving a heartfelt sigh, she embraced the shuddering oblivion, letting her tormented reality disappear into its whirling, mindless void.

With a frustrated oath at Ivy's escape, Drake spent himself within her pulsing body, the need to prolong the passion to wrest an answer from her now gone. Groaning more in defeat than in satisfaction, he collapsed heavily upon her.

As soon as the last tremor subsided, Ivy's mind abruptly returned to the reality from which she had temporarily escaped. She became aware that Drake's body still intimately claimed her as he lay sprawled on top of her.

Their coming together had seemed an urgent, mutual need to escape the grimness of the world around them. But where she had desperately needed comfort and support, Drake had sought something entirely different.

"All you wanted was answers," she choked. "Answers you hoped I would spill while my mind was so distracted. While I . . . I—"

A terrible emptiness swept through her, worse now than before, and Ivy again began to cry.

Drake heard the anguish in her sobs and saw the emptiness reflected in her tear-filled eyes.

He felt just as empty.

He had wanted a confession he could live with but had gotten nothing. And the act of love, which before had been as satisfying to his soul as it had been to his body, had this time only satisfied the most basic of needs. Even in the midst of passion, he had been unable to forget that Ivy might have been part of the plot that had killed his best friend.

The faint sound of approaching footsteps made them both tense, aware that Drager must have returned with the miniature and that Cauldron was coming to get them.

Hoping the new portrait would contain something that proved things one way or the other concerning Ivy, Drake was anxious to see the contents. He hurriedly rolled off her and reached for his breeches, tossing Ivy her cotton shift as he stepped into his pants.

Afraid Cauldron would burst in without knocking, Ivy hastily jerked the shift over her head. No sooner had the material settled around her then the door swung wide open.

"Is Drager back, Keils?" Drake asked, fastening his breeches as he turned toward the hallway. But instead of Cauldron, Allen stood there, the pirate captain's gold-trimmed pistol in his hand cocked and ready to fire.

Chapter 22

Allen took in the scene before him, the passion that had occurred only moments before obvious from the rumpled bed and Ivy's and Drake's state of dishabille. What disturbed him the most was the tears glistening on Ivy's distraught face as she sat in the middle of that passion-tumbled bed.

"Did Drake force you this time, Ivy?" he demanded, his fingers tightening around the trigger of the pistol he kept leveled at the pirate.

Gentle as Allen was, Ivy sensed he would kill Drake if he had taken her against her will. But Drake hadn't. She had been dazed and upset, her emotions taken advantage of, but she certainly hadn't been forced.

Shamed to have her betrothed find her fresh from Drake's embrace and even more shamed to have to admit she had again been willing, she answered in a wavering voice, "No, he didn't."

Allen's eyes flickered momentarily over Ivy's tear-stained face. "Get dressed. I'm getting you out of here." He kept the pistol carefully on Drake while Ivy gathered her clothes and retreated into a shadowed corner to put them on.

"Where's Keils?" Drake demanded.

"Locked in the cellar," Allen answered him, "which is where you're going to be, too." He had originally thought to lock Drake in this room, but the pirate looked brutishly powerful as he stood there clad only in a pair of breeches, and Allen knew it wouldn't be adequate. The man could easily kick down the door.

"If you think I won't shoot you because I'm a clergyman," Allen added with fierce determination, "you'll find you'll be dead wrong! To save Ivy, there's *nothing* I wouldn't do. Particularly when it comes to dealing with *you!*"

The intensity with which Allen spoke convinced Drake. He stayed still, waiting for the clergyman's next move.

"You ready, Ivy?" Allen asked.

"Yes."

"Then let's go." Allen addressed the words to Drake as he stepped to the side to make room for the pirate to precede him.

Drake considered rushing him, but the steady way Allen held the gun on him gave him no opportunity. "How did you manage to lock up Keils?" he asked instead, playing for time as he walked toward the door. He hoped the darkness of the hallway would give him a chance to break away, but the lamps in the corridor were lit, a testimonial to Allen's forethought.

Before answering, Allen motioned to Ivy to follow. Carefully keeping Drake covered, he followed him down the hall.

"He wanted something strong to drink," he explained,

"so he took me with him to the wine cellar, which is kept behind a locked iron lattice." An ironic grimace touched Allen's mouth. "People never seem to think a clergyman is any kind of a threat, and he was no exception. When he took his eyes off me for a moment, I was able to hit him over the head with a bottle and then lock him up."

"Is he all right?" Ivy asked in concern. Despite everything, Cauldron was her father and his welfare was important to her.

"I wouldn't seriously hurt a man you claim is your father, Ivy," Allen chided her gently. "He'll just have a headache, that's all." As he watched Drake look back over his shoulder, obviously weighing his chances to get to the pistol, he snapped, "*You*, I don't feel as charitable toward, so *don't tempt me!*"

Again, there was a sincerity to his words that made Drake believe him. And even if he hadn't, Allen gave him no chance to relieve him of his gun as they made their way down into the wine cellar. The flickering light of a wall sconce showed that Cauldron, locked behind the latticed door, was still unconscious as he lay on the stone floor.

"Are you sure he's not hurt badly?" Ivy asked worriedly.

"I didn't hit him any harder than I had to," Allen reassured her. Unlocking the door, he motioned with the pistol to Drake to step inside. At that moment, Cauldron's groan showed he was beginning to revive.

"He's coming to now, Ivy." Allen snapped the metal door in place, swiftly locking it with one turn of the key. Through the decorative bars, he viewed the two occupants with satisfaction. "These doors were designed to protect a fortune in wine. Though they were meant to

309

keep people out, I'm sure they'll do just as good of a job keeping people in."

As Ivy watched Drake kneel by Cauldron, helping him to a nearby cask so he could sit while his head cleared, the way the pirate captain groggily rubbed at the back of his head concerned her.

"Are you all right?" she asked him.

Cauldron looked up at her, his eyes narrowing, accusing slits. "You might think you're escaping, Ivy," was his answer, "but I'll find you. No matter where you go, where you hide, I'll find you." Then he turned his harsh gaze to Allen. "And you too, Reverend," he promised, "for helping her."

They were frightening words, but at least they showed Ivy that Cauldron had all his faculties. She hadn't thought her escape could brand her as guilty in the pirates' minds, but looking into Drake's eyes and seeing the same accusation, she knew it was true. Their harsh expressions told her that nothing she could say would make them change their opinions about her.

"You should have believed Ivy," Allen reproached the pirates, slipping his arm around her in comfort. "About everything! When she told you she wasn't involved in a spy plot, you should have believed her—no matter how incriminating the evidence—because Ivy *doesn't* lie! And when she claimed you as her father"—this he said to Cauldron, still sitting on the cask—"as much as I don't like the idea, you should have believed that too! But your thirst for revenge made you suspicious, where no suspicion was due."

Having gotten that tirade out of his system, Allen started to turn away and then stopped, facing the pirates again.

"I wish I could give you to the authorities," he said with feeling, "because I hate piracy, but since they've agreed to pardon you, I guess it would be fruitless." He sighed in resignation. "Not that Ivy would let me turn you in anyway," he added, "not when Keils Cauldron is her father."

It was the kind of considerate statement that so characterized Allen, Ivy thought as he glanced down at her with a tender smile. In so many ways, she realized again why he was so right for her.

"We better leave," Allen said, drawing Ivy toward the stairs leading from the cellar. "Drager will be coming back soon. And once these men are free . . ."

As Ivy looked back over her shoulder, she knew the two pirates would forever have a place in her heart— Cauldron as her newfound father and Drake as her ill-fated lover. A deep feeling of loss washed over her at the way everything had turned out.

A few minutes later, she and Allen were galloping down the long drive, heading away from the mansion, she on her black gelding and Allen on Drake's roan stallion. The silvery light of the full moon, low in the sky, lit up their way.

As they rode, Ivy realized she was still wearing the diamond and amethyst band Drake had bought for her. Once again, she should have left the glittering piece of jewelry behind, but as with her escape from the *Sea Maid*, everything had been too rushed to remember such a thing.

The sight of it brought back the memories of the unsanctioned passion she and Drake had shared. He had taught her how to love—and how to regret that she had done so. The affair was over, the emptiness lingering inside her told her that, but so, unfortunately, was any future relationship with her father. Her running away branded her as guilty, a thought that greatly bothered her.

At the entrance to the drive, Allen pulled his mount to a halt, allowing Ivy to come up alongside him. "I have an idea where to go to be safe," he said. "We'll—"

Ivy raised her fingers to his lips to stop his words. "It will be best if I don't know your plans," she said softly, coming to a decision. "I don't want anyone to be able to force me to say where you are."

Allen looked at her in disbelief. "You're not coming with me?"

"If I run away, it will make it look as though I'm guilty."

"If you don't run away, you could die!" Allen's words were an urgent plea. "They're already responsible for two men dying and they think you're part of the same plot!"

"But I'm *not* part of the plot," Ivy reminded him. "By coming back instead of running away, it will help prove my innocence. And even if something inadvertently connects me to that conspiracy, I have to trust that when Cauldron really examines everything, he'll get to the truth."

"Perhaps that could happen," Allen had to admit. "But Cauldron is only part of the problem." He paused and then added meaningfully, "There's also Drake."

Ivy knew the name evoked images for both of them, images neither one wanted. "I was like my mother when it came to him," she said after a moment. "But there's nothing but emptiness between us now. It's over, for both of us."

Allen believed the softly spoken words, but Ivy's decision to stay deeply worried him. "It's too much of a

312

gamble," he insisted. "Please come with me."

Ivy shook her head. "Even if we got away from Cauldron, the government would want me for treason—and you, too, for helping me. I could never live with that." She placed her hand on his, letting it rest there.

"I must stay, Allen. Not only to prove my innocence, but also to prove to Keils Cauldron that he's my father. That's important to me too."

Allen sighed in defeat. "If you're determined to do this," he said in resignation, "then I'll stay too. I'll help you see it through."

"This is something I must face alone." As Ivy saw an objection form on Allen's lips, she added, "And you being there would only make it harder for me. Cauldron would punish you for hitting him and then helping me escape. I don't want to have to watch that."

Allen knew he had lost the battle. "Oh, Ivy," he said unhappily, "I'm going to worry about you."

"In the end, everything will turn out all right," Ivy said with certainty.

"I'll be there for you when it is." It was a promise.

"I know that, too, Allen." Ivy raised her lips for the gentle, caring kiss he placed upon them. "I think when everything is resolved in Norfolk, Cauldron will forget his anger at you. But until then, stay in hiding. I don't want anything to happen to you."

"I'll keep you in my pray—" Allen broke off in alarm as Drager, astride a dark mount, emerged from a grove of pines on the far side of the clearing that separated him from them.

For a moment, all three were shocked into stillness, and then Drager, kicking his horse into a gallop, headed straight toward them.

313

"Go!" Ivy hissed to Allen. "And I'll ride in the opposite direction. He'll chase me, not you, and it won't matter when he catches me since I was going back anyway!"

Seeing Allen's hesitation at leaving her, she brought her hand down hard on the stallion's rump to make the high-strung animal leap forward. As the animal did so, she headed her gelding toward a heavily wooded area, crashing through the branches as she tried to gain as much time for Allen as she could.

From behind her, she could hear Drager, a much better rider, swiftly catching up. She swept between two closely enmeshed pine trees, through a shallow stream of icy water, and then galloped wildly across a meadow filled with matted, brownish grasses. Despite her efforts, from the sounds of the fast-approaching hoofbeats, she knew Drager was almost upon her. Just as she was about to enter another packet of trees, he caught up, roughly grabbing the reins from her hands.

"Where's the Capt'n?" he shouted, bringing her gelding to a sharp halt.

Ivy could tell from the harsh tone that Drager expected the worst. "He's in the wine cellar with Drake," she quickly reassured him.

"Dead?"

"No."

"That better be true."

As Drager hauled her gelding back toward the mansion, Ivy hoped Allen would make it to safety before the sharp-tempered pirate came back out to get him. At the front entrance, the man was none too gentle as he yanked her from the horse and marched her down to the cellar.

At the sound of footsteps, both Drake and Cauldron

rose to their feet, expecting to see Drager, returning with the miniature. The sight of Ivy clasped hard within the man's grasp was a total surprise.

"Open up the lock, Ivy," Cauldron snapped at her.

Ivy flinched as Drager gave her a hard push toward the latticed door. "I can't. Allen has the keys."

"Drager," Cauldron growled, "shoot the damn thing open!" When the pirate had done so with one deafening shot of his pistol, Cauldron burst from the makeshift jail. "Where's that clergyman?" he demanded.

"I had t' chase this one down first." Drager gave Ivy a shake hard enough to rattle her teeth. "And she was ridin' like the devil hisself to get away." He handed Cauldron the miniature he had been sent to retrieve. "But now I'll get that preacher!" Giving Ivy a shove in Drake's direction to turn her guardianship back over to him, he turned to the steps and took them two at a time.

Ivy stumbled hard against Drake's chest. As she tried to straighten away, his fingers clamped harshly on her arm, keeping her captive. She looked up into eyes that were hard with suspicion.

"I had already decided to come back," she tried to explain.

"I might have believed that if you had come back on your own, with the keys, and freed us." Cold disbelief scored each of Drake's words. "But since Drager had to chase you down and drag you down here, I can't."

Her situation was worse, Ivy realized with alarm. Much, much worse. "I just wanted to give Allen a chance to get away, that's all. But I *was* coming back." Despite her explanation, she could tell neither man believed her.

"He won't get away." Cauldron's words were a grim vow. "Not with Drager tracking him down."

Saying a silent prayer that it wouldn't be so, she watched worriedly as Cauldron turned his attention to the miniature and pried off its golden back. As he read the folded page within, Ivy added another prayer that it wouldn't contain any mention of her as a courier for the last missive. The way the men felt about her now, it might be all they needed to seal her fate here in the cellar instead of waiting for Norfolk.

"This letter shows the information goes from Norfolk to the Bermuda Islands," Cauldron said, not looking up as he scanned the information. "Being British, that makes sense."

Ivy shifted uneasily when Cauldron finished reading and looked up to meet her eyes.

"There's nothing about you."

Ivy sagged in relief at the words. She would have a reprieve until they talked to the last spy in Norfolk. And when they did, she would have to hope that nothing would inadvertently connect her to the plot. If that happened, she no longer felt that Cauldron would look past the first incriminating evidence and dig deeper to get to the truth.

The mood was grim as they all returned to the drawing room to wait for Drager's return. When he came back empty-handed, the mood became even darker.

"Where did Allen go?" Cauldron's question was fierce as he turned to Ivy.

"I don't know. I told him not to tell me." The look in Cauldron's eyes made her fear he might use force to test the truth to those words. To her relief, he didn't, though his expression became grimmer yet.

Drake knew what Cauldron's worry was. "You better hope that Allen," he said to Ivy, "being the godly man he

316

is, doesn't decide to beat us to Norfolk to save the life of that last spy. Because if he does, you won't want to know what will happen to him."

Such a deed hadn't even occurred to Ivy, and she hoped fervently it wouldn't occur to Allen either, though such an action would certainly be in his nature. But as she thought more on it, she knew she had no worries in that direction.

"He won't go to Norfolk," she said with confidence. "Not that he probably wouldn't like to. I'm sure he'd rather see Simon Whittaker turned in to the authorities than have him brutally killed. But he would have to know that getting involved could hurt me, and he would *never* do it for that reason alone."

Drake gave Cauldron a nod, showing he believed her. When it came to Ivy, he didn't doubt the clergyman would put his concern for her above all else, for it was obvious how deeply the man cared for her.

Cauldron had no choice but to hope Allen wouldn't meddle since the clergyman was already gone and he didn't want to lose any more time by hunting him down.

"Let's return to the *Sea Maid*," he decided. "The full moon will enable us to set sail immediately for Norfolk."

Chapter 23

The trip to the *Sea Maid* was a silent, grim journey for Ivy. Since Allen had made his escape on Drake's stallion, Drake took her gelding, making her ride pillion with him. Neither he nor Cauldron said anything to her and she was equally disinclined to talk.

When they reached the ship, Drake brought her to his cabin. "I'm going to lock you in here while I'm navigating the ship downriver," he said, his words curt. "We'll be traveling all through the night, so you best get some sleep. Tomorrow might be . . . unpredictable."

It was a euphemism that didn't do anything to dispel Ivy's worries. So much had changed since the last time she had entered the captain's quarters of this ship, she thought, looking around at the luxurious cabin. And none of it had changed for the better. Her innocence, both of her soul and body, was now gone—the one lost to Cauldron's accusations and the other lost to Drake's passion.

Her eyes settled on the bed. The covers, still rumpled, brought back unwanted memories of the night that had begun that loss of innocence. As she glanced at Drake, she could see from the way he was staring at the bed that he, too, was remembering that fateful night.

If only she could undo all that had happened, but, of course, that was impossible. She had only to look into Drake's eyes and see the suspicion there to know she was in danger. And she had only to look beneath those tangled covers and see the stained sheet to know her virginity was forever gone.

She knew she couldn't face sleeping between those particular sheets again. "Could . . . could I have fresh linens?" she asked awkwardly.

"I'll get some."

The abrupt way Drake answered and then went to find new bedding showed Ivy he knew all too well her reasons for asking and felt the same. As she waited for him to return, she stripped the old sheets from the bed, wadding them into a tight ball to hide the story they so plainly told.

"Here."

Ivy took the new linens and then watched uncomfortably as Drake picked up the old ones. "What will you do with them?" she felt compelled to ask. The idea of one of the crew washing them and then showing his findings to the other rough crew members was more than she wanted to contemplate.

"What we shared was private, Ivy." The words were quiet. "And it will stay that way. I'll burn these in the galley stove."

Ivy knew she could believe him. After the door closed behind Drake, she made the bed and then changed into her nightgown. When she untied the two remaining miniatures from her cloak, setting them out for moral

320

support, the absence of the third tiny piece was a grim reminder of all that had happened.

After she slipped under the covers, anxiety kept her awake as the ship moved down the river, bringing her toward a fate she was afraid to meet. Though she had had no part in the plot, she found herself obsessed with the idea that something would make it seem she had been. Hours later exhaustion finally claimed her, letting her find some peace.

The sound of a loud explosion jolted her back awake. Outside the windows, a bright red glare lit up the dark sky.

"Oh, my God," Ivy cried out loud, throwing aside the covers so she could scramble from the bed, "we're under attack!"

A hand clamped around her wrist, stopping her.

At the unexpected assault, Ivy screamed. She thought the ship must have already been boarded and lashed out at her attacker, hearing him grunt as she connected with his face. Hoping to take advantage of his pain, she jerked savagely at her captured wrist to try to free herself.

Instead, she suddenly found herself pinned to the bed, her other wrist held just as tightly as the first as the assailant rolled on top of her to stop another blow. She screamed again, thrashing wildly beneath his grip.

"It's me, Ivy," Drake gritted, letting his full weight rest upon her to stop her flailing movements.

"Drake?" Ivy hadn't realized he had come to bed. Relief surging through her, she stopped fighting. "I thought you were someone from the ship that's attacking us." Fear made her voice rise as the words spilled forth. Expecting the marauders to burst in at any moment, she struggled to sit up so that she could at least face them.

Drake tightened his fingers around her wrists to keep her where she was. "We're *not* under attack."

"But the explosion!"

Drake could feel the wild beating of her heart. "We're in the Chesapeake now and that was a signal for the *Black Cauldron*. We'll be sending them off as we sail, and when the ship sees one, she'll know to meet us back at Cay's Cove so we can reboard her."

As the fear of an attack faded, Drake's words replaced it with fear of her future. "That will be after the stop at Norfolk."

Though Ivy voiced it as a statement, Drake could hear the question—and the dread—in her words. "Yes, it will," he conceded. "And it will work out well with our plans. A pirate ship can't sail right into Norfolk, but this one can."

Ivy couldn't help but wonder if she would still be alive when the exchange of ships took place. She felt her heart pound even harder at the thought.

Pressed so tightly against her, Drake was aware of every frightened beat of Ivy's heart, every worried breath she drew. He hadn't thought he could still desire her, not when she might be guilty of so many terrible things, but as he became aware of the softness of her body beneath him and the way her breasts pillowed the hardness of his chest, he knew he still did.

Ivy felt Drake's heart suddenly begin to beat at a pace that was as rapid as her own. Since she knew fear wasn't the cause of his quickening pulse, that only left one reason. . . .

"Let's forget everything but now," Drake murmured, finding her lips in the darkness.

Ivy, afraid of her future and panicked by her past, found herself wanting that too. But when Drake's mouth caressed hers, it was Allen's face that came to her mind, making her think of his gentle, farewell kiss and the promise he had made to always be there for her. Troubled by the image, she pulled away.

Even as Ivy withdrew from the kiss, Drake had already begun to withdraw, too, at the memory of Geoff.

"Neither of us can forget what stands between us," he said softly, raising his head.

"No," Ivy agreed as Drake rolled away, stretching out alongside her in the bed, "we can't." They both were silent as they dwelled on what the morrow would bring.

When another signal went off, Ivy flinched at the explosion, the sound a harsh reminder of how soon her fate would be sealed.

"Could you hold me, Drake?" she asked hesitantly, knowing from his restless movements he was still awake. "Just hold me? I'm afraid."

"I'm afraid, too, Ivy," Drake confessed, his words heavy. Turning toward her, he brought her into his arms, trying without success to reassure himself as well as her that everything would go well in Norfolk.

When Ivy woke, Drake was gone and it was long past sunrise. Because of the loud signals during the night, her rest had been sporadic, but her tiredness immediately evaporated when she remembered their approaching destination.

As the hours passed, she restlessly watched through

the windows for the first sight of Norfolk until it finally came into view. By the time the ship had docked at one of the many piers, she was a jumble of nerves.

Her unease grew worse when Drake brought her onto the deck and Cauldron thrust the miniature of the one-eared man into her hand.

"Take this," he said.

Ivy looked at it in dread. "Why?"

"We're hoping Simon Whittaker might not have known exactly when you would show up with this thing and that maybe he's still expecting you."

They wanted to see the man's reaction to her, Ivy thought bleakly. "Jonathan might have written to Simon about me," she tried to impress upon him, "so he could know my name and even have a description of me."

The answering look Cauldron gave her showed Ivy he thought she was already making up excuses for the way Simon would react to her. He hailed a coach, and as they sped toward the church, she tensely listened to his instructions on what to say.

"You better hope," Cauldron ended grimly, "that Allen didn't decide to stop us from taking the law into our own hands. Because if we get to the church and find out he somehow beat us there, he will regret it."

Knowing Allen as she did, Ivy was sure she didn't have to worry about that. It was small comfort, though, for she still had much to agonize over. All too quickly, they arrived at Christ Church.

Finding no one in the chapel, they proceeded to the offices that lined a short hallway in the rear.

"May I help you?" asked the rector from behind his desk as they stopped at his door.

Ivy felt Drake nudge her with his fingers. "I'm here to

see Simon Whittaker," she said.

The rector rose from his chair. "He recently left this church," he apologized.

Had Allen somehow beaten them here after all? Worry poured through Ivy at his fate if that were true. And hers too. Since she had helped Allen escape, she knew Cauldron's anger would be directed at both of them.

From behind her, she heard Cauldron's low growl of frustration at the news and then felt another nudge from Drake to continue. Though she was afraid to hear the answer, she had to ask the questions the pirates wanted.

"When did Simon leave?"

"Over a week ago."

It was shortly after her capture, which cleared Allen, Ivy realized with relief. As her spirits began to lift at the unexpected reprieve of Simon being gone, another low growl from behind her showed how frustrated Cauldron was over this new development.

"Did someone come for Simon?" Ivy asked the question without hesitation, knowing Allen wouldn't be named.

"Not that I was aware of."

"Do you know where he went?"

"No, I don't. He left suddenly, with no explanation, leaving the church with no one to take over his duties."

Ivy couldn't believe her luck, for if the pirates couldn't find the man, it would probably be better for her own future. "Well, thank you," she said, eager to end the conversation.

"Where did Simon live while he worked here?" Drake suddenly asked, breaking the silence he had maintained. "Perhaps someone there knows where he went."

The rector shook his head. "He lived in one of the

325

buildings on the church grounds and kept to himself. When he left, everything he owned was gone."

"Can you tell us where he hailed from or where else he might have worked?" Drake persisted. As the rector frowned, obviously starting to wonder at the barrage of questions, Drake added smoothly, "We were supposed to deliver this miniature to him"—he gestured to the one Ivy was holding—"and I'd hate to not have him get it."

The rector nodded in understanding. "Looks like a lovely piece and he was very fond of those little portraits." He pursed his lips as he thought. "He worked in Georgetown before coming here, and I believe he originally hailed from Coverton, South Carolina."

Knowing where the man had been didn't shed any light on where he might go, Ivy thought with satisfaction. She didn't see the look Drake was exchanging with Cauldron behind her.

The two men nodded in silent agreement. The little Carolina town had been where Cauldron had been born and raised, and it was also where his great-aunt had lived before moving to Georgetown. They now had their answer as to how the spies had found out about the aunt's connection to the pirate captain when they had plotted his death.

"One last question," Drake said to the clergyman. "What does Simon Whittaker look like?"

"He's around forty. Short, thin, with thick hair the color of a carrot."

"Thank you," Drake said. "You've been a great help."

As they left the church, Cauldron said thoughtfully, "Where do you think Simon went?"

Ivy knew Cauldron's question wasn't addressed to her. But she was sure that after a brief discussion, both men would realize Simon Whittaker would be a hard man to trace, especially since he would be taking great pains not to be found.

"I'd probably go to the place I'd feel was safest," Drake replied. "And for Simon, that would be British soil."

"Where the miniatures went?" Cauldron mused. "The Bermuda Islands?"

"It's as good of a place as any to start," Drake conceded. "If he's not there, we'll just have to hunt until we find him."

They weren't going to give up, Ivy realized in dismay. They were determined to find their prey even if they had to search the earth for him. In many ways, it was an ominous thought.

"Sooner or later we'll find him," Cauldron vowed. "He's the one who told the others about Martha. And because of that, Geoff died. He'll pay for it."

Their need for revenge was frightening in its intensity. Ivy suddenly didn't doubt they would eventually find Simon Whittaker. And when they did, if the man said anything at all that linked her to the plot, even indirectly, she knew that fierce vengeance would be turned on her.

Cauldron gave Drake a slap on the shoulder, eagerness to start the hunt apparent in its motion. "Let's head for Cay's Cove, so we can reboard the *Black Cauldron*," he said with anticipation. "We're going to need her to get safely past all the British ships between here and the Bermudas."

The pirate vessel, alerted by their signals, was already waiting for them when they entered the secluded inlet at Cay's Cove. Leaving only enough men on board the *Sea*

Maid to keep it safe until they returned, everyone else was quickly shuttled to the larger, well-armed ship. It was with a feeling of dread that Ivy found herself once again on board the infamous schooner, its sails full as it sped toward the British islands.

As she unpacked the canvas bag, bringing out all three of the miniatures, she placed the ill-fated one at the bottom of her trunk, not wanting to be reminded of its existence. The other two, of her parents and Allen, she set once again on top of the drawers, needing their comforting presence more than ever.

As she put the rest of her belongings back into her trunk, her eyes grew troubled as she placed the lovely silk gown Drake had bought her on the top. He had said it would be for the celebration Cauldron would have if he accepted her as his daughter. She remembered answering with asperity at the time, "What do I wear it to if he doesn't accept me? My funeral?"

It was beginning to look now as though she might have inadvertently foreseen her future. More and more afraid, she wondered how the forces the three miniatures had set into motion would finally turn out.

Chapter 24

The shift from cold, overcast days to warm, sunny ones as they approached the Bermudas was the only thing Ivy enjoyed about the short voyage. By the end of the second day, she didn't need her cloak when she was up on deck, and by the following morning, she could have easily worn a light cotton dress, had she had one with her.

But the sun climbed higher the closer they came to their destination, and the balmy weather that had been the one, alleviating factor turned traitor as well, becoming too warm. By the time they entered the aqua waters that surrounded the pink, sandy beaches, discomfort was the only word that could describe the way Ivy's woolen clothes felt against her skin.

Dressed in the right attire, it would have been different, for the air was pleasantly warm, not hot. But with only wool dresses and one totally inappropriate silk gown to choose from, she had nothing lightweight to wear. The men fared much better. Able to shed their coats and simply wear a flowing white shirt, they were dressed far more suitably for the balmy setting.

Alone in Drake's little cabin, Ivy sat wearing only her cotton shift, not wanting to put on her wool dress to go ashore until she had to. To best search the area to find if Simon Whittaker was there, the *Black Cauldron* was widely circling the tightly clustered islands, dipping at intervals into isolated coves to covertly drop off small groups of men. At the end of the day, they would all meet at a certain tavern in Tucker's Town to discuss their findings.

Cauldron, impatient to begin the hunt, had gone ashore at the first landing. Several other stops had occurred since then, so Ivy knew it would soon be time for her and Drake to be put ashore. All she could hope was that Simon wouldn't be there.

The trip to the British-controlled islands had been uneventful, the English vessels they encountered shying away from the infamous pirate schooner that had taken so many of their ships. And the nights had remained uneventful as well. Though she and Drake still slept in each other's arms, each seeking what comfort they could from the other's presence, the barriers between them had kept them distant.

The sound of the anchor being lowered signaled that another longboat would soon be launched. Just then, there was a rap at the door.

"You ready, Ivy?"

"One moment, Drake." Reluctantly, Ivy donned the lavender dress. Its woolen fabric, though finer than her other wool dresses, immediately felt as though it was sticking to her skin, itching where it touched bare flesh instead of the cotton of her shift.

Following Drake out into the bright sunlight, she hoped the trade winds would help keep her cool. But as they were rowed toward a secluded cove and dropped off on the pink sand that edged a mass of exotic rock formations, she knew she would soon be sweltering.

As she and Drake headed inland, the rock and sand at the water's edge were replaced by lush patches of cedars and palmettos. Ivy pushed aside one of the fronds.

"How long before we reach Tucker's Town?" she asked, already feeling the effects of the heat.

"With the villages we need to stop in to ask questions, maybe two hours."

Ivy felt a trickle of sweat run down between her breasts, and she tried not to think about how she would feel by the end of the day. Already she was hot and thirsty and, at the mention of villages, was looking forward to a refreshing drink at one of them. Half an hour later, though they had passed a number of limestone cottages along with an occasional pyramid-shaped outbuilding, there was no evidence of a village.

"Where *is* that first town?" she asked, her hot dress beginning to feel suffocating.

"It's still a ways yet."

Although she felt uncomfortable, Drake looked fresh and unaffected by the warmth, but that was undoubtedly due to the billowy white shirt he was wearing, cut open to the waist. As Ivy trudged along beside him in discomfort, she paid scant heed to the colorful birds, the lush foliage, or even the little lizards that scampered out of their path. But when they passed by a pink-tinged cottage, the line of clothes strung from its stepped roof over to a red cedar caught her eye as nothing else had. On it was a yellow gauzy island dress, its material obviously dry as it flapped in the warm breeze.

The cost of such a garment would have to be minimal.

"Drake," she said suddenly, pointing toward the line, "could you buy me that yellow dress from the people who own it? I really need something cooler to wear. I'll pay you back, of course."

For the first time since the contents of the miniature had been discovered, Drake felt a smile come to his lips, both at Ivy's suggestion and at her usual promise of payment.

"Of course," he agreed automatically even though he knew he would never accept Ivy's money. Then his smile faded as he wondered if Ivy would have a future in which to consider paying off her debts.

When Drake's expression grew somber, Ivy had no trouble guessing his thoughts, for on making the promise, she herself had wondered if she would be able to keep it.

"If I can pay you back," she amended, her words awkward.

Not wanting to dwell on that possibility, Drake turned his attention to Ivy's request. It was certainly valid, considering the wool she was wearing.

"You should have something lighter," her agreed. "Let's see if the people who own that dress are home."

As they made their way toward the cottage, they had to shoo away the chickens that were roaming freely around the small yard. At the door, Drake knocked. There was no answer.

"Looks as if no one's here," he decided, "but that won't stop us." Going to the line of clothes, he pulled the yellow dress from the wooden pins that held it.

"We can't just *steal* it, Drake."

At that heartfelt protest, Drake reached over, lightly touching Ivy's cheek. "Even with all the damning evidence against you," he said softly, "I have a hard time believing you could have been involved in that plot. You always seem so honest."

For a moment, the mood was as it had been before everything had gone so wrong. Ivy gazed into Drake's eyes, her own eyes pleading for him to believe in her.

"I *am* honest, Drake."

But she could see too much had happened for him to accept that. The mood broken, she stepped away from his touch.

"I guess I can't convince you of that, but, nevertheless, I won't steal this dress. I don't want it if you intend to just take it."

"You always think the worst of us pirates," Drake gently chided her. "I wasn't going to steal the dress." He fished into his pocket for a coin. "I was going to leave some money."

"Oh." As usual, she had thought the worst even though neither Drake nor Cauldron had ever done anything to deserve that lack of faith. She had given them far more reasons to doubt her integrity.

Those gloomy feelings were pushed aside when Ivy saw the coin Drake meant to use. Very large and made of gold, it was worth much, much more than the simple island dress, making her already considerable debt still larger.

Even as she told herself the amount she owed might not matter, given her dire circumstances, she knew for the sake of her sanity she had to believe she had a future.

"Don't you have a smaller coin than that?" she asked.

"Afraid I don't." Drake tossed the gold piece up and down in his hand. "It's this or nothing."

Ivy was far too uncomfortable to pass up the dress. "Leave the money," she said in resignation.

With a flick of his hand, Drake tossed the coin toward the door, making it land on the limestone stoop beneath it.

"I need a place to change," Ivy said as he handed her the dress. Though they had yet to reach a village, there were enough cottages in the area to threaten the privacy she needed.

"There's no lock on the door," Drake said, nodding toward the cottage. "Considering the amount of gold we're leaving, I'm sure the people who own this place wouldn't care if you used their house."

"That wouldn't seem right, to walk into someone's home," Ivy decided. "I'll change when we reach that first town."

The next bend brought them to a field full of laborers.

"I'm going to question them," Drake said, veering toward the workers. When they reached the first group of men, he asked a number of discreet inquiries about Simon Whittaker.

To Ivy's relief, Drake's questions brought no information as they moved through the field from one group to the next. Her luck finally failed when Drake hailed one last laborer at the edge of the field of crops.

"I saw a stranger with red hair yesterday," said the perspiring worker, eying Ivy's warm wool dress curiously as he spoke. "A short man, as you said."

Ivy flinched at the news, her hope that Simon had not gone to the Bermudas crumbling.

"Could you tell where he was heading?" Drake asked.

"East maybe. Couldn't really tell."

As they moved away from the field, Drake frowned when he looked at Ivy's lavender dress. In his flowing shirt, he looked no different than the male islanders.

Nothing marked him as a pirate, so he would draw no inquiring glances in town. Ivy's hot wool dress would be in sharp contrast to the gauzy cottons worn by the island women. She would bring unwanted attention to them that would hamper their search.

"Before we get to the first town," he told her, "I want you to change at the first private place we come to. Your wool dress is already drawing too much attention."

As they walked, Ivy was silent, thinking about the ramifications if Simon was found in the near future. From the way Drake was equally quiet, she was sure his thoughts were on that serious topic as well.

Less than a quarter mile farther, they found the private place Ivy needed to shield her from prying eyes. The collapse of one of the island's many underground caves had left behind a clear pool of salt water surrounded by jagged formations of limestone indented from the rest of the terrain. They had to pick their way down through huge chunks of stone.

"I'll go behind there," Ivy said, indicating an arched piece of stone that was large enough to hide her from any islanders passing by. The area was accessible by taking just a few steps into the shallow water of the pool to go around the side of the arch. Ivy removed her shoes, lifting the hem of her dress to walk through the ankle-deep water. It felt marvelous on her hot feet.

Once behind the limestone wall and onto a dry, smooth sheet of sandstone, she placed the island dress over a jagged remnant of a once-proud stalagmite and then lost no time stripping off her woolen garment. Free of its cloying weight, she immediately felt much better.

Going to the spot where the sandstone sloped into the water, she scooped up a handful of the crystal-clear liquid, splashing it over her throat and arms, not caring if her shift became a little damp in the process.

"Ivy."

At the unexpected word, Ivy straightened with a start, surprised to find Drake standing at the edge of the limestone wall that had separated them. His boots were off, his feet bare and wet from the shallow water. After the emotional distance existing between them the last few days, she certainly hadn't expected him to invade her privacy.

"I keep telling myself I shouldn't still be interested in you," Drake told her softly, "not when you could be part of the plot that killed Geoff. But I can't seem to help myself."

The words made Ivy's heart constrict. "I keep telling myself I shouldn't still be interested in you," she answered, her words just as soft, "not when you're a pirate and I'm betrothed to another. But I can't seem to help myself either."

Drake opened his arms to her. Ivy came into them, letting her face rest against the hardness of his chest as he hugged her to him. The barriers that had been between them, even as they had shared the same bed, suddenly seemed unimportant as they faced what the day could bring.

"I'm afraid of what's going to happen today," she whispered.

Knowing that Simon was somewhere on the island and would undoubtedly soon be found, Drake shared her fears.

"I am too, Ivy." He brought his hand to her hair, lacing his fingers through the long, silky strands at the base of her neck. "I am too."

Though neither of them voiced it, they both knew they would soon be sharing passion, perhaps for the last time. For a long, long moment, they just clung to each other, finding solace in the other's presence.

Then they both became aware of the other's need to complete the union that would bring a small measure of comfort to their aching souls. Drake felt Ivy's nipples harden beneath her damp cotton shift, pressing into his chest. Ivy felt Drake's arousal, heavy and warm beneath his breeches, pressing into the softness of her loins.

"I can't resist you," Drake breathed as he drew Ivy's shift over her head, tossing it onto the rock that held her clothes. "Not now, when so many things could change."

Naked, Ivy slipped her hands around Drake's neck. "I can't resist you either," she said with a catch to her voice. "Not now."

Drake scooped Ivy up into his arms, carrying her through the sun-warmed pool to where the water met the sloping stretch of sandstone. He laid her down on its smooth surface.

Cool stone greeted Ivy's shoulders and head; warm, shallow water greeted her hips and thighs. Aroused by the sensuous combination, she watched impatiently as Drake stripped off his clothes, tossing them onto the rock to join hers.

Chapter 25

"You look like a sea maid," Drake murmured as he stared down at her, "lying half in the water like that, with your breasts bare and your long hair streaming around you."

Once such talk would have embarrassed Ivy, but now the words made her feel feminine and desirable. Her eyes moved slowly over Drake, looking so virile as he stood naked before her in the shallow water. His readiness was apparent and it excited her to know she was its cause.

"Then we make a perfect pair," she murmured back, holding out her arms to him, "because you look like a sea god, rising from the water."

Drake stretched out alongside her, his torso half covering hers as he came into her welcoming arms. Ivy gloried in the feel of his warm body, the muscles so taut under the golden flesh that covered them. And she gloried in the feel of his thickening arousal, straining now in readiness against her thigh. Her body, heated before by the warm air, reached a new peak as she anticipated receiving his passion.

Drake let his fingers run slowly over the lushness of Ivy's body. He already knew what a soft cushion her breasts would make for his chest when he made love to her. And he knew her hips, so sweetly rounded, would allow him to love her without restraint on this smooth sheet of sandstone, their soft curves absorbing and then returning each passionate thrust of his body.

Ivy gave a long sigh as his fingers continued to travel the length of her body, touching her in ways that were meant to excite. The water, just deep enough to lap gently against her hips, tantalized that part of her that was now yearning for his possession.

Scooping up a handful of the clear liquid, Drake let it dribble over Ivy's breasts. The nipples, already swollen with desire, glistened in the sunlight that streamed in through the tall, jagged rocks that surrounded them. Bringing his lips to one upthrust crest, he encircled it with his tongue, aroused by the slight saltiness that was only partly caused by the water.

Ivy felt her breasts swell beneath his touch, their tips growing tight with wanting. But as Drake rasped his tongue over one then the other, as wonderful as that felt, she knew what she really wanted was to have him inside her, merging their bodies as well as their souls.

"Make love to me, Drake." The words were a soft plea as Ivy parted her legs, welcoming him.

Moving between those parted thighs, Drake entered her with slow deliberation, the shallow water of the sun-warmed pool a sensual caress to the intimate joining of their loins.

Their bodies came fully together, creating the most intimate of bonds. As Drake began to move, his hips strongly thrusting into her, Ivy felt the water surge around them, emphasizing the power of his possession and her willingness to accept it.

She knew there could be no greater pleasure than what Drake was giving her. In return, she gave herself with total abandon, wanting to give as much pleasure as she received in this last, bittersweet lovemaking.

"Love me." The words were a moan as Ivy lifted her hips time and again to meet Drake's. Sparkling drops of water flew wildly around them, making their bodies glisten as they strained to ignite that final, shuddering release.

Suddenly Ivy's senses were whirling, her body shaking as she and Drake reached that pinnacle together. The water splashed wantonly as their bodies heaved with the force of their fulfillment. Then, as their frantic movements finally stilled, the water settled into a quiet calm.

As Drake lay heavily atop of her, catching his breath, Ivy held him tightly, wanting to keep reality at bay. Finally, Drake raised his head, his eyes already shadowed by what the day could bring.

"I wish we could stay here forever, Ivy," he said with heartfelt regret. "But we can't, not when there are questions that need to be answered if either of us is to find peace."

They were words Ivy wasn't ready to hear, but as Drake pulled free from her body, bringing her to her feet, she knew her uncertain future had to be faced. While they washed away the traces of their passion and then dressed, they were both engrossed in their own solemn thoughts.

Attired in her gauzy island garb, Ivy at least felt cooler if not at ease. The simple yellow dress, gathered peasant-style about the shoulders, fit well, tapering at the waist before flaring out in a long, billowy skirt. Folding the lavender dress into a neat square, she then followed Drake out of the shelter of their private haven.

A short while later, they were in a small village. Though they had stopped at a number of places, there was no further information about Simon Whittaker. Nor did they get any response at the next small village. But with so many of Cauldron's men combing the island and knowing that a red-haired stranger was indeed around, Ivy knew with grim certainty that someone would find him.

When they reached Tucker's Town and located the narrow alley that housed the tavern where they were all to meet, her worst fears were confirmed as Cauldron, waiting for them at a table in a dark corner, waved them over.

"We found where Simon is," he said triumphantly. "He's been spotted at a deserted guard tower north of here."

Though she had expected to hear such words, Ivy's stomach still twisted at the news, for the confrontation she had dreaded would soon occur.

Cauldron pushed aside the mug of bibby he had been nursing. "Let's go get him," he said, eagerness filling his words. As the men around him started to rise, he motioned for them to stay where they were. "I don't want him warned off by a troop of men approaching," he said. "Just Drake and I—and Ivy—will go. Wait here until the rest of the men arrive and then go to the ship. It should be at the rendezvous point by now. We'll set sail as soon as we finish here."

Ivy hardly noticed as Drake took the bundle of clothes from her hands, handing it to one of the crew to take back with him. As they left the tavern, she had no thoughts except for what would happen when they reached that deserted guard tower.

The journey wasn't far. When they arrived at the battered ruins, they saw a high turret looming over the rocky crag. The ocean, at the bottom of the drop-off, made a moaning sound as its waves surged around the sharp rocks at the base.

"Supposedly, Simon is staying in the room at the top," Cauldron said, staying in the concealment of a thick patch of cedars as he led them toward the structure.

With a sense of doom, Ivy looked up at the guard tower. By the time they had quietly made their way up the circular, steep steps to the top, she was short of breath, but she knew it was from fear rather than exhaustion.

Motioning for Ivy to step forward, Cauldron reached for the doorknob of the room before them. When he pushed it open, he and Drake stepped to the side so that anyone within would see only Ivy standing there.

As the door swung wide, it revealed a small room whose outer, rounded sides were made of latticed metal. In its middle was a crumbling fireplace and through a narrow doorway on one of its latticed walls was a circular, roofless guard ramp that surrounded the top of the tower. Held up by metal beams that angled upward from the tower proper, the circular ramp seemed almost suspended in space since the metal walkway that had connected it to the inner room had long since rusted. Spanning the chasm between the two now was a makeshift, wooden plank.

Kneeling by the fireplace as he checked the contents of a large satchel was a man with fiery red hair. Ivy watched as he scrambled to his feet, obviously startled by the door's unexpected opening. For a long moment, he stared at her blankly and then, to her dismay, she saw recognition flare in his eyes.

"Ivy Woodruff!" he exclaimed.

Ivy could only hope that Drake and Cauldron would believe that Jonathan Moore, as she had feared, had given Simon a description of her. Her heart sank further when the man stepped forward, speaking as though he knew her.

"Last I heard, you were still Keils Cauldron's captive! What are you—"

Simon's words came to a halt at the sight of Cauldron and Drake standing on either side of the door. Immediately, he went for the pistol tucked into his waistband.

Drake leveled his own weapon at the man before he could draw it. "Don't try it!" he snapped. Simon froze. Drake carefully approached him, taking no chances as he relieved Simon of his gun. With no one else to prove or disprove Ivy's involvement, he didn't want to risk this last spy dying before they got the information they wanted.

With his prey disarmed, Cauldron moved closer. "I can see you recognize me, even with this beard," he told Simon. "And your actions tell me you know I wouldn't be here unless I had found the miniature Ivy was going to deliver and connected you to the plot that killed my son." He stared hard into Simon's eyes, seeing the man blanch beneath his gaze.

"We have already killed Samuel Hockett and Jonathan Moore," he continued roughly, "so we know about their part in the plot." He paused. "Now we want answers. If you give them, you'll go free."

344

At the words "go free," Simon's face lost a little of its pinched, scared look. "About what?" His voice cracked a little as he spoke.

"You grew up in Coverton, South Carolina." It was a statement not a question.

Simon knew better than to deny something that Cauldron had obviously unearthed. Slowly, he nodded.

"That's where I grew up too," Cauldron added, his words grim. "As did one of my relations, Martha Gainsby, before she moved to Georgetown." He jabbed a finger into Simon's chest. "You were the one who knew of her connection to me, weren't you? And passed that knowledge along to your friends to lure me to my death?" His face was as grim as his voice as he ended the question.

Simon's hands were trembling. "All I did was mention that I knew about her relationship to you! After that, it was the others who planned to kill you. Not me!"

"What others?" Cauldron growled the words.

Simon's eyes went to Ivy. "*She* was part of it."

It was an accusation that went far beyond Ivy's worst fears. "All I did was carry the miniature!" she protested sharply. "Nothing else!"

"No?" Simon sneered. "She was the one who suggested that Jonathan and Samuel kill you—not only to help England but also to pay you back for what you did to her mother!"

Ivy's face drained of all color at the lie.

"And when your son died instead of you," Simon continued, "*she* was the one who suggested she try to claim you as her father to get herself named as your new heir! And then she planned to see you hanged for piracy!"

"Those are lies, all lies!" Ivy moaned in despair.

"No, they're not!" Simon flung back at her. "How

345

could I know all that if it weren't true?" He turned toward Cauldron, his eyes hopeful now that he had provided information that would appease the pirate captain.

Instead, he found himself caught in a strangulation hold as Cauldron dragged him toward the plank that led to the open guard ramp.

"If it weren't for the information you gave," Cauldron spat, "my son would still be alive."

Simon thrashed wildly as Cauldron dragged him over the chasm to the outer ramp. Drake added his strength to Cauldron's so there would be no chance of Cauldron also falling.

"But you said you would let me go if I answered your questions!" Simon screamed as he was hauled right to the outer edge of the narrow ramp.

"I lied." With one strong heave, Cauldron flung the man over the railing. Ivy's scream of horror merged with Simon's as he fell through the air, striking first the edge of the drop-off below and then tumbling down its steep side to crash on the jagged rocks at its base. The ocean surged around the broken body as its waves foamed among the boulders.

For a moment, Cauldron looked down at the torn body in satisfaction, then he turned toward Ivy, his eyes full of pained betrayal.

"I didn't want to believe it of you, Ivy," he said, dragging out the words he didn't want to say. "I hoped it wouldn't be true." He took a tortured breath. "But it is." Only the chasm separated her from him and he took a step toward the plank that spanned it.

"You mustn't hurt her!"

The sharply spoken words, coming from the stairwell, made everyone turn toward it in surprise. Allen stepped into the room, a leather traveling bag in his hand.

"Allen!" Ivy cried in disbelief, the sight of him bringing her a much-needed feeling of support. Then that feeling faded as she realized the implications of his being at the guard tower. "Why are you here?" she ended in an unhappy whisper.

"I would think that's pretty clear right now," Cauldron grated, his pistol already leveled at the clergyman. "And from the traveling bags Allen and Simon both have, it looks as if they were ready to move on to the greater safety of England. Unfortunately for them, we got here first."

Ivy didn't want to believe the accusation. "It's not true, is it, Allen?" she pleaded. "That you were part of the spy ring?"

"It's true," Allen said without hesitation or shame. "But only Simon was leaving," he added intently, addressing the words solely to Ivy. "He heard a treaty is being discussed that will end the war so he wanted to return to England. I wasn't going to join him until everything with you was resolved," he stressed, wanting her to believe his motives. "I was just using this place to hide until then. I was coming up to tell Simon about the ship he would be taking, when I heard him being flung over the edge." He paused and then added with deep sincerity, "I couldn't let that happen to you."

Ivy was shaken by his confession. "How could you be part of all that, Allen?" she asked. "Your vows . . . our betrothal . . ."

"I was only involved with gathering information to help England win the war. My heart is on her side, it always has been." Firm conviction emphasized his words. "I thought with your English background you

347

would still cleave to me when it was all over and the truth came out. But I *wasn't* part of the killing, Ivy. I didn't even know about that. And I *didn't* know Jonathan gave you the miniature to deliver. I swear I didn't! I never would have involved you in any of this."

He turned to Drake and Cauldron, still standing on the outer walkway. "And that's why I came in here just now instead of running away. Ivy was never part of this. Never!"

"Simon Whittaker recognized her the minute he set eyes on her!" Cauldron ground out.

"He recognized her from the miniature I have of her!" Allen lifted the bag he held, indicating the piece was in there. "After I got away from Havenrest, I stopped by the church to pick up my personal belongings before going into hiding. The miniature was among them."

Cauldron's harsh expression didn't change. "Simon also said she was part of the plot and gave us enough facts to make it clear he knew what he was talking about!"

"He knew the situation from me!" Allen stressed. "All he was trying to do was save himself. It's not true about Ivy! I'm the person you want, not her!" He let his bag fall to the ground as he raised his hands in surrender.

"Oh, I want you all right," Cauldron said with deadly intensity. "Just as I want everyone who was involved in the scheme that killed my son! You're going to join your friend Simon at the bottom of the cliff!"

As he prepared to cross the plank, Ivy knew she couldn't watch Allen die. Her foot shot out, catching the end of the board. Sliding clear of the edge, it dropped downward, hitting one of the metal beams that supported the walkway from underneath. For a moment, it teetered there, then it dropped again, speeding toward the ground below.

"I can't let you kill Allen!" she cried. "If he says he didn't have anything to do with Geoff's death, then I believe him! And so should you! He could have killed you at Havenrest when he had the pistol, but he didn't!"

She felt Allen tug at her arm, dragging her behind the shelter of the latticed metal wall as the pirates cocked and aimed their pistols.

Though she could see through the metal strips that made up the wall, its construction made it impossible to fire a bullet through, not without risking the danger of its ricocheting back toward the person who fired it. For the moment, she knew she and Allen were safe, for the chasm couldn't be jumped, not without a running start, and that was impossible on the narrow walkway.

The only way the pirates could get back into the guard tower now would be to climb down the metal beams that held the walkway in place and then hoist themselves back up to the doorway beside her. As high as they were, it seemed an impossible feat.

Cauldron swore as he lowered his pistol. "I'm sure Allen didn't kill me," he gritted, "because he was probably hoping you could still claim me as your father and become my heir. Since there wasn't any definite proof at that point to connect you to the plot, it could have worked!"

"It wasn't like—"

"We'll get the two of you," Cauldron promised, cutting Ivy off as he looked down at the framework of beams that would have to be scaled to get back into the tower. The height or the maneuvering didn't intimidate him, not with years of climbing rigging on a pitching ship.

"This won't take but a few minutes for us to scale," he told her, gesturing to the beams, "so don't think we won't catch you!"

Ivy threw Allen a worried look, believing Cauldron. Instead of looking daunted, Allen pointed toward the cove. A schooner was now sitting in its waters.

"All we need is a few minutes, Ivy! That's the ship Simon was going to catch. That's what I was coming up here to tell him, that she had arrived! She'll be sending in a longboat!"

"Then go!" Ivy cried the order as she watched Drake and Cauldron scanning the framework, obviously planning their climb. "Quickly, before they get over here!"

Instead of obeying, Allen looked at Ivy in stunned disbelief. "You couldn't be planning to stay, Ivy! Not this time!"

At the words, Ivy was aware the pirates had stopped surveying the scaffolding to listen to what was being said.

"I'm not guilty," she stressed, "of anything!"

"And they don't believe you, do they?" Allen shot back. "Even with both of us saying it's not true. They didn't believe you before and now they'll *never* believe you! You must come with me—to England, where we'll be safe!"

"But I'm an American," Ivy protested.

"There's *nothing* for you there," Allen said urgently. "Not any longer! Keils Cauldron doesn't accept you as his daughter and Drake did nothing but steal your innocence!"

He also stole my heart, Ivy thought bleakly to herself. "I gave him my innocence," she reminded Allen softly.

Allen sensed the emotions still binding Ivy to her

pirate lover. He caught at her shoulders, determined to convince her to put all that behind her.

"Drake and Cauldron are like forbidden fruit, tempting women into situations they shouldn't succumb to. Your mother would agree if she were here."

"Yes," Ivy murmured, "she probably would."

"And like your mother, your involvement with a pirate will make tatters of your reputation. In England, no one will know about your time with Drake. We can begin anew."

Ivy looked at him with uncertainty in her eyes. "This is like history repeating itself."

"Your parents had a good marriage in spite of your mother's time with Cauldron."

Slowly, Ivy nodded. "Yes, they did."

"We can have a good marriage too."

Ivy brought her hand to her stomach. "But like my mother, I might already be carrying another man's child."

"And like Ian Woodruff, if that's the case, I'll accept that child as my own and love it as much as if it were mine. Come with me, Ivy," Allen ended in a plea. "We could be happy together."

Ivy cast a look toward Drake, her eyes meeting his. Though they burned into hers, he said nothing, and Ivy knew it was because Geoff's death still hung between them.

Allen made her face him again. "All that's here is death," he reminded her. "Death for something you didn't do!"

Ivy glanced at Cauldron, seeing the revenge still raging in his eyes and the accusation stamped into the lines of his face. Though her emotions told her to stay so she could try to prove her innocence, the deadly reality of the situation made her give in to Allen's plea.

"I'll come," she conceded, her words an anguished whisper. When Allen, picking up his leather bag, drew her toward the door, she hesitated, looking back. The pirates were still watching her, not yet attempting to cross the beams.

"I *wasn't* involved in the plot that killed Geoff," she told Cauldron, her voice breaking. "And though there's no proof I'm you're daughter"—the words caught even more—"I am. I'm sorry I couldn't convince you of that . . . Father."

With tears in her eyes, she then faced Drake. "I . . . we—" Unable to continue, she began to cry, the tears coursing down her cheeks. Pulling the diamond and amethyst ring from her finger, she placed it on the ground. "When I can"—her voice choked with emotion—"I'll pay you back . . . through Elizabeth . . . for the other things you bought me."

Allen tugged urgently at her arm. "Ivy, *let's go!*"

Chapter 26

Blinded by her tears, Ivy let Allen hurry her toward the stairwell. From behind her, she heard the sounds of Drake and Cauldron climbing onto the metal beams.

"Where is Cauldron's ship?" Allen gasped as they raced down the steps.

Ivy brushed futilely at her tears, trying to think only of the future, not the past. "On the other side of the island."

"Then if we can only get to this ship, we'll be safe," Allen said between long breaths. "Cauldron will never be able to catch up with that kind of a lead. Especially since he thinks this ship is going to England, when it's really going to New Zealand! We'll have to stay there for a while," he explained, "until we're sure Cauldron has finished searching England for us, but when it's safe, we'll return to our mother country. I've been promised a position in the same church where my uncle once presided." Reaching the bottom of the guard tower, he ran with her toward the jagged drop-off that slanted sharply down to the ocean.

At its edge, they stopped, gasping for breath as they looked down over the side. The wind, whipping up the incline, made Ivy's long hair swirl around her face. Out in the cove, she saw the schooner was lowering a longboat—a safe haven if they could only reach it. As she looked down at the steep climb that awaited them, she shuddered at the sight of Simon's body, battered and bloody, lying on the sharp rocks at the base, the waves foaming around it.

Allen set down his leather bag as he peered over the edge to look for the safest way to proceed. Though parts of the incline were unclimbable, some places appeared manageable if they followed a zigzag path to the bottom.

"It won't be easy, Ivy, but we have no choice," he finally said. Sitting down on the edge, he carefully let himself slip down onto the first ledge. Narrow and slippery with moss, it made for dangerous footing. One look down to Simon's body made it clear that death would be their fate, too, if they made one careless step. The jagged rocks at the bottom would be deadly. Gripping a rock for support, he reached one hand up toward Ivy.

"Come on down," he urged. "Very, very carefully."

"Should I hand your bag down first?"

"Leave it."

"But your personal—"

"I have you, and that's all I really need," Allen said emphatically. "With this climb, I want both my hands free to help you. It's not going to be easy for you, wearing a dress."

As Ivy sat down, letting her legs dangle over the side as Allen had done, she looked up at the building looming above her. Drake and Cauldron were traversing the network of beams, quickly making their way back into the

354

tower. She knew it would be only a matter of minutes before they reached their goal. Taking a steadying breath, she let herself slide down into Allen's waiting grasp.

"Don't look down," he warned.

"I won't." Holding onto the jutting rocks, Ivy concentrated on her feet, each step made treacherous by the moist rocks and moss. Although her long, billowy dress made it difficult for her to see where she stepped, she moved as fast as she could, guided by Allen.

"There's another ledge we'll have to drop down to," Allen said a few minutes later. Using the same method he had used before, he lowered himself over the edge. As Ivy prepared to follow him, she heard Drake and Cauldron reach the top of the drop-off. She looked up, meeting Drake's eyes. They were filled with something foreboding as he gazed down at her.

Ivy let herself slide down to Allen.

He caught her in his arms, holding her close so she wouldn't slip off the narrow, slippery ledge. Ivy looked up once again. Above them, Drake was lowering himself down onto that first ledge, with Cauldron preparing to follow. He moved with the sureness and grace of a cat, landing on the ledge with dangerous ease. Ivy felt her breath catch at the sight of him coming so determinedly after her.

She looked back to Allen, at the familiar, attractive face that was so close to her own. He was her betrothed, and she cared for him deeply, but as she looked into his eyes, she finally realized that while what they felt for each other was warm and tender, it wasn't the kind of love a husband and wife should share.

It wasn't enough, she suddenly knew with certainty. For her mother, returning to Ian Woodruff and marrying that gentle clergyman had been the right decision. She had been happy, able to put her passionate affair with Keils Cauldron behind her to go on with her life.

For herself, it wouldn't be the same. She wouldn't be able to forget Drake and the passionate love they had shared. It would be his face she saw when Allen took her to bed and his children she wished she was carrying. Though Allen could solve many of her troubles, she knew her future couldn't be with him. It wouldn't be fair—not to him and not to her.

It was Drake she loved. She had tried to deny it, tried to convince herself that it was simply an attraction that had brought them together, but it was more than that. It was love, a love she felt despite the fact that Drake Jordan was a pirate. And though they had no future, not as things stood, they still shared a past—a past that also involved Keils Cauldron. She knew she had to face that past and accept the consequences.

"Allen," she said with soft regret, stepping away from him, "I can't go with you. I really can't. No matter what awaits me here, I have to face it."

Allen could hear the conviction in her voice and see the determination in her eyes. "But I love you, Ivy," he pleaded.

"Is it love?" Ivy questioned gently. "Or am I just another stray kitten you want to protect? You deserve a woman who can love you with her heart and soul, not someone who gave those to another."

"Ivy—" Allen's fingers curled through hers in an involuntary desire to keep her with him. "They'll kill you if you stay."

Ivy took another step away, shaking her head to stop further entreaty. As her foot came down on the slippery moss-covered stone, it slipped and made her lose her balance. Feeling herself start to topple, she tightened her fingers around Allen's in a desperate effort to regain her footing. But a clump of ferns beneath her feet suddenly gave way, and she dropped hard, hitting the edge of the ledge.

Clutching wildly to Allen's hand, she tried to pull herself back to safety, but the rocks beneath her crumbled, and she fell again, sliding over the side. Held only by Allen's hand, she swung perilously over the sharp, jagged rocks at the bottom.

Ivy was aware that Allen, holding his position above her, had grabbed onto a rock jutting from the side of the escarpment. As she tried to keep her grip on his fingers, she felt him try to pull her back onto the ledge. The pressure increased, and her fingers began to slip.

Suddenly Ivy was unsure if Allen was trying to pull her to safety or to free his hand from her grasp. Now that he knew she wouldn't share her life with him, had he decided it would be better for them both if she died now instead of later at the pirates' hands? It would be a quick, easy death, and he could begin a new life without fear that the pirates would force her to reveal his whereabouts. Having seen the fate of his fellow conspirators, he already knew death would be his fate as well if Cauldron and Drake ever caught up to him.

Her life was literally in Allen's hands, and Ivy realized she really didn't know him as well as she had thought, considering his involvement with spying.

As she hung there, looking down at the sharp rocks beneath her, a part of her almost wanted to have it end, have the strain and uncertainty finally be over. But another part wanted to prolong her life—at least a little

357

longer—until she had a chance to speak one last time to the two men who had become so important to her.

Only Allen was in a position to control which fate was to be hers, and she said a quick prayer that God would help him make the decision best for her.

Abruptly, she found herself jerked upwards, partially reaching the ledge. As Allen gave her another strong pull, Ivy grasped at a nearby rock, helping him bring her the rest of the way. She collapsed in his arms, holding him as hard as he was holding her.

"Ivy, oh, Ivy," Allen murmured, pressing his cheek to hers. "I thought I was going to lose you."

She never should have doubted Allen's motives or his basic goodness, Ivy realized, no matter what plot he had joined. He would never cause her harm, even at the price of his own safety.

"You'll never really lose me, Allen," she said tenderly, cupping his face with her hands. "Because a part of my heart will always be with you."

She came to her knees then, looking up at how close Drake and Cauldron were to them. They were rapidly reaching the ledge above them.

"You must go now, Allen," she begged. "Quickly."

"Not until I say one more thing that may change your mind," Allen insisted. "Once I escape, Cauldron and Drake won't get their pardon. That's going to make them even angrier with you."

Ivy hadn't thought of the effect the escape would have on the pirates' future. There would be no pardon, no chance for a different kind of life. In so many ways, she hated to think of those plans coming to an end. Cauldron had told her he was looking forward to a new existence, an existence that would now have to be forsaken. And

Drake had talked of opening his plantation, a plan that could never be fulfilled.

But Allen's life was more important than dreams of a new future. If she had to be held accountable for the pirates' change of plans, then that was the way it had to be.

"I'll face whatever must be faced," she told Allen, gently refusing his final plea.

Allen saw the unshakable determination in her eyes to stay behind. "If you stay—"

"My fate will be in God's hands." Ivy pressed her lips to his in a last kiss that was as gentle as it was loving. "Now go!"

Allen came to his feet, her hand still in his as she knelt on the ledge. "May God protect you, Ivy."

"And may God protect you, Allen."

With a bittersweet smile of farewell, Allen let her fingers slide away from his. As tiny pieces of rock cascaded around them, showing how dangerously near the pirates were getting, he turned his attention to the narrow ledge, quickly working his way downward. No longer slowed down by helping Ivy navigate the rough terrain, he made fast progress, sliding roughly down the final steep incline. Standing on a boulder whose tip just cleared the foaming surf, he looked back up toward Ivy, cupping his hand to his mouth to call up to her.

". . . love you . . . Cauldron . . ."

With the wind snatching his words, Ivy could only make out a few, but she could tell they conveyed his love and his concern as he said his good-bye.

"I love you too, Allen," she called, but she knew her words, like his, were lost to the wind around them. As she raised her hand in a final farewell, she wondered if she would ever see him again.

She watched Allen, with a wave of his own hand, turn toward the ocean and leap from rock to rock as he made his way to the deeper water. When he could go no further, he drove off the last large boulder, swimming with long strokes as he headed toward the longboat that was coming in to get him.

He was going to get away, Ivy thought in relief. Suddenly, she realized Drake was lowering himself onto the ledge on which she sat. She rose to her feet as he dropped down beside her.

"You didn't go."

Though it wasn't a question, Ivy could hear the question in his voice. "My fate lies here," she said simply, resigning herself to whatever came. "Not with Allen." Below them, the longboat hauled Allen inside, then turned toward the safety of the ship.

When Cauldron dropped down, flanking her on the other side, Ivy addressed her next words to the two of them, as she stared out at the bobbing longboat.

"If you want to punish me for treason," she said, trying to keep her voice steady, "at least now there's truth to it since I helped Allen escape." She glanced down at the jagged rocks beneath her where Simon's body lay so still and lifeless. "But I won't betray him to you. No matter what happens to me."

For a moment, Cauldron was silent and then he said quietly, "You could have run away with Allen, but you didn't. You decided to stay even though you knew you could be facing your own death."

Ivy met Cauldron's eyes. "Running away would have been a death of sorts too," she answered, her voice just as quiet. "I couldn't have lived with myself knowing you

360

thought me guilty of Geoff's death. It would have torn me apart." Taking a ragged breath, she then turned toward Drake.

"And a part of me would have died," she told him softly, "if I had followed in my mother's footsteps, trying to forget a past that can't be forgotten."

As both men remained quiet, she again faced the ocean, staring blindly out at the water. The sun was setting, its long rays touching the waves, making their tips golden, but Ivy didn't notice the beauty.

"I *am* innocent." Ivy felt tears form in her eyes as she spoke. "I know that's impossible for you to believe, not with everything that's happened, but I had to stay anyway to say that to you both."

The tears began to fall as she looked down at the jagged rocks below. "And if that's to be my fate, then so be it." Not wanting her final destiny to be at the hands of either one of the men she had come to love, she stepped forward, choosing to put an end to it herself.

Chapter 27

On each side of her, she suddenly found her arms clamped in a bone-crushing hold that yanked her away from the precipice.

"I believe you!"

Both men spoke at the same time.

Ivy was shaken, as much by what she had almost done as by the words she was hearing. "You do?" she said unsteadily.

"May I go first, Drake?" Cauldron asked, turning Ivy toward him. "I don't know what I would have done with you back at the guard tower," he confessed, "but death wouldn't have been one of my choices. When you decided just now not to go with Allen, it ended my suspicions. I don't need you stepping off a cliff to prove your innocence."

For a moment, Ivy closed her eyes in relief, saying a brief prayer of thanks. As she thought of Allen's future, they were still filled with worry as she opened them again.

"What about Allen?"

Cauldron glanced out at the schooner where Allen was now standing at the gunwale as he looked toward the cliff at Ivy.

"You seem to believe he had nothing to do with Geoff's death," he finally said. "That, combined with the fact he saved your life, will save his. As far as I'm concerned, I got my revenge on the people who deserved it."

He placed his hand on Ivy's shoulder, the gesture a little awkward. "I'm sorry I doubted you about that plot," he added sincerely. "I hope you can forgive me."

There was still a reserve between them caused by Cauldron's certainty that she wasn't his daughter. Though it hurt Ivy to see it, there was nothing she could say to prove her heritage to him. All she could hope was that one day the lack of proof wouldn't matter.

"I can forgive you," she said, meaning each word.

Cauldron's expression lightened considerably. "I'm glad." Giving her shoulder a caring squeeze, he then turned toward the cliff, reaching up to grasp the ledge above them. "Let me give the two of you privacy," he said as he hoisted himself onto it. "I'm sure you have things to say to each other. I'll meet you at the top."

As they faced each other, neither speaking, it was Drake who broke the silence.

"Can you forgive me too, Ivy? For not believing you?"

"I would have thought the same," Ivy answered without hesitation, "had I been you."

Drake reached over, his hand caressing her cheek. "You said that a part of you would have died if you had followed in your mother's footsteps, trying to forget a past that can't be forgotten." He paused, his eye questioning. "Does that mean you can finally accept the life I lead?"

Without the pardon, Ivy knew there would be no other choice, for Drake would still be a pirate. But she also knew she would cleave to this man and face their future—whatever it was and wherever it took them—together. What she felt for Drake was a commitment, a commitment she was finally ready to take despite the differences in their lives.

"There was a time I didn't think I would be able to accept what you are," she admitted with candor, "but now I can."

Drake drew her toward him. "My piracy will be all in the past," he promised. "Once I get the pardon, I'll open my plantation, make it thrive again."

"But you won't have the pardon," Ivy said awkwardly as she realized Drake hadn't yet considered the ramifications of Allen's escape. "Not with Allen gone." Expecting him to look disturbed over the news, she was surprised when he simply shook his head.

"No one knows about Allen but you, me, and Keils," he reminded her. "And none of us is going to turn him in."

Ivy looked out toward the ship, to where Allen still stood watching her. "No," she agreed, her eyes full of tenderness, "none of us will."

Drake knew Ivy would always care for Allen and that Allen would always care for her in return. But when it came to Ivy's love, he knew he no longer had a rival. Slipping an arm around Ivy's waist, he lifted his hand in a salute to the clergyman to let him know Ivy was safe and that she would never come to harm while in his care.

Allen waved his hand in return, and the schooner's sails began to billow as the ship prepared to set sail and head out toward the sea.

"Ivy," Drake said softly, looking down at her lovely face, "when we get back to my plantation, will you marry me?"

In answer, Ivy simply lifted her lips to his.

The sun had long since set by the time they made their way to the isolated cove where the *Black Cauldron* awaited them. As they boarded the ship and then went down the steps leading to their cabins, Cauldron handed Ivy the leather bag Allen had left behind.

"Thank you for letting me keep this," Ivy said. "I know Allen will want me to send his personal things to him when I can."

"I'm sure he'll want the miniature of you." There was no rivalry in Drake's words.

"I hope it wasn't damaged while we were running." Ivy unfastened the bag's clasp to find the delicate piece. At the very bottom of the satchel, wedged beneath a Bible, was the miniature. "It's not broken," she said as she removed the leather-bound scripture to get to the small portrait.

A folded, faded piece of parchment slipped from inside the Bible, fluttering down to the floor. Probably Allen's ordination paper, Ivy thought as she picked it up. When she saw her father's handwriting, she took a startled breath. It took her only seconds to read its contents.

"My God," she finally whispered, her hand coming to her mouth.

"What is it?" Drake asked in concern. "Is something wrong?"

Too stunned to speak, Ivy simply handed the paper to him.

Taking a quick glance at it, Drake said, "You better have a look at this, Keils."

Cauldron took the parchment nearer to the lantern nailed onto the passageway wall, holding it into the light so he could see it better. The words were written in a very tidy handwriting. Even before he glanced at the signature at the bottom, he knew whose name would be there: Ian Woodruff. The entries in Ivy's family Bible and the old church records had been entered by the same neat hand.

Taking his time, he read the letter, absorbing the words that revealed that Ivy was indeed his child, not Woodruff's. When he was done, he raised his eyes, meeting Ivy's, which were shining with happiness.

"Allen must have found that when he was hunting for his own personal papers," she said breathlessly. "When he shouted good-bye, I caught only a few words, including your name, but I thought he was just voicing his final concerns." She gave a delighted laugh. "Instead, he must have been trying to tell me about the letter!"

As Cauldron watched her undisguised happiness and her growing excitement, the words he had been about to say died on his lips. The letter was a forgery, the ink not as faded as the parchment on which it was written. It would take someone knowledgeable to such things to detect it, but in the course of his piracy he had gained such expertise. He could only surmise that Allen had created it to ensure Ivy would come to no harm while she was being held by him. The clergyman had probably meant to somehow get it to her, and today, as he had fled, he had finally found that opportunity.

There was no proof Ivy was his daughter—and considerable evidence pointing to the fact that she wasn't—but as she looked at him with unmistakable love in her eyes, he suddenly knew it made no difference, for he had come to love her, too. They had both overcome the obstacles that had separated them—she, her dislike, and he, his suspicion—and it had filled a gap they both had in their lives. She needed a father and he needed her, and that would be enough.

He held out his arms.

Without hesitation, Ivy fled into them, burying her face into his shoulder. "Oh . . . Father." Tears of joy filled her eyes.

As Cauldron bent down to hold her close, he didn't know if the moisture on his cheeks was hers or his. He had lost a son, and that was something that would always leave a certain sadness in his life, but that sadness was now tempered as he held Ivy in his arms. A contentment he had never thought to feel again washed over him, along with a newfound sense of protectiveness. Ivy had been through so much.

Abruptly, he straightened, his brows coming down in a frown as he looked toward Drake, standing there smiling as he watched the two of them embrace.

"Drake," he said sternly. "What exactly are your intentions toward Ivy?"

Drake's lips twitched at seeing his friend suddenly turn into a protective father. He realized Cauldron was deadly serious with his question and he answered just as seriously, "I mean to marry her, Keils."

Satisfied, Cauldron then raised Ivy's chin to look into her eyes. "And is that what you want?" he asked, his voice suddenly gentle again.

Shyly, Ivy nodded.

"Ivy and I already discussed it," Drake told him. "We plan to marry as soon as we get back."

"That's not soon enough!" Cauldron challenged him. "As captain of this ship, I'm going to marry the two of you as soon as we get underway!"

Immediately, he regretted saying the abrupt words, which came out as an order rather than as a request, knowing Drake didn't like others making up his mind for him.

But Drake, instead of taking offense, simply held out his hand to Ivy. "Will you marry me today," he asked, his words softly formal, "with your father presiding over us?"

Ivy entwined her fingers through his. "Yes," she answered just as formally, "I will."

Cauldron beamed. "Ivy can get ready in my cabin," he suggested. "I'll have one of the men prepare a bath." He looked at her yellow island dress, soiled and ripped from the climb down the escarpment, and then thought of her other dresses. "I wish I could buy you something really fancy for this occasion," he added with real regret.

Ivy's lips turned up in a smile. "I do have something fancy. Something Drake"—she glanced at him, her eyes full of love—"insisted I buy in case of a celebration."

A short while later, Ivy was ensconced in a steaming tub of water that had been brought into Cauldron's cabin. Hanging on the wall next to her was the silk dress, its graceful, pale orchid folds now looking smooth and sleek as the steam from her bath removed the wrinkles. Her hair already washed and toweled, she let its long length trail over the side of the tub as the balmy island weather dried the damp strands.

At a discreet knock on the door, she rose from the tub,

feeling her excitement grow as her wedding approached. In a matter of minutes, she was dressed, her hair gleaming as she gave it a final combing.

Cauldron looked proudly at Ivy and Drake standing before him, ready to exchange their vows. The orchid shade of Ivy's silk gown emphasized the gemlike color of her eyes and acted like a foil to the beautiful raven hair flowing down her back. Drake, dressed now in buff-colored leather breeches and a shirt of fine white cambric, was equally striking.

"Dearly beloved," Cauldron began, "we are gathered here . . ."

As Cauldron said the words that united her in marriage to Drake, only those opening ones were familiar to Ivy. Obviously the first marriage ceremony her father had ever performed, he simply spoke from the heart, saying words that expressed his deep emotion.

Ivy thought it the most stirring ceremony she had ever heard. And from the way Drake reached over, taking her hand and lacing his fingers through her own, she knew he found it equally touching.

"You may now place the ring on your bride's finger."

Caught up in marriage plans that had developed so quickly, Ivy hadn't given thought to this part of the ceremony. She didn't know what Drake would place on her finger, for when they had all returned to the ship, she realized now he hadn't stopped back at the guard tower to get the ring she had removed.

When Drake pulled the diamond and amethyst band from his pocket, she looked up at him in surprise. "You picked it up as you came after me," she breathed.

"Even then, I was still hoping that somehow everything would turn out all right," Drake answered, raising her hand to his lips. "And it did." He placed the glittering band on her finger. "I'm glad to put this back where it belongs," he murmured, "because I love you."

Ivy's eyes shone with happiness. "I love you too."

Cauldron was watching them fondly. "You may now kiss the bride."

Drake was already moving to do just that. Slipping his hands around Ivy's slender waist, he pulled her close, lingering over the kiss that finally bound them together as husband and wife.

When the embrace finally ended, Cauldron smiled indulgently. "If I can just have your signatures on the marriage paper I made up, everything will be complete."

As Cauldron handed her a quill and a piece of parchment containing carefully drafted words that detailed the particulars of this very special event, Ivy had to smile when she saw several other discarded papers on his desk, showing her pirate father had wanted to make this particular document perfect. She signed her name to it with a flourish, hardly believing how wonderful everything had turned out. A moment later, Drake was scrawling his signature as well.

Cauldron laid the document aside and poured them each a small glass of fine wine. "Today," he said, handing out the glasses, "I joined the two people who mean the most to me together in marriage. May that bond be everything you wish it to be." Their glasses clinked as the three of them touched them together.

"I'll take your cabin for the rest of the journey, Drake," Cauldron suggested as they sipped at the wine. "My quarters will make a better bridal bower than that small cabin of yours."

Drake looked at Ivy to see her reaction. At the slight shake of her head, he exchanged a private smile with her.

"I think we'd rather stay where we are, Keils. It's kind of cozy there."

The becoming flush rising to Ivy's cheeks at the sultry tone of her new husband's words told Cauldron he had detained this loving couple long enough. He gathered Ivy to him in a final hug.

"I love you, Ivy."

"I love you too, Father." Once again, Cauldron was clean-shaven, his handsome features revealed, and Ivy pressed her cheek to his smooth one in a gesture of love before giving it a kiss.

Feeling himself growing misty-eyed, Cauldron stepped back to let Drake take his rightful place at Ivy's side.

"You're a fine man, Drake," he said fondly, taking both Drake's arms in a clasp that was as loving as the hug he had bestowed upon Ivy. "I know you'll take good care of her."

"I will." As Drake stepped back, he slipped his arm around Ivy's waist, smiling down at her. "And that's a promise."

Love was a special and wonderful thing, Cauldron reflected as he watched them leave the room, their feelings for each other obvious in the way they held each other. It made him think of Elizabeth, and how much he missed her. As he glanced over at the newly signed marriage document lying on his desk, he had a feeling there could easily be another wedding—his own—in the not too distant future.

*　　*　　*

Inside Drake's small cabin, Ivy looked down at her hand, gazing thoughtfully at the expensive ring that again adorned her finger.

"This is the ring I made you buy me," she said hesitantly. "I meant to pay you back for it—"

"I never would have taken your money," Drake interrupted. "Not for the ring and not for the dresses."

"I would have paid you back anyway."

There was a certain prim promise to Ivy's words that, as usual, strongly appealed to Drake. "I'm sure you would have tried," he agreed.

"We needed a ring for the ceremony, but this one is terribly expensive." Ivy began to remove the glittering band. "I'm sure you'll want to exchange it for something simpler."

Drake placed his hand over hers, stopping her. "That's the ring I wanted you to have then, and it's still the ring I want you to have now." His words were firm, brooking no protest. "It was meant for you, meant to be a bond between us."

As Ivy gazed into his eyes, she knew he meant every word. The ring truly symbolized the feelings they shared. Though she had always liked the look of it, now it had so much more meaning to her.

"I never thought I would ever have such a pretty piece of jewelry," she shyly confessed.

Drake raised her hand to his lips, kissing each of her fingers. "I intend to shower you with all kinds of pretty things, Ivy."

"That's not necessary, Drake."

Drake smiled at the response so characteristic of Ivy. "I know it's not *necessary*, but I want to do it anyway. Indulge me."

"I don't know if I'll feel comfortable with that."

"I'm sure you won't," Drake agreed with some humor, "but let's give it a try anyway." He gave her hand another kiss, this one slow and lingering in the center of her palm. "And now," he murmured, "we have a honeymoon to think about."

Ivy felt shivers of anticipation course through her, but before they consummated this marriage, there was something she had to attend to.

"First," she said, gently drawing away her hand, "there's something I must do." Feeling Drake watch her curiously, she went over to the miniatures of her parents and Allen. Before, their presence had given her the strength and support she needed when her destiny had been so unclear. Now, she was confident of the path she was taking—and their presence on this very special night would be an intrusion.

Picking them up, she opened her trunk, carefully placing the one of Allen inside first. "I know you're wishing me well, wherever you are," she whispered. Then she felt her heart grow full as she set the one of her parents beside Allen's.

"Mama," she murmured to the lovely lady in the tiny portrait, "you made a different decision in your life, but for me, this is the right one. I know you and Papa would have given me your blessing."

After she closed the lid of the trunk, she turned to Drake, ready to begin a new life with him at her side. As he held out his hand, she slipped hers into it.

"Are you ready for bed now?" Drake murmured.

Ivy nodded.

"If you look behind that blanket"—Drake nodded toward the material that formed the partition—"you'll find something to help make our wedding night special." Giving her hand a squeeze, he then released it.

Curious to see what he had put there, she stepped behind it, and a broad smile came to her lips when she saw what was waiting for her.

The white satin nightgown that Sarah Weaver had given her when they had commandeered her farmhouse was hanging from a peg on the wall.

"It's perfect, Drake," she breathed, holding it up to herself, her hands going over its satiny folds.

"I've been wanting to see you in that nightgown from the moment I saw it," Drake confessed, speaking to Ivy through the blanket. "There's something about picturing you in white satin that makes me want to caress every curve of that pretty body of yours."

It was an arousing image. "Then I guess I better put it on," Ivy said with a sudden breathless excitement to her voice.

It didn't take her long to get the lovely nightgown in place. It clung to her body, its tiny shoulder straps and low-cut front making it far different from her flannel nightwear. The feel of the satin against her bare skin made her nipples harden and boldly jut against the fine, clinging material. It was a sensation Ivy found highly sensual.

"I'm ready," she called to Drake, and she knew she was indeed ready, both to come out from behind the partition and to join herself to him in their marriage bed.

"I am too," Drake answered, reaching up to turn down the wick. Instead of dousing the light entirely, he only turned the flame low, letting it softly illuminate the cabin.

As Ivy stepped from behind the blanket, his eyes

moved appreciatively over her. Her hair flowed long and free, its silky blackness a beautiful contrast to the white of the satin she wore. The material molded sensuously over her body, emphasizing the curve of her hips, the narrowness of her waist, and the ample swell of her breasts, their fullness accentuated by the twin peaks that thrust provocatively against the delicate fabric.

"My pretty, pretty sea maid," he said with a wanting rasp to his voice. "You look beautiful in that nightgown."

Ivy thought Drake looked rather magnificent himself. He was already in bed, the sheet drawn up around his waist, his torso naked. In many ways, she mused, this night was similar to the first they had shared, but this time, she knew he would be as naked beneath that sheet as the rest of him. It was a thought that made her pulse quicken.

"Come have a toast with me," Drake suggested, reaching down to the floor where two glasses of wine were ready. He picked them up, handing one to Ivy as she sat on the edge of the bunk.

"To us," he said, lifting his glass to touch hers.

"And to our future," Ivy added softly. Together they drank to the life they would be sharing. Her body, already warmed by the quickening of her pulse, grew warmer as the wine added its heady effects. When Drake set aside their glasses and then raised the sheet to welcome her beside him, the sight his naked loins, already showing his body's taut readiness, made her eager to once again feel his embrace.

Always before, she mused, it had been Drake who had instigated the caresses they had shared. She had luxuriated in the passion and had given herself freely in response, but she had never been the initiator. The passion had been too new and the circumstances too uncertain.

Tonight, she felt different—both very married and very bold.

Bringing her hand to Drake's chest, she let it run slowly down the corded muscles. The sharp intake of his breath as he sensed her destination showed his surprise and his pleasure.

"Before," she murmured, "you loved me. Tonight, I'd like to love you." She paused uncertainly. "But I'm not sure how."

Drake groaned as her fingers moved lower, finding him. That part of him that was already eager to love was suddenly straining for release.

"You're doing just fine, Ivy." The words came out strangled.

As she felt Drake swell more beneath her touch, Ivy realized with a heady sense of pleasure that she was doing fine. Her touch, at first a little hesitant, grew bolder as she saw the effect it had on Drake. His pleasure would be her pleasure too, she knew, for she would be the recipient of that growing, pulsing desire.

She felt her thighs grow moist with her own readiness and heard her breathing turn as ragged and wanting as Drake's. She suddenly found she wanted to give him the same kind of ecstasy he had once given her.

Drake's hips jerked as Ivy's lips touched his bare flesh. Though what she was doing was highly provocative, he didn't want his primly raised bride to think she had to pleasure him in such a fashion just because he had once

377

pleasured her so.

"Ivy," he protested, pulling away, "you don't have to do that!"

Ivy gazed at him with eyes already shadowed by passion. "I'm only doing to you what you did to me."

"I'm me and you're you," Drake said emphatically. "Things that were proper for me, aren't—"

"Some things, Drake," Ivy interrupted in a throaty whisper, "aren't meant to be proper. They're only meant to be enjoyed." Before he could make another protest, she brought her lips to him once again. She knew her instincts were right as Drake, after a moment's tenseness, gave in to her caresses, lying back as his hips began to arc with desire.

When Drake felt his passion spiraling to a near-bursting point, his fingers tangled in Ivy's raven tresses to stop her sensuous siege. He hauled her up across his chest, breathing heavily.

"I want us to consummate this marriage together." His words were a groan as he feverishly tugged the satin of Ivy's nightgown up around her waist. Parting her legs, he let her legs straddle him as she lay on top of him. The feel of her readiness, so evident as her loins pressed closely to his, showed he didn't need to delay any longer.

Expecting to be rolled over so that she would lie beneath him, Ivy was surprised when she felt Drake butt intimately against her, his body boldly seeking entrance to hers. But when he claimed her completely, her surprise turned to pleasure as she realized the freedom such a position would give her. Pushing herself away from his chest, she straightened so that she was sitting fully astride him. It brought him deeper, the sensation a highly arousing one for her.

378

"My lovely sea maid," Drake breathed, gazing up at her tenderly. "You fit me as nicely as your wooden likeness fits the prow of my ship."

The comparison was one Ivy found as arousing as the feel of him within her. "You have quite a prow of your own," she teased, a catch of desire to her voice.

Drake smiled at her newfound boldness. "And you, my beautiful sea maid"—he brought his hands to her breasts, caressing their fullness through the satin— "grace it beautifully."

Ivy arched her back, letting her hair spill backward over her shoulders as she luxuriated in the touch of his fingers.

"I love the feel of satin on your skin," Drake murmured, his fingers stroking over the nipples that seemed to beg for his touch.

Ivy brought her eyes back to him. "And I love the feel of your touch," she said softly. "It excites me."

"Then this is only the beginning," Drake promised, thrusting his hips sharply upward.

The movement took Ivy's breath away. Then as she felt the rousing effect of the rhythm he was setting, she began to move her hips as well, glorying in the way she could give free rein to the passion Drake was igniting within her.

Letting her instincts guide her, she threw any remaining primness to the wind, her body responding with primitive abandon as she sought to bring both herself and her pirate mate to that ultimate shaking pleasure.

When it came, with Drake's hips bucking and her hips whorling, the pleasure was more intense than any lovemaking that had come before. Her mind reeling, Ivy's body went wild as she felt Drake's seed explode in a series of hot gushes deep within her.

It was a long, long while later before either could speak.

"I think we can say you loved me," Drake finally managed as he held Ivy close to his chest. "If Keils doesn't get a grandchild out of *that,* it will be a miracle."

Ivy felt a blush touch her cheeks. "I felt bold," she whispered, nuzzling her face into his shoulder.

Drake stroked the long raven hair that trailed over him. "You felt beautiful."

Ivy sighed in contentment, luxuriating in the lulling aftermath of their passion. As she curled her fingers through the wiry golden hair that covered Drake's strong chest, her eyes were drawn to the glittering diamond and amethyst ring that now permanently adorned her finger. Knowing it was now a real wedding band and not make-believe brought a contented smile to her lips.

Married. Being so had added a special new feeling of closeness to their lovemaking that had greatly enhanced her pleasure.

"There's something about being married that made everything better between us," she confessed.

Drake smiled as he began tugging at the satin night-gown to get Ivy as bare as he was. "I noticed." Pulling the garment over her head, he tossed it aside, his eyes darkening with new desire.

"You loved me," he whispered, rolling her over to place her beneath him, "and now, *Mrs. Jordan,* I'm going to love you."

He was teasing her, but the strong, answering desire Ivy felt as Drake dropped a smattering of kisses across her breasts showed her he wouldn't be disappointed by her uninhibited response this time either. Then, an unsettling thought occurred to her.

"Drake," she murmured, almost reluctant to voice the thought for fear the answer wouldn't be what she wanted to hear, "with my father being a pirate—"

"He won't be one for much longer," Drake reminded her, his lips returning to the dusky crest he was arousing.

Ivy sighed, the sound one of both pleasure and concern. "I know. But until the pardon goes through, he's still a pirate. Do you think the wedding was legal, considering that?"

Drake raised his head so that he could look down into the delicate beauty of Ivy's face. "Pirate or not, we're at sea and he's the captain. It's binding."

Ivy drew in a slow, relieved breath. "Then what we're doing is—"

"What every newly wedded man and woman are supposed to be doing," Drake murmured, bring his lips to hers. "Making love."

Inside his cabin, Cauldron picked up the marriage document, wanting to put it safely away. As his eyes moved over the paper, they suddenly widened in shock as he saw the way Ivy had hurriedly signed her name. The v and y of Ivy were reversed, making the name misspelled.

He sank into a nearby chair, his limbs suddenly feeling weak. He couldn't remember how many times he had made the same kind of mistake himself, when he had been distracted or his mind hadn't been on the task at hand. The number of times he had reversed the letters of his own name over the years spilled through his thoughts.

It was just too much of a coincidence that he and Ivy shared a trait that had haunted him all his life. She had to be his daughter after all. . . .

He leaped to his feet, heading for Drake's cabin to tell her the exciting news. But as he raised his hand to knock at the door, he suddenly knew it wasn't necessary. He had already given his heart to her and this bit of evidence didn't change that.

Besides, he mused, letting his hand drop to his side, he would certainly be intruding. He turned to the steps leading above, deciding to take the wheel for a while. He needed the feel of the wind and spray on his face as he thought about the future. For the first time in a long while, it looked bright.

Dear Reader,

Zebra Books welcomes your comments about this book or any other Zebra historical romance you have read recently. Please address your comments to:

Zebra Books, Dept. WM
475 Park Avenue South
New York, NY 10016

Thank you for your interest.

Sincerely,
The Editorial Department
Zebra Books

THE BEST IN HISTORICAL ROMANCES

TIME-KEPT PROMISES   (2422, $3.95)
by Constance O'Day Flannery

Sean O'Mara froze when he saw his wife Christina standing before him. She had vanished and the news had been written about in all of the papers—he had even been charged with her murder! But now he had living proof of his innocence, and Sean was not about to let her get away. No matter that the woman was claiming to be someone named Kristine; she still caused his blood to boil.

PASSION'S PRISONER   (2573, $3.95)
by Casey Stewart

When Cassandra Lansing put on men's clothing and entered the Rawlings saloon she didn't expect to lose anything—in fact she was sure that she would win back her prized horse Rapscallion that her grandfather lost in a card game. She almost got a smug satisfaction at the thought of fooling the gamblers into believing that she was a man. But once she caught a glimpse of the virile Josh Rawlings, Cassandra wanted to be the woman in his embrace!

ANGEL HEART   (2426, $3.95)
by Victoria Thompson

Ever since Angelica's father died, Harlan Snyder had been angling to get his hands on her ranch, the Diamond R. And now, just when she had an important government contract to fulfill, she couldn't find a single cowhand to hire—all because of Snyder's threats. It was only a matter of time before the legendary gunfighter Kid Collins turned up on her doorstep, badly wounded. Angelica assessed his firmly muscled physique and stared into his startling blue eyes. Beneath all that blood and dirt he was the handsomest man she had ever seen, and the one person who could help beat Snyder at his own game.